JULIANNA DRUMHELLER

THE MAIDEN TREE

DHP
DREAMHARROW PRESS

THE MAIDEN TREE
Copyright © 2020 Julianna Drumheller

ISBN 978-1-7357481-0-8 (Kindle ebook)
ISBN 978-1-7357481-1-5 (EPUB)
ISBN 978-1-7357481-2-2 (paperback)

This book is a work of fiction. Names, characters, organizations and places are products of the author's imagination.

Cover art by Julianna Drumheller
Interior design by Julianna Drumheller

Published by Dreamharrow Press, in the United States of America
www.juliannadrumheller.com

To all of those who have grown too old for imaginary friends,
but not for imaginary demons.

CHAPTER ONE

I NEVER MET THE OLD MAN who died beneath our elm tree. He was a vagabond, my father said, and though we did not know him, we had a duty to put him to rest. In my own childish way, I thought the funeral blaze might finally set things right, and mark the end of the dark times that had come upon us. I was eight years old that summer, and eager for everything to go back to normal, the way it had been before the epidemic.

"The ashes of the magpies were still swirling on coat-breezes when he was found," said one of the gardeners, and his cryptic muttering became an oft-repeated phrase by many who heard the story.

"Will they burn him on the same pyre as the animals?" one of the laundry maids wondered aloud to another, as they picked up the linen baskets for the week.

The pyre they spoke of was scant yards from the tree under which the old man had died, just beyond the reach of its branches. The tree's outer leaves were as smoke-singed as the paintings in old chapels, for the tenants had lit many fires there already. Night and day, smoke drifted across the open fields as the farmers burned the corpses of infected animals.

I'd heard stories of people dying of arrhemia in the village, but this was the closest I'd come to witnessing it. A tenant had found the old man, covered in spidery black marks where the cruorflies had bit him. I had never seen the dreaded marks myself, but I heard they bruised just the same on the bellies of the calves and goats that died of the disease.

Afterward, long after the summer ended and the infection waned, I would come to understand how the funeral was only the beginning of a new normal, that things would never go back to the way they were. It wasn't the old man's fault—at least, I didn't think so, not at the time. Perhaps the Queen of the Dead was riding through the hills that day, and reining in Her smoke-gray steed She sniffed the air and caught the scent of our burning pyre. And She was drawn to it, and decided to stick around for a while.

Or perhaps I'd been marked at birth for Her attention, and nothing I could have done would have averted it.

ഇൗരു

The heat of the day had not yet lifted as we made our way down the lane to the fallow pasture where the elm tree stood. The sun flashed through a line of trees, diffusing through the scrim of my veil. We turned off the road, the tree looming before us. It was a sprawling, solitary thing, flung up on the hill to gather in the dusk, and I couldn't stop looking at it, imagining the violent shudder that must have taken place beneath its silent boughs.

The thought was suffocating. I struggled to breathe beneath my corset and petticoat, and the protective netting my nurse, Hespa, had draped over me. Every step was like slogging through heavy mud, and the coutille cage round my middle, though not laced so very tight, pressed uncomfortably against my ribs. I wondered if this was how the old man had felt when his lungs began to fail. That was how it ended with arrhemia. I wanted to turn round, to run back to the safety of the house. But then my father would know he'd made a mistake in allowing me to witness this, in treating me like a grownup.

I reached for Hespa's hand as we trailed behind him. Maslin, my father's valet, walked at his side, bearing an unlit torch; some of the other servants carried buckets of water. The neighbors had come from their cottages in the lower court, their faces concealed by funereal half-masks, the women veiled. Father Parquar strode a few paces ahead of the main group. He was the first to crest the hill, taking the path that had been trampled in the long plumes of wild oat grass, and as he looked over at the elm tree, its branches seemed to rustle with reproach.

Not far away, the old man lay within a cage of dried, bent boughs, placed over an open frame. Beneath the frame, bundles of wood had been arranged in pyramids, like rows of sharp teeth. The smell of charcoal still lingered in the air as we took our places in a half-circle round the pyre. People moved carelessly round me, with no thought to my view, and I squirmed, craning my neck and standing on my toes to see. I caught glimpses of a threadbare coat, a stained cotton shirt, patched trousers, a pair of well-made calfskin shoes. Those shoes I had seen many times, sitting outside my father's door.

Perhaps it was the veil playing tricks on my vision, but for a brief, terrible instant I thought the man in the bier *was* my father. I had to look round and find him again to reassure myself that he was yet among the living. And there he was, speaking in quiet tones to Maslin, his face partially obscured by a simple black half-mask. But he looked like a stranger to me with his pomaded hair, drawn from the temple and held neatly in the back by a cord, the furrows of the comb visible in the sweep back from his forehead. His hair thus anointed, it appeared almost black, not the undistinguished blond which reminded me of the color of the fields during the frostmoon. Instead of his usual rolled shirtsleeves, he wore a black jacket with a broad lapel, of the sort gentlemen wore, spun of the finest wool. This was how he presented himself whenever he wished to remind people who he was, which wasn't very often.

The sun was close to extinguished now, and when the light in the west had dwindled to almost nothing, my father nodded to Maslin and he lit the torch. The other onlookers had begun to shuffle and murmur, the torchlight reflected in their eyes, glittering through veils and flickering in the holes of their funereal masks.

"Does anyone know his name?"

"It started with a P, I think."

"Pico? Pilo?"

"Some Velan name, wasn't it?"

"His name was Pelico," my father said. Everyone quieted at once. He took the torch from Maslin and stared at the leather strap unraveling from the grip. I waited for him to speak, hoping he had the right words in him, and that he would find them in time.

He cleared his throat and scanned the small crowd. "He...came up to the house a few times, looking for a meal. I only spoke to him once or twice. He'd not always been so unfortunate. He used to be a bookseller in Tarbonne. But I suppose he didn't get many customers there, more's the pity."

My father's kennelmaster spat on the ground. "Man was a drifter. A footpad, most like. I told you, sir, I would sic my dogs on him if I ever caught him creeping round here again."

There was a low murmur of agreement in the assembled throng.

"He brought no harm to us," my father said, but now the women had joined in the admonishment.

"How dreadful to have such men about," one lady whispered, anonymous behind her veil.

"To think of the *child*," another said, looking at me.

My father held up his hand, but I could see he was losing them. Beside me, Hespa had drawn up her veil and was staring out at the gathering darkness. Her profile had a stony look about it, the way it always did when someone round her was speaking nonsense, and she was in no position to refute them.

My father was left holding a sputtering torch. When it became clear that he had nothing more to say on the matter, Father Parquar stepped forward.

"Friends and neighbors." He clasped his hands before him and went on, "These are the last moments of Pelico. We hold up this torch in the darkness, to shine one last time on the moments we shared with him upon this earth. He lived and died in the light of Aneidis, as do we all. He had his debts, as have we ours. Let us lighten his load by accounting for him now."

My father touched the flame to the top of the pyramids stacked beneath the bier. As the fire burst upward, the priest gestured to the men and bade them, in turn, to say a good word about the dead man.

"At least he didn't die far from the fire pit," said the first.

"A considerate chap, that one," his neighbor agreed.

"*I* think it's rather morbid," a woman said. "Why anyone would wish to draw his last breath in such a place, I'll never understand."

The priest lifted his hands and spoke a few words under his breath, and the fire engulfed the wooden cage. A gust of wind raised the flame even higher, and debris from previous fires scattered outwards, ashes and feathers taking to the air.

The ashes of the magpies were still swirling on coat-breezes, I thought, and the phrase made me shiver despite the intense heat radiating from the bier. The grownups seemed to approve of the fire's hunger, searching within it for inspiration, as each were called upon to speak. At first they tried to be sincere, but eventually someone cracked a joke, and one of the gardeners uncorked a bottle of wine, which gave off the tang of vinegar.

"Pelico has paid his final debt. Let us now return him to his place in the sun," the priest intoned.

We stood watching as night fell around us. The pyramids had become a maw of fire, snarling and snapping through the dry wood. I saw one of my father's shoes catch flame as Hespa drew me back from the heat and the smoke. The smell of burning wood and feathers and pig bones, and something else, savory and stomach-turning, rose on the wind. Then one of the planks of the frame collapsed, sending up a shower of sparks. I huddled next to Hespa and grasped her hand, but I could not avert my eyes from the sight before me. I was looking down through the cage as the wood beneath the man's head began to shift, and for a moment he seemed to rise up inside the bier. Sparks flew and wreathed his head, like a glowing mass of insects taking wing, and then they seemed to form into the figure of a woman with her head flung back, her hair a long ripple of flame. I squeezed Hespa's fingers tight and turned to look at her, to see if I was alone in my perception, in my sudden unease.

I could read nothing in her face. But behind her, the elm tree had become a solid black, hunkering thing, and it seemed to thrum with a patient, wakeful force.

My thoughts were interrupted by the deep boom of a drum. Outside the half-circle of the funereal party, a few of the neighbors were preparing to play a requiem. I watched in fascination as one unwrapped a fiddle from an oil cloth. My father sometimes listened to symphonies on his paleophone, all grand works which I knew by now by heart. But I had never closely watched anyone play. I did not know how the sound was made, and it held for me a deep mystery, like a kind of sorcery.

The musicians consisted of two women and a man. Both women were veiled, and the man wore a full mask with a long nose that looked like a crow's beak. In his arms he cradled a flat stringed instrument I didn't recognize. He plucked at the strings, making adjustments of the pegs. One woman held her drum before her on a broad strap, her back arched from the weight of it as though she were with child, and she began to sway, swinging two soft mallets together. The second woman, the fiddle player, drew her bow across the open strings, letting out a low, mournful sound. I waited in rapt fascination for the real music to begin, but at that moment my father walked over to Hespa and spoke something in her ear, and she in turn guided me round by the shoulder.

"It's time we went back," she said.

"But I want to stay and listen to the music," I protested.

"That we shall not do."

"But *why?*" I asked, even as she was herding me down the hill toward the lane.

"Because your father says so," Hespa said.

"I don't see why I shouldn't listen to the music," I grumbled.

She stopped in the lane and turned to look at me. "Listen to me, kit. Your father only wishes to protect you. I know it must be difficult to understand, but that is the heart of it."

"Protect me from what?" I asked. "The cruorflies? But you said the fire keeps them away."

Hespa didn't reply. I couldn't fathom what could be so dangerous about listening to some village musicians. Why *now* was he reacting this way, after allowing me to see the old man burn?

I tried to walk as slowly as possible, but my nurse was wise to my tricks and hastened me onward. I could hear the music in the growing distance, the thrum of the drumbeat, the high, keening notes of the fiddle as it floated down the hill. The sound made me shiver, not in fear, but in unexpected delight, exciting all of my senses. It anchored me in the moment, giving every detail of my surroundings new vividness and import, making me ache with the need to capture it. I wanted to remember everything, just as it was.

A crescent moon rose above the flush fields, hanging over the house like a shining blade. Bats circled overhead and crickets hummed, and fireflies danced in the long grass beside the lane. I had a sense, even then, that it was all to pass away. And I longed to wrap it up somehow, like a box of sweets, so I could have the pleasure of unloosing the ribbons once more, of drawing back the crinkling paper and renewing my delight. But I had no art to accomplish this; I knew that now, as I listened to the music fade away.

In the thicket beside the road, I caught sight of a pair of glinting eyes, and I paused to see what animal lurked there. There was a rustle of undergrowth as the long, lean body of the small predator bolted away. As I peered into the darkness to see where the creature went, Hespa turned round and put her hands on her broad hips.

"Amardine Sophia! Stop your shilly-shallying. We must get back to the house."

It wasn't like her to speak to me in such a harsh tone, and I shrank from her, more confused than ever. Everyone seemed to have sharper edges that summer, though. First a cluster of deaths in Tarbonne, and now this old man had died under our elm tree. My father was also worried about his treasured pardesu trees and his mood swallowed everything, turning the whole household into a gauntlet of despair and rebuke. At least, that was how it felt to me.

"Hespa," I said, feeling my throat swell up and close off my tears, "I think I just saw a *spight*."

She stared at me, her body tensed as though she might scold me again, but then she let out a sigh and patted me on the head, careful not to upset my bonnet and veils. "Never you mind, kit. I'm sorry I ever gave you such ideas. You know your father would say that's just superstition."

The music was fading. The house loomed ahead, its solid walls promising shelter and safety. On the veranda were pots of herbs and pitcher plants to trap flies, and the windows were lined with marigolds and lemon balm to ward off other unwanted pests. Spider silk curtains spanned the windows of the nursery, tacked into place, so that nothing bad could get in.

But my father was still out there, and he was all that stood between me and the nameless terrors that lay in wait, out there in the world. He had put the torch to my mother's funeral pyre once as well, and I wondered then, of a sudden, if they had burned her on the same spot, beside that same restless, unquiet tree.

෨෬

I was still thinking of my mother when I went to bed that night, and I dreamed of a woman burning in a wooden cage, of smoke and ashes on a hot wind. Her voice called to me from within the inferno, but I couldn't understand what she wanted. I awoke before dawn and crept out of bed, my limbs still languid with sleep. But my mind was clear. Some energy in the house had shifted during the night, set in motion the previous evening by the ritual of flame.

Hespa shared a room with the cook, Marguerite, next door to the nursery. She usually awakened early, but she was still snoring behind the door as I padded out into the little vestibule that lay outside our rooms. There was a clatter of activity in the kitchen below. I picked up a small potted tree from the side table and held it before me, humming softly.

The melody bubbled up without a conscious thought, but I could sense it resonating throughout the tree, connecting with its spirit. I continued to hum for about a minute, until I could feel a tiny pulse running through the trunk. "*Light*," I whispered.

The white blossoms on the tree seemed to swell with luminescence. The light was faint, but it was enough. I'd discovered this trick rather by accident one evening, in the dark of the nursery. It had proved useful when I wanted to stay up reading past bedtime, or creep round the house undetected. The light was more subtle than a candle, and it didn't flicker or strain the eyes. But I understood that it wasn't normal to sing to trees and make them light up, so I kept this ability a secret.

My first thought was to have a look at the aetherscope on the wall in the drawing room. That would tell me if there had indeed been an energetic shift, or if I was just imagining things. I crept down the hall, listening for the sound of footsteps on the kitchen stairs. It wouldn't do for the servants to find me skulking round in the dark—they would only shoo me back to bed before my investigation could even begin.

The hallway led straight to the great drawing room, where sofas and chairs sat clustered round thick Crimori rugs. The tall windows were shuttered still, but even in the light of the glowing tree, I knew it was all perfectly ordered, the chairs neatly arranged, the tea table set. On the wall, the aetherscope was glowing dimly, and I crossed the room to examine it. It was a basic model, designed to detect local flux in the aether and umbra.

While most people are aware of these energies swirling round us at all times, competing for dominance, their influence is usually subtle and not well understood without formal study. An excess of aetherial energy could increase one's mental focus, but it could also cause irritability. A preponderance of umbra was known to produce melancholy and strange dreams, to awaken creative insights and violent impulses.

Though at the time I had only a vague understanding of such things, I knew that most people didn't favor the umbra, and in fact feared its sway. In my provincial village, it was considered bad luck to make contracts during an umbral moon, when large energy clouds swirled in the firmament, making the moon glow purple. Horses spooked more easily during such times, it was said, and all manner of accidents increased in number.

I squinted up at the aetherscope, hanging on the wall above my head. It looked like a small clock, except instead of a ring of numbers it contained two concentric circles of inlaid crystals. Fourteen to represent the aether; fourteen for the umbra. Each was calibrated to react to varying levels of energetic flux, the most sensitive crystals lighting up first. Now, eleven crystals in the umbral ring glowed purple; three in the aetherial ring shone a pale gold.

If only I'd thought to look at it the day before, to see if it had changed. Was this high level of umbral energy from a lingering miasma, or had it spiked during the night? The images from my dream flooded back to me, of the woman burning in the wooden cage. I shivered, and as I stood in the darkness of the drawing room, I thought I heard a voice upstairs, singing.

It was a woman's voice, high and keening. I looked back at the aetherscope, but it hadn't changed. *You're imagining things*, I told myself sternly, in my father's voice. *That's what the umbra does, if you don't discipline your mind. It can drive you to madness, if you let it.*

I hesitated, both thrilled and terrified by what awaited me upstairs. Perhaps it would wake my father, and he would investigate. Perhaps I ought to knock on his door and alert him. But somehow neither of those outcomes seemed right to me—I couldn't help but feel, instinctively, that the singing was meant for me alone. I could not ignore the call.

I padded over to the foot of the staircase and made my way up quietly, pausing on the landing where another little seating area sat empty. The leaves of the potted ferns ticked against one another softly, as though tut-tutting about the light waking them before dawn.

Onward, to the second floor. There was nothing but silence in the gallery, which lay between my father's room and the one my mother had slept in. Her room was never opened except for brief airings, but beyond her door, the singing sounded more clearly. My heart pounded as I touched the painted ceramic knob. Forget-me-nots. A splash of blue paint on white porcelain.

An image flashed in my mind then, part of the dream that had woken me. I was lying down, and two hands, slender and white, were weaving gestures above my head. The same voice I heard now sang in the distance, high and sweet. But there was a second note, a dark harmony, that rang with it. *Just a dream, kit,* Hespa would have said. And yet, she was always on the lookout for signs and portents, for *spights*, as she called them, and threw salt over her shoulder as a first line of defense.

I had to go in, to stand in the room I imagined her dying in, to scour the darkest corners for some sign of her presence. I half expected to find her sitting at her dressing table, or laying out her gowns on the bed. I imagined her turning round, her face lighting up with a smile. "Come here, darling," she would say, as she caught me lingering in her doorway, and she would throw her arms wide to draw me into her embrace.

I pushed the door open. The moment it swung in on its hinges, the singing went silent. The room was unoccupied.

I stepped in and gently closed the door behind me. I held out the little tree, letting its light shine on the four-poster bed, neatly made; on the dressing table and washstand, on the wardrobe and painted screen in one corner. The room smelled slightly musty, the air stale as dead rose petals. "Mama?" I whispered. I didn't expect a response, and received none. But still, I felt she must have called me to this place.

Was this the first time I had ever stood in this room? I couldn't remember. I had often looked through the open doorway while it was being cleaned, but I didn't think I'd ever really gone in. I felt like an interloper. But I stepped forward anyway and walked alongside the bed, running my fingers over the wooden top of the dressing table. Too late I saw that I'd left a trail in the fine dust. I tried to wipe it away with my fist, but this only disturbed the dust more, leaving an oil mark from my skin, like a rosette. The short sleeve of my nightdress wouldn't do, either. I looked to the towel rail near the wash basin, but it was empty. Perhaps there was something in the wardrobe.

I went round the foot of the bed and pulled the doors of the wardrobe open. Nothing. Just wooden pegs and empty space. But there was a drawer in the bottom. I knelt down and pulled it open, trying not to make any noise, but the wood had become warped from disuse, and it gave an ominous creak.

I saw clothing, first. Curiously, not ladies' gowns—though perhaps that shouldn't have surprised me, for my aunt had mentioned once that the gowns had been auctioned off. This clothing was made of rougher material, and as I pulled out the first item, I saw that they were breeches, sized for a boy significantly older than me. There were shirts as well, like small versions of the ones my father wore. I sat back, confused. Did I have an older brother? But no one had ever spoken of him. Perhaps he had died? If so, what was his name; where was his reliquary? But that made no sense, I realized, for these weren't baby clothes. Surely my parents couldn't have had a child old enough to wear such attire, who died before I was even born.

Perhaps they belonged to some other relative, then, or

even to my father when he was young, though why my mother would have held on to them was a mystery.

I folded the clothes as neatly as I could and arranged the items in piles on the floor. Then I searched the drawer further. Beneath a couple of leather belts, I found a book, a small wooden box, and a leather folio. I took out the book first—a thick volume entitled *The Courtly Language of Flowers*. The binding cracked as I opened it. On the first page was an inscription—*To my dearest Sephonie, with love always. Martel.* I smiled as I imagined my father giving my mother this book. I paged through it, wishing I had more time and more light to absorb its contents. From what I could make out, it was all about coded messages in floral bouquets, an idea I found thoroughly intriguing.

I set the book aside for the moment, and turned my attention to the wooden box, lifting it out of the drawer and opening the lid. Against the dark velvet lining lay two small phials of scent, their hoses entwined, their bulbs resting together. I withdrew one of the phials and found it empty, but the second still held a bit of scent. I squeezed the bulb gently and it gave way, like the flesh of an overripe fruit. A faint perfume filled my nostrils, a familiar scent, musky and tenebrous, delicate as a blush rising upon a woman's cheek. Her scent, my mother's scent. I inhaled deeply, feeling light-headed, as a picture of her formed in my mind.

She had died when I was about a year and a half old, of a complication of the lungs, my father said. He didn't burden me with the details, but I imagined her spending her last days resting pale beneath white sheets, delicately coughing up blood onto starched handkerchiefs as he alternated between pacing the sickroom and wiping her brow, ever with a tortured look upon his face. The tortured look was not difficult to imagine; I had seen it many times growing up, especially when I chewed my food too loudly, or let the ducks into the nursery.

My father's moods were a mystery to me, but I thought he must be pining for my mother. He kept a small portrait of her on a table in the library, and it was this picture that fueled my imagination now. There, she looked a fragile wisp of a woman, the sort who could compel favor with one glance over a bared shoulder. She had huge, glittery dark eyes, veiled by the shadow of her lashes. Her pale hair was blown back like a cloud, the up-sweep misting over the tips of her ears. Her ruby lips were slightly parted, revealing the white crescent of her teeth, as though she could still be surprised by the adoration her beauty commanded. But I knew she was an actress. She was the darling of the regional opera houses, the perpetual ingénue, known for her clear, haunting soprano vocals. Even in those days, marrying a stage performer was hardly considered respectable for a gentleman of employ. But my father was a different person then, or so I've heard.

The portrait made me uneasy, to tell the truth. I didn't see in it a devoted mother, but rather an impossibly beautiful woman who had lived a life beyond my wildest dreams. Yet I couldn't stop myself from looking at it whenever I was in the library, though it made me feel small, unworthy of her legacy.

I shook myself from my reverie. There was more to be found in the drawer, so I set aside the wooden box and lifted out the bulging folio. The leather was cracked and worn away in places, and the strap nearly came to pieces in my hand when I unwound it. Inside was a collection of playbills and bound libretti.

I took the wooden box, the book about flowers, and the libretti, placing the clothes neatly back in the drawer as I had found them. Then, tucking my stolen goods under my arm, I tip-toed out of the room.

I put everything inside one of my hat boxes in my own wardrobe. Over the next few days, I would take the items out whenever I was supposed to be napping or keeping quiet. From behind the silk screens of the nursery windows, I sang tuneless little hymns to myself and paged through the libretti, transfixed by pictures of doe-eyed ladies dressed too prettily to be real.

At night, I dreamed often of her rising from her pyre, and sometimes, in that transition from sleep to wakefulness, I thought I heard her singing, clear and sweet. When I told Hespa, though, she warned me not to speak of such things, at least not round my father. "I knew you oughtn't have gone to that funeral," she replied. "It's lit a fire in your imagination, that's what."

"What's wrong with that?" I asked, and though she

grumbled in response, I knew her disapproval was only an act. Still, I waited until she left the room before once again retrieving my favorite libretto from its hiding place and paging through its contents.

There, alone and cross-legged on my bed, I puzzled out stage directions and arcane lyrics, as though they were instructions to some magical ritual that would reverse whatever bad things had been done, and somehow bring back my mother's love.

CHAPTER TWO

THE SUMMER OF THE ARRHEMIA EPIDEMIC, the pardesu trees stewed in the greenhouses, growing flagrant and wild. The gardeners moved through their ranks with a constant *snip-snip* of their shears, draping the precious bowers with cappa sprigs to absorb moisture from the humid air. My father turned over every leaf and seed pod, sought and destroyed rotten crowns, and grumbled about the exorbitant price of the mechanical ventilation system he had put off purchasing earlier that spring. He rotated the smaller hanging plants on their racks and wheeled the larger ones into the arcades, where a faint breeze might stir from one end to the other. If you have heard the name Desmarius, then you may begin to understand my father's burden. Perhaps you have a bottle of pardesu extract in your larder, kept under lock and key. If it bears my family sigil—a miniaturized, flowering topiary—then you will know it is the real thing, the liquid gold of spices.

Guildenflore was, in fact, the name of our family estate. The greenhouses were the jewel in the crown, as they contained the priceless pardesu trees, but much of the land was given over to farming and pasture, and my father remained heavily involved with this aspect of production as well. Sometimes he took to his study to obsess over a great map of the estate, pocked with so many pinholes that parts of it had to be patched and redrawn. It was as though he were a general directing troops in some endless war that raged only in his own head. He would fume behind closed doors to his manager when the tenants disregarded his precise grazing rotation schemes, though I never saw him lose his temper in front of them.

My great-great-grandfather Sebastien Desmarius was the first to bring the pardesu tree to these shores and learn to propagate its fruit, though my family had cultivated the land for nine generations. The great house was at least as old as the family business, but it was rebuilt upon the foundation of a more de-fensible structure, older even than my family's claim to the land. Two arcades ran east to west, connecting the main structure with two smaller residences, enclosing the courtyard. Now they mostly provided protection from the summer sun. They did little to suppress the mounds of wild lantana that burst over the courtyard walls, or the sable-leaf ivy that crept up to the sills, or the mulberry trees bristling against the old stonework, whose fruit, when it dropped, littered the walkways like bloody thumb-stumps.

By contrast, the indoor plants of my father's prized collection were trim and shapely, and had every appearance of being civilized. As a child, I became obsessed with taking care of them. I scrutinized, adjusted, watered if necessary, and gave an air-pat to each one that needed attention. I knew which ones I could leave alone for a spell. I filled the empty perfume bottle with water to mist the plants, as judicious in my applications as a good cook. I would circle round the edge of the drawing room, nimbly picking my way across the backs of chairs and sofas to reach the spider plants and lamb's ears hanging from their brackets. From there I would make my way to the dining room, where the twisted trunks of my great-great-grandfather's pardesu trees filled a sky-lit alcove, blooming in the summer with hundreds of fragrant white blossoms. Finally, I would run upstairs to the gallery, where musicians once played, from which the amardine flowers of my namesake trailed like delicate shooting stars.

It was an idyllic place, in many ways, but for my own apprehensions, and of course the danger of the cruorflies. At dusk, they rose from their sodden feeding grounds in dark, virulent waves. Men came into the courtyard and spilled rainwater from open pots into a drain, leaving them standing on their rims. Like vandals, they overturned the great stone mortar which must have stood for centuries, growing mossy with disuse. But it was all for our protection, I knew. That was why Hespa insisted on cocooning me in layers of veils when I went out of doors, for the cruorflies brought fever on black wings of death.

My father tried to assuage my worries. Cruorflies were mostly active at dawn and at dusk, he told me. Arrhemia mostly affected livestock, and those who worked closely with the animals. That was why meat had all but disappeared from our table. But he took no measures to preserve his own health, for he couldn't move, couldn't see, couldn't breathe, beneath such restrictive attire. And he had important work to do.

Sometimes my thoughts would spiral round and round over what would happen to me if he died. I imagined my aunt arriving with a retinue of servants to take over the house and empty the wine cellar. I imagined her sitting at the head of our great Hresbine dining table, deciding what was to be done with me.

I began checking the aetherscope every day, as though that might give me some warning of things to come. Three of the umbral crystals had gone dark a few days after the funeral, from eleven down to eight, indicating only a slight imbalance in the flux that held steady for the next week. The strange dreams subsided, and no more did I hear my mother's voice, calling to me from the edge of sleep. Perhaps, I began to believe, those incidents had meant nothing after all, reflecting only a passing cloud of umbral madness.

ℰᏣ

Every so often, visitors would come to stroll through our gardens and reception rooms, and to sneak a glimpse at the greenhouses. We were on a list, a record of old homes deemed especially picturesque by the peers of the realm. Ours was noted for its botanical specimens. Most of the visitors were ladies of rank, on some errand or another, perhaps paying a call to my aunt, the Viscountess of Rivene, who lived in her own great house six miles away.

One morning, about a week after the funeral, I was making my way round the salon with my perfume bottle when I heard women's voices in the hall beyond. I knew I wasn't supposed to disturb them. And while I had every desire to obey my father and avoid his censure, I couldn't deny my curiosity, my hunger for knowledge of the outside world. I resolved this conflict by crouching amid the potted ferns, hoping that my striped green and white frock would provide ample disguise. After all, I reasoned, I could hardly be a bother if I was neither seen nor heard.

Two women entered the room, their skirts filling the doorway. The taller woman stepped in front of her more diminutive companion, her sapphire blue skirts swishing as she strode in. Her black hair was piled high upon her head, like a wave cresting before the prow of her tiny feathered hat. Her full-length black cruisse flowed down her back and flared out, rippling round her elbows like long maiden tresses, shocking me with the immodesty of its near-transparent construction, which barely concealed the back of her neck. She passed my hiding place, shading her eyes with one arm, as she took in the room at a glance.

The second lady followed her in, fanning herself with a pamphlet. She had rounded shoulders, a sallow complexion, and silt-colored hair that was already beginning to lose its shape, though it wasn't yet noon. Her dress, the color of a burnished copper kettle, did little to brighten her features.

They paused for a moment to appreciate the view out the doors to the pergola, wedged between the two wings of the house and open to the courtyard beyond. They breathed in the savory fragrance of basil and lavender and lemon balm. Neither of them spotted me. I tucked my head down and tried to keep perfectly still as the ferns tickled my cheeks.

"Such a charming view," remarked the taller woman. Her voice had an almost girlish quality, as though she perpetually spoke round a bright smile. "I do love these old houses, don't you, Leda? With their big airy courtyards and arcades. You don't see them much anymore outside of the marches." She sighed dreamily. "It must have been wonderful for entertaining in its day."

"In its day?" asked the one named Leda, flipping open her pamphlet. "Has the owner abandoned the house?"

"Oh, no. He lives here, but he doesn't socialize. You saw how we are treated here—like customers at a public house. No personal welcome, no grand tour. Quite a superior attitude, if you ask me."

I looked up for a moment. Leda spooned a coffee bean from an urn on the side table and asked, "What do you suppose that maid of theirs is going to *feed* us?"

"Aneidis only knows. I'm going to clip one of those lovely peonies for our table. I have to have one."

Leda cracked the coffee bean and chewed it carefully as

her friend bustled out onto the pergola. "Why doesn't he socialize?" she said, raising her voice. "Do you suppose he's hiding something?"

From outside on the pergola, I heard a pair of all-purpose ladies' shears go *snip snip*, and I cringed inwardly.

"I don't think it's anything so sensational as that. He's just peculiar, that's all."

"Do you recall what happened to his wife? The opera singer?"

From my hiding place, I stopped breathing, afraid to miss a single word of the other woman's response.

"Oh, there were all sorts of wild rumors about that. The family, of course, says it was a lung infection." The lady in blue appeared in the doorway, holding a single bloom.

"It's always a lung infection," Leda said, as she plopped down on the divan, right across the narrowest part of the room from where I crouched. I was close enough to make out the box-stitch detail on the hem of her skirt. As she reached out for the little coffers of food offerings on the table, the scent of the peony filled my nostrils, making them tingle. *No, no, don't sneeze*, I thought, holding perfectly still as the sensation waned. I had to know more.

"It's a wonder though he didn't remarry," Leda continued thoughtfully. "Without a son to carry on the business, who knows what will come of it?"

The lady in blue leaned into the doorway, so that only her head was visible. "I heard she was so beautiful, she ruined him for other women," she said. "If you believe such a thing is possible."

"I don't believe it," Leda said.

"No?"

"She may have been a beauty, but such charms only captivate a man for so long. Once he grows accustomed to them, there's little difference between a thistle and a rose."

"Your cynicism astounds me, cousin," said the lady in blue. "But surely a woman's talents must count for something."

"They count for nothing, once the marriage contract has been sealed."

The lady in blue had finished rummaging in the garden and appeared fully in the doorway, back-lit against the brilliant sun. Another wave of scent hit my tingling nostrils, and I tried to breathe slowly as the sensation intensified. *Don't sneeze, don't sneeze, don't sneeze...*

"I am shocked and dismayed," she said. "Such a view runs contrary to the most basic tenets of the Ladies' Betterment Society. For what good is self-improvement if not to strengthen the marital bond? To maintain such a low opinion of man's attachments—why, it degrades our own sex just the same—"

"*Achoo!*" The sound burst from my throat like a startled songbird, high and delicate.

Leda gasped and leaped to her feet in a rustle of taffeta silk, then advanced round the table and thrust a finger out at me.

"There is a child in here! She was concealing herself. Spying on us!"

The lady in blue, still standing in the doorway, began to laugh. "Don't be a loon, cousin. Why, that must be the man's daughter. Ellinora's niece. Let me see her. Did you ever see such eyes and ears on a child? It puts me in mind of one of those little sand cats in Lady Valin's menagerie. Come out, child, don't be frightened. Come have a pretty flower. See what I brought for you? Seven mercies, whatever were you thinking, hiding from us like that? We won't bite, I promise, we only wish to see your curious little face."

I rose to my feet, taking some encouragement in her tone, which was the same tone all grownups used to indicate they were friendly toward children. I smoothed my skirts as best I could and dropped into a neat little curtsy, looking from one to the other. I smiled, though not too much, and clasped my hands behind my back. But even with such niceties, Leda did not appear won over. Her mouth was set in a grim line that offered me a glimpse of her future visage.

"What's your name?" asked the lady in blue, ignoring her cousin's irritation.

I told her my full name.

"Do you like flowers, Miss Amardine?" she asked.

I wasn't sure how to respond to such a silly question. Without answering, I took a tentative step toward her and examined the mangled stem of the peony, thinking how best to preserve the bloom.

"Go ahead, take it. I've an idea—why don't you tell me about the flowers here?"

"Truly?" I asked, as Leda's mouth twitched at the suggestion. No one had ever offered me such an opportunity before. I launched into rapid speech, aware that either of them could cut me off at any moment, for any reason, and send me back to the nursery. "Did you see the dwarf magus when you came in? We have three different cultivars, but my favorite is the one in the vestibule. It's blooming now—it's the one with the spiky red flowers that spiral out from the center. Did you know that each one has five spirals in one direction, and eight in the other? They're actually the bracts, though, not the flowers. I can show you the difference, if you'd like." I reached out for the flower, intent on teaching them to identify the various parts of its anatomy.

"What is that?" Leda asked, pointing at my right hand, in which I held the bottle of perfume.

I held it out for inspection, proud to be the owner of such a beautiful glass bottle.

The lady in blue said sharply, "What are you doing with that, child?"

"I knew there had to be something," Leda said, in an ominous tone.

"Let us see the bottle, child," said the lady in blue, her voice taking on the edge of command.

My hand reached out; my fingers loosened. "I didn't steal it," I protested, as she took it away from me.

"No?" she said. "Whose scent is it, then?"

"I don't know. It isn't perfume, it's only—"

"Playing with scent is no childhood pastime. And who cut your skirt? I can see your petticoat. You're too tall for that frock."

"How old are you, child?" Leda demanded.

"Eight," I said, and couldn't help but add, "I was only misting the plants."

She looked round, took in the dozen or so pots of greenery in this room alone, and shook her head. "Does anyone else know you have this? Your governess? Your alma? Your *father?*"

"No—I mean, I don't have a governess or an alma."

Leda turned to her cousin. "No governess and no alma! And wearing perfume at such an age!"

"But it isn't perfume," I repeated, flinging up my hands in frustration. "You can go ahead and try it! Go on!"

"Don't get excitable, child. That will never do."

I edged toward the door. This was not how the visit was supposed to proceed. All I wanted was to be away from these baffling women, alone with my piles of books and velveteen kittens. To my great relief, Hespa appeared at that moment in the doorway, balancing a heavily-laden tray in one hand.

"Amardine Sophia!" she scolded. "What are you doing, bothering these ladies? You know you're not supposed to be in here when your father has visitors." She started to apologize to the women, but the one in blue interrupted her.

"Is this child in your charge?" she asked Hespa.

"Yes, my lady."

"What do you know of this?" she asked, holding up the bottle.

Hespa didn't blink. "It's a perfume bottle," she replied, her face as bland as custard.

"Do you think that's *appropriate* for a girl her age?"

"She says she has no governess and no alma," Leda put in. "It seems the task of guarding her against her own nature falls entirely to you."

"Oh, I don't think—" Hespa began to say, but the lady in blue cut her off.

"It isn't just the perfume. She's forward in other ways, as well. You ought to have heard her go on about steeples and brackets! Children ought to show more restraint."

"And she was spying on us when we came in," Leda said.

"Forward *and* sly. Not a good combination," said the lady in blue, shaking her head.

Hespa didn't argue any of it. She just stood there, frozen, as the women continued to talk about me, as though I wasn't even there. Why didn't she say something to exonerate me? I waited, but she kept silent as she placed the tray down on the side table, her face betraying nothing.

"I'll take care of the bottle," she said.

The lady in blue handed it to Hespa, who dropped it into her apron pocket.

"Go on, then," she said to me. "We'll speak later."

I wasn't even out of the room when the lady in blue said, "She ought to have an alma."

"*I* would send her to an almary," Leda replied. "Creeping and spying, and wearing perfume. I wouldn't take any chances with that one."

I retreated to the nursery, in shock. I had done something terrible and these women thought Hespa was to blame. They thought I didn't belong here. They thought Hespa wasn't fit to bring me up. What if they had the power to send me away, against my father's wishes? But he would never send me away, I reasoned. Who would look after the house? He must know how much time I spent, taking care of the greenery. I played the conversation back in my mind, still unsure where I had gone wrong.

Trying not to cry, I sat down at the dressing table where I kept my stationery. It didn't have my name on it yet, but it was a stiff, formal looking paper. On a fresh, new piece of paper I wrote down everything the women had said, as closely as I could recall it. I'd developed a habit of doing this, to Hespa's chagrin. She had caught me at it one evening last frostmoon when I was supposed to be doing my lessons—I was waiting for the ink to dry in the chill, damp air, and had no time to conceal the papers. She had told me never to do it again. I told her I would only write down my impressions of things, so I could paint pictures of them one day. "Goodness," was all she said to that, as though she'd never heard of anyone doing such a thing. But she let me keep scribbling away, and even gave me three colored pencils in lieu of paint.

Now I took out the pencils and began to sketch the ladies. They were out in the courtyard now, the one in blue chattering like a jackdaw under the trees. I remembered her face, so pretty and perfect, until her mouth had twisted with scorn and her eye glinted with disappointment. I tried to capture the way she had looked at me, as though this would allow me to throw it back on her like some sinister mirror spell, but I couldn't get it right.

I was still scribbling away when Hespa brought my lunch. She set down the tray and then, without a word, took the bottle out of her pocket and laid it on the dressing table.

"Take it back, I don't want it any more," I said.

"You can just keep it here with the bric-a-brac," she said. "There's no harm in that, surely. You said it was only water, after all."

"It *was* only water," I replied, still feeling sulky. "But those ladies said I oughtn't play with such things. And I don't care about it, in any case." I went back to my drawing, but I'd made it even worse, so I scratched it out and then ripped it in half for good measure.

"Where *did* you find this bottle, kit?" she asked.

I didn't reply.

"Listen to me," she said. "You did nothing wrong. I'm sure I've seen bottles of pretend scent in the shop windows, right next to little girls' bonnets and hair ribbons. But you mustn't play with real perfume. Scents have power that you don't understand. And if your papa were to smell it, it would only bring him up old memories, and make him sad."

"They want to send me away," I said.

"That's none of their business. Your papa wouldn't send you away for the world. Don't you worry about such nonsense."

Because we had visitors, she didn't stay and eat with me. After she left the room, I picked up the bottle and uncorked it, then brought it up to my nose. Just as I'd told the ladies, there was nothing in the bottle except water from the basin cupboard. But a faint scent still remained, so indefinite that I doubted either Leda or the lady in blue would have detected it. They would smell ridiculous wearing it, I thought, with some satisfaction. They weren't worthy of the scent, and I was sure everyone would know it.

But their criticism left me with a lingering anxiety no ritual could relieve. That night I dreamed they returned to the house and cut off all of my fingers, convinced beyond all doubt that I was concealing claws. I screamed for my father to help me, but he was nowhere to be found. I woke thrashing in the darkness, still calling out for him, but it was Hespa who came for me, a candle illuminating her ruddy face, her hair glinting like rusted lambswool in a nimbus of light.

CHAPTER THREE

I KEPT MY WORD TO HESPA, leaving the "real" perfume bottle safely in my hatbox. But my curiosity would not be so easily appeased. The following day, I crept upstairs while my father was in his workshop. I paused before the door, hearing the sounds of his paleophone, then kept going, down the hallway to the gallery. I had to look into my mother's room once again. There was still light outside, though it was starting to fade, and I thought I might discover something I had missed before, when I'd had only a faint-glowing tree to aid my investigation. But just as I was approaching the door of the blue room, it swung open, and Hespa emerged with her dustrag.

She sighed when she saw me. "What do you think you're doing, miss?"

"Nothing," I replied.

She shook her head, knowing me too well to accept such a response. "You know your father doesn't want you poking round back here," she said. "Why don't you see if you can be of help to him in his workshop?"

"Do you think he might like that?"

"You won't know until you knock on the door," she said.

I scurried off, satisfied by her reasoning. He didn't answer my knock, but the door was unlocked, so I pushed it open and peered inside.

He was hunched over his workbench, his back turned toward me. I didn't call out to him right away; I wanted to take in the grandeur of the room. For to call it a workshop, although accurate, didn't do it justice. It had been a ballroom once, in some bygone age when people still held fêtes here, but now the shadows of the white pillars lay stretched across an empty floor. I had read of dancing, and knew what it was, but I had never seen it demonstrated at Guildenflore.

My father had "withdrawn from public life" sometime after I was born. At least, that was what my aunt, Lady Ellinora Pendrake, liked to say when she was in her wine-steeped lamentations. That summer was even worse than usual. My father was nervous about the excessive heat and rain, and about the cruorflies culling the herds and dropping the magpies from their roosts. And though he hadn't announced it, I knew he was nervous about a dinner party.

Once a year we hosted dinner for the harvesters and their families, and all the folk of the lower court. The neighbors and cousins also attended, no matter what the absence of an invitation might indicate to some. They would draw up on foot or in sedan chairs, leaving their servants to look uncomfortable and ill-prepared. Then they would circle round the tables and wait to be scandalized by some family drama, which was inevitable. Usually Grandame was the one who planned the menu, readied the house, and tried to make certain everyone was attended to and didn't go home with too much to talk about. But she had remained far away, in Ildecia, to manage certain affairs with a family property there. So it was that my father was left to do everything, and as of now he had done close to nothing that I could ascertain.

I thought he hadn't heard me enter the workshop, but before I could approach he said, "Come here, Amardine."

I closed the door behind me and stepped forward, my slippered feet making no noise on the parquet floor. As I approached the workbench, he rose and stretched, setting aside the small pardesu tree he was wiring, and went over to a cart where three others were awaiting his attention.

I sat down in the chair next to his. My father plucked one of the trees from its familiar pot and carried it round the workbench, over my head. I sensed the furtive grasping of its roots; the little pardesu tree was scrabbling to make a pact with the earth. Dirt rained down on the white puffs of my sleeves, but he was looking at the tree and so it didn't upset him.

"The pruning shears, Amardine," he said, holding out his other hand with palm upraised. Solemn as anything, I pretended

I was completing some religious ritual as I placed them into his hand. I waited for him to say something suitably mysterious or profound, but his attention was fixed on the tree.

"Why must you hurt them so?" I asked, as more dirt crumbled away from the trembling roots.

"Don't be nonsensical. I'm trimming and re-potting the specimen, that's all. Pardesu trees have to be kept stunted for the extract to reach maximum potency."

"It looks to me like you're cutting its roots off," I said. "How would you feel if someone cut off my feet the way you're doing to that tree?"

He gave me a sideways look, the sun-weathered skin round his eyes crinkling. "I suppose I'd have to bury you in a planter and see if flowers sprouted from your head."

"You're the one who's nonsensible," I retorted.

"Non-sen-si-cal. And I didn't ask you to keep me company."

I watched him silently for a while. There were things I wanted to ask him, but every time the questions rose up in my throat, I found myself swallowing them back down again. And then, as the moments passed, the questions sunk deeper and deeper, until they were buried completely, like seeds.

"When are you going to harvest the pardesu?" I asked, finally.

"Within the fortnight. We'll need a couple of clear days for the drying process. Father Parquar expects we'll get a break in the rain soon." He glanced up at the pillar next to his workbench, where he had stuck his daily-recorded readings from thermometer, barometer, and aetherscope. I squinted over his shoulder to read his tiny print, noting that there had, in fact, been an increase in umbral flux just after the funeral for the old man. But the high spike during that night hadn't been recorded, presumably because he hadn't witnessed it.

"What about the umbra?" I asked.

"What about it?"

"Isn't it rather high?"

He turned to look at me, his expression bemused. "I didn't realize you took note of such things. It has been a bit high this last week, but not so out of balance as to affect the harvest."

I nodded, wanting to prolong this line of inquiry, but I didn't know enough about the subject to think of better questions. Instead, I turned to the matter of the upcoming dinner party.

"Don't we need to air out the tents?"

"We will, but there's no sense in doing it now."

"What are we going to eat?" I asked.

"The usual fare," my father said.

"Is everything ordered already?"

He looked at me then, furrowing his brow. "Why so many questions about the dinner party?" he asked.

"I just want to make certain it's a success," I said, earnestly.

He laughed. "You don't trust your papa, do you?"

I felt the heat rise in my face. "No, I mean, it's not that, Papa." But I couldn't resist asking one more question. "Are you going to give the toast this year?"

"Do you think I shouldn't?"

"No," I said, but it sounded too emphatic to my own ears. I tucked my legs under me and leaned forward, watching him as he went back to his work. I imagined the tree curling into itself, crushing its own branches from within. That was what must happen if you were prevented from growing outward, I thought—the rings would wind tighter and tighter until your whole self was squeezed between them. I felt my senses attune to the tree, with hardly a conscious effort. I perceived an unexpected level of distress—more than the reaction to the trimming, I thought. There was a toxin, spreading up through the braid of its trunk. The tree wanted to weep, to flush it out. I could feel it, almost like a tingling in my own hands. I willed the sap to run free, and instinctively I began to sing, very softly, in a nonsense language, helping it along.

My father's hands froze. He turned to me, his expression flat and unreadable.

"Where did you learn to sing that?" he asked.

"I don't know, I just felt like singing it."

"You must have heard it somewhere. Did Hespa teach you?"

I pressed my thumb into the palm of my other hand, anxiously tracing the whorl of lines inscribed upon it. "No, Papa. No one taught me."

Stupid, I thought, cursing myself for my carelessness. I hadn't thought he would actually recognize the song. I *had* made it up, I was sure of it.

"Don't do it again," he said. "Especially not round the servants, do you hear?"

"But why not?"

"Because I told you not to."

He stood up, brushing bits of twig and leaf from his trousers. "I'm done here for the evening. Clean the floor and table if you please, and lock the doors behind you when you leave."

"Wait," I said.

His shoulders tensed. I wanted to ask him about the things I'd found in my mother's room. But this was a bad time. I'd already ruined it.

"Never mind, it's nothing," I said.

He regarded me for a moment, then turned on his heel. Then he was gone, the door thudding hollowly behind him, his booted steps receding down the stairs. I was alone in the vast ballroom.

But the tree—the tree was screaming for my attention. I gathered it up from the workbench, cupping the roots in my hands and willing it to heal. Sap ran from newly-opened wounds in the bark, discharging the ailment. Tiny white flowers blinked open and glittered like crystals in the light of the aetherlamps, as though in silent gratitude. My father denied that a tree could possess intelligence, but most people thought that of children, too.

"Even a little tree ought to have a fine pot to grow in," I said. I placed it back in its proper container, and the leaves seemed to shiver with relief. I smiled, forgetting, for a brief moment, my father's strange reaction.

But only for a moment. I replayed the exchange in my mind, recalling how his light teasing had changed in an instant, as soon as I began to sing. He didn't lose his temper often, instead preferring the weapons of silence and withdrawal. I had made him uncomfortable, and for that, I must be punished.

The day's rain had finally subsided, but it was still drip-dripping from the eaves, from the balcony beyond the screened door. I slipped the latch and went outside to stand on the long platform, looking out over the courtyard, to the far end where Grandame's little house stood, and across the iron gate to a second unoccupied cottage. This second house had long been the residence of my great-aunt Rosamund, but she lived in a sanitarium now, her mind having gone soft shortly after I was born.

I worried my father might think my mind was going soft, as well. Those things ran in the family, people said.

The smell of woodsmoke clung to the damp air. It reminded me of the elm tree, where the old man had died, and how its branches rose up like a multitude of arms, frozen in the midst of casting some powerful spell. But that was just the sort of fancy I knew my father wouldn't appreciate. So I kept my own counsel, listening to the unbroken drone of the bullfrogs. I walked the length of the balcony, pulling down the silk screens, letting them cloud my view. I was enclosed now, but I could still smell verbena, a citrus tang that sharpened my senses to a knife's edge. Through the haze of the screen, the glow beetles flickered in the grass like candles in a fog.

It might have been a perfect summer evening, and I wish I could remember it that way. But as I turned and gathered up broom and dustpan to clean up my father's mess, all I could think was that I had displeased him.

☙❧

A few nights later, through the open doorway of the washroom, I watched Hespa soak her gnarled feet in a basin of salts. I liked the soft sound of the water purling round her ankles, as she lifted one foot, then the other, patting them dry with a towel.

Hespa had come from a place called Ungria when she was a girl, and worked for my aunt before I was born. She had a broad, pinkish face, and eyes that were reassuringly bovine in their constancy. Her burnt-red hair was softer than it looked: almost fleecy where it appeared all wire sponge springing from beneath her wimple. She was the largest woman I had ever seen, taller than most men, including my father, and was sturdy and guarded in her nature. But sometimes, when we were alone, she would tell me stories she'd learned as a child.

She bent down, the locket she always wore slipping out from beneath her collar. Its gold chain glinted in the light of the oil lamp. I stole into the room and drew up the little wooden stool to sit before her.

"Hespa, will you tell me the tale of the Witch in the Wode?"

"That one again, kit? You won't sleep a wink tonight."

"I won't be scared."

She curled her toes in the water, making them pop up out of the surface like the roots of some ancient tree. "I oughtn't have filled your head with such things."

"Well, you did, and you can't very well take it out of my head now. Please, Hespa."

She sighed. "All right, then. Once, there was a young girl who lived in the forest. Her name was Tarsha, and she was a few years older than you. She was the eldest of her siblings, with a younger brother who'd been sickly ever since he was born. Their parents didn't think he'd live to see his tenth birthday. But Tarsha would go out every day and gather herbs to make her brother a special tea. She loved her brother so much that she made a vow that she would one day learn how to cure him of his disease. One day, she promised him, he would sit a horse and ride and hunt with their father.

"One afternoon when Tarsha was out in the forest, she spied a figure moving through the bracken. The figure was a hunched, ugly old woman with a basket, and she was gathering herbs as well. They met in the bracken and Tarsha explained why she was there. Then the old woman surprised her by offering to help.

"*Such an old, feeble woman,* Tarsha thought, *how can she help me?* But she followed her back to her home in the forest all the same. She entered the old woman's hut, which was dark and cramped and filled with all sorts of odd bits and pieces."

"Was she scared?" I asked.

"A little bit," Hespa replied. "But she would have been more scared if she'd known what the old woman was."

"She was a witch," I said, reveling in it.

Hespa nodded. "The witch said, 'I have been looking for an apprentice for some time. I will teach you what I know about herbs and potions if you work for me every day. And in exchange, I will give you a phial of medicine to take home to your brother. He must keep drinking it or he will waste away.'

"Tarsha agreed to this arrangement. She was excited to learn about herbs and potions. She helped the witch make the medicine for her brother, and each evening she would ride her horse back home and give him the potion. The witch taught her how to make it, but left one ingredient out of the recipe, which she would add herself at the very end. Try as she might, Tarsha couldn't get the witch to tell her what the secret ingredient was. 'One day, when you're older, I will teach you everything I know,' the witch promised, 'even my most secret powers, which you have never seen.'

"'I don't believe you have secret powers,' Tarsha told the witch."

"Why didn't she believe her?" I asked.

"Perhaps she did believe her, but she wanted to needle the witch into showing them to her," Hespa said. "But the witch wouldn't be vexed so easily. She told Tarsha, 'When you're older, I will teach you my secret powers, but only if you work hard and do everything I ask of you. And above all, you must never, ever open the door to the cellar.' Tarsha was a good worker, and as she had no reason to go in the cellar, she agreed. She worked for the witch for nearly five years, growing into a lovely young woman. Each day she faithfully brought her brother his potion, and he grew stronger as well. By now he could ride a horse with their father. He passed his tenth birthday, and the whole family celebrated.

"But one day, while the witch was out in the forest gathering herbs, Tarsha was left behind to stir the cauldron. And it was then that she heard a knocking on the cellar door." Hespa rapped on the door of the washroom with her knuckles, three resounding knocks that made me jump.

"Are you too frightened to hear the end, kit?" she asked.

I shook my head. "No, I want to hear it."

"Very well. But don't say I didn't warn you."

"I like being scared," I said.

"Well, Tarsha didn't enjoy it as much as you do. She was so frightened by the noise, she nearly dropped the sachet of herbs she was carefully sprinkling into the cauldron. She stopped and listened for a moment, and then the knocking came again.

"'Who's there?' she called out.

"'A prisoner,' came the answer. It was a man's voice. 'Please, let me out.'

"'I can't let you out,' Tarsha said, going to the door. 'I'm not supposed to open the cellar door.'

"'Why do you do the bidding of an evil woman, who keeps an innocent man locked in her cellar?' he asked.

"'How do I know you're innocent?' Tarsha said. They went back and forth several times, and as they spoke, she began to question what the witch had told her. She could hardly allow someone to be imprisoned unjustly. She was curious, too. Finally, she agreed to open the door just a crack, to see the prisoner.

"She found the witch's ring of keys, which she had left hanging on a hook by the door. Tarsha found the one that unlocked the cellar and put it in the lock. Then she opened the door, just a little bit, and gasped.

"Even with just a glimpse, he was the most handsome man she'd ever seen. Without thinking, she opened the door wider and stood before him, spellbound. He was tall and trim, and had long, golden hair and eyes the deep gray of a winter sky.'"

"What is winter?" I asked.

"It's like the frostmoon, except colder, and it lasts for months on end," Hespa explained. "Snow falls from the sky and blankets the ground. Sometimes it can even bury houses."

I shivered.

"But it wasn't winter yet. It was only autumn. And Tarsha was in love."

"With this man she'd only just met?" I asked, skeptical.

"It happens in the stories," Hespa said, sounding defensive. "Besides, she was young and had never been in love before. You'll understand someday."

"I doubt it," I said. "But I want to hear the rest."

"Once Tarsha came to her senses, she realized what she had done. 'My brother!' she said, starting to panic. 'Once my mistress returns and sees what I've done, she'll cast me out of her house. I'll never learn the secret ingredient I need to keep my brother well.' She tried to explain the problem to the man, and after listening, he said, 'I know what the secret ingredient is.'

"'What is it?' asked Tarsha.

"'The blood of a prince,' said the man.

"Tarsha gasped as the man rolled up the sleeve of his fine coat and showed her the marks in his skin, marks made by a small, sharp knife. 'You see, your mistress has been using my blood in her potions. She intends to keep me here in her cellar until I have no more blood left to give.'

"Tarsha was horrified that she had been a part of such a thing. And yet, her actions had saved her brother. She put her hands to her face and began to weep.

"'Don't cry, lovely girl,' said the prince. 'You have freed me, and so I owe you a debt. You know how to create the potion, do you not?'

"'Yes,' Tarsha answered. 'Now I know every step and ingredient.'

"'Then the solution is simple. I will freely offer my blood to treat your brother, if you agree to be my bride. You and your brother shall return with me to my kingdom, and he can be your knight.'

"Tarsha lowered her hands and stared at the prince, not sure she had heard him properly. 'But I am just a simple girl,' she said. 'Surely there are others more suitable to be your bride.'

"'None as beautiful or as brave as you,' said the prince. 'But you must make your decision quickly. That old hag will return soon and imprison me once again.'

"Tarsha was charmed by the prince's words, but she still felt she owed her mistress an explanation. She wrote a note telling her that she had to leave, and thanked her for all of her many lessons. Then she put on her cloak and led the prince to the shed where her horse was tied up. 'We'll need to go back to my house to get my brother,' she said.

"'Of course,' said the prince. He got on the horse behind her, and they began to ride out into the forest."

Hespa lifted her feet out of the basin and began to dry them with a towel. "Now you have to decide which ending you want," she said.

"I want the real ending," I said. "The one your grandame told you."

"Very well," Hespa said. "But first you need to get ready for bed."

She helped me out of my clothes and gave me a clean night shift to slip over my shoulders. Then she sat me down at my dressing table to comb the knots out of my hair. "Tell me the rest of the story," I pressed, as she began untangling the ends.

"Tarsha and the prince rode out into the forest," Hespa continued. "She had traveled this way hundreds of times by now, and knew the route like the back of her own hand. They took a familiar path, crunching through the fallen leaves. But soon, she began to feel uneasy. The landscape seemed to shift round them. The familiar path seemed different somehow, the trees growing more close, their bare limbs reaching out to snag her hair with their spidery branches. An hour passed, and Tarsha then knew that something was wrong. She ought to have reached her house by then, or at least seen smoke curling from its chimney, but there was no sign of anyone around them. Even the birds had gone silent.

"Tarsha cursed herself for her own foolishness. How had she got them lost, when she had taken this path so many times? She decided not to say anything, fearing the prince would think her soft in the head. Perhaps they would stumble upon some familiar landmark soon, and she would find her way back to the proper path. As the path wound round a bend, she saw that it continued through an archway made of many sticks bound together with twine. She'd never seen anything like it before. Again, she felt uneasy. The horse sensed her fear and stopped in the path. She almost spoke up. But then the prince gave the horse a kick, prodding it into motion, and the moment passed.

"They continued on," Hespa said, as she worked her way up the ends of my hair. I winced as she hit a snag. "They passed beneath the archway. And then, everything changed."

"They went into the Umbra," I said. It was this part of the story that always made me shiver with a mixture of terror and delight.

She nodded. "The Umbra wasn't an evil place, not altogether. But it could be shaped by those who passed through it, those who had the will to do so. Of course, Tarsha knew nothing of this. She only knew that she had passed into a realm of silvery twilight, where the trees grew twisted and close, and terrible, bat-winged creatures with the faces of old men flew shrieking from the branches. She covered herself with her hood and shrank away from them as they clawed at her head. She grabbed at the mane of her horse as it reared in terror. All the while, the prince sat calmly behind her.

"'Don't be afraid,' he said, but his voice had changed. It had become deeper, raspier, and the words did nothing to quell Tarsha's fear. 'We're almost there.'

"Tarsha turned her head to look at the prince. What she saw made her faint dead away, and she would have fallen from her horse if the creature hadn't grasped her tight."

"What did it look like?" I asked.

"The creature Tarsha knew as the prince no longer appeared like a handsome young man. It had a man's face still, but one that had aged about seven decades. Black veins stood out against its pale skin, and its eyes bulged out of its hairless head. It had no neck, and its head bobbed about a foot above its body, tethered by a black, shadowy substance that rippled in the silvery light. Tarsha knew at once that the creature was a demon, and that she had followed it back to its domain."

Hespa spoke softly, without theatrics. Somehow that chilled me even more than if she had put on an entertainer's voice.

"What happened then?" I whispered.

"What happened? The witch, meanwhile, returned to her hut and found the cellar door standing wide open. Then she found Tarsha's note. She burned the note, letting out a curse that allowed her to sense Tarsha and move in her direction. Then she took her sword from the wall of her hut."

"She had a *sword?*" I asked. I didn't recall this detail from the story.

"She does now," Hespa said, round the hair pin she'd stuck in her mouth. "She wields it in both hands."

I felt a painful tug and suddenly realized what she was doing with my hair. "You're not putting it all up in pins, are you?" I asked.

"You were being so still, kit, listening to my story," she said. "Don't you want to hear the end?"

I sighed. "Yes, but I don't see why I need curls. I don't want to go to sleep with pins in my head."

"I saw it in an advert. I thought we might see how it looked, before the harvest dinner," Hespa said.

I tried to imagine Hespa poring over the latest fashion adverts in the newsstand at Meliflore's.

"All right," I sighed, if only to get back to the story. "What happened after the witch picked up her sword?"

"She got on her horse and rode into the forest. With her spell, she could track Tarsha even though the demon had changed the landscape. Soon, she came upon the archway made of branches, and knew that's where they had gone. She rode into the Umbra and called upon the good spirits to protect her."

"There are good spirits in the Umbra?" I asked.

Hespa nodded. "Whenever you feel happy for no reason, or help another person, it creates good spirits in the Umbra. They look like motes of light, but if you look closely, you can see that they're made up of many glowing eyes. And they swarmed out of the darkness to light the witch's path. As she traveled, she was beset by the bat-winged creatures, but she got off her horse and stood her ground. Her horse reared and bit at the creatures, stomping them into the dirt. The witch fended them off with her sword, stabbing a number of them before the rest flew off. Then she got back onto her horse and continued on her way.

"At last she came to a clearing where a single tree stood, and at its base, the demon was circling, marking the ground with a stick. Through the branches, the witch could see Tarsha, trapped in a cage made from the living boughs of the tree, laced together like giant hands. The witch knew she had to interrupt the demon before it could finish making its circle. If it was completed, the demon would be able to bend the tree's spirit to its will and have it crush Tarsha. So she kicked her horse and charged straight ahead. The demon was so surprised to see the witch that it dropped its stick.

"The witch stopped short of the demon and looked at Tarsha. She was alive, but unconscious, slumped in the branches of the tree. Raising her voice, she called out to the tree, her words a magical charm to ask the tree spirit for aid. Normally, she would hear the spirit rustling in her mind in response, but this time, there was no reply. The demon laughed, a terrible, grating sound that echoed through the clearing and rang through the distant ring of trees.

"'Foolish old woman,' said the demon. 'Your feeble spells won't work here. This is my domain. Go home and die in your own world.'

"The witch thought about what to do. She didn't want to fight the demon with her sword, for the demon had long, sharp claws and was much stronger and faster than her. Still, she couldn't leave her apprentice to her fate.

"'Spare the girl,' the witch said. 'Let her go, and I won't destroy you.'

"The demon laughed again. 'As though you could destroy me, old woman. You might have been able to overpower me in your world, but here I am the stronger. You have no means to kill me. Your sword is useless against me. Even your spells cannot hurt me.'

"'Are you so certain of that?' the witch asked.

"'Your spells would bounce off of me,' the demon taunted. 'You know this is so—else you would have destroyed me when you had me trapped in your cellar. Even your glyphs of binding will not work here.'

"The witch's shoulders slumped. She knew the demon spoke the truth, for she had studied all manner of demons. 'Spare the girl,' she said again, 'and take me in her place. I know you plan to sacrifice her. But I am an old woman, and have lived long enough.'

"'That is what you think? Of course the girl needs to die. But she will be reborn in this tree as my consort, to remain at my side for all of eternity. Why would I trade her for an ugly old crone?'

"At that, the witch cast a spell. Not to attack the demon, which she knew was fruitless. Instead, she changed her form, becoming the most beautiful woman the world had ever seen. Her skin became perfectly smooth, and her hair grew out in long, thick waves. Her back straightened; her limbs lengthened. She stood tall and proud. As pretty as Tarsha was, no mortal woman could rival the witch's new form.

"The demon looked her over. 'How do I know you won't change back as soon as the sacrifice is complete?' it asked.

"'Because whatever form that is sacrificed is made permanent,' the witch reasoned. 'Isn't that so? Else your young bride would grow old one day, as well.'

"The demon knew this to be true. 'Very well,' it said, after some consideration. 'Your apprentice can watch you die on her behalf.' And with that, it pulled Tarsha from the tree's grasp, dropping her to the ground. Tarsha groaned and began to wake. Then the witch climbed up in the tree to take her place.

"Once the witch was inside the demon's circle, touching the tree, she tried again to connect with the spirit of the tree. This time, the tree responded. The witch asked the tree to reach out with its branches and ensnare the demon. At once, the branches began to shake, and long, sharp thorns sprouted out everywhere except on the limbs that cradled the witch. The tree uprooted itself and descended on the demon, which was trying to flee. But the tree called to its friends at the edge of the clearing, and they rushed in as well, attacking the demon, stabbing it with ten thousand thorns.

"The demon's screams woke Tarsha, and she sat up on the ground to see a flurry of movement as the trees clubbed and stabbed the evil creature to death. When it was finished, they all went back to their places, and the witch dropped out of the tree. Tarsha could hardly believe what had happened.

"'Mistress, how can you ever forgive me?' she asked. 'I was foolish and didn't trust you, even though you saved my brother and have taught me these last five years. But now he is sure to die.'

"The witch found Tarsha's horse grazing at the far end of the clearing, and they prepared to return home. 'What makes you think your brother is going to die?' she asked.

"'Because the demon's blood was the secret ingredient, and now the demon is no more,' Tarsha said, getting on her horse.

"'Is that what the demon told you?' asked the witch. 'Have you learned nothing, child? All demons are liars. The blood is not the secret ingredient.'

"'Then what is it?' Tarsha asked. 'Will you tell me if I work extra hard and promise never to disobey you again?'

"'I will tell you now,' the witch said, as they passed back through the archway and returned to their familiar forest. 'The secret ingredient is a wise heart, tempered by the sorrows of the world, the very soul of the witch who has learned to turn her melancholy into passion. You have suffered at the hands of a demon, and yet you survived, and returned home. You have everything you need to heal your brother.'

"Tarsha had nightmares for many years afterwards. But she never forgot what the witch had said to her. She couldn't be fooled by anyone. She became a powerful healer, singing dark, mournful songs to evoke her magic. Her brother grew up strong and her family thrived. When the old witch died, peacefully in her sleep, Tarsha hung wooden chimes in the trees outside her hut. To this day it's said her spirit whistles through the chimes, protecting the grove from evil-doers and soothing the hearts of those who suffer."

I sighed with satisfaction. "Hespa, you ought to write this down in a book."

"Oh, no, kit," she said. It was difficult to tell with her complexion, but I thought she might have blushed. "I doubt anyone would wish to buy such a tale for children. You mustn't repeat it round your cousins, either—they might be too frightened."

By now Hespa had nearly finished pinning my hair. I looked like a stranger to myself with my scalp bristling with pins. *Like some creature from the Umbra*, I thought. That reminded me of something.

"Hespa, do you remember those ladies who came to the house?"

"Last week, you mean?"

"Yes. The ones who yelled at me about the perfume."

"It wasn't right of them to do that," Hespa said.

"They thought I was strange-looking," I said, leaning forward to peer at my face in the mirror. Were my features overly large? Were my ears truly like that of an animal in a menagerie? I tilted my head to examine them. They folded over at the tips, giving them a slight tulip shape. That was odd, I realized, with a growing sense of unease. My father's ears didn't look like that. I turned over my palm, to stare at the whorl of lines spiraling out from the center. That was strange too, wasn't it?

Hespa sat very still, on a stool behind me. I couldn't read her expression in the mirror.

"You do look a bit different from other children," she said, with her characteristic bluntness. "You know of the Feym-ri, from the stories?"

"I thought they were just stories," I said, my stomach tightening.

She shook her head. "They're people, just not from this world."

"What do you mean?" I asked. "Where do they come from?"

"From—the Umbra," she said, hesitating. "They've lived among us for thousands of years, since the Age of the Titans. At least, that's what my grandame told me, when I was a little girl."

A little shock ran through me as I thought about the story she had just told, about all the stories she had told me over the years. How long had she been waiting for me to make that connection?

"From the Umbra? You mean like the demon? You mean it's a real place?"

"It's as real as anything," Hespa said. "It's where umbral energy comes from, leaking into this world through cracks in the firmament. The Feym-ri were there first, though. The demons were created by the hate and greed of humankind."

She went to the bed and turned the covers down, then gently patted the mattress. I rose obediently and got under the sheet and coverlet, drawing my knees up to my chest.

"Your father ought to be the one to talk to you about this," she said, as she sat down on the edge of the bed.

"You know he won't," I said. "He never tells me anything."

She sighed. "I know, kit."

"Was that—what my mother was, then?" I asked.

"She had the blood. Feym'ari, they call it, when there's a human parent. That's what you are, too."

"What does that mean?" I asked. "Is it good, or bad?"

"It is what it is. It's nothing that ought to bring you worry or shame," she said. "You see how I'm different, as well? In the country where I come from, many people are descended from the giants. Or at least, that's what they say."

"Truly?" I asked. "I just thought you were very tall. Were there Feym-ri where you came from? Did you ever meet one?"

"I did. They were travelers, mostly. They find refuge in the forests, living off the land and trading in the villages. Some people think the Feym-ri are naturally wicked. That they traffic with demons. That's what the priests said. But they don't know the truth of it. The demons invaded their home; that's why they came to our world. They've guarded the umbral pathways for thousands of years. It was the priests who brought trouble to my land, when they drove them from their posts."

"Is that why you left?" I asked.

She nodded. "I traveled with the Feym-ri for a time, along with some of the other children from my town. They helped us get down the river, to the city of Cerelune. We knew they wouldn't talk to the priests."

"Why not?" I asked.

"They have no love for Aneidis. That divide goes back a long, long time."

"Father Parquar is a priest, and he's always been kind to me," I pointed out. Then another thought crossed my mind. "Do you suppose he doesn't know about me? About me being—" I paused, the word sitting awkwardly on my tongue—"feym'ari?"

"He knows," Hespa said. "But he's a good man, and you can trust him."

"How do you know?" I asked.

"The men who came to Ungria were different. They were war-priests, sent from Achalion, a city far to the east. They're more strict about how they worship there."

I stretched my legs out beneath the coverlet, wishing she would keep talking, but I sensed her reserve building again. I felt as though we were two castaways deserted together in a foreign land, and we ought to cling to one another for mutual support. But we were more than that, of course. She was a servant, and I was child. Neither of us had the luxury of speaking freely.

Nevertheless, I couldn't resist asking one more question. "Is that why Papa doesn't go to chapel? Because he married a feym'ari woman?"

Hespa leaned over my bedside table and blew out the lamp. She rose to her feet, her silhouette towering against the moonlit silk screens on the windows, and I could easily imagine that she was descended from giants, with her broad shoulders and statuesque figure. I imagined that with a sword in her hand, she could dispatch anyone who tried to hurt me. But unlike the witch in her story, she had no sword, only the blunt instruments of her station, and I was beginning to suspect that these would never cut through to the truth I sought.

"One day, when you're older," she said, "you can ask him yourself."

CHAPTER FOUR

I DIDN'T WANT TO WAIT UNTIL I was older. I wanted to beat my fists against the door of my father's workshop and demand answers. *Why won't you talk about her? Why won't you talk to me?*

But I could already imagine his reaction. I could see the dead eyes, the mouth down-turned with faint disgust. "Calm yourself, Amardine," I imagined him telling me, in that stern tone of voice that always made me feel like an unruly animal in need of discipline. "I won't be moved by tricks and tears." That was another one of his favorite sayings.

I was to remain calm, always.

Very well, I thought, deciding to go about my quiet work on the second floor. I would search my mother's room more thoroughly. Hespa was outside on the veranda, beating the carpets with her thick wooden paddle, so the way was clear. But then, just as I was about to mount the second flight of stairs, I spotted something on the wall that didn't belong. My slippers skidded on the wooden floor, which was currently bare of its usual area rug.

There, half concealed in the shadow beneath the edge of a picture frame, was a small bubble in the wallpaper. When I touched it, it moved. To most people, it might not seem such a terrible thing, but I understood its implications. I couldn't imagine how it got there. I'd never seen wallpaper bubble before—this was the sort of thing that could only happen in disordered houses, where no one made the beds until after breakfast.

Was it part of a pattern? Was it an omen? A *spight*, as Hespa would call it? I tried to recall how she'd explained it to me. "It's a sign that something's a-tapping on the walls between our world and the next, trying to find weak spots, trying to find a way in." She'd been dusting the upstairs hallway when she first told me about spights, and as she spoke, she stepped in front of the window at the end of the hall and her whole form turned dark and flat against the streaming light, the edges of her body glowing like an open doorway. The effect made me so uneasy, I didn't go up to that hallway for a long time afterward.

Once again the curious dread arose in me, as though I'd uncovered the end of a fine silken thread, only to feel the tug of the unseen spider at the other end.

My father mightn't worry about a spot of dirt tracked upon the floor—that could easily be swept away by someone else —but a shoddy design, a flaw in craftsmanship, could pitch him into a disgruntled fever that could last for days. Once, he purchased a new set of drawing room chairs and discovered, upon their delivery, that the backs were not made of solid mahogany, but rather had been artfully veneered. His contempt for the furniture had been impossible to bear, and in the end, he had returned it. It made me wonder what he might decide about me, should he ever find me so lacking.

He never would have decided on his own to hang our clean, plastered walls with aggrandized flower designs, especially not ones which were drawn by someone who clearly lacked botanical knowledge. No, this was Lady Pendrake's idea. My aunt had pestered my father all the previous year to have his drawing room papered, saying it was very much done in the great houses of Cereval, and our family home ought to reflect something of the modern age.

He was a stubborn man, but his only means of resistance was doing nothing. And one day, Lady Pendrake sent a wallpapering crew to the house. Hespa had loaded up the service trolley and offered them tea, and from that point on he could not work himself up to throw them out. It was too awkward, I imagine, once they started measuring windows and cornices, and got their fingers stuck in the fine handles of the porcelain.

And so he suffered them to paper the drawing room and the stairwell like a Yfandish bank. I thought it was dreary and stifling, but Lady Pendrake insisted, "It will respond beautifully to the warm glow of an aetherlamp."

I couldn't afford to let him see the bubble in the wallpaper. Already he worried about the harvest and the cruorflies and the dinner party, and I had felt the effects of it, in the frequent repetition of "Not now, Amardine." Already he feared meat and shunned water, taking brandy in the evenings and weak wine throughout the day. He had begun sipping his morning coffee on a little-used balcony, behind a screen, as though he could no longer bear the view. In the drawing room he sat and smoked cheroots, his head nodding back against the wall, letting his fingers drape and all feeling leave his leaden eyes.

No, there would be no tranquility in the house, not even a rare moment, when the bubble in the wallpaper was discovered. I could imagine, just by way of his discontent, the walls of the house fracturing, slumping into the mud, the very foundations cracking beneath the weight of his dire predictions. There was nothing I could do about the harvest, or the cruorflies, or even the dinner party, but perhaps I could solve this one thing for him.

I crept downstairs, silent but for the dead-leaf rustle of my skirts. Night had not yet fallen, and the sky through the windows was woolly with rain. Marguerite would be in the kitchen with her daughter Esmay, preparing dinner. I went straight down the hall, past the front door, past the salon and the library, then turned to the left, all the way to the end of the corridor, where my father's office was located.

I looked for an ink roller and, after a sudden insight, a piece of stationery paper. I had watched my father's valet with the clothes iron, pressing out wrinkles in his shirts, and it occurred to me that a roller might do the trick for the wallpaper. I was pleased with myself for thinking to put a piece of paper under it, in case there was still ink residue on the roller. It was the sort of careful forethought my father would admire. I stole over to his desk, in search of the items I required, but paused as my eyes settled over a small, worn-looking book, sitting tidily in one corner.

The leather cover and binding was swollen with water damage, and so old the title was worn away. Its pages, too, were waterlogged, and some were encrusted with dirt. I had never seen this book before, and could not imagine my father taking so little care with any book in his collection. I picked it up gently, the pages crinkling, the binding cracking as I flipped open the front cover.

The title page had been ripped out. But the table of contents, though stained and faded, was still legible. As my eyes scanned down the page, I tried to absorb its contents, but it was so bizarre, so unexpected, that I had to read it several times before comprehension dawned.

"*A Sacrifice For a Good Harvest*," read the first line. Then:

"*Reading Eggshells to Predict Weather*"

"*Cures for Poisoning*"

"*A Tonic for Grief*"

"*A Binding for the Spirits of the Umbra*"

"*Speaking with the Dead*"

"*Words of Warding*"

"Rituals of Passing: Safe Journeys of the Spirit"
"Watered in Blood: A Guide for the Dying Magus"

How had my father, who disparaged both religion and super-stition, come to be in possession of a book like this? What was he doing with it? Was I holding in my hands an actual spellbook? I stood beneath the window, holding the book against the fading light. I imagined I was a sorcerer's apprentice, innocently cleaning my mentor's tower when I stumbled upon some forbidden grimoire tucked away in a secret cupboard.

My father's startled voice rang out behind me, interrupting my flight of fancy. "Amardine!" he shouted, and I let out a mouse-like squeak and whirled to face him. In an instant, I'd forgotten I was supposed to be a sorceress.

He stood in the doorway, looking alarmed and oddly flustered. I tried to hide the book behind me, but I was so rattled at being discovered that I hit the side of my leg with it and dropped it onto the floor.

He looked from my face to the book. I picked it up and stepped forward, handing it over to him.

"Here's your book," I said, calmly.

"What are you doing in here?"

"I was just looking for the ink roller," I said, hoping he wouldn't pry into the details. "Why do you have this book, anyway?"

He set it on the desk and affected a casual stance that was at odds with the look of alarm I'd seen cross his features ear-lier. "One of the tenants brought it to me," he said, evenly. "He found it in his wine cellar. It's all just old superstitions. But I shouldn't have left it out where you could find it. That was my fault."

"You're not angry with me, then?"

"No, but I will be if you go through my things again. You don't need this sort of nonsense clouding your mind." His glance strayed once again to the book. "I ought to burn it, I suppose. I don't need it falling into the wrong hands. The next thing I know we'll have potion peddlers on every corner and goat sacrifices in the town square."

"Oh, please don't burn it!" I said, without thinking. "I mean, it's wrong to burn books, isn't it? You always said burning books was a 'pastime for savages.'"

"I said that?" he asked, sounding genuinely surprised to hear his own words issuing from my mouth.

"Yes. You were talking about it with Father Parquar. The Church took some family's house and burned their books. You said it was a pastime for savages, I remember." I'd written it down, too, because I'd rather liked the phrase. And because I'd got into the habit of recording the things my father said, in case he denied them later.

He shook his head, at a loss. "I meant what I said about going through my things. I'll be very angry with you if you do it again. I will refrain from burning the book, but you must agree not to meddle with things that aren't your own. Do you understand?"

I nodded.

"Go, then. I'll see you in the dining room for supper."

The rain was falling again by the time we ate our dinner. It came in a last great torrent that sluiced down the glass like the blade of a cleaver, and I was glad of it, for it drowned out the clink of the silver. My father didn't mention the book, or my indiscretion, and for once I was grateful for his silence. My head was a jumble of thoughts, none of which would be welcomed at the dinner table. I couldn't stop thinking about the book—what was he doing with it? Did I believe his explanation, that a tenant had found it in a wine cellar? I tried to remember the headings listed in the table of contents. *A Tonic for Grief. Speaking with the Dead.*

Was this about my mother? Was he trying to reach out to her in the spirit world? But that was old magic, forbidden, and it was dead now in any case, its weakened fragments dismissed by learned people like my father as nothing more than superstition.

Superstition. The spight. I had forgotten what had started all of this, the bubble in the wallpaper, moving as though something lay behind it, trying to break free. I picked up my fork and pushed the food round on my plate, pretending I hadn't seen the look in my father's eyes when he saw me clutching that worn-out grimoire, as though I were a stranger to him, some misbegotten changeling left unjustly in his care.

ଌଠଓଌ

The following morning dawned dry and clear, with a patch-work of blue shining through the clouds. After that came a blast of dry heat, as though some Titan from Hespa's stories had just let open a great oven door.

In fact, we'd only just finished breakfast when Hespa made reference to that very thing. I was in the drawing room watering the houseplants when Milo Meliflore, one of my father's cousins, rapped on the open door frame. He was a grocer from Tarbonne, come ostensibly to look at our rhubarb garden, but it had been a long walk in the sun, he said, and a cup of tea would fortify him for the march back to town.

"Of course," Hespa said, and rang the bell for the kitchen. "It's bound to be a hot one. Must be bread day in the cloud cities."

The man made a short braying sound of amusement, but he seemed tense. Hespa asked him to sit down, but he just stared at her, then said he'd like to listen to the paleophone. Of course Hespa wouldn't let him go near it without my father present. The man kept darting glances over at the corner of the room, where the instrument sat on its intricate wooden stand. Hespa was polite, engaging him in light conversation while Esmay brought the tea, but he was not going to get round her, and he knew it.

When he finally left, she watched him go, as though to make certain he was truly on his way. Then she turned to me, muttering.

"I don't know why he thinks he can just walk in here and use the paleophone," she said, indignantly. "There's not much I can do, though, if he's truly determined."

"You could fend him off with a stick," I said.

"I'm not about to start some family feud," she said, as though my suggestion was in earnest. She was as restless as I was, I realized. The break in the rain had finally come, and the lawn sparkled with the blinding aura of rain drops sizzling in the sun. "I need to go to town today," she went on. "Will you be a good girl and stay close to the house while I'm gone?"

I nodded. "You ought to stay a bit longer, though."

"Oh?"

"If you go now, you'll catch up to that man, and then you'll have to talk to him all the way to town."

Her face had a way of going blank when she was forced to endure unpleasant company, and it did so now, just thinking about it. I noticed she was in no hurry after that to finish straightening the room.

"You stay off the main road too, kit," she said. "And out of the swamps."

"Yes, Hespa."

"Keep away from the boardwalk, as well."

"I will."

"Don't go into the woods, either. And make sure to wear your veils."

I sighed. "I will, but I need help with them. I thought I might go see Father Parquar."

"That sounds like a good idea," Hespa said.

Father Parquar had the peculiar quality of being generous in conversation, even with children. Whenever I spoke to him, he listened and responded as though I'd said something wise and grownup. It wasn't in his nature to keep secrets, and yet, I trusted him as a confidant. If anyone would give me the answers I sought, it was he.

His bungalow was just down the lane that led to the lower court. Once I was outfitted to Hespa's satisfaction, I set out through the courtyard, covered from head to toe except for my face. I was glad I didn't have to walk far, for the heat was merciless.

I spied Father Parquar in his garden, bending to place some small objects in a birdbath. He waved me over, and I unlatched the gate and entered the yard, which had been taken over by raised vegetable beds. He smiled at me as I slipped the latch, beckoning me over to where he stood.

"Fine day, isn't it?" he said, his eyes crinkling. Beads of sweat stood out on his forehead, under thick strands of salt-and-pepper hair.

"I suppose so," I said. Across the road, up on the hill, the branches of the elm tree were swaying in the breeze. I wondered how long before the pyre was put to use once again, and if it would be laden with animals, or someone from the fields, or the lower court, or from my own household.

He followed my gaze to the tree, to the pyre, and his expression grew thoughtful. "Your father wasn't sure you were old enough to watch a funereal rite," he remarked. "Did it frighten you?"

"No," I said, quickly. "Only—I had a dream afterward. About my mother."

"Ah, I see." He untied a leather pouch from his belt and loosened the drawstring. "What was she doing in your dream?"

"She was calling me."

"Here, hold out your hands."

I did as he asked, and he poured into my open hands a jumble of river stones, all painted different colors. They looked like game pieces of a sort.

"Go ahead and put them in the water," he said, pointing to the birdbath.

"Why?"

"So the bees have safe places to land. That way they won't drown trying to get a drink."

I placed them carefully, making a spiral pattern with the stones. Father Parquar watched me without commenting. When I'd finished, he asked, "What do you think she wanted to tell you?"

"I don't know. I think she was only just waking up. Perhaps she's been in a dream, as well. Do you think that dead people dream?"

"That's a rather sophisticated question," he said. "And unfortunately, I don't know the answer. But some part of us lives on after death, this I do believe."

The bees were hovering round a nearby sage bush now, and

it wasn't long before one of them dipped down to land on one of the stones, crawling over to the water.

"You know my mother was a singer, don't you? Did you ever hear her sing?"

"Not in the concert hall," he said. Unlike my father, he didn't sound alarmed by my questions, and I took encouragement from that. "But I heard her sing, yes. She practiced often. She had a beautiful voice. It had a rather unique quality I can't quite describe. Almost as though she was harmonizing with herself. Some fancy technique she learned, I suppose."

"How did she and my papa meet?" I asked.

"I believe she wanted to create a signature scent. Something with pardesu blossoms. She was charmed by the house and the gardens. She was quite young when she and your father met, but she'd already lived a full life."

"You mean on the stage?" I asked.

He nodded. "It's not an easy life. It may look glamorous on the surface, but I think there was a lot about it she wanted to escape."

"Did they love each other?" I asked.

"I believe they did, in their fashion," Father Parquar said. "But I don't think she ever truly adjusted to country life. I think she liked the idea of it. But she had such a passion for life, like no one else I've ever known. I don't think either of them quite knew what they were getting into."

"Do you think my papa misses her?"

"I'm sure he does."

"He's not very happy, is he?" I asked.

"No. He's not been the same since your mother died."

"Is that why he's so hateful?"

"Hateful?" Father Parquar frowned.

He might as well have slapped me, for the level of mortification that set in. I realized at once I'd overstepped with my questioning. He was my father's friend, after all—his only friend, for that matter. He would surely think I was imagining things, trying to cause trouble.

"I don't mean hateful," I recanted. "It's only—I wish I knew what he was thinking."

The priest gave a dry chuckle. "He does like to keep his own counsel," he said, moving toward the gate. "I was about to go see Whistler. You ought to come; he's been missing you."

Whistler was Father Parquar's horse. He was kept in a pasture across the lane and was said to be the oldest horse in the county. I followed Father Parquar to his grazing area and as we approached the fence, the horse lifted his head and ambled over to us, sway-backed and stumbling, looking for treats. Father Parquar reached into his pocket and produced a radish. The horse sniffed at it, curling back his lips to reveal rows of yellowed teeth. He took the offering, chewing it with a satisfying crunch.

"Is Whistler going to live longer than you?" I asked, as the horse dipped his head down and pulled out a shoot of alfalfa.

"It's possible," the priest said, with a shrug. "He has been mightily fortified by a special diet. The secret is in the pasture, in the soil."

"What do you mean?" I asked. He sounded serious.

"This is a special place," he said, gesturing outward to indicate the expanse of fields and groves spreading below as the road dipped down to the lower court. "It may not seem so to you, but your family has created something rather marvelous here. It may not be as exciting as an ancient castle ruin, but it's a legacy, nonetheless."

"What's a legacy?" I asked.

"A gift. From parent to child. Your father has given his life over to this land. I know he's cross sometimes, with the burden he carries. But I see how he cares about every corner of it. He takes pride in the well-being of his tenants, keeping their homes in good repair, hearing their grievances, handling their disputes fairly. He refused to let even a vagabond meet his maker without a proper rite and proper shoes. Someday, it will be your turn, and I'm certain you will manage this land and its people with the same care and attention."

I said nothing.

"But that's a long way into the future," he said, with an apologetic smile. "And it doesn't help in the moment, when you're faced with Master Sourpout, Esquire."

"I'll be sure to call him that the next time I see him," I said, rolling my eyes as I reached out to pet the horse. "Hespa says his bark is worse than his bite. And that I'm 'a child of keen feeling.'"

"Then it just hurts all the more," he said, and I nodded.

"Perhaps I could talk to him," he said.

"Would you?" I asked. "Do you suppose it would help?"

"I don't think it could hurt."

"If you do talk to him, you ought to ask him about his book."

"What book?" he asked.

"He has a book of old magic," I said.

He turned to me, waiting patiently for me to continue.

"I saw it. He told me a tenant brought it to him. It had real spells in it, for talking to dead people and all manner of other things. You ought to ask him about that."

"You know he doesn't believe in those old spells," Father Parquar said.

"It looked as though he dug it up in the ground."

"Perhaps he did. I told you this place was special," he replied, with that secretive smile of his, which let me in on the fact that he was joking, but only a little.

"So it's real?" I asked. "It's not dead? The magic in that book, I mean?"

"Magic cannot truly die," he said. He looked out over the pasture, to the hill that rose up behind it, where the elm tree stood. A light breeze rustled the leaves, betraying their shining undersides, like golden coins scattered upon the wreath of a reliquary. "It can change forms, and be used in different ways. Its energies can be scattered, but they cannot be destroyed. The old magic you speak of is still present in our world. It's evoked through art and music, through dance and poetry. It is the magic of the heart, as opposed to the magic of the intellect.

Does that make sense?"

"Yes," I said, thinking of Hespa's story. A vision flashed before my eyes, as though someone else had put it in my mind, and I imagined the secret ingredient wafting in the air over the witch's cauldron, like perfume.

Like perfume.

"I have to go," I said, climbing down from the rail of the fence. "Thank you, Father Parquar."

CHAPTER FIVE

SINCE MY DREADFUL ENCOUNTER WITH THOSE two ladies of rank, I had not touched the perfume bottle. I had every intention of leaving it alone. The women's scorn and suspicion had made me feel sullied beneath the skin, where it couldn't be washed out by a hot bath. Even now, as I recalled their sharp words, I had to repeat to myself that I'd done nothing wrong, denouncing their accusations in my mind.

I didn't know if Hespa had told my father of that incident. Perhaps he would have simply laughed it off—I could never predict what he might do in any given situation. Most of the time, I took the cautious approach, but that morning I felt inspired, my purpose narrowed, my focus clear.

It had seemed such an easy decision, to leave the perfume bottle hidden in the hatbox. I'd hardly thought about it in days.

But that was before Father Parquar's words had evoked the vision.

I'd always had an active imagination, but this had felt different, like a waking dream, as though I were receiving a message from beyond. It was as though someone was whispering in my ear, reminding me of the untapped potential tucked away in my wardrobe. I didn't stop to wonder, then, what otherworldly being might be speaking to me, though even if I'd known, it probably wouldn't have changed anything.

I raced back to the house, and finding it empty, inquired in the kitchen about Hespa. Of course she hadn't yet returned from Tarbonne. I retreated to the nursery and closed the door, then withdrew the hat box where I'd stored my stolen goods. Out came the perfume bottle, the one that still held scent.

Just a little bit, I told myself. *Just enough to know for sure if I'm imagining things. If nothing happens, I'll put it away forever.*

I pressed the bulb and it let out that intoxicating fragrance, a fine mist dispersing into the air. I leaned in, closing my eyes, inhaling deeply. Images of my mother flashed into my mind—I imagined her at Pendrake Hall, singing in my uncle's drawing room, her voice rising above the crashing notes of the pianoforte. I thought of her meeting my father for the first time, in the febrile stew of the greenhouses. I pictured my father, softspoken and shy, removing his workman's beret and brushing back the lank strands of his hair. And my mother, that mysterious ingénue—I could almost feel the heat of the sun feeding her loveliness as she dropped her gaze beneath flowers the size of parasols.

As I breathed in, the scent drew me in deeper. And then I was looking down at a blue-eyed baby, cradled in my arms, and I *was* her; I felt love and warmth flowing through her to a child that must have been me.

I snapped my eyes open. The pictures evaporated, like rain on sun-lit fields. These were not my own thoughts, I was sure of it now. There must be some enchantment at work, some part of my mother's spirit contained within the bottle.

I squeezed the bulb again, an impulsive reaction, borne of a desperate need. This time I pointed the nozzle in the other direction, toward myself. On my neck, on my wrists, in my hair. I sprayed it indiscriminately, with a child's lack of artifice. By the time I recovered my senses, I understood my mistake. The scent overpowered everything. Light and color exploded in my mind, the pictures snapping in such rapid succession I could make no sense of them. A cacophonous roar echoed through my head, as though every aria my mother had ever sung was replaying at once. I squeezed my eyes shut and clamped my hands over my ears, but I couldn't shut it out. Pain shot down my spine. I ran shrieking to the washstand and dumped a full pitcher of water over my head. The shock of it momentarily disrupted the flash of imagery, and the water in my ears dampened the sounds. But I could still smell the perfume on me and I didn't know how to wash it off.

Tears filled my eyes, blurring my vision. I called out for Hespa, then remembered she wasn't there. I ran out into the courtyard, into the brilliant light of the afternoon sun, screaming for help.

I crossed the courtyard to the gate between the two empty houses, my ears ringing, my head feeling as though it was going to explode. I'd had headaches before, but nothing like this—I thought I might vomit from the pain. I shielded my eyes from the bright light, and as I hurried past my great-aunt's un-occupied home, shadows seemed to waver in the darkened windows, as though someone was moving about inside. *This is what madness must feel like,* I thought, remembering the old woman's fate. Packed off to a sanitarium, her house left to collect dust and memories. I stopped at the gate, my hands on the wrought-iron bars, as the dread rose up in me again, like razor-winged butterflies cutting my insides to ribbons. *What if he sends me away, too?*

Panic drove out my fear of my father's reaction as I crossed the lawn to the first of the three long greenhouses. The light sparking off their glass exteriors seared my eyes, leaving dark spots dancing in my vision. After a brief, frantic conversation with one of the gardeners, I was let inside the building where my father was working. The heat hit me even as I entered the screened-in vestibule. Once I passed through the second door, it nearly staggered me. My eyes took a long time to adjust to the relative dimness of the interior. Greenery closed all around me, the narrow path-ways between the rows of pardesu trees littered with white blossoms. I pushed aside encroaching branches and the long tendrils of ferns. Everything had a place here; everything was part of the greenhouse's complex scheme. Everything except me.

One of the workers led me to my father. At first my distress didn't seem to register with him. I gabbled at him incoherently as he stood before me, tools in hand, looking baffled at my sudden appearance during the workday. But then he began to understand. Perhaps if the pardesu trees had been flowering then, he wouldn't have even noticed the reek of scent. But they had all fallen weeks ago, crushed underfoot, stamped of their odor and their essence.

"God's teeth, Amardine!" he shouted at me, when comprehension finally dawned. "What have you gotten yourself into?"

Some of the other workers nearby paused to take in the family drama unfolding in their midst, then pretended they hadn't noticed. My father took me by the hand and practically dragged me out of the greenhouse behind him. I stumbled along the path, trying to keep up with his long strides. Once we were outside, he rounded on me. His face contorted, his normally handsome features twisting with rage, his anger rising like a thick, black cloud. It was horrific to behold, as though I were watching him turn into a demon before my eyes. I shrank away from him, half-blinded with pain, overcome with fear.

"Where did you get that perfume?" he demanded.

I trembled and opened my mouth to speak, but the words spilled out unintelligible.

"I want answers, Amardine."

Then the tears came, a flood of wrenching, ugly sobs. I put my hands to my face, as though that might hide my excessive display of emotion.

"Stop that," he said, and the coldness in his voice wrenched something inside of me, dropping me straight to the ground, where I curled up and tried to shield myself from the onslaught.

"Stop that," he said again. "You know you did wrong. Own up to it. Don't you dare try to work me with your hysterics. Look at me. Look at me!"

I couldn't look at him. All I could do was press my face against the grass and cling to that small comfort of softness and warmth. *This is it,* I thought. *He really will send me away now.* There was something terribly wrong with me, sickeningly wrong. Hadn't I been warned? Why hadn't I listened? Wasn't I just as bad as those ladies had said?

I gave one last shuddering cry, then drew myself up to hug my knees. But I couldn't bring myself to look at my father's face.

"Are you done now?" he asked.

I nodded, wiping the tears from my face.

"Go in the house," he said. "Get that bottle of perfume and leave it on my desk. Do not touch anything else, do you hear me?"

I nodded miserably.

"Run along, then. Get one of the servants to clean you up. I've work to do."

I fled, almost preferring the yelling to his controlled, stony wrath. I was crying again by the time I reached the house, and found Esmay in the kitchen garden. She ran a bath for me, and washed my hair, and as I was scrubbing away, Hespa returned from her errand.

When I was clean and dry, and no longer reeking of perfume, she brought me tea with honey and some sweets from the kitchen. It was exactly the sort of display my father would have despised, a reward for bad behavior, and I felt guilty even as I let her coddle me.

Once the proverbial dust had settled, I was eager to comply with his instructions, to show him that I wasn't such a hopeless case after all. Alone in the nursery once again, I took the perfume bottle from its hiding place in the hat box and ran my fingers over its beveled edges. But even as I was preparing to relinquish it, even after all the trouble it had caused, I felt inextricably drawn to it. Now that I understood its power, how could I simply hand it over, never to be seen again? Perhaps just one more whiff, one tiny spritz of the beaded bulb.

No, I told myself sternly. *You mustn't ever, ever do that again.*

In my mind, my own blue eyes blinked up at me, like huge river stones. A baby's face, smiling, reaching out its tiny hands, knowing how to grasp for love. I shook my head. My mother was gone, and nothing could change that. I tore my gaze from the perfume bottle and let it drift out across the room. And then my eyes fixed on an object on my dressing table, an identical bottle, grimy with old residue, a splash of water filling the bottom.

No, I told myself again. *Don't even think about it.*

But I had thought about it. And once the thought came, I couldn't dismiss it.

I got up from my bed, my limbs moving mechanically, and retrieved the bottle on my dressing table, the one that held only water. I emptied it into the basin, then picked up the other bottle, which I had tossed carelessly onto the bed. I removed both stoppers, and, trying not to breathe, poured a small amount of scent into the now-empty bottle. Now both contained the perfume.

I placed one bottle back in the hatbox and buried it beneath my spare blanket and pillow. A small act of rebellion, perhaps, but it weighed heavily on me. *I'll just leave it there for now*, I told myself, a sort of mental compromise. *I won't touch it again.*

Then I picked up the other bottle and made my way down the long corridor to my father's study. I set the bottle on his desk, which was clear except for a paperweight, a fountain pen, and a blotter. The strange book was nowhere in sight.

I walked out of the study feeling as numb as a sleepwalker. The decision had been made; there was no going back now. I had set myself against my father's will.

I dreaded dinner that night. I kept silent as we ate our salads, taking tiny bites, trying not to irritate him further. After Hespa brought the main course, he finally spoke to me.

"You're sulking, I see."

I nearly choked on a bite of roasted aubergine. "No, Papa," I protested. "I thought you were still mad at me, that's all."

He looked down at his plate and his face seemed to crumple, confusing me all the more. "No doubt you think I'm like a monster out of Hespa's stories."

"No, of course not!" I said, quickly. "I'm sorry for what I did. You're not a monster, Papa, truly."

After that, he acted as though nothing had happened. And though I was careful not to make him feel bad about himself, a seed of defiance had lodged in my chest, beginning to pulse with life.

He had come to a decision too, I discovered, not long afterward. For the next time I tried the door to my mother's room, I found it locked.

CHAPTER SIX

A FEW DAYS LATER, I STOOD on the eastern wall of the courtyard, where it joined the balcony of the house. The tents were spread flat on the lawn to air, not far from the white road that snaked between the hills and copses of trees. Beside me, Father Parquar sat smoking a cheroot, his long legs sprawling over the edge of his wicker chair. He was "taking a moment," he'd explained, before chaos descended upon the household. It seemed we were of like mind in that regard.

I was dressed in my second-best frock, a light blue-and-white pinstriped ensemble that had my cousin's initials sewed into the collar. I remembered Hespa's words as she'd dressed me that morning: "You remember what we practiced, kit, about addressing your cousins?"

I'd nodded, but hadn't volunteered to demonstrate.

"You've an important duty today. You're not such a little girl anymore, that you can hide in a book when company comes. Lady Pendrake will have her hands full with preparations, and she'll need you to keep Miss Beatrice and Miss Bianca entertained."

And so I stood, watching the road with a gnawing apprehension, enjoying my last few moments of peace.

Father Parquar considered the cheroot between his fingers, which was nearly burned to the nub, then carefully tapped out the remaining leaf into a small box. He unfolded himself from his chair and stood up. "I think I see your uncle's carriage coming round the bend," he said.

I brushed my skirts and made my way down the stairs in the courtyard, then through the iron gate and glass doors under the pergola, bringing me to the entrance hall. From the front windows I spied an unfamiliar carriage, mud-splattered and wobbling on narrow wheel rims, jouncing up the drive. I recognized the horses, though, with their blue and silver bridle plumes. The Pendrakes had arrived, and behind them, there would likely be a wagon-load of foodstuffs and extra cutlery and plates, and a retinue of servants to carry it all.

The carriage crunched to a stop on the gravel drive, and the doors popped open. Bianca was the first to emerge, flying out in a flutter of pink lace.

Bianca was a year younger than me. She had big brown eyes and delicate features, with freckles and a shock of brown curls that shone red in the sun. She would remove her hat when adults were in attendance and smile sweetly as they passed her from hand to hand, but you could tell the attention ruined her, for she was always fussing in the background.

Right now, however, her wild temperament was on full display. She was scowling, her face and collar spattered with mud. "I saw it!" she shrieked, as she scuffed her shoes in the gravel. "I saw it, I saw it, I saw it!" Lady Pendrake took her hand, hastening her toward the house, just as my father walked across the lawn to intercept them.

I slipped out onto the veranda to listen, and prepare myself for whatever was about to unfold. My aunt's face was frozen in a smile and she gave a helpless shake of her head. "We need to use the washroom. I'm so sorry, Martel. I'll only be a few minutes."

"I'll get one of the servants to see to her," my father said.

"No, no, that won't be necessary." As she spoke, the vakra feather in her sapphire blue hat teetered precariously in the breeze. "We just had a bit of a mishap in the carriage. I *told* Bianca not to lean out the window, but do you think she would listen? Well, you understand how it is with little girls. We just need to get freshened up, that's all."

"Stay strong," my father said, gesturing her toward the house. She hurried past me with nary a glance, as I descended the steps and walked out to greet my elder cousin.

Beatrice was still departing the carriage. She was a large girl, with a short fringe of black hair above her brow, a small red mouth pinched between full cheeks, and creamy skin so perfectly even it might as well have been a mask. I envied her hair, because it looked like a black curtain falling round her shoulders, very dramatic, like a heroine in a storybook. But I would never tell her so. She was three years my elder, and thought I was a hopeless fool for knowing the wrong things, like the classifications of flowers instead of the branches of the royal tree. She kept an illustrated book of the royal personages, and could point out those she had spied drinking from thimble glasses, sprawled out in open carriages on parade. Sometimes I would catch her staring at me from beneath the stubble of her lashes, as though she were wary I was embarking on some dangerous transformation.

Nevertheless, it was my duty to be a gracious hostess. I smiled at her as she brushed herself off and surveyed the grounds with a blank, dissatisfied air. My father was nearby, speaking to Lord Pendrake as the driver helped the older man out.

"New carriage?" my father asked, looking unimpressed by the mud-spattered contraption.

"The latest and greatest," Lord Pendrake said, fondly patting the side panel, as though it were a cherished steed. Then he looked at his gloved hand, frowned, and flicked away a spot of dirt. "May I introduce you to the newest model of the Cartouche?"

"How does it do outside of town? It seems a bit light for these roads," my father said.

"Ah, Desmarius. I knew you'd say that. You've no appreciation for flash; you'd drive a turnip cart if you thought it would save you a whit. But I do plan on having some alterations done.

There's a carriage-maker in Vincosa who can fit the Cartouche with wider wheels, and I know Lady Pen has a few ideas of her own for the interior."

"No doubt," my father replied, dryly.

I turned to Beatrice, who was standing uncomfortably nearby. She was wearing a red checkered dress pinned with a brooch. I squinted to read it. *LBS Junior Recruiter.* "How do you do?" I asked, remembering to greet her properly.

"Awful," she said. "The road was miserably hot. And Bianca was even more annoying than usual, bouncing the whole time and trying to hang out the window. I don't know why she can't behave like a lady."

"Let's go inside," I suggested. "We can sit in the breezeway and drink cold tea. Hespa made some this morning."

Beatrice shrugged without enthusiasm, but followed me into the house nonetheless.

"What's your pin for?" I asked, pointing to the brooch.

She made a face. "Oh, this? It's one of Mother's ideas. I'm supposed to ask all the girls I know if they want to join her society. The Ladies' Betterment Society, that is."

"Can I join?" I asked.

"No," she said.

"Oh—all right."

"I mean, if you really want to. I just didn't think you'd be interested in that sort of thing."

"What do you do? Do you have meetings?" I asked.

She nodded. "We all have to learn a talent and show how

we've improved upon it. Mine is the pianoforte. And we have recitals to raise money. But you have to be good at something if you want to join."

Down the hall, Bianca was wailing in the privy closet. There was a scuffle of shoes on the tile floor, a hissed word, and then silence.

"Where are your servants?" Beatrice asked. "You said we could have cold tea."

"I think Hespa is down below, in the kitchen. Let's go look for her."

"What, go down in the kitchen?"

I stared at her, feeling my face prickle. "Or we can use the bell."

Before she could reply, Bianca came running down the hall, still sniffling. The front of her dress looked damp, but clean. Lady Pendrake emerged behind her, a serene smile plastered on her face.

"Darling," she said, kissing my cheeks. "I am so sorry I couldn't greet you properly outside. You look very pretty today. But then, you always do. Very neat and well-mannered, unlike this one." She flicked her hand at Bianca.

"Thank you, Lady Pendrake," I said, uncertainly. "Would you like to sit in the parlor and drink tea with us? I have my own tea set."

At that, she laughed and pinched my cheek. "What a sweet girl you are, to offer me refreshment. And from your very own tea set!" She turned to Beatrice. "Isn't she a sweet girl, Honey Bee?"

"Very much so," Beatrice said, glaring at me.

"Bianca, come say hello to your cousin," my aunt said.

In response, Bianca rolled up her skirt and wadded it into the waistband of her pantalettes. Then she dropped to all fours and loped down the hallway, barking like a dog.

Lady Pendrake's composure evaporated in an instant. "Bianca!" she exclaimed, but the girl was already gone, knocking into the furniture in the drawing room. "What is the meaning of this?" she asked Beatrice. "What is your sister doing?"

"She likes to pretend she's feral," Beatrice said, rolling her eyes.

"You must get her under control. You are her elder sister! I won't have her tearing up *my* family home!"

"Do you want me to put a leash on her?" Beatrice asked.

"Do as you must! I have to go see to the arrival of the servants." She put a hand to her forehead. "This is not what I need today, Honey Bee."

"Don't worry, Mother, I'll take care of it," Beatrice said.

"Thank you, darling. You girls have a nice time together, won't you?"

ॐ

They would not sit and work at embroidery—they did enough of that at home. They did not draw or paint. Though Beatrice played the pianoforte, it was of little use, since my father had got rid of ours some years ago—"that great beast of burden," he'd called it. In desperation, I brought my cousins to the library, hoping they might find some books to keep them occupied.

We sat on cushions round a low table, sipping tea with honey and eating from a platter of fruit and cheese. Bianca was still pretending to be a dog, crawling on all-fours and occasionally coming over to sniff at us. We tried to ignore her at first, but when she flicked out her tongue and licked Beatrice's elbow, the elder Pendrake sister finally had enough.

"Stop that!" she shouted, cracking Bianca on the forehead with the blade of her hand. Bianca reeled backwards, collapsing onto the floor in a heap. Undeterred, she began barking loudly.

Beatrice turned to me and said, "I've had enough of her stupid games. Let's tie her up in the courtyard, if she wants to be a dog so badly."

"I don't think I have a rope," I said, trying to forestall her. I picked up a fig and held it out to Bianca.

"Sit," I told her.

She picked herself up off the floor and sat cross-legged before me.

"Good dog," I said, dropping the fig into her open mouth. "See, if you're quiet and calm, you can have more treats."

"And if you're *not* good, we really *will* tie you up outside," Beatrice said, glowering at her sister.

"She's being good," I said, patting Bianca on the head.

"You oughtn't be nice to her when she's like this," Beatrice said.

"But she's being quiet and polite," I objected.

"She's acting like a *dog*."

Bianca panted and yipped.

"That's it," her sister said. "No dogs allowed in the house!" She stood up and grasped her sister by the arms, trying to drag her toward the door. Bianca kicked and growled, and Beatrice lost her balance, tumbling into her. The two of them rolled about on the floor, snarling and snapping, trying to grab at each other's hair.

"Stop it!" I cried out, as Bianca's head cracked against one of the side tables, the one my mother's portrait sat on. It toppled over and fell to the floor, landing face-down on the rug. My cousins paused, and before I could retrieve the picture, Beatrice picked it up, still panting with the effort of the tussle. She turned the picture over in her hand.

"That's your mother, isn't it?" she wheezed.

I reached out for the picture, but Beatrice held it back. "Yes," I said.

She placed the picture back on the table and primly retied her hair ribbon. After taking a deep breath to steady herself, she said, "I remember when she died, you know."

I tried to form a response, but all the words stuck in my throat.

"I'm sorry, you probably don't like talking about her," Beatrice said, picking up the teapot. She poured another cup for herself. I watched the brown liquid flow from the spout with a sort of glazed fascination, unable to look her in the eye.

"It's all right," I said, weakly.

"I met her, you know. Isn't that funny? I can't remember what she was like, though, except how pale she was. I think she must have been dying already by then, because she was as pale as a ghost."

Bianca rocked forward on her haunches and plucked the honey dipper from its pot. "That's because she *is* a ghost."

"I thought you were supposed to be a dog," Beatrice said.

"I'm a talking dog."

"If you want to talk with us, you can't be a dog of any sort."

Bianca held the honey dipper under her chin. It caught the light from the windows and cast a glow in the hollow of her throat. She turned to me and said, "Dogs can see ghosts, and I saw one, on the way here."

"You did not," Beatrice argued. "There are no ghosts. Alma Monti said what people think are ghosts are just empty echoes of the past."

But I was transfixed by the intensity of Bianca's expression. She leaned forward, her eyes blazing with fervor. Her grip on the honey stick seemed to lend her words an unholy power. Beatrice's protestations were drab by comparison, easy to dismiss.

"Where did you see a ghost?" I asked, a chill skittering down my spine.

"It was hanging from a tree," Bianca said, with the ease of certainty. "I saw it when we were driving here. I tried to lean out of the carriage to get a better look, and that's when the mud hit me."

"You are such a liar," Beatrice said. "You were squirming and bouncing the whole time."

"What do you mean, hanging?" I pressed, ignoring Beatrice.

"Like, upside down. From its feet."

"Was it a man, or a woman?" I asked.

"A woman."

"What did she look like?"

Bianca's expression went vacant for a moment. She stared into space, and at first I thought she hadn't heard the question. But then she said, "I don't know. Her dress had fallen down over her face." She grinned, wickedly. "Her pantalettes were showing. But since she was a ghost, it was all sort of a blur of white light."

"You saw all that while you were driving here?" I asked, not sure what to think.

Bianca fell down on the floor, shrieking with sudden laughter. "I did, I did!"

"You won't get anything from her when she's like this," Beatrice said, with an authoritative sniff. "She doesn't mean anything by what she says. She just likes to 'test the air for sound.'"

The way she enunciated it made it sound as though she was repeating the words of someone else. "I'm not sure what you mean," I said.

"That's what Mother calls it. 'Oh, that's just our little B, testing the air for sound!' You wouldn't know what it's like, though. You don't have a sister."

"I wish I did," I said.

"Well, you can have mine," Beatrice said, giving Bianca a savage nod. "I wish I had a real dog, instead. A little dog with very fast legs, that I could fit inside my reticule." She looked me over speculatively. "What sort of dog would you choose, Amardine? If you could get one?"

"Oh, my papa would never allow it," I said, turning to Bianca, who had crawled over to the fireplace and was sniffing into it on her hands and knees. "I'd like to know more about what you saw, Bianca. Do you think you could show me where it was?"

"She didn't see anything," Beatrice insisted. "She's just trying to ruin the conversation. This is what she does, all the time. She's a liar."

"But why would she say that about the gown, and the upside-down hanging?" I asked.

Beatrice shrugged. "Perhaps she saw it in a book. It doesn't really make sense, though, does it? If you wanted to hang someone, you'd do it by the neck, not the feet."

"I suppose it depends on the purpose," I said, thoughtfully.

Beatrice popped another fig in her mouth and wiped her hands delicately on her napkin. "It *is* funny, though, talking about your mother. I probably remember her better than you do."

She might as well have reached beneath the table with a knife and sliced it across my heel.

"I don't think she was quite as pretty as people make out," Beatrice went on.

As I was trying to form a response to this, Bianca nudged my shoulder. I turned to find her crouching beside me, kneeling in the pool of silk my skirts made on the floor. A dark shape draped from her drooling mouth as she growled for my attention.

Beatrice's mouth wrenched open as though by some unseen force. Beside me, the dark shape dropped onto my skirts. It was a dead magpie, its eyes still bright and mocking, its feet curled tightly as though they were trying to cling to life itself.

"Where did *that* come from?" I exclaimed, leaping to my feet.

"You had that in your mouth!" Beatrice screamed. "You had that in your *mouth!*"

It was too much for Bianca to stay in character, and she squealed with laughter, stabbing her finger at the fireplace in answer to my question.

"I'm telling Mother about this!" Beatrice fumed.

Gingerly, I picked up the small feathered corpse and placed it inside a footstool, thinking I would leave it there until I could ask Hespa what to do with it. I felt a stab of unease, and thought again of the bubble in the wallpaper—the thought kept returning at odd moments, laced with a power I'd unwittingly bestowed upon it.

"Amardine, what are you doing?" Beatrice's voice cut me from my reverie.

"I was only thinking," I said.

"We ought to have a funeral for it," Bianca said.

Beatrice crossed her arms over her chest. "We are not having a funeral service for a dead bird."

"Why not?" I asked. It would keep them occupied for a good hour, at least. And it didn't sit well with me to just leave a dead bird inside a footstool. Suppose one of the maids found it before I could dispose of it? They would get the fright of their life, and they might think I was keeping it for morbid reasons.

"We don't even know how to have a proper funeral," Beatrice said.

"I do," I said. "My papa let me watch one."

"Burn it, burn it, burn it!" Bianca agreed. "Maybe I'll see Ghost Lady again."

"You need to stop talking about ghost ladies," Beatrice said. "If the servants heard you, they would think you were born in some old horse barn."

"How do you know I wasn't? Were you there?" Bianca retorted, sticking out her tongue.

"You see? She has *no* pride," Beatrice said.

"Where did you say the Ghost Lady was hanging?" I asked, as a sinking, queasy feeling pooled in my stomach. I felt certain I knew what Bianca was going to say, could see it clearly in my mind's eye: a woman in white, upside down, stretching out her arms to grasp the roots of a great elm tree.

"I'll show you," Bianca said.

CHAPTER SEVEN

THE PICNIC BASKET WAS PACKED WITH everything we needed: candles, matches, old broadsheets, and a dead magpie. We threw a towel over top of the items, and I led the way out the front door, onto the veranda. Bianca slammed the door behind her, and a few moments later the clatter of footsteps sounded on the floorboards. Lady Pendrake and another woman appeared, swirling their wine glasses, just as I was about to descend the front steps.

"There they are!" the newcomer squealed, as she made a rush for the Pendrake girls. "Big B and Little B! How *are* you, darlings? Do you remember me? I'm Miss Hathervale, your mother's—I don't know, what is it, Ellinora? Fourth cousin, I think? We grew up side by side in the gourd patch, as they say. And my grandmother was a Pendrake, did you know that?"

The three of us all stared at her. I looked to Beatrice as an example of how to respond, but she had adopted her customary sullen expression, conceding nothing.

Lady Pendrake's mouth stretched wide, her teeth glinting. "They're so shy!" she said, glancing round as though it was all supposed to be in confidence. "They hardly speak! Do you, girls?"

Bianca beamed at Miss Hathervale and dropped into an exaggerated curtsy.

"But what is wrong with the other one?" she asked. "She doesn't smile at all!"

Lady Pendrake let out a dribble of laughter. "She has a sun allergy."

"Are you girls having a picnic?" asked Miss Hathervale, pointing at the basket. I deftly stepped away from her, trying to forestall any idea she might have of pawing through it.

I nodded. "We thought we might go for a walk."

"A walk!" She turned to Lady Pendrake. "But surely not in this heat. Especially if one of your girls has a sun allergy."

"She's right," Lady Pendrake said. "Go back in the house, girls. You'll get burned up, walking on a day like this. Not to mention you'll spoil your clothes."

"Oh, *Mother*," Beatrice grumbled.

"Don't you 'oh, mother' me. Go inside the house." Lady Pendrake indicated the direction with a tilt of her wine glass, nearly sloshing it over the side.

Beatrice let out a huff, but she turned obediently, and we all followed her through the front door.

"*Big B!*" Bianca whispered gleefully, as soon as we were in the entrance hall. She repeated it, making it a single word: "*Bigby! Bigby! Hahaha!*"

Beatrice rolled her eyes. "What a monstrous woman. I can't believe she actually grew up with Mother. Calling herself 'miss' when she's so old and ugly, it's ridiculous. If you're not married by the time you're twenty-five, you oughtn't call yourself *miss*. Everyone knows that."

"Nobody will ever marry you," Bianca said. "Bigby."

"I'm *practically* engaged already," Beatrice retorted.

"Truly?" I asked. "To whom?"

"Our cousin, who lives in Carabilos. My father's heir."

"Aren't you his heir?" I asked, confused.

"No, Amardine, I'm not," Beatrice said sharply. "When you live in an important house like mine, there are rules about who can be the heir. It would have been my brother, if he'd been born. But he wasn't, so our house will go to my cousin."

"I didn't know you had a brother," I said.

"It was before Bianca was born. But mother lost him."

"Who cares," Bianca said, tapping her foot on the tiles. "If he was all that special, I would have seen his ghost. Let's go to the Burning Hill."

Hammers rang out in the courtyard, punctuating the sound of deep voices as the workmen assembled the drying platforms for the pardesu pods.

"We can go out through the courtyard," I said. "The men won't bother us."

It was true—no one paid us any mind as I led my cousins around where the men were working, past a mound of unhappy lavender, and onward to the gate. The three of us slipped out behind the house and then Bianca took the lead, bringing us to the lane that looped round the house and led to the lower court. I wasn't surprised when she stopped at the base of the hill where the elm tree stood, but felt a frisson of recognition go up my spine, all the same.

"This is where I saw the Ghost Lady," Bianca said, pointing to the tree. "She was hanging from that limb, right there."

"I still don't believe you," Beatrice said.

"I don't care what you believe. I know what I saw. She was all lit up, like from within. And then the carriage passed by and when I looked back again, she was gone."

I suddenly remembered how she'd called it the Burning Hill. "Did you know we burned the dead on this hill?" I asked.

Bianca shrugged. "I know a lot of things."

The wind shifted and the leaves of the tree shivered, but only blue sky pierced through. I sniffed the air as a faint charnel smell hit my nostrils, the scent of ashes and burned flesh.

Bianca brushed past me and bounded up the hill, her skinny limbs flailing at odd angles, red hair flashing in the sunlight. Beatrice hung back, looking suddenly fearful.

"I don't think we ought to do this," she said. "We'll get our dresses dirty going through that grass."

"You can go back if you like," I said.

"Well, if you're going up..."

I turned from her and began picking my way up the hill, the long grass snagging at my ankles. Bianca was already at the top, waving her arms and emitting an unearthly wail. "*Whoo, whoo,*" she keened, kicking up her skirts, like some demonic owl flitting about in a pink petticoat.

I ignored her performance and approached the remains of the wooden cage that had held the old man's body. Bits of bone were strewn among the rubble and ash. The skull was still partially intact, half buried in the dust. Tufts of feathers lifted on the breeze, swirling round my feet. I nudged the rubble with a toe, uncovering a broken wooden tube with small holes drilled into it. Crouching down, I picked it up and blew the ash from the holes. The wind sent it back in my face, and I dropped the object, coughing violently.

"What are you doing, Amardine?" Beatrice asked. She had crept up behind me, and was digging one toe in the dirt, prodding at the bones. "Is that a person's skull?"

"Yes," I said, standing up.

"Gross," she said, wrinkling her nose.

"Haven't you seen a funeral rite?"

"No, and I'm sure I wouldn't want to. It smells awful when the tenants are burning their dead."

Bianca cracked a stick against the trunk of the elm tree. A flock of jackdaws burst through the canopy in a flurry of movement. As they took to the sky, a single black feather floated down, landing upon the twisted mass of roots.

I picked up the basket and went to retrieve the feather,

careful to stay clear of Bianca's stick. She was hooting with laughter over the birds' sudden exodus, waving the stick as she called out in imitation of the jackdaws.

As I bent to pick up the feather, I noticed small, oval-shaped paw prints crisscrossing the ground near the trunk of the tree, as though they had circled it many times. A fox, perhaps? Perhaps there was a den hidden in the roots, I thought, peering into the dark crevices for some sign of a burrow. The branches above me shifted in the breeze, and sunlight glinted off of something metallic hidden in the roots. Then a cloud passed overhead, and shadows pooled in the hollows.

Had I found a cache of coins? Perhaps the old man hadn't been destitute, after all. Perhaps he had left a secret treasure beneath the roots of our elm tree. Excitedly, I reached in to pull the object out, my fingers digging in the dirt. I felt something hard and round—not coins, after all, but something more like a finial. I tugged at it, but it remained lodged in the earth. What if there was a secret *door* under the tree? My fingers trembled as I imagined the possibilities. That would be even more exciting than buried treasure.

"What are you doing *now?*" Beatrice asked, with an exasperated sigh.

"There's something under here," I said, tugging harder. I felt something slide out of the dirt, and I toppled backward on the ground as I finally pulled it free.

It was a tarnished metal stake, topped with a bulb that did indeed look like a door handle.

Beatrice and Bianca were both watching me now, as I stood and brushed the dirt off of my discovery.

"It looks like a diald," Beatrice said.

"What's a diald?" I asked.

"You don't know what a diald is? Haven't you ever seen them at chapel?"

I shook my head. "We don't go very often."

"Well, you know how there's a wooden railing in front of the altar, with holes in it, and all different metal stakes dropped through the holes?" she asked.

I nodded, recalling a vague image of such a thing from my few visits to the chapel in Tarbonne.

"They come in pairs," Beatrice went on. "One stays at the chapel, and the other is for your devotions. It's so you can always stay connected to the chapel in your mind. I'll be getting mine in a few years. They have real magic in them."

"Real magic?" I asked.

"From the priests in Achalion." She reached out as if to take it, but I drew it closer, turning away from her.

"It probably has a name on it," she said. "They all have inscriptions."

"It's too dirty to tell," I said, shrugging, trying to sound disinterested. In truth, I was dying to brush it off and find out who had left such a thing in the roots of our tree. Would a vagabond carry a diald? Perhaps the old man had planted it there as he sat dying under the elm, contemplating his final destination.

I turned to drop it into the picnic basket, only to find Bianca ransacking it, throwing the towel aside to lift out the dead magpie. She held it over her head like a sacrifice. "Who cares about a stupid metal stake," she said. "I want to *burrrn* something."

Beatrice rolled her eyes at her sister's theatrics. "Give me the matches. Little girls like you two oughtn't play with matches."

"We ought to make a pyre," I said, but by then I was the only one still committed to the idea of a proper funeral. Bianca drop-kicked the bird into the tree while Beatrice made a torch from a rolled broadsheet.

"Stop that, Bifa, and bring it here," Beatrice said. Her sister held the bird aloft while she tried to put it to the torch. A few of the feathers smoked and burned up, crinkling in the hot air, but the broadsheet burned faster, and Beatrice was soon hopping up and down, shouting for help as she waved the flaming torch about. Finally she dropped it, and I rushed forward to stomp it out. I was glad my skirt was a few inches too short, or else I might have set myself on fire.

"Why won't it burn?" Bianca said, in a wheedling tone that was surely lost on the elements she was petitioning. Then she kicked the dead bird down the hill, where it rolled and bounced against the field stones.

"What the devil?" The voice floated up from the road below. It was my uncle, Lord Pendrake, flanked by my father and Father Parquar. Bianca dropped to her stomach in the long grass, and then Beatrice and I followed suit, my elder cousin grumbling the entire time about ruining her new frock. The dead magpie continued its descent, landing in the grass near his feet.

"I heard a scream!" Lord Pendrake said, as my father peered into the grass where the bird had come to rest. Then my uncle pushed past the other men and began clambering up the hill, his arms windmilling as he nearly lost his balance, not to mention his cane.

"Sir, I don't think—" Father Parquar began, rushing forward to keep the older man from tumbling down the hill. My father started forward as well and there was a brief struggle as they tried to restrain him in a respectful manner.

"Folly and villainry! I won't allow it on my family's land!" Lord Pendrake bellowed, shrugging off well-meaning hands.

Beatrice, Bianca and I huddled down in the grass shoulder to shoulder, watching the scene unfold below.

"Your father doesn't carry a sword, does he?" I asked, anxiously. He was wearing a long, sleeveless coat of spidersilk, which could have concealed such a weapon.

The two of them snickered.

"Papa with a sword. Imagine!" Beatrice snorted.

"He'd murder all the furniture!" Bianca said.

"He probably would, too, thinking a chair was a crouching footpad in the dark," Beatrice agreed. "Hush, though, here he comes."

"Come out, come out!" Lord Pendrake shouted, advancing on our position. His bald, liver-spotted head gleamed in the sunlight like a vakra egg.

"Let me investigate," my father said, rushing forward as well. He would have easily overtaken my uncle, except that at that moment, Lord Pendrake let out a cry of triumph, and my father stopped short.

"What is it?" my father asked, brushing aside the long grass with his walking stick, as though looking for a snake or some other offending creature.

"We've got the bastards. Fresh tracks in the dirt, see?" Lord Pendrake let out a loud chortle. "I may be old, but I'm not blind. My hunting days aren't over yet!"

Father Parquar stepped up to examine the tracks, brushing aside a tangle of grass. "They look...rather small," he observed.

"The size of the quarry matters not," Lord Pendrake said. "A weasel may be small, but it's a vicious species in close quarters."

"I'm not in the habit of wrestling weasels," my father said.

"Ha! I bested the lot of them in my days at Whitscape. You hear me, villains? I'll put you down for the sport of it!"

Beside me, Bianca began to giggle.

"Do you hear that?" Lord Pendrake asked his companions. "Be still and listen."

Bianca let out a loud "*whoo-whoo*" in response, then dissolved into loud, cackling laughter.

"I think we may have found a witch," Father Parquar said.

"A truly dangerous creature. Perhaps I ought to go forth and confront her."

Beatrice sighed and stood up, brushing off her dress. At her sudden movement, Lord Pendrake startled and fell back, and my father had to catch him to keep him from sprawling down the hill.

"Father, it's just us," she said, as she made her prim descent down the hill.

"Beatrice, my girl! Has someone hurt you?"

"No, Father. We were only playing."

"I distinctly heard a scream. Where is your sister? I won't be satisfied until I see her free and unharmed."

Beatrice turned and put her hands to her mouth. "BIFA!" she shouted. "GET DOWN HERE THIS INSTANT!"

"Come on," I said to Bianca, who had put her head down in the dirt and was shaking with laughter. "I suppose we ought to show ourselves." I practically had to drag her to her feet and we both nearly tumbled down the hill.

"God's teeth, what have you been doing?" my father demanded, upon seeing me. I realized my dress was stained with dirt and grass and I probably still had ashes on my face. My cousins' clothes hadn't fared much better.

"We were just having a funeral for a bird," I said.

My father looked at me as though I'd gone mad. "It's nearly suppertime," he said. "And then we need to sort the pods onto the drying platforms."

"You're going to let me help this year?" I asked, flushing with sudden, unexpected pride.

"You're all helping this year. It's about time you stop these silly games and learn something of the family business."

℘℧

The servants had arranged drinks and a canopy over one end of the drying platform. Normally Grandame sat at the head of the table as the final arbiter of quality, though this was more of a ceremonial duty which concluded with her signing off on some papers; my father and the other workers always finished the sorting process over the next couple of days.

My father and aunt had quarreled before supper over some wine she had pulled from the cellar, which he had been saving until it reached its peak. She had accused him of being vicious and insensitive; he had accused her of imbibing too freely. I was rather surprised she came out with us to the drying platforms, for by that time she had to hang on to her servant's arm to steady herself. In her other hand she held a wine glass, tilting precariously between her finger and thumb. But she was determined to show her dedication to the family business, hushing Beatrice when she complained about having to sit out in the hot sun.

My father preceded them to Grandame's empty chair, placing a hand on the back of it. But he didn't sit down. Instead he pulled the chair out and stood behind it, waiting like a gentleman for a lady to be seated.

Lady Pendrake fanned herself as her servant adjusted the angle of her parasol. She looked at my father and a surprised smile spread over her face. "Well! Aren't you gallant, Martel. I'm glad to see your years of bachelorhood haven't eroded all of your courtesies."

"No, indeed, they have not," my father said. "I remember you once said a lady ought to sit at the head of the sorting table."

"Once!" Lord Pendrake guffawed. "She's said it more than once, believe me."

"It's a tradition," Lady Pendrake said. "We've always done it that way. And for good reason, too. A lady's eye is more discerning."

"Indeed," my father said, looking at me. "Amardine, take your place, please."

I didn't move. He couldn't actually be saying what I thought he was—but then again, he must, for he stood in front of the chair even now, blocking Lady Pendrake's advance.

"You've a discerning eye," he said to me. "Sit, please."

Lady Pendrake's fan gave one final flutter, like the death rattle of an ailing bird.

But it was Lord Pendrake who replied: "Oh, ho! I see what you're up to, Desmarius. Yes, let the little feym-blooded girl do it. I don't know why I didn't think of it. I'll have new labels printed, get a portrait artist out here to render her likeness. Just a loosey-goosey sketch is all we'd need—I know the man who did the adverts for Strutt & Swagger, he has a studio over in Cordair, on the canal. Maybe he'd put a picture of the moon on it, too."

"Keep your moon," my father said crossly, cutting my uncle off as he was gathering his breath. "I'm not pandering to the sort of people who are impressed by a drawing of the moon. Now, Amardine, take your place."

I stepped forward and cautiously took my seat. I ought to have been pleased with his unexpected approval, but it didn't feel right. Everyone was looking at me, and any pride I might have felt dissipated under the weight of their hostile and curious stares.

"Wait just a minute," Beatrice said. "Why does *she* get to sit *there?* I'm older than her, after all."

"Hush now, Honey Bee," Lady Pendrake murmured.

Cheeks flushed, Beatrice claimed one of the other chairs. When she turned away she had tears in her eyes, but she managed to drag her chair back from the table with a semblance of valor, as though it were the carcass of some great wild beast she had killed. Arms crossed over her chest, she sat outside the protection of the canopy for all of about three eye-blinks, before one of the servants went out and planted a parasol next to her in a wrought-iron stand. From beneath the parasol she glowered at me, her eyes promising pain.

I didn't think much about her reaction at the time. I was too busy wondering what had come over my father. Perhaps Father Parquar *had* spoken to him. Perhaps he was determined to start anew, had at last begun to take my contributions seriously.

He poured a basket of seed pods onto the table, and they skittered everywhere, like insects. Then he sat next to me and explained the task of sorting the pods. He showed me the very best pods: bright yellow, with no separation along the seam, and no brown spots. He showed me which ones were acceptable and which needed to be discarded, and explained that I was to find anything he missed.

It wasn't difficult work, for my father missed little. I asked him questions when I wasn't sure why he'd sorted a particular pod into one basket instead of another, and he patiently explained. Mostly, all I had to do was shovel seed pods with my hands, dropping them into the baskets with a satisfying clatter. Lord Pendrake insisted that we bring the paleophone out, so we even had music, and the servants brought fresh lemons and ice for the carafe on the tea table. It would have been pleasant, but for the black cloud of resentment I sensed rising from Beatrice, who had not rejoined the group at the table.

I wished my father had not singled me out. He didn't understand Beatrice, not like I did. She never forgot a slight. As the sun sank and the shadows stretched across the courtyard, the servants lit the scent lanterns to keep the cruorflies at bay, and I could see the flames smoldering in her dark eyes. Finally, my father announced that it was too dark to continue with the work, and Beatrice walked back to the house without speaking to me.

She and Bianca were sharing a room in the guest suite, fortunately, leaving me alone in the nursery. I was so preoccupied by my cousin's rancor that I nearly forgot about the diald, which I had stashed in the wardrobe while changing my clothes. It all came back to me as Hespa was preparing me for bed, and after she left the room, I retrieved it from the hatbox in which I kept all of my secret treasures.

The moon was full and bright, glowing a faint purple that tinged the clouds. *An umbral moon*, I thought, reminding me that I hadn't checked the aetherscope that day. It hadn't fluctuated much over the last week, but a full umbral moon would likely shift the energy.

I wiped the diald with a towel and cracked the door open to the courtyard, so I could fling the dirt outside and see the strange object more clearly. Now I could see the grooves of an inscription, but it was still too dirty to read. Undeterred, I took a clothes brush from my dressing table, dampened it in the basin, and began to scrub the diald clean. It was still dark with tarnish, but at least I had unearthed the inscription.

What was the old man's name? Pilo? Pelico? I turned it over in the moonlight, expecting confirmation of my theory. What I saw, however, defied my assumptions and left my hands trembling.

Sephonie Desmarius, née Mira, b. 822, the inscription read. *My gods are the trees, and I am the veins in the leaf.*

CHAPTER EIGHT

THE FOLLOWING DAY, EVERYONE WAS PREPARING for the dinner party that evening. The tents had popped up on the south lawn like giant mushrooms, and the children of the workers ran foot-races and played tug-of-war with a giant rope, the sound of their laughter ringing in the air. Meanwhile, Beatrice and I hung the insides of the tents with garlands of wildflowers, cappa sprigs, and ivy. Bianca had claimed to be ill, and was in the house, resting, much to Lady Pendrake's chagrin.

"I don't see why we have to do this," Beatrice complained, as she stood on a footstool, fussing with the work I had just finished. At least she was speaking to me again. She'd been silent all throughout breakfast, giving me dirty looks over the rim of her cup as she sipped her milky lavender tisane. "Why should we have to do the work while the other children play?"

"Everyone has to do something," I said. I was sitting cross-legged on one of the tables, untangling a knot of ivy. "And anyway, they were picking pods yesterday, while we were playing."

"What of it? We've every right. It's supposed to be a feast day for *everyone*. Yet here we are, practically ladies of the court —well, I am, that is—and we are the ones having to work?"

I looked down at the string of ivy in my hands, secretly glad the task would take most of the morning. I feared being left with the Pendrake girls with nothing in particular to keep them occupied.

Perhaps "fear" wasn't the right word. I reminded myself that Beatrice and Bianca were my cousins, and on that account, would never actually harm me. It was just my own poor manners. I didn't know how to amuse them properly. No doubt I frustrated them, when they were used to an endless parade of amusements.

Beatrice stepped down from the footstool and hopped up on the table beside me. She opened her reticule, which she had left nearby, and sifted through its contents.

"Do you want to see the latest fashion plates from *Pattern Living*?" she asked, pulling out the magazine. She flipped it open to show me a picture of a lady wearing an elaborate gown, with a pleated hemline and swags of contrasting fabric draped over a full skirt.

"Ooh, very pretty," I said, giving the picture a dutiful glance before going back to my work.

"It's styled after the gown Princess Eveline wore at her first Sugar Ball," Beatrice said.

"What's a sugar ball?" I asked.

She gave me a pitying look. "It's one of *the* most important social events in Cereval. I want to go when I'm sixteen, but Mother says I have to wait until I'm eighteen. I don't suppose you'll go at all. You need a special invitation if you're not a real lady."

"I suppose not, then," I said.

Beatrice frowned, picking up a strand of ivy and turning it over in her hands. "How much longer do we have to do this?"

"Until it's done," I said. "Let's just try to finish it. We can talk about everything we wish we were doing right now, and just act it out in our minds."

Beatrice frowned at me. I saw that dark look flash in her eye, the one she'd been sustaining most of the prior evening. "You're a very strange girl. My papa said something last night. 'The little feym-blooded girl.' That's what you are, aren't you? I asked my alma once, Alma Monti. And she said she thought you were one."

"Yes," I said, feeling my stomach tighten as I went back to my work.

"What does that mean, exactly?"

I kept my head down as I considered my reply. Even if I had an answer, I didn't feel inclined to discuss it with her.

"Do you have magical powers?" she pressed.

"Like what sort?" I asked.

"I don't know, reading minds, turning into animals, that sort of thing. I know—you could tell me what I'm thinking right now."

"You're thinking that you're bored, and you wish I was more amusing, and—and that I couldn't possibly know what you're thinking right now."

Beatrice leaned back, narrowing her eyes. "That *was* what I was thinking," she said, in a slow, ominous tone. "Alma Monti was right."

I sighed and shook my head. It was only a guess, of course, but Beatrice seemed to lack the sort of imagination that takes the mind down more obscure pathways. I swung my legs over the side of the table, letting the string of ivy fall from my lap. "Will you help me drape this? You're taller than me."

She was still staring at me, her expression shuttered. "You oughtn't read people's minds," she said. "It's not polite and you ought to be punished for it."

"I won't read your mind again, even if you ask me to," I promised.

"Good," she said, picking up one end of the trailing ivy and snapping it in her hands, as if to test its strength. Was it strong enough to strangle a small girl? That was what I imagined her thinking, in that moment. "Because I don't like freaks in my own family. We're not a circus, you know."

I looked away as Hespa entered the tent with some of the Pendrake's servants, to finish decorating and lay the tables.

Beatrice and I were shooed out to greet the guests as they trickled in from neighboring farms. The Hubor relations mingled with the Meliflores, and the Ladossa cousins skulked round the edges of the gathering, swooping in to ambush the servants carrying drink trays and platters of finger foods. They swarmed round the front of the house, leaving the workers, for whom the dinner was intended, standing at the fringes of the crowd.

My father was nowhere to be seen, but Lord and Lady Pendrake were holding court on the veranda. I could hear my aunt's high, piercing laughter as she leaned in to share a joke with another woman. They were all dressed magnificently for such a hot day, I thought, and the flutter of fans was a constant sight. As soon as one lady started up, the others in her coterie would join suit, the fans snapping out and wavering in the sticky air like giant bobbing butterflies.

Beatrice cut through the crowd on the lawn and swept up the stairs to the veranda, taking her place at her mother's side. I followed and slipped unnoticed into the house, where I spent a pleasant afternoon reading a book and listening to the sounds of my father and Father Parquar talking in the drawing room. When I heard them preparing to go out, I followed.

Everyone grew silent as my father emerged from the house. I watched from the side, hoping he would make a good impression on the guests.

"Thank you, all," he said, projecting his voice. There was a low murmur at the edges of the crowd. My father paused, toying with his wine glass. "You know, I almost decided to cancel this whole affair. The dinner, I mean." Those closest to him exchanged glances. "But I knew most of you would find your way here anyway, so I thought I might as well have a meal prepared."

On the veranda, someone tittered—I thought it might be Miss Hathervale, who had once again latched on to Lady Pendrake. My father went on, "It's been a bad year, we all know it. The herds are thin, and we've all grown accustomed to the smell of smoke and charnel fires. I doubt I'm the only one who's developed the habit of checking my skin for cruorfly bites. Not that finding one would do much good, since there's no cure for it."

He paused, scanning the crowd, which had gone perfectly silent. "As many of you know, a man recently died of arrhemia, on this very land. You're probably all breathing in his ashes, as we speak. It makes you think, though, doesn't it? Yesterday my dear sister Ellinora reminded me of the preciousness of life, the need to seize the day, to drink the good vintage before we're all ashes and dust."

I pressed my thumb into the center of my hand, tracing the whorl of lines on my palm, a nervous habit I couldn't seem to break. He continued: "But we must not let the terror of paralysis and possible asphyxiation rule over our lives. We must go on and do what needs to be done, even if that means hosting a dinner party."

This was turning out to be very different from the toasts Grandame made. Everyone was so still, I began to think someone had cast a spell to freeze them in their place. There was real fear in Lady Pendrake's eyes; I could see it winking like the diamonds in her cruisse as her gaze fluttered over the crowd.

Then Father Parquar stepped forward, touching my father's elbow lightly, gently displacing him. The priest cleared his throat and smiled at the baffled assembly. His voice carried clearly, and as he began to speak, those in the back ceased their shuffling.

"I think what our esteemed host is trying to say is that before we celebrate a successful harvest, we ought to take a moment to reflect on this singularly difficult truth: that so much of our success is dependent on the whims of fate. Drought, excessive rain, epidemics, accidents—at any moment, all the good we have achieved in life may be snatched away from us. Any one of us might be crushed by the vicissitudes of fate, and come to ruin.

"And yet, by coming together, by celebrating together and renewing our connections, we remind ourselves that our neighbors and friends are here for us, to share our burdens and our joys. It is the tradition at harvest-time to make an offering of our bounty. We do this in accordance with the will of Aneidis, who warns against hoarding the surplus of our fortunes. With this offering we ask for His blessing, so that we may be spared for another year. So let us not despair or fall into apathy. We are alive, right now. We are the lucky ones. So we will not close down the kitchen. We will not cancel the dinner party. We will set up more tables, find more chairs, and offer the good vintage, to all of you, today."

My father frowned a bit at that last statement, but everyone else raised their glasses and cheered. I let out the breath I'd been holding, and sidled up to Lady Pendrake.

But she wasn't looking at me directly when I approached, and she mistook me for a servant. "More wine, please," she said.

"I'm sorry, Madame, but I'm not allowed to serve wine," I replied.

"Well, find someone who is!" she said, then turned fully and saw me. Her eyes widened with astonishment and she immediately went to fixing one of the bows on my neckline. "There you are, child! Never mind what I just said! Come, let us go to the tent together. Where is Beatrice?"

"Here, Mother," Beatrice said, coming round the side of the veranda.

"Go check on your sister. Tell her it's almost time to eat."

Bianca was dragged from her bed, sniffling with a summer cold, and Lady Pendrake laid a hand to her forehead, a line of worry furrowing her brow.

"I could have done without all that talk of sickness and catastrophe," she said, straightening Bianca's frock. "Aneidis knows, I've been hearing enough about it from the ladies —they're such nervous nellies, you'd think they spent their days milking goats and washing their clothes by the river. But that's my brother for you, all doom and gloom. He didn't used to be like that, you know. I remember when we had string quartets playing on this very platform, all summer long. And everyone said he had such easy manners. It's a shame, really."

"What happened to him?" I asked.

"Your *mother* happened to him," Lady Pendrake said, swirling the dregs of her wine glass. She dabbed at the powder sheen on her face with a napkin, then smiled and pinched my cheek. "Never mind that, though. You're such a sweet, bright little girl. Not like her at all."

I looked down at my feet. I didn't want to be sweet and bright, not if it meant being compared in such a manner. At that moment, though, the dinner bell rang out—two of the children from the lower court had been given the honor, and they pulled the rope with gleeful abandon. Lady Pendrake staggered to her feet, pulling her husband up beside her. As they walked together, she seemed to do a sort of box step, shuffling four steps for each one of his. She twirled round, looking back over her shoulder, and struck out her arm to me, as though to draw me into her circle of light. I trailed after her long, emerald green skirts, the airy chiffon billowing up from beneath a layer of gold silk. There was a sort of glamour about her that I found enviable, yet at the same time made my stomach turn. My father dismissed her as a mere nuisance —sharp-tongued and overwrought—but as I followed her across the lawn, I wondered if he underestimated her.

When I stepped into the tent, though, all of my anxious thoughts scuttled away, replaced with awe. The servants had transformed the inside of the tent since Beatrice and I had left it, not so long ago. It wasn't yet dark outside, but the sun was casting long shadows over the lawn, and the leaves of the trees were beginning to shimmer molten as they caught its dying rays. The golden light spilled into the tent, a fiery backdrop against a series of long tables, which were dressed in white linen, and aglow with candle flames strung out like beads.

As I took my seat at my family's table, more people entered the tent, stirring the air. That was when the scent hit me, that of dozens of table bouquets, rich with roses and spiked with datura. Lanterns had been hung with incense to ward off flies, and the smoke curled up toward the tent poles like swirling gray wraiths.

Everyone agreed the wine was excellent, and the servants, many of them on loan from the Pendrakes, brought out tray after tray of small plates topped with salad greens dressed with delicate herbs and citrus flavors, leek cakes in ginger sauce, terrapin soup, and spiced lamb with mint. There were other dishes that I didn't even recognize, perhaps dreamed up by the Pendrakes' chef, and I tried one of everything, except for the lamb. Lady Pendrake noticed the plates stacking up at my elbow, and praised me for my adventurous palate. "I wish my girls would eat like that," she said, looking pointedly at her daughters. "This one"—Bianca—"turns her nose up at everything we serve her, and that one"—Beatrice —"would eat honey cakes for supper every night if she could get away with it."

"Yes, we all know how perfect our cousin is," Beatrice said, not quite rolling her eyes.

Lady Pendrake refused to dignify the comment and instead turned toward my father. "I wasn't going to say anything," she said, "but honestly, brother. That toast."

"I thought it a fine toast," Lord Pendrake said, in a boom-ing voice that caused several people at the next table to turn their heads and listen.

"You act as though you're above all of the fanfare, but I

know you secretly enjoy it," she said.

"What's not to enjoy?" my father replied. "Aside from your astute observations about my character, that is?"

She shook her head. "Do you really check yourself every day for cruorfly bites? You said yourself it wouldn't do any good."

"At least I would have the thrill of anticipation," my father said, with a shrug.

"Not me," Lady Pendrake replied. "I'd rather not think about it unless I have to. In any case, I suspect the number of deaths is greatly exaggerated. Why, I don't know a single person who has succumbed to arrhemia."

"You had six deaths on your estate last month," my father said. "I read the tally in the broadsheet."

"Well—yes, but I didn't *know* them."

"Three of them were children."

"Exactly," Lady Pendrake said. "They were probably running round in the mud. Almost all cases of arrhemia in children could be averted if the parents had a bit of sense and minded their little ones. Speaking of little ones, you must let me bring Amardine to Pendrake Hall."

I glanced up from my plate, my eyes fastened to my aunt's face, to her shoulders, to the hollow in her throat that moved when she spoke.

"Surely you must see how lonely the child is. She has no one here."

"And what makes you think her life here is so unfit?" my father asked.

"Oh, I could go on," Lady Pendrake said, taking a sip of wine. "Though I suppose if I had to point to something, I'd start with your toast."

"Yes, yes, a fine toast," Lord Pendrake interjected, as though he'd heard nothing else that was said.

"I wonder what sort of manners she's learning from you. It's one thing for a man to be peculiar, but imagine a lady telling her guests she nearly canceled their dinner! All this doom and gloom will give our guests indigestion. And I pity my poor niece, having such a surly grouse for a father."

Lord Pendrake let out a "*Ha!*" that sounded like a cork exploding from a bottle. "Let the man be a surly grouse! He's earned the right to it, more than any other I can say! Isn't that the fact, Desmarius?"

My father drew in his breath and said nothing. I sensed the words tumbled up behind the closed door of his mouth, and my stomach seized up.

"It's her education I'm concerned about," Lady Pendrake went on.

"She has a tutor," my father said, through clenched teeth.

"A village schoolmistress? Surely you can do better for your only child. And no alma, I see."

"No," my father said. "We needn't talk about this here, Ellinora."

But my aunt had an uncomfortable way of pushing against such social mores, especially after she'd had a couple glasses of wine. She wouldn't let up about the subject, and there was no way for my father to silence her without creating a larger spectacle. "I was thinking," she said, brightly, "that it might be nice to start her in the choir. I don't doubt the girl has a lovely voice."

I could see the veins pulsing in my father's temple as he struggled to maintain his composure, though what precise e-motion he was trying to rein in, I couldn't say.

"You can't be serious," he said, in a low voice.

"I'm absolutely serious. My girls have already started. What sort of young lady will she grow up to be if she hasn't sung in a choir?"

"A perfectly content one, I should think."

"Are you going to forbid her from learning music, then?" Lady Pendrake asked.

"Why shouldn't I learn music?" I asked.

They both turned to stare at me, as though they'd forgotten I was there.

"I think it's about time we make our rounds with the guests," my father said. He stood up, and Lord and Lady Pendrake did the same. There would be a break in the courses while they circulated among them, leaving us children to our own devices.

"I can teach you how to sing," Beatrice said. She pushed back her chair and stood at the head of the table, facing everyone in the long tent. Then, folding her hands in front of her, she began to bellow at the guests. I supposed the song was probably a hymn, judging by its heavy, sustained tones, but then again, perhaps that was just how she sang it.

Everyone stopped talking at once to exchange amused glances. Then Lord Pendrake began to sing, his baritone drowning out the sound of his daughter's voice. Beatrice turned furiously on him and sang even louder. Lord Pendrake lifted his hands, inviting everyone else to join in, which they did, all except for me. I didn't know any hymns. People were standing up, teetering to their feet, singing with drunken exuberance. When the song ended, someone—I thought it was Milo, the grocer—began singing a different sort of song, more lively, one that inspired clapping and laughter. This time the ladies blushed and didn't join in. After that, half of the guests milled round the tent, while the other half remained in their seats, and I heard someone say there would be dancing in the lower court later that night.

Then the flap of the tent opened, and Hespa appeared, cradling a brightly-painted egg the size of a giant's skull in the crook of one arm. She bore a small round table in the other hand, like a torch. Lady Pendrake, who had gradually worked her way back to her original table, clapped her hands. "Oh! Here is the boiled vakra egg. Let us tap the shell. Which of you little lambs will make a wish?"

It took a few moments for the guests to return to their seats and quiet down. The appearance of the vakra egg signaled the final round of dishes, and the singing had whet their appetite. Maslin, following Hespa, handed Lady Pendrake the silver spike and mallet as Hespa placed the egg, in its cup, atop the circular table. Lady Pendrake rose to her feet and gave one swift tap against the top of the egg, reducing the exquisite painted design to a web of splinters. There were shouts of "Brava!" and much clapping, and then one of the servants who possessed the necessary deftness for the task peeled away the fragments and placed them on a tray to be passed down the length of the table.

Father Parquar stood up and delivered a blessing as the egg was cut into pieces and served on tiny tea-set plates. Everyone else bowed their heads in silence. I tried to listen to the priest's words, but a vague ripple of unease had passed through me. I thought about Bianca's Ghost Lady, and the dead magpie, and the spight in the wallpaper—which might not really be a spight, now that I had some distance to think about it—but all of it locked into place in my mind, as though I had a box of terror built out of everything that had ever happened to me, and it all *had* to fit together because if it didn't, it meant I was going mad.

The priest finished his blessing and took up the tray of vakra egg fragments. Solemnly, he said, "We now begin the dispersion of Allotments." Without looking at the tray, he handed one of the pieces to Lady Pendrake, then to Lord Pendrake and my father. He moved silently behind the row of diners, placing shell fragments into waiting palms. When he came to me I was afraid he would notice my palms were sticky with sweat. But he just dropped the shard into my hands and moved on.

Hespa had told me once that her people could read omens in the entrails of animals, and I wondered if the egg shell had served a similar purpose in those long ago days, when people had practiced the old magic. My own shard was generous in size, decorated with blue flowers as bright as lapis. The inside of the shell was mottled brown, but there was a pattern to the color variation, one that had never been rendered by an artist's brush. It looked like a spiral, a whorl of sorts, almost flower-like. There was a familiarity to it that took a moment for me to recognize, but when I did, I only felt more puzzled, more uneasy. I had a similar pattern in the lines on my palms.

My head began to buzz, drowning out the sound of laughter around me. My hair grew damp and clung to the back of my neck as little dark spots exploded in my vision. The voices of the other diners grew distant, and strange thoughts bloomed in my mind, disconnected from reality, dissipating the moment I tried to catch hold of them.

"Amardine, darling, would you like me to keep your piece of the shell?" My aunt's voice cut through the disorienting haze of my mental landscape. "Are you all right, child?"

I nodded, not trusting my voice to work properly.

"We can put it in our petition box to take to chapel on Ordas next. I know your father doesn't observe such practices, but there's no reason you ought to be left out of it. What do you say, Miss Amardine? Would you like me to deliver your piece of shell to our chapel in Rivene?"

"I think I'd like to keep it," I said, faintly.

"Child, sweeting, you're not supposed to keep it. You're supposed to put it in your petition box." She shot my father a look. "Didn't anyone teach you that?"

"But then it will be gone," I protested.

Lady Pendrake's face took on a mournful, pitying look, and she pressed her palms together beneath her chin. "No, it *won't* be gone, I'm afraid. It will sit on the mantel forever, and Father Parquar will never be able to offer your petitions to Aneidis. Do you want that, sweet child? To be overlooked forever by Aneidis because your father is too stubborn to observe a basic sacrament?"

"That's enough, Ellinora," my father said.

"Am I so wrong to be concerned about my niece's Allotment?"

"She can keep the damned egg shell," my father said. "Good God, woman."

I'd barely noticed that the main course had been served —Marguerite's famous white duck, roasted with a wine sauce, along with a creamy rice dish with mushrooms and a side of long green beans. Perhaps the plate had been set in front of me when my vision was dark. I felt weak and slightly queasy. Across the table, Lord Pendrake cleared his throat.

"I had a most interesting conversation the other day with a gentleman from Cereval," he told my father, before Lady Pendrake could express the outrage brewing in her dark eyes. "The consortium is interested in producing a cosmetic eyedrop that's found a bit of infamy in the Port of Pheres. I shan't disturb your digestion right now with business, but it involves eaveswort. Do you have experience with the plant?"

"*Eaveswort?*" my father burst out. "That's an invasive species. A blasted weed. Anyone can grow it; it takes a sort of black alchemy to get rid of it."

"He was only asking," Lady Pendrake said, as she summoned more wine.

Lord Pendrake said, "No, that's good to know. But perhaps a superior specimen could be cultivated, yes? If, for example, a man with the right reputation had the proper funding?"

"I have no interest in such a thing," my father said, flatly.

Lady Pendrake clucked her tongue. "Stubborn, as always."

He rounded on her. "Why? Because I choose not to sully the Desmarius name? We have no peer in the production of pardesu extract. The family has built its reputation for over a century. And you think I ought to jump into the business of cosmetics, to chase some fad that will be over in a few years?"

"Yes, and I am so very pleased with your concern for the family's reputation. Too bad you weren't concerned about that a decade ago." She smiled tightly round the rim of her glass.

"This again." My father's voice was chillier than I'd ever heard it, even more than the time he'd caught me with the perfume bottle. "Is it ever going to end? Sephonie's dead, Ellinora. What more do you want?"

I watched in dread fascination as the color drained from my aunt's face. She'd always had a fair complexion, and she liked to enhance it with powder, to contrast with her silken black hair, which she wore roped together in a chignon at the nape of her neck. Tears prickled in the corners of her eyes, and she fumbled for her handkerchief to wipe them away.

"I'm sorry," she said, in a broken voice. "I never meant to suggest..."

"You never do," my father said.

She shook her head, sniffling. "You wound me terribly. I would never—I only want what's best for my niece. To see that she's raised properly. I don't wish to see her spiraling down the same dark path."

Spiraling. Spiraling. The word kept ringing in my head. I looked down at my plate, to the pattern emblazoned on the inside of the egg shell. Suddenly, my stomach heaved. I got up and ran from the tent, managing to make it to the lawn outside before purging the last seven courses behind a honeysuckle bush.

CHAPTER NINE

THE BONFIRES BURNED IN THE LOWER court until late into the night, and shouts and laughter rang out over the sound of the drums and pipes. I stood upon the balcony of my great-aunt's vacant house, which connected to the courtyard wall, wishing I was out there, skulking at the edges, observing the wildness of the celebration.

My cousins were already asleep, in a guest room on the second floor. I understood that I was supposed to be like them, not like the children of the laborers, who shrieked with laughter as they ran races and tumbled in the grass. But I wasn't like any of them, truly. I thought about what Lady Pendrake had said, about spiraling down a dark path. Was that what was happening to me? Could she see it somehow, in my face, in the way that I spoke? When she looked at me with her mocking black eyes, did she see herself reflected in some otherworldly mirror?

I'd told no one about the strange feeling that had come over me during dinner, about the near blackout I'd experienced. Nor had I said a word about the pattern on the eggshell, not even to Hespa. I certainly couldn't bear the thought of my father looking upon me with pity, or disgust, as he concluded beyond all doubt that I had indeed gone mad. I cringed as I recalled his reaction to the perfume—the look in his eyes, the cold tone of his voice. I felt again that shrinking feeling, the sharp twist of my heart. His methods had been effective, though, for I hadn't touched the perfume bottle after hiding it in the hat box in my wardrobe.

Now, though, as I thought about it, as tears stung my eyes and made the stars a blurry smear across the sky, I felt a sliver-prick of anger. I had felt so ashamed by what I'd done, and worried so much about displeasing him again, but there was a small part of my soul, a tiny spark, that raged against such treatment. I had tried to smother the blaze, but it flared again now, burning as bright as the fires in the lower court.

I needed answers, and no one would give them to me. Perhaps it was time to commit to my transgressions, to forget about being the good girl for once. I could never seem to get the knack of it, anyway.

I turned from the sight below me, from the smoke and the merriment, thinking of a different fire I'd witnessed, not so long before. Was that when the strange feelings had started, the thoughts of spights and bad omens?

The walls of my great-aunt's house, unoccupied for as long as I could remember, bristled with ivy, giving it a hairy appearance in the dark. I passed along the top of the wall, over the gate, and down the stone steps to the courtyard, where the pardesu pods were drying on their platforms.

Too late, I caught the glow of a cheroot in the darkness, and realized my father was out there as well, sitting under the pergola and staring out at the fruits of his labor. He rose to his feet as I descended the stairs.

"What are you doing out here at this hour?" he asked, as I crossed the courtyard to stand before him. He sounded more curious than annoyed.

"I wanted to look at the stars," I said, "and listen to the music."

"I can't keep you away from it, can I?"

"I only wanted to listen."

"But you don't, do you? You want to learn to sing, to play an instrument. Isn't that right?"

Was this a trick question? Would he be angry if I told him yes, that was exactly what I wanted?

"Your aunt thinks you ought to sing in a choir. Did you know that was how your mother started her career?"

I shook my head. "No, Papa."

"That was where the impresario found her, the one who lured her away from home at the age of fifteen. I'm sure her parents thought her safe enough, singing for chapel services. But she packed a single valise and left home without so much as a word to them."

"Was she so unhappy at home?" I asked.

My father exhaled a curl of smoke, and said nothing.

"I would never leave home like that," I said, earnestly. I wanted to ask him what an impresario was, and what happened to my mother after she was lured away. He was rarely so forthright with me, and I thought perhaps the night had something to do with it, and the solitude of the courtyard under moonlight, so quiet and still after the flurry of activity over the past few days.

He withdrew a small ivory box from his pocket and tapped the last bits of unburnt leaf into the container. "I hope not," he said.

I shivered, feeling again the nagging sense that I was missing some part of a pattern. Some invisible thread was winding itself round me, and I couldn't seem to find the end to unhook it.

"I want to learn to sing," I said. I had an idea that it would help somehow, to give me a sort of clarity. Perhaps that was my secret ingredient, I thought, recalling Hespa's story.

My father nodded, his shoulders slumping. I felt as though I had defeated him somehow, without any knowledge or intent to do so. "I suppose I can arrange to have an alma come and teach you hymns. Perhaps that will satisfy your aunt, as well. She's been talking about sending you to Pendrake Hall for a proper education with your cousins."

"I don't want to go to Pendrake Hall," I said. "I told you, I want to stay here. She can't make you send me, can she?"

"No. But I must admit, she's made some good points. You're very alone here, Amardine."

"I don't mind," I said. I watched a bat circle out over the mulberry trees, where a set of wind chimes murmured. I wished suddenly that I could be out at night all the time, when everyone else was asleep and the world lay at peace under its cloak of darkness.

"That's what concerns me," my father said. "Go on inside, then. You ought to be in bed at this hour."

"Yes, Papa," I said, as he swung the wrought-iron gate, thick with roses in the full bloom of summer, then slid open the glass doors behind it. I stepped into the front entrance hall and padded through the drawing room, down the corridor to the nursery. Hespa was snoring in the room next door, a reminder that I was truly alone, left to my own devices. I wasn't quite ready for sleep.

Instead, I went to the wardrobe and pulled open the doors, careful that I didn't let them squeak. I needed no light to find the hat box; the moonlight spilling in through the spider silk curtains was enough. I took out the perfume bottle and carried it over to the window, then unpinned one side of the curtain from the frame. The night air whistled through the window, making the fine fabric billow up into my face. I peered out across the row of drying platforms, afraid my father would see that the curtain had come undone. He'd pinned it in place to keep out the flies, and though the herbs planted round the courtyard were sufficient to keep most of them at bay, it would be just like him to charge in and insist on fixing it.

I put the pins back, all but one, so I could get a bit more

air. Then I sprayed the perfume out through the gap in the curtain and leaned forward to take a sniff. I was determined to be more careful this time. I didn't want any trace of it to linger in the room, or in my hair, or on my night dress. Nor was I prepared for the barrage of images that had assailed me the last time I'd used it.

Again, I caught the familiar musky scent, just as it was whisked away on a night breeze. I closed my eyes and let the visions creep in.

At first, I thought nothing was going to happen. Images flashed behind my eyes, but they were only disjointed memories from the events of the previous days—Bianca crawling about with a dead magpie in her mouth, Hespa cradling the giant egg, my father giving his toast. But then my mind began to quiet, and the pictures dissolved into mist. My head began to thrum. And then something flashed across the void of thought—a golden pendant, spinning on a chain in the darkness. The spinning slowed and a hand reached out to clasp it, then opened the palm to reveal the sun-and-sword of Aneidis. The links of the chain flashed, reflecting candlelight. A woman's voice, whispering over and over, *"Forgive me, forgive me, forgive me, oh, God, forgive me."*

Then the image was gone. A jumble of thoughts crowded into its place: mundane, anxious thoughts, the same old fears and familiar disquietude. I was alone again in my head, for better or worse, and it was beginning to throb with a violent ache. Try as I might, I couldn't expand the vision, couldn't reconnect to that place I'd found in the darkness.

I was about to put the perfume back, but the sight of all the items I'd collected, arranged on the bed, distracted me: the book on floral arrangement, the libretti, the fragment of egg-shell, the diald. It was this last item that caught my attention now.

Beatrice had said that the diald contained magic, that it was wrought in a far-away city by powerful priests. These priests were of a different lot than Father Parquar, of this I felt certain. In my mind, they were distant, dignified figures with long white beards. I couldn't imagine them leaving stepping stones for thirsty bees, or cherishing the oldest, ugliest horse in the county, if they noticed such things at all. But no one disputed that the magic of the priests was real.

Even my mother had been a devotee—this surprised me. For some reason I had not thought her religious. Perhaps I associated her too much with the old magic, had made assumptions about her because of who she was—or *what* she was. But I knew it was her bejeweled hands that caught the spinning pendant. She had held the symbol of Aneidis as she murmured her prayers. She had used a diald in her practice. She must have known something about magic, about the divine.

These things she had left behind would have to be my guide.

I would need to experiment. I had no textbook, no teacher, but for this tenuous connection with my mother's spirit. I returned to the window and did a second trial, spraying a bit more scent through the gap in the curtain. The courtyard was empty now; my father had at last gone inside. I inhaled deeply, holding my breath. Then I sat on the bed and picked up the diald, letting it rest across my open palms.

I sat with legs crossed and eyes closed, feeling the weight of the metal stake in my hands. The now-familiar swirl of thoughts rushed into my head, unimpeded. My mind was no longer a separate island, floating in an aetherial sea. Thoughts burst in upon me which weren't my own. As the blood pounded between my ears, I sank deep into a vision. I saw the same jeweled hands reaching out before me, grasping at the roots of the elm tree. My body was stretched, and I realized I was hanging, just like Bianca had said; I could feel the rope tied round one ankle, the strain of my own weight on my joints. In my other hand I held the diald, slick with blood, and I understood that a sacrifice had been made. I braced myself against the roots, spinning one way, then the other, and plunged the stake into the earth. The spinning stopped. My vision darkened. A voice cried out, bubbling up as though from underwater, from a great distance. *What have you done, child? What have you done?*

The darkness beckoned, promising union, comfort, a soft place to land. I wanted to let myself be pulled into its undertow. Never again would I need return to the glaring daylight and the sharp edges of reality. This was the place where I belonged—the darkness wouldn't judge me strange or mad.

But then I felt my hands grow warm—my actual, child

hands—and blinked, disoriented, as my own room returned to focus. The heat was radiating from the diald. That was what had jarred me from my reverie. I dropped the metal stake onto the bed and shuddered, which started my whole body shaking uncontrollably. My head ached with a vengeance. What *had* I done?

I put everything back in the hat box. *That's it*, I told myself, in my sternest governess voice, the one I adopted whenever I feared I'd gone too far astray. I had seen enough of the visions. I could let the objects rest now, safely hidden in the wardrobe. *They are in their proper place*, I thought. To which the school-mistress in my head replied, primly, *And so are you, child.*

છ૭ભ

The Pendrakes left the next morning after breakfast. I watched from the veranda as their black Cartouche, which had been wiped down until it gleamed in the sunlight, made its way down the road. It made it all the way to the treeline at the edge of the lawn before coming to an abrupt halt, its frame dipping down, narrow wheels spinning in the mud. A momentary sense of dread came over me as I thought they might be stuck there until the road dried out, and have to take up residence at Guildenflore in the meantime. But a couple of the gardeners rushed out and gave the carriage a good push, and they were soon on their way.

I sighed with relief, glad that everything could finally go back to normal. I even looked forward to returning to my lessons with the schoolmistress. She wouldn't arrive until mid-afternoon, after the village school was out, and until then I was free to do whatever I pleased. I thought about borrowing one of Hespa's sensation novels. She liked to practice her reading with them, and usually left them under her bed, within easy reach for inquisitive minds. But then I heard Father Parquar speaking to my father in the courtyard, and my thoughts returned to the metal stake. Perhaps he would know what to do with it.

From the salon, where I sat in my favorite reading chair, I could hear their conversation clearly. After about a quarter of an hour, they parted ways, and then the iron gate squealed as my father entered the house. His footsteps thudded up the stairs, and I raced out of the house to catch up with the priest, metal stake hidden in the deep pocket of my pinafore.

Father Parquar was just about to close the gate at the far end of the courtyard as I called out his name. He paused, holding the gate for me, then closed it behind me as I stood catching my breath in the shadow of the stone wall.

"Is something wrong, child?" he asked, his brow knitting with concern.

"I'm not sure," I said, feeling the weight of the diald pressing down into my pocket. I withdrew the stake and held it out to him.

He took it and turned it over, reading the inscription. "Where did you get this?"

"I found it," I replied vaguely, not willing to give up all of my secrets. "It was my mother's, wasn't it?"

"It certainly appears that way." He turned it over again, thoughtfully. "I've never seen this before, though."

"Beatrice says she ought to have a second one at chapel," I said.

"Yes, that's right. But I'm sure this never had a companion at the chapel in Tarbonne. I would have remembered it."

"Why? What's so special about it?" I asked.

"I don't think this was created by the priests in Achalion."

"Why not?"

He paused, frowning. "Because dialds are made from cold-wrought iron. This looks like it's been plated with silver."

"What does that mean?" I asked. "Why would she have it, then?"

"I don't know. Silver is traditionally used to kill spirits that have crossed over from the Umbra or the Aetherial." He turned it over one more time, then held it out, the final pointing toward me. I shivered, despite the warmth of the day. I wasn't sure I wanted it, after what had happened the night before.

"Perhaps you ought to keep it," I said. "Shouldn't a priest have a silver weapon?"

"It's yours, by right," he said.

Gingerly, I grasped the finial, and with one last dubious glance, dropped it back into my pocket.

"I'll give you some silver polish," he said. "It will clean up nicely, I think, if you take care of it. It's a valuable keepsake."

I nodded and turned to go back to the house, more

confused than ever. I felt certain my father would never have allowed me to keep such a thing, and I couldn't shake the feeling that I was committing some transgression, despite having the blessing of a priest. Perhaps I ought to have told Father Parquar about the visions. Perhaps that would have changed his decision.

And perhaps, if I had, I would never discover the truth I sought.

I passed beneath the pergola and entered the house through the iron gate, going through the entrance hall to the empty drawing room. I was trying to make sense of my fragmented religious education when the petition box on the mantel caught my eye.

It was about the size of an ample jewelry box, made of white ceramic with a lock on the front. It was fashioned to look like bands of people and animals—horses, dogs, oxen, even elephants—were marching round the outside of it, ascending celestial stairways to the top. At the top there was a narrow slit into which one would drop the petitions. No one ever touched the petition box, not even Hespa when she was dusting the mantel. Although my religious education had been sparse, I knew it was only to be touched by the head of the household, that only my father could bring it to a priest, as he was supposed to do regularly, so that the petitions could be removed and read by the holy intercessor.

Do you want to be overlooked forever by Aneidis because your father is too stubborn to observe a basic sacrament? My aunt's words came back to me as I stood before the mantel, peering up at the box. I'd never thought much about Aneidis, but my mother apparently had, judging by the pendant she had worn.

Footsteps sounded in the hallway, and Hespa appeared with a tray. She began gathering up plates and wine glasses scattered about the room, still left from the previous evening when dozens of people had milled through the house.

"Hespa, do you ever write petitions?" I asked.

"I never have," she declared, straightening her back. "When I was young, I worked for a Crimori lady who wrote letters to her sisters. Pages and pages of letters, a fortune in parchment. I couldn't imagine it. How much was there to say? When I want to pray, kit, I do it in my head. That way you don't have to bother anyone."

"Do you pray to Aneidis?"

She paused, balancing the tray on one arm. "I pray to whoever will listen. But not too often, mind. It's dangerous to court the gods."

"Do you think I ought to start writing petitions?" I asked.

"Why do you ask such a thing?"

"I don't know. I just thought—maybe it would help."

Once, when the Pendrakes were visiting, Beatrice had asked me who my alma was, and I hadn't known what one was. I'd tried to cover my ignorance by answering as succinctly as possible.

"I don't have one," I'd said, with a nonchalant little shrug.

"Why not?" she asked.

"Some people just don't need one."

Beatrice had given me one of her slow, calculating looks. "What's *that* supposed to mean? My alma's already taught me twenty-five canticles. How many do you know? I'm going to sing at chapel this spring, Mother says so."

That had made me imagine a glamorous-looking woman with flushed cheeks and a throaty voice, swaggering about on a stage. But it turned out an alma was a sort of religious instructress. And I'd never had one.

Perhaps that was what was wrong with me. Perhaps, if I'd had such an education, I could make sense of the nagging feeling that I was missing something, some thread of cosmic logic.

By now, Hespa had gathered up all of the glassware, and was heading toward the open door to the hallway. "If you think it will help, kit," she said, echoing my thoughts. She didn't sound convinced.

Then a door opened upstairs, and my father's footsteps sounded above me. He had a heavy tread, despite his wiry build, and his boots thundered on the stairs. They paused above the landing, and I heard him curse under his breath.

Oh, no, I thought. *He's finally found the bubble in the wallpaper.* With all the activity in the house, I'd dared to think that perhaps it might go unnoticed. I stood motionless in the ensuing hush, not even daring to breathe. The clock on the mantel ticked gently. The voices of the servants carried on quietly below. As he dropped the last step to the landing, his feet coming into view through the banister, I scuttled to the far end of the room, out of sight.

His footsteps paused for several moments, and then came one more footfall, landing softly on the rug, like the last drop of rain to fall down a pane of glass.

A moment later, I heard a *wrrriiitching*, tearing, rending sound, as though some monstrous scarab was thrashing about up there, husking off its old skin. I knew what that meant: the hated wallpaper was finally coming down.

There was a pause. A silence. Then my father's voice came bellowing down the stairs. "Amardine!" he shouted. "Get up here this instant!"

Reluctantly, I ducked out from behind a row of ferns and made my stand at the base of the stairs. He stood on the landing, looking down at me. From there I could see nothing out of the ordinary, aside from the long curls of wallpaper he'd torn down. Now he would have to do the whole drawing room, I thought, with a bit of panic. That would take forever, and he would no doubt make a production of storming about the house, cursing to the end of time.

He sounded *truly* upset, though; I couldn't tell if it was anger in his voice, or fear, or something else.

"Come up here," he said, beckoning me with his hand.

"What is it?" I whispered.

"I want you to look at something."

"Why, Papa?"

"I want you to tell me what you see."

I gathered my skirt and started up the steps. I was looking down, trying not to trip on the long hem of Beatrice's most recent hand-me-down, so I didn't see right away what had upset him. When I finally did, I had to stare for several moments before it made any kind of sense.

"Well? What do you say to this?" my father asked.

Revealed on the wall was a picture, or perhaps an intricate symbol, about a foot in diameter, inscribed with what appeared to be blue paint. It was a flower, its pinwheel petals made up of smaller pinwheels, which in turn contained even more minute renderings. The shape of it was familiar to me, and once I got over my initial dull shock, I realized why. That was the pattern, in greater detail, that I'd found in the egg shell. Which I'd also seen before, on my own hand.

"What do you say to this?" my father repeated.

"I don't know," I said.

"You do know," he said, dropping down and grasping my shoulders. "Did you put that there?"

Behind him, the whorl of blue slid into focus, and I thought about how painstakingly it must have been rendered. "No, Papa," I said. "I don't know how to paint like that."

He seemed to consider that for a moment. The vertical line in his forehead, the only true mark of age borne on his face, furrowed deep. He let go of me and stood up straight, turning to the vandalized wall.

"You didn't see who did it?" he asked.

"No, Papa." I was just as baffled as he was, but for

different reasons. For a moment, I thought about turning over my palm, holding it out to him and saying, "Look here, look at what's happening." He could draw his own conclusions. Then he would figure out the problem and fix it, and everything would be all right.

I clenched my fist at my side, instead.

"You're absolutely certain you've seen nothing unusual in the house?"

I swallowed hard and said, "Have you, Papa?"

He didn't reply. Instead, he pushed past me and continued down the stairs, crossing the drawing room to the wall where the aetherscope hung. I followed in his wake, digging my thumb into my palm to quell my anxiety, standing in his shadow as we both stared silently at the device. All fourteen crystals in the umbral ring were glowing purple, a full circle.

"Is that bad?" I asked finally, my voice barely more than a whisper.

"It's not good," he said. "It's never good."

ℰↄ�℞

My father didn't speak to me much for the next few days. He had the wall painted over, and just as I'd predicted, tore down the paper in the drawing room, as well. The room was off-limits to me while this work was being done. If more mysterious symbols were discovered beneath the offensive display of convolvuli, I never heard about it. And I suspected I *would* have heard of it, given the shortness of his temper.

Hespa, on the other hand, had gone on full defense against "the forces that lie in wait," as she liked to call them. She left a bowl of salt on my nightstand and burned incense in the stairwell, and instructed me to stay on the first floor. "Demons and spirits of the Umbra like to use landings and stairs to get into this world," she said. "It's because they're in between one space and another. It's the same reason they prefer dawn or dusk."

"Maybe it's a good spirit, and it's trying to talk to us," I said one night, as she was hanging a bunch of fresh fennel in the door frame of the nursery.

But she shook her head. "Good spirits don't try to scare people like that."

"What if it doesn't know any better? What if—" I dropped my voice to a whisper—"what if it's my mother's ghost?"

She finished securing the herbs from the nail she had pounded into the wall the day before. Then she came over and sat by my bed, where I sat up on the pillows, far from sleep.

"I know you want to think that, kit," she said, gently.

"It might be," I said.

"It might be," she conceded. "But spirits of the dead don't act like that, not usually. They don't have the power to make marks on walls. They come to us in our dreams, most often. That's the easiest place for them to reach us. And even then, they have to wait for the right time."

"Then—you think it's something else?"

"I don't know."

"Are you scared, Hespa?" I asked.

"A little," she admitted, reaching out to smooth my hair. "But try not to worry. My grandame taught me a few tricks to keep evil spirits at bay."

She blew out the lamp, and I lay awake for hours afterward, hoping my mother's spirit would send me a message through my dreams. But when I did finally succumb to sleep, it was heavy and undisturbed.

A few days later, as I was sitting down to a meal of honey cakes and Minz melon, my father ghosted into the doorway of the breakfast room, as though he'd been lurking silently nearby. He stood watching me for a moment, leaning on one arm against the doorjamb.

"I need to speak with you," he said, finally.

I swallowed a bite of honey cake and set down my fork. He pulled out a chair, letting its legs scrape across the flagstones, and sat down.

"What is it, Papa?" I asked.

"I've decided to send you to your aunt's for a time," he said.

"No," I blurted out, before I could think. I winced, feeling my face grow hot.

"No?"

"I mean—I'd rather not, if you don't mind."

He placed his hands flat on the table. "I'm concerned about you, Amardine."

"I didn't draw that picture on the wall."

"I know you didn't. It must have been one of the wallpapering crew."

I knew he was lying. He didn't believe that for a moment.

"Then why are you sending me away?"

"I'm not trying to punish you," he said. "I just think a change of scenery would be beneficial. You ought to spend more time with your cousins."

"Papa?"

"Yes, Amardine?"

I turned my fork over in my hand, staring at the mark on my palm.

"Nothing," I said. "It's just—I don't know what to talk about with my cousins."

"Just try to take interest in the things they like," he said.

"I don't think they like me very much," I confessed.

"Give them a chance. Make an effort. Perhaps they don't know what to say to you."

He was giving me that look again, the one that said *you are the stranger; you are the one who doesn't belong.* He was already resolved to send me away. I had to be more careful, lest he decide to make my exile permanent.

Then he heaved a sigh and rose from the chair. "I know I'm not the best example to you. I don't know what else to do. They're your cousins, your only close relations. You need to have some connections in the world. Your aunt was right about that, at least."

He turned on his heel and left the room, the sound of his boots on the flagstones fading behind him. I didn't move for a long time. Finally I picked up my fork and stabbed it into my half-eaten honey cake. I took a bite, but the cake had lost its flavor. All I could taste was the sugar, and it made my stomach turn. I put the fork down, my hand trembling.

How long would I have to be away from home? Spending a single day with my cousins was torturous enough. Would I even be allowed to go for a walk by myself, or read a book? Would I be required to talk to them from sunup to sundown? I didn't know how I would survive this nightmare. How did grownups do it, when they entertained company for weeks at a time? I'd always wondered this, when Lady Pendrake spoke of visiting friends in distant counties. Perhaps they had a schedule, or wore a special hat when they didn't want to talk to anyone. If so, I would have to ask Hespa about having one made.

There was but one thing I knew for certain, as I traced the spiral on my palm with my right thumb: I had no confidantes at Pendrake Hall.

CHAPTER TEN

I AWOKE THE MORNING OF MY departure to Pendrake Hall with my stomach in knots. I'd been dreaming the night before, the sort of dreams from which I awoke tossing and turning, my mind spinning like a wooden top. I'd dreamed of a murky, underwater voice, but the words had bubbled away as soon as I'd opened my eyes.

"When do dead people talk to you in your dreams?" I asked Hespa as she packed my trunk, removing each dress from the wooden clotheshorse and folding it neatly on my bed.

"Goodness, child. It's too early in the day for such questions," she said, pausing to examine an ink stain on one of my pinafores.

"If it was nighttime, you would say it was too late."

She sighed and draped the pinafore over the back of a chair. "Amardine Sophia, how many times do I have to tell you not to put stained clothes in the washing? Those girls in the village never spot clean anything. Now I'll have to treat it with lard, and you won't have it at Pendrake Hall."

"I have another one," I said.

"Yes, but it has a patch in it."

I realized that I'd forced her to send me away looking shabby, and felt a pang of guilt. "Don't worry, Hespa. I'll take the one with the ink stain, and just drop a bottle of ink on my lap the moment I get the chance. That way Lady Pendrake will have to lend me a new one."

"Don't you dare, kit," she said, but she snatched it up again and began folding it into a neat white square.

"You never answered my question," I complained, watching her work.

"About the dead, you mean? It isn't wise to try to talk to them, kit. They're not the same as they were in life. They get confused. Sometimes they're angry."

"But you *can* talk to them?" I pressed. "How?"

She sighed again. "I don't know. And I don't think I would tell you, even if I did."

"Has a dead person ever talked to you in a dream?"

She picked up her packing list and stared at it for a long moment, as though she'd not heard the question. I thought she wouldn't answer, but at last she set it down on the dressing table and said, "Only once. But I was very ill at the time. It might have been a fever dream, after all."

She wouldn't elaborate on it, even after I continued to press her. She worked efficiently, and soon announced that she had checked the last item off the list. I trailed after her as she carried my trunk to the front hall.

"Can't you go with me?" I asked.

"You know I'm needed here, kit. Besides, you surely won't want your nursemaid minding you every moment."

"What if I need to ask you a question?" I asked.

"If it's an important question, I'm sure someone else can answer it."

The clock in the drawing room struck nine. Hespa fretted over not finding my hat right away in the hall cupboard, but eventually produced it, though it was a bit flat from having been pinned to the floor by the tip of a parasol. The hat was ordinary in every way, possessing no special ability to ward off unwanted conversation, but that had ever been a fanciful hope.

Hespa tied the ribbons under my chin and stepped back, regarding me with an expression of grim pride.

"There," she said. "Now you look like the toast of the town."

"Why would I want to look like toast?"

She sighed a third time in the span of an hour. "Never mind, kit. Be a good girl for your aunt and uncle. Try not to ask them questions about dead people."

I hadn't even thought of that, but now I considered it. I knew my aunt liked to talk, especially after she'd had a few glasses of wine. Perhaps she would be more forthcoming about certain questions my father refused to answer. I started to feel a bit better about the whole ordeal of going to Pendrake Hall, now that I'd found a purpose in it.

The carriage rolled up the drive a few minutes later. I thought my father would send me off, but he didn't appear. He was probably busy with the pardesu extraction. I knew it was an exacting process, one which he had to supervise closely. Hespa carried my trunk out and the driver hopped down from his seat and loaded it in the back. It was strange to travel by myself, with a driver I didn't know. I'd never done anything like it before.

The carriage was plush and comfortable, at least until it started moving. Then it jolted over every dip and rut in the road, making my teeth hurt. Fortunately the road smoothed out once we got closer to Tarbonne, and I began to relax into the journey, watching the countryside roll past. The carriage passed signs for a blacksmith, a milliner, a wine importer, and a café. A couple of old men sat at a table outside of the café, smoking cheroots and playing a game with tiles, but they didn't look up when I fluttered my hand in greeting. I spotted Milo Meliflore loitering outside the grocery, but I didn't bother waving to him.

Soon the village was behind us. The carriage wound through shady stands of poplar trees and cedar orchards, past rows of bee boxes. We came upon a group of boys and girls walking in the road, swinging baskets as they were herded by a schoolmistress.

"Look, there's a girl in there!" one of the boys announced, and everyone smiled and waved up at me.

I could now imagine how Bianca had got in trouble hanging out the window of the Cartouche, for there was so much in the world to see. And we hadn't even reached Rivene yet. After about an hour, as we made our gentle descent toward the town's outer limits, I caught my first glimpse of it.

The rooftops were a patchwork of tiles, shimmering in the heat-haze of the late morning sun. The mosaic was cut through the center by the river, a silver ribbon of water, trailing velvet stillness. I suddenly wished I had someone to describe it to, and then I remembered the children I'd seen on the road earlier, and how they'd looked so happy together. They were strangers to me, though.

The carriage slowed as we entered the press of traffic. The road was pebbled here, and taller wagons passed by the carriage so close they became a bright-colored blur. I kept my head well inside, ducking behind the curtain whenever I sensed the thunderous approach of one of the wagons. I didn't wave to anyone here. I sensed that I was becoming invisible, just one of many passengers being ferried from one place to the next. In a strange way it was comforting, I thought, as we paused to wait for a stopped delivery cart to resume its route. One could even become a different person, and hardly anyone would ever know.

When the traffic cleared, the carriage entered the main thoroughfare, a two-lane street with a sidewalk lined with market stalls. There were shops, too—real shops with plate glass windows. In one window, three mannequins were draped in diaphanous gowns with wide silk ribbons tied about the waist, posed round a table as though they were taking tea. The carriage paused again, and I peered through the plate window at the mannequins, imagining I was listening in on their conversation behind the glass. *My dress was made by the finest dressmaker in Bavil-Figonea,* one announced. It was the most fantastical place I could think of. *Well, my shoes are made from moon rocks carved into slippers,* said another. "Why on earth would you want shoes made from rocks?" I asked, taking on the character of the third mannequin. I hadn't meant to speak aloud, though. Worse, at that very moment, the door of the shop had opened and two elegantly-dressed ladies emerged, laughing among themselves. They stopped laughing as soon as I spoke.

"What did that child say?" one whispered. The other just shook her head. Then they took in the carriage and stepped closer, scrutinizing me, as though I were a ruffian or a stowaway who didn't belong in such a fine contraption. Did my hat look shabby? I wondered, remembering how it had been partially crushed in the cupboard. Perhaps it was shabby. It had a patchwork look to it, its soft top puffing up from a wide, stiff brim, like a muffin. By contrast, the women's hats towered atop their heads, vakra feathers bobbing in the breeze. I looked down at my own clothing, and then at the people walking on the street, seeking out girls my own age for further study and comparison. *How could I have ever thought of bringing my ink-stained pinafore?* I berated myself. Hespa had *tried* to warn me of the shame, but at the time, I was too focused on getting her to talk about dead people.

The carriage jolted forward then and crossed the bridge, leaving the two sour-looking women behind. It wasn't long before the road opened up again, winding through hemlock groves and passing a crumbling stone wall. After about a quarter of an hour, we came to the edge of the trees, where they appeared frozen in retreat from the looming edifice of Pendrake Hall.

My father had said it was newer than Guildenflore, which surprised me, because I associated such grandeur with ancient days. The house had two symmetrical wings that extended from its central hub, and the whole of it rose from a smooth blanket of grass atop a green plateau. The road cut straight down the middle of the lawn, diverging only to go round the edge of a pond. A flock of vakras clustered round the pond, but as the carriage made its way toward the house, they scattered across the lawn. I'd never seen the birds up close before, and I withdrew from the window as one ran alongside the carriage, its long neck outstretched, pitching it forward, its short wings flapping. It looked somewhat like a wild goose, if geese could grow to be the size of ponies.

The carriage finally came to a stop before the steps of the house. I stepped down onto the gravel, and the driver waved me up the steps as another servant appeared from a door on the ground floor and took my trunk. This was it, I thought, as I ascended the steps. I was out in the world on my own for the first time, and I was determined to make a good impression. I slowed my stride, gathering my dignity, and knocked on the door.

An older man with a lantern jaw, wearing a uniform of blue-gray, answered my knock. He bade me wait in the entrance hall while he informed Lady Pendrake of my arrival. His shoes clicked on the marble floor as he strode across the room and disappeared through a door, and I was left alone in the hall. Muffled voices rang out from a distant room, up the great staircase that stood before me. There was nothing to do but wait, so I traced a slow path along the walls, which were the same pale blue-gray as the servant's uniform, broken into separate panels by gilt molding. Each panel was dominated by a huge oil painting. The paintings were mostly of men standing round in shady groves with their hunting dogs, or women sitting amid huge skirts, looking away from whoever was painting them.

I hadn't long to wait before my aunt swept down the stairs to greet me.

"Don't you look like a proper little lady," she said, smiling, as I curtsied before her. She bent down to kiss my cheeks, pausing to wipe a spot of dirt from my collar. "There. Now you're perfect. Did you have a pleasant journey, darling?"

"Yes, Lady Pendrake," I said.

"You must call me Aunt Ellinora," she said, grandly. "There's no need for such formalities here. My home is your home."

"Yes, Aunt Ellinora," I said.

"You look ill," she said, frowning. "Did you sleep well last night?"

"Not very well," I said. "I had strange dreams."

"Yes, I understand that you're plagued with those from time to time. I hope you won't have any bad dreams here. I want you to have only fond memories of your visit. Rivene isn't such a large town, but there are some lovely shops for a girl your age. Have you ever been to a real dressmaker?"

"No, Aunt Ellinora. But my maid, Hespa, has made a few things for me."

She smiled and patted my head. "That's what I was afraid of, dear."

I thought of my ink-stained pinafore, packed away in my trunk, and felt the shame creep in once again.

"Come, let's find your cousins," she said. "I'm sure they'll be excited to see you."

I followed her out of the entrance hall. The voices up the stairs rose again. One of them sounded vaguely familiar, but I couldn't place it.

"Do you have company, Lady—Aunt Ellinora?" I asked, trying to sound polite and grownup.

She turned to me and smiled again. "Why, yes, darling. Two of my dear friends were in the neighborhood, and they're staying with me for a little while. Today they're meeting with our local chapter of the Ladies' Betterment Society. You'll get to meet them too, don't worry."

"What is the Ladies' Betterment Society?" I asked.

She led me through a door on the right side of chamber, and we entered a gleaming corridor lined with windows. "Oh, it's just a little group of us women trying to do our part to make the world a better place," she said. "'Bettering ourselves, bettering our future!' That's what we like to say." She gave a light laugh. "It may sound a bit ambitious, but I do hope to make a difference, don't you?"

"I suppose so," I said.

"Perhaps you could join the junior chapter with my girls," she went on. "You'd love it, I'm certain. The girls sing songs and go on outings together, and they even host their own little fêtes in the ballroom. I'm sure Beatrice will tell you all about it, though."

"She told me about it, I remember now," I said, thinking of my cousin's brooch.

"Oh, I'm glad to hear it. I know she can be a bit shy about such things. That's why I made her a Junior Recruiter, to coax her out of her shell."

We found my cousins in a parlor, finishing their lessons. Lady Pendrake gave them permission to quit early and take the rest of the day to show me round the house. Bianca sprang from her seat immediately, nearly knocking over her tutor, a rail-thin elderly woman with spectacles. Beatrice was more languid, rising to greet me with her customary bored expression.

"How do you do, Amardine?" she asked, stiffly.

"I'm very well, and you?"

Lady Pendrake beamed at us. "Aren't you two exquisite? I'll leave you to your devices. I'm sure you have so much to talk about."

"Come on," Beatrice said, after my aunt left. "Mother says I'm supposed to give you a tour of the house."

I followed her and Bianca out of the room. "Show her the ballroom!" Bianca said. "It's really fun to slide round on the floor. You'll see."

Beatrice rolled her eyes. "She's too young to understand the proper use of a ballroom," she explained to me. "Have you ever been to a real fête, Amardine?"

"I don't think so," I said.

"You would probably know if you had."

I followed my cousins up the great staircase to the second floor. A hallway ran across the top of the stairs, looking down into the entrance chamber below. More family portraits lined the opposite wall, and Beatrice was quick to point out all of her ancestors that differed from mine. It was strange to think how closely we were related, yet we were almost from different worlds entirely. Beatrice talked of going to Cereval once the weather cooled—the city was ghastly in midsummer, she told me, with an air of authority; no one stayed in town if they could help it. But in the fall, there were parades and festivals every week, and dances on Bergamot Green, where all the ladies of quality gathered to meet respectable gentlemen.

"You're too young to go to those sort of dances," Bianca pointed out.

"I'll be old enough soon," Beatrice said, pushing open a pair of heavy wooden doors, which were carved with roses and acanthus leaves and polished to a high shine. Light spilled into the room from a row of high windows on the opposite wall. I'd always thought the ballroom at Guildenflore was grand, but this was even larger, and was furnished as a ballroom ought to be, with mirrored walls, plush chairs and low tables lining the outside edges, a raised platform with a pianoforte and paleophone, and an open floor for dancing.

"I have my dancing lessons in here with an instructor from Queen's Conservatory," Beatrice said. "She's young and very beautiful, and she knows all the latest steps."

"What is Queen's Conservatory?" I asked.

"It's a school in the mountains where the most talented girls and boys go to learn music and dancing. It isn't easy to get in, but I've been practicing the pianoforte so I can apply when I turn twelve."

"Mother will never let you go to that place," Bianca said. She flung her arms out and skipped over to the wall of mirrors.

"Why not?" I asked, as Beatrice and I followed.

"She might meet a boy."

"Is that a bad thing?" I asked.

Beatrice sighed. "I'm already engaged. I thought I told you that, Amardine."

I recalled what she had said about her cousin, her father's heir, but the particulars didn't much interest me. "How do you apply to the school?" I pressed.

Beatrice picked up a book lying on one of the tables and placed it on her head. She studied her reflection in the mirror, then began walking slowly across the floor, trying to keep the book from falling. "You have to go there and audition," she said.

"Audition?"

"It's like a recital, but much, much bigger."

"How do you get to audition?" I asked.

Beatrice frowned as the book began to slip. "You need a recommendation from someone."

"Do they teach umbral magic there?" I asked.

Beatrice reached up to adjust the book. "What's that?"

"The Umbra is a world beyond this one," I said, "where bad dreams take the shape of demons. And there's magic that can be shaped through music and stories. My maid, Hespa, told me about it."

"Is that where ghosts live?" Bianca asked.

"There are no ghosts," Beatrice said.

"Yes there are," Bianca insisted. "Mother even sees them, up in the Ghost Gallery."

"The Ghost Gallery?" I asked.

Beatrice started to shake her head, but stopped when the book moved again. "She calls it the Ghost Gallery, but there's no such thing."

"Go ahead and ask her!" Bianca shouted.

The book fell, slapping onto the ivory tiles. The sound echoed throughout the room. Beatrice looked at it, scowled, then walked off toward the platform. I picked up the book and set it back on the table, trailing after her, my mind still full of questions.

Bianca twirled, her hair flying about her face. "You wouldn't get into the Conservatory anyway," she teased her sister. "Even if Mother did allow it."

"What makes you the expert?" Beatrice shot back. "Alma Monti says I play *quite* well for a girl my age. It isn't fair that I'm not allowed to apply. If Mother had inherited *your* house, Amardine, I could go to the Conservatory and marry whomever I wanted."

"I don't see why you couldn't still learn music," I said.

"That's what *I* said," Beatrice replied. "But Mother says I can learn just as well at home."

"She thinks if Beatrice stays at home, she won't get into trouble," Bianca said, finishing her dance. "But she doesn't know Beatrice. *I* know Beatrice."

"What's *that* supposed to mean?" Beatrice demanded. "You're the one who's always ruining things. What about the time you picked all the flowers in the east garden?"

"I was hungry," Bianca said, with a shrug.

"And then you were sick. It serves you right, too."

"I was pretending to be a very small pony," Bianca explained. "Like the ones Princess Violet and Princess Eveline ride in street races."

Beatrice turned to me, shaking her head. "Do you see how ridiculous she is?"

"You oughtn't eat flowers," I said. "You could die if you ate the wrong ones."

"Really?" Beatrice asked. "Which ones?"

I was so pleased by her interest that I nearly blurted out a list of toxic plants. But then I thought the better of it. "I don't know," I lied.

"You're not very useful," Beatrice said. "I was thinking of poisoning my maid. I don't like the way she cuts my hair. No one my age wears a fringe any more." She gave a chilling shrug, then plopped down at the pianoforte and began flipping through the scores.

"Can you sing, Amardine?" she asked, twisting round on the bench.

"A little." I'd only had a few lessons thus far.

"I wish I had something from an opera," she said. "Like your mother would have sung. But all Alma Monti gives me to play are hymns. Do you know anything else?"

I shook my head. "All I've been learning are hymns, too."

"That's too bad," Beatrice said, turning back to the music. "You can sing along if you like. Try not to sing too loud, though. I don't like being drowned out."

☙❧

As the rest of the day crawled by, I was acutely aware of each hour that passed. But I remembered what my father had said, and tried to engage Beatrice by asking her questions about fashion. At first she scorned my ignorance, but soon warmed to the topic, and insisted on showing me her wardrobe. She and Bianca had a suite with its own sitting room, a feature that secretly impressed me. In their large shared bedroom, Beatrice hauled all of her dresses and hats from the wardrobe and arranged them over her coverlet, which soon disappeared beneath a mound of silk, taffeta and lace. I murmured my admiration, and was told that the dresses I most admired were at least a whole season out of fashion. "Mother says I can get something new at the shop next time we go to Rivene," she said. "I'm so sick to death of pleats."

Finally it was time for dinner. I learned that my cousins didn't eat their evening meal with the grownups, at least, not while they entertained guests. I couldn't wait to be free of them, to bask in the luxury of solitude. There were rules here I didn't understand, and with each moment my anxiety wound tighter, making me feel restless in my own skin. I told myself it would surely get better, once I was familiar with the household routine. Even so, a sense of dread squeezed my gut every time my attention drifted from their conversation, as though the house held some dark secret that was just waiting to reveal itself.

It was late when the dishes were finally cleared. One of the servants showed me to my room. Inside, beyond the circle of her candlelight, I could just barely see the foot of the bed. The woman crossed the room and opened the shutters, which extended almost to the floor. A flood of moonlight streamed in, bathing the white coverlet that lay across the bed. There sat my velveteen kitten, all plush upon its pillow, waiting for me.

Try to be happy, I told myself sternly, as I picked up the kitten and held it to my chest. *Don't ruin everything.* I tried holding onto an image of the shop window as I finally drifted off to sleep, but all I dreamed of was home.

CHAPTER ELEVEN

THE NEXT MORNING, ONE OF THE maids woke me and helped me dress for breakfast. "You have an invitation from Lady Pendrake," she said. "She would like for you to meet her friends this morning in the sun room." It sounded very formal, so I picked out my best frock and hoped my appearance wouldn't disappoint her.

As the maid led me down the stairs and through a hallway, the sound of voices echoed from somewhere beyond. When I entered the sun-lit breakfast room, I found the table occupied by three men and three women, including the Pendrakes. I recognized the women immediately; they were the ones who had come to Guildenflore and scolded me about the perfume bottle.

I tensed, waiting for them to tell my aunt that I was a bad child, not to be trusted. But they merely smiled and gave no indication that they had ever met me before.

"Ah, you're awake," Lady Pendrake said, beaming at me. "How did you sleep last night?"

"Very well, thank you," I lied. In truth, I'd been awake most of the night, tossing and turning in the giant bed.

"My niece," she said, for benefit of her friends, and I dropped into a curtsy. "Amardine is the sweetest child you will ever meet."

"Surely not sweeter than your own lovely girls," said the woman I'd known as the lady in blue. She was wearing a light yellow dress with pink flowers this morning, her dark hair pulled back in a loose chignon.

"Oh, well, there's no comparison to my girls," Lady Pendrake said. She introduced me to her company, and I learned that the "lady in blue" was Lady Beryl Chandray, the Countess of Vincoshar. She was the most important person I'd ever met, notwithstanding her husband, the Count, who smiled tolerantly beside her. Then there was her cousin, Lady Fairlion, whom I knew as Leda, and her husband, the Viscount of Lomn. The men nodded as they were introduced and then returned to their own conversation about an upcoming election, but the women clearly weren't done with me yet. Lady Chandray crooked a long finger at me and bade me come close.

"Let me have a look at you," she said, and I went to stand before her. "I've seen this child before," she said, and turned to her cousin. "We both have."

"Have you really?" Lady Pendrake exclaimed.

"At Guildenflore," she said, giving Lady Fairlion a conspiratorial look.

"You didn't tell me you'd been to Guildenflore," my aunt said, her hand fluttering to her throat with mock outrage. "And how did you find it?"

"Your brother was very rude to us," Lady Chandray said. "He didn't welcome us at all. But your niece made up for her father's poor manners. She told us all about the houseplants. Every last one of them. Isn't that right, cousin?"

"Oh yes, she was quite the thorough hostess," Lady Fairlion said, with a short laugh.

I looked down at my feet, feeling my face grow hot.

"Why don't you sit down, Miss Amardine?" Lady Pendrake said, indicating the end of the table, where three empty chairs waited. Presumably the other two were for my cousins. Where *were* Beatrice and Bianca? I almost welcomed their company, if it meant taking the scrutiny off of me.

"It seems my girls are late, as usual," my aunt said.

"I do think it's wonderful that you're taking such an interest in your niece," Lady Chandray said, as I sat down and smoothed my skirt over my knees. "Her nature might have turned out very differently otherwise."

"I do what I can," Lady Pendrake replied, giving me a fond little smile. "It's a terrible thing for a child to grow up without a mother. Almost as terrible as a mother losing her child."

The other women nodded soberly and there was a brief moment of silence round the table, broken by the arrival of

Beatrice and Bianca. They shuffled through the doorway and curtsied to the guests, then took their seats and eyed the empty sideboard.

"I'm *starving*," Beatrice said, picking up her fork. Her mother laid a hand on hers, pinning it to the table.

"We were waiting for you, darling," she said. "And please don't use that word in this house. No one here is starving."

She nodded to the footman, who was standing nearby, and he left the room, returning with breakfast. He went round the table serving us, but I didn't take much from the first platter, which consisted of sliced meat covered in gravy. I wasn't accustomed to eating such heavy dishes at breakfast. When a platter of fruit and cold meats came round, I picked a thin slice of melon. Beatrice stared across the table from me and snickered.

"You're not supposed to eat that," she said.

I froze, fork and knife hovering in mid-air. What had I done wrong this time?

"That's just a garnish," Beatrice explained.

"Now, Honey Bee, let's not embarrass our guest," Lady Pendrake said. "If she wants to eat the melon, that's her choice." She turned and smiled at me. "Perhaps you would prefer bread and milk?"

"I'm not very hungry," I said, wishing they would all stop staring at me. Lady Fairlion gave me a distinctly critical inspection.

"I was taught that children eat what they are given," she said.

"Amardine is our guest," Lady Pendrake said. "She shall eat whatever she likes."

"*I* wanted bread and milk," Beatrice piped up. "I'm sick of eating dinner for breakfast."

"Dinner for breakfast! Don't be a silly goose," Lady Pendrake said.

"I want the kind of bread we usually have at breakfast. Why can't we have that?" Beatrice asked.

"I do hope you didn't put yourself out for our sake," Lady Chandray said, giving my aunt a cool little smile.

"Oh, no, not at all," Lady Pendrake said. "Beatrice is just trying to be amusing. Her sense of humor requires a...certain degree of familiarity."

"I don't think young ladies ought to put on comedic airs," Lady Fairlion put in. "It only makes them look desperate for attention."

"It isn't natural," Lady Chandray agreed. "*I've* certainly never met a woman who was naturally amusing."

"I wasn't trying to be funny," Beatrice said, with a scowl.

"And you were succeeding admirably, Honey Bee," Lady Pendrake said.

I was glad they had forgotten about me, though I could practically feel Beatrice's rage emanating across the table. As she stabbed at a piece of meat with her fork and brought it grudgingly to her mouth, I began to understand why she always seemed so caustic.

After breakfast, we children were dismissed to the care of

my cousins' governess, Mistress Kettering. For their first lesson, Beatrice worked at her embroidery while Bianca read aloud, sounding out simple paragraphs from a primer. Then Beatrice recited the lineage of the royal family and named all of the dukes and counts of the realm, pointing out their holdings on a map. I'd never heard of any of them, except for the Count of Vincoshar, whom I'd met earlier. For all of Beatrice's fawning over titles, I was surprised she hadn't tried to make a better impression.

After that, we all worked at our penmanship until lunchtime, copying poems from a book. I enjoyed the exercise, sounding out the words under my breath as I wrote. I was fascinated by how they all fit together, and thought I might try writing my own as soon as I had a chance.

We took a break for lunch, and then, with our energy renewed, ran upstairs to the ballroom for a dancing lesson. There I met the girl from the Conservatory. I had to admit, Beatrice hadn't exaggerated her charm. Her name was Miss Vil, and she was everything I'd been taught a young lady ought to be —beautiful, graceful, patient, ever-smiling. She led me through the steps as we listened to a cheerful gavotte on the paleophone, uttering not a single harsh word, even though I kept making mistakes.

"See what I mean?" Beatrice asked, when the lesson was over. We were on our way back to our own rooms to take respite. Even the servants were napping, and the house was eerily silent. "That's why I want to go to the Conservatory."

"Are all the ladies there so beautiful and kind?" I asked with a sigh, as we reached the door to my cousins' room.

"Why do you ask that?" Beatrice snapped.

I turned to her, confused.

"Do you think I'm not pretty enough to get in? Is that it?"

"No, of course not," I said. "You have the most lovely complexion and hair. I wish I had raven black hair like you. You're like a heroine in a story-book."

She scowled bitterly. "Stop laughing at me."

"I'm not," I protested. "Next time you come to Guilden-flore, I'll show you some of my books. You'll see."

She didn't reply. To my shock, I saw that her eyes had filled with tears. I opened my mouth to speak, but before I could say anything further, she balled up her fists and angrily wiped the tears away.

"I don't care about your stupid books," she said, then turned on her heel and wrenched open the door to her room, slamming it behind her.

☙❧

After respite, I rejoined my cousins in the parlor to wait for our last lesson of the day. Beatrice practiced on the pianoforte —the Pendrakes possessed not one, but two such instruments, as well as a large harp, which no one in the house knew how to play—while Bianca and I worked on our embroidery. I hadn't slept at all during respite, my nerves too frayed to allow such tranquility of mind. I startled at the sound of the clock as it struck the hour, my stomach fluttering as the butler opened the door to admit our instructor.

She was an elderly woman, sharp-featured, wearing a long gray robe and a wimple. She looked at me, sitting next to Bianca on the divan, and raised a thick eyebrow.

"You are the cousin, is that correct?" she asked.

I rose from the divan and curtsied. "My name is Amardine, Madame," I said.

"*Madame?*" she repeated, her eyebrow arching even higher, like a furry caterpillar that had just spotted a juicy-looking leaf. "Is that how you address an alma?"

I looked to my cousins for support, but they were exchanging glances with each other, their hands over their mouths, trying to hide their laughter.

"I am Alma Monti," she said, in a dignified tone. "You may address me as Alma."

"Yes, Alma," I said, bowing my head. "I'm sorry, I didn't know."

"She's never had an alma," Beatrice said.

"Is that so?"

I shook my head.

"That is a shocking omission, I must say," Alma Monti said. "But then, I imagine your upbringing has been rather irregular."

"I suppose so," I said.

"You look nervous, child. What disturbs you?"

"I'm—I'm not, Alma Monti. I'm just tired, that's all. I didn't sleep much last night."

"And what preys upon your mind, that you do not sleep?" she asked, sharply.

"Nothing in particular," I said.

"Nothing? Nothing at all? I find that difficult to believe."

"I don't know what else to tell you," I replied, trying to mask my irritation.

"Young people ought to sleep well at night," she went on. "They have no reason not to, unless it be a bad conscience. Perhaps you have something you wish to confess."

Baffled, I turned once more to my cousins, though I ought to have known they would be no help.

"It's true, Alma Monti," Bianca said, her hands clasped in her lap, her skirts falling perfectly even round her ankles. "Amardine is a witch and I'm sure she feels just awful about it."

"I am not!" I cried out.

"She is," Beatrice put in. "She can even read minds. She did it to me just last week."

"You don't truly believe that," I said, glaring at her.

"She knows how to poison people," Bianca said, "and about umbral magic."

Alma Monti's nostrils flared as she sucked in a breath. "Umbral magic! What do you know of such things, child?"

"Nothing," I said, perhaps too forcefully. "I mean, I've only heard stories from my maid."

"Stories from your maid! What sort of woman would be telling you such things? And with your bloodline, no less! This is even worse than I imagined! And here you were, standing before me, such a neat little thing, and all along you head was filled with—with such *impurity!*"

I felt a white-hot rage bubble up from the core of my being. "How dare you speak of Hespa that way?" I said, my voice rising, going shrill. Not just Hespa, I thought—my mother, too. "Who are you, anyway? You're not my family. I won't sit here another moment and listen to you!"

After the words rushed out of me, I felt a hollowness in the smoldering pit of my stomach. What in the world had come over me? Alma Monti's mouth had fallen open, and she stared at me, gaping like a fish. Even my cousins were shocked into silence. They sat with their hands over their mouths, eyes wide, as though waiting for the next shoe to drop.

Finally, Alma Monti recovered herself. "Go, then," she said. "I thought it good of your aunt to bring you here, but now I question the wisdom of letting you mix with your cousins. You're a bad seed, Miss Desmarius, that's what you are. There's no denying it."

I turned and fled from the room, my slippers skidding in the hall outside as I nearly collided with one of the maids. She gave me a questioning glance, but I didn't wait round for her to interrogate me. I ran blindly, searching for an escape, any place I could be alone.

Rounding a corner, I found myself back at the now-empty breakfast room. A door on the far wall led outside; on the other side of the great glass windows lay a terrace and gardens.

I slipped out the door and tried to orient myself through the tears that blurred my vision. I thought I was facing out from the side of the house. Keeping a wary eye for vakras, I descended the steps of the terrace and took cover in the garden.

My heart was still pounding from the shock of what I had done. I had never spoken to any grownup in such a manner, let alone an alma. I wished I could just disappear into the hedges. The garden wasn't large, but its paths were twisted and ran close together in unexpected ways, and the foliage grew dark and impenetrable. I came upon a small, circular clearing, where a stone bench ringed a statue of a weeping woman. There I sat for a long time, sobbing in solidarity with my stony companion.

No matter how hard I tried to be good, I couldn't seem to help myself. Was it true, what the alma had said about me? What I'd done was truly bad, there was no denying that. I'd lost my temper and yelled at an alma. An alma, of all people! What would she do? Would she tell Lady Pendrake?

I had to leave, that was all there was to it. There was no place for me at Pendrake Hall. I couldn't even trust myself. If I could get my trunk from my room—no, I couldn't manage the trunk by myself. I'd just take my velveteen kitten and leave everything else behind. I could walk into town, it wasn't that far. Once there, perhaps I could find someone who was going to Tarbonne. There might even be a public coach. I'd need money for that, though. Would the coachman take my silver-backed hairbrush in exchange for fare? I'd bring that, too, just in case.

As I mounted the steps to the terrace, a racket sounded across the lawn. It was the vakras, honking and braying like some demonic cross between a goose and a donkey. I'd have to get past them, somehow, but it was best not to think about that quite yet. I slipped into the empty breakfast room and made my way down the corridor toward the main staircase. From the first-floor salon came muffled laughter and conversation. A door opened, and the sounds grew louder. Hard-soled shoes clicked on the marble floor. I ducked round a corner and hid in a statuary niche just as a tall woman in a flowing chiffon day dress strode past, patting her cheeks with a handkerchief.

When she was safely past and out of sight, I crept up the stairs and made my way to my room. There, I found the bed neatly made, my velveteen kitten sitting on the pillow as it had been the first night. I considered a moment, then stripped the pillow of its case, my nerves jangling as I stuffed the kitten, the hair brush, and a few other sundries into the cloth sack. I knew it was wrong to take it, but I hoped Lady Pendrake would understand that I intended to give it back.

I gathered my things, clenching the open end of the pillow case in one hand, and eased the door open. The hall was empty. I slipped out of the room as footsteps sounded on the stairs, and familiar voices rang out.

"You're being ridiculous, Bifa. I'm sure she didn't get eaten by a vakra. She's probably just in her room, sulking."

Bianca giggled in response, her feet thumping hard on the floor as she closed the distance between us. There was no time to duck back into my room and close the door before she rounded the corner, stopping short in the corridor. "There she is! I found her!"

Beatrice caught up a few moments later. I held the sack made of the pillowcase at my side, partially concealed behind my skirt.

Beatrice's gaze fell upon it immediately. "What are you doing?" she asked. "Why are you carrying round a pillowcase?"

"I just needed it to carry a few things," I said.

"You're not *leaving*, are you?" Beatrice asked. "You can't leave yet."

"I don't think I ought to be here," I said.

"You haven't even seen the whole house," Beatrice said.

"I've seen enough."

"You haven't even seen the gallery!" Bianca said, holding one leg behind her and hopping on the other foot.

"You shouldn't have said those things to Alma Monti," Beatrice went on. "Her face went red as a beet after you left. She was so mad, I thought she was going to choke. She just kept muttering things like, 'Well, I never!' and 'The nerve of that girl!'"

Bianca threw her head back, letting out a peal of laughter. "I've never seen anyone's face turn so many colors all at once!"

"Do you think she'll tell Lady Pendrake what I said?" I asked.

"Oh, I doubt that," Beatrice replied. She paused, and a slow smile crept across her face. "But I might."

"Please, don't tell Lady Pendrake," I said. I hated to beg of her, of all people, but I couldn't see any way round it.

"I won't tell her," Beatrice said. "Just so long as you promise to do something for me."

"What would you have me do?"

"I haven't thought of it yet. I'll let you know when I do. But you're not allowed to leave until I say so."

I hate her, I thought, my stomach churning.

Bianca twirled, letting her skirts fly out. "Show her the gallery!"

"You mean the hall with all the paintings, where I came in?"

"Not that gallery," Beatrice replied.

"The Ghost Gallery," Bianca whispered.

"That's right," Beatrice said. "What do you think of that, Amardine? Are you scared?"

Not of the ghosts, I thought. I was more afraid of Beatrice setting a trap for me, for the sake of her own twisted glee. But if I refused to go, they would think me weak.

"I'm not scared," I said.

Beatrice's mouth tightened into a smile. I tried not to flinch as she reached out and put a clammy hand on my arm, as though we were chums. "Mother keeps the door locked," she said, her strange, flat gaze boring into me. "But I know where she keeps the key."

CHAPTER TWELVE

THE GHOST GALLERY, AS BIANCA CALLED it, was on the third floor of Pendrake Hall, but to get to it, Beatrice told me, we had to go all the way downstairs.

"The door to the stairs is in a cloakroom. We'll have to go nearly to the kitchens," she warned me, as though we would be crossing enemy territory. "Don't let the servants see you."

I trailed after her, Bianca creeping along behind us, quiet as a cat. Beatrice made her way down the main staircase with a slow, dignified air, which I sought to imitate. We had to appear extra serious to make up for Bianca's slinking, which looked highly suspicious.

Fortunately, no one was about. Lady Pendrake and her coterie were having apéritifs on her balcony, Beatrice assured me, and her father, if we ran into him, would just assume someone with authority had sent us to the kitchens. I could tell she was accustomed to making such calculations. And so we managed to get downstairs and take refuge in the cloakroom before anyone spotted us.

Beatrice opened a door in the back, and Bianca and I followed her through, into a stairwell dimly lit from above. The steps creaked beneath us as we made our way up toward the light, dead beetles crunching underfoot.

"Mother only comes up here once a year," Beatrice said, as Bianca and I trailed a few steps behind. We reached the first floor, which opened into an unfinished room, empty but for an old chest of drawers, and a tangled mat of rope which might have been the remnants of a cot.

"Does someone live in here?" I asked.

"Not anymore. This used to be a servants' room. But now it just goes to the gallery." The stairs continued on the other side of the room, making a turn on a landing, bringing us to another long, empty room with an identical layout. We crossed this room to yet another stairwell, leading us to the third floor. At the top of the stairs was a heavy wooden door.

Beatrice pulled out her borrowed key.

"Are there really ghosts in there?" I asked, imagining a corridor filled with floating, semi-transparent shades, like layers of sheer curtains.

"I suppose we'll just have to see," she said, as she put the key in the lock and turned the doorknob.

The door creaked open. The corridor beyond was brighter

than the stairwell, and as I followed Beatrice in, I was disappointed by how ordinary it appeared. A wide hallway stretched before us, littered with dead leaves. Light spilled in from a rosette window at the far end, illuminating large, heavy picture frames lining both walls. The first eight frames on the left wall held paintings, but there were about a dozen more blank frames. The first couple of paintings depicted Lady Pendrake holding a baby. The rest were of a small child, appearing slightly older in each successive painting. In the last one, the child—a boy with rosy cheeks and coal-black curls—looked to be about eight years old. He sat on a pony, holding a ripe plum in one hand, a challenging expression writ across his cherubic features.

"Who is this?" I asked.

Beatrice stepped up beside me to stare at the last painting. "That," she said, "is Theore."

"Who is Theore?"

"My brother," Beatrice said.

I looked at her, confused. "I thought he died."

"He did," Beatrice said. "He didn't just die—he never lived in the first place."

"But how does the painter know what he would look like?"

"Mother knows," Beatrice said. "The same way she knows he would have been a boy. He even has his own room, too. I can show that to you, as well, but it's not all that interesting. Bifa and I aren't supposed to go in there. *We* don't get our own separate rooms in the children's wing and it's all because of *Theore*."

"I jumped on the bed once," Bianca said, with a grin.

"I never knew any of that," I said, my gaze drifting back to the painting. "Lady Pendrake must be terribly sad to do all of this."

"She has his portrait painted every year. Nobody knows who the artist is. She doesn't even want to know. That way the connection is more spiritual, she says." Beatrice rolled her eyes. "Now you see the rubbish we have to live with."

"I don't think it's rubbish," I murmured, my attention fixed on the beautiful child before me. The artist had done an expert job, as far as I could tell. I could almost imagine the boy was real. Perhaps Lady Pendrake was *making* him real, bringing him back to life with a magical spell. What if she knew something about contacting spirits?

"Poor Lady Pendrake," I said.

"*Poor Lady Pendrake*," Beatrice scoffed. "She cares more about Theore than she does about us."

"That's because Theore is perfect," Bianca said. "He never does anything wrong. He never runs in the house or scuffs the furniture. Also he speaks three different languages."

"Does he?" I asked.

"Of course he does, he's a boy," Bianca said.

"I'm sure Mother would let *Theore* go to Queen's Conservatory if he wanted to. Or even King's, for that matter," Beatrice said.

"It isn't fair," Bianca said. "Nothing we do is ever as good as Theore."

"Why don't you have any other brothers or sisters?" I asked, stepping away from my cousins to walk the length of the gallery.

"Mother tried for a long time," Beatrice said. "She used to take all sorts of tisanes. But I suppose she can't any more."

"Have you ever tried to summon his spirit?" I asked.

"Seven mercies, no."

"I have," Bianca said. "But I couldn't get it to work."

"That figures," Beatrice said. "You know ghosts aren't real. Alma Monti says so."

"Why do you call it the Ghost Gallery, then?" I asked.

"Bifa started calling it that. Sometimes her imagination gets the best of her."

I continued walking the length of the gallery, until I reached the window at the end. Sunlight streamed through the stone mullions and tracery, illuminating patches on the canvases. The child's gaze seemed to follow me from within the heavy frames. Looking more closely at Theore's baby picture, I noticed that his eyes were completely black. Was that what babies' eyes looked like? I wondered. What had first appeared to be a scene of domestic tranquility now seemed vaguely sinister.

"Maybe we should go back down," I said, shivering.

"Not so brave now, are you?" Beatrice said.

"I just thought we could do our hair and dress for dinner," I said. "In case the Countess drops by."

Beatrice smirked. "You don't fool me, Amardine. The paintings are weird, just admit it."

"They *are* weird," I agreed. I edged toward the door, fearing Beatrice would block my way out, but she let me go and followed me downstairs. The paintings had so filled my vision that even now, when I blinked, I could see them, seared onto the blank walls of the stairwell. The young boy, so full of hope and promise, and the beautiful lady with bundle in arms, her face stricken with stillborn joy.

That was what it was, I decided. It must be my aunt's sadness that lent the pictures their eerie aspect.

I thought of the story Hespa had told me, of Tarsha and the witch. *The secret ingredient is a wise heart, tempered by the sorrows of the world*, she had said. And then I thought: *I need to talk to Lady Pendrake*.

ഇൗന്ദ

After dinner, we children were sent to my cousin's room to get ready for bed. Their maid gave us each a thimble glass of syrupy-green liquid. It was too sweet for my taste, so I only pretended to drink it, then poured it discreetly into a hardy potted fern. Beatrice downed hers as she sat before a child-sized dressing table, unpinning her hair and brushing it out.

"Why don't you let your hair down, Amardine?" she said, looking at me through the mirror. "We can compare locks."

I hesitated, sensing there would be no positive outcome in doing so. Beatrice turned on her stool.

"Well?" she said.

Reluctantly, I took my hair pins out and shook my hair loose. It fell over my arms, pooling in the crook of my elbow. Beatrice rose from her stool and went to sit on the divan, between Bianca and me. She lifted a strand of my hair and ran it through her fingers.

"Your hair is longer than mine, but mine is thicker," she observed. "I'd rather have thick hair, wouldn't you? Thin hair just makes you look like a witch."

I glanced down at the lock of hair pressed between her thumb and finger. Maybe she was right, I thought, though I did like my long hair. I liked how Hespa would put a drop of rosemary oil in the palm of her hand and rub it into my scalp, and then comb it through the ends, like a nightly ritual.

Beatrice dropped the ends of my hair and turned to her sister, who was slumped over the arm of the divan, her eyes closed, the tonic sticky on her chin. Slowly, her hands fumbling, she untied the satin ribbon in Bianca's hair. Then she began to smooth the curly locks with her fingers, murmuring to her in an unprovoked display of sisterly affection. I thought she was acting strangely, so I remained silent, watchful, until her head fell against Bianca's, and the two of them lay splayed together on the divan, their legs curled beneath mounds of taffeta glinting in the yellow glow of the aetherlamps.

"Beatrice?" I whispered. She didn't answer. Bianca began to snore loudly. I picked up her empty thimble glass from the dressing table, sniffed it, then set it down, feeling as though I'd escaped some dire plot. But why had my cousins' maid wanted to put us into such a stupor? I stole out of the room before she could return and insist that I take the medicine as well. The hallway outside was unlit, but an aetherlamp at the end illuminated my way well enough. The house was strangely quiet. I heard no laughter coming from the salon, no clink of billiard balls downstairs, no clatter of footsteps on marble.

I considered going to my own room, but the paintings in the third-floor gallery were still troubling me. I turned the other direction, toward the opposite wing of the house, where Lady Pendrake had her private reception rooms. I'd never been in this area of the house before. I listened closely for the sound of voices, but heard nothing.

A door stood open, leading to an unoccupied room. I slipped inside, where the aetherlamps were burning under thick frosted globes, their yellow light melting into the shadows. I flitted past gilt-framed mirrors and shelves of bric-a-brac—all figurines of naked, winged children. Beyond that room was another parlor, and within, its occupants were draped in their chairs like mannequins. The curtains swirled on a sudden draft, and moonlight spilled in, glinting on empty wine glasses. For a moment I lost my nerve, ducking back into the room with the mirrors, prepared to make a dash back to the children's wing. But then a thready voice called out from the darkness.

"*Wendeland.*"

The unfamiliar word hung in the air, giving me pause. It was my aunt who spoke; I recognized the voice despite its timbre, and I crept back to the doorway to find her struggling to draw herself up on a divan.

"Wendeland," she said again. "That was the name of the opera."

Her hat was on the tea table next to a silver carafe and a stack of magazines, and her hair had become slightly mussed, the chignon loose enough to let one black spiral curl fall free. Deep shadows pooled beneath her eyes, and the veins at her temple twitched in the moonlight. At the other end of the room, near the cold fireplace, Lady Chandray and Lady Fairlion dozed, one of them giving a little cough. The scent of incense hung in the air, not the same as the kind my father used to ward off insects, but something woodier, smokier.

I slipped into the room and sat down on the edge of a stuffed velvet chair. Lady Pendrake regarded me from across the tea table.

"I knew it was you," she said. "I saw your shadow. My own girls would never afford me such a silent approach."

"What are you doing in here, Lady—Aunt Ellinora?" I asked. "Are you unwell?"

"Do I look unwell?"

I considered how to answer this, then decided it was best to say nothing.

"Where *are* my girls?" she asked, her eyes suddenly darting.

"They're asleep," I told her.

"That's good," she said. "But what are you doing, child, flitting about in my private reception rooms? Shouldn't you be asleep, as well?"

I swallowed nervously, thinking about the tonic I'd refused earlier. "I...I wanted to talk to you."

"Of course, little one. I'd hoped we might have a chance to speak in private."

"Lady—Aunt Ellinora," I began, glancing round to make sure no one else was listening in. The other women still appeared to be in a stupor. "Are you...are you doing magic?"

She gave a little laugh, which turned into a cough. "Magic? Whatever do you mean?"

"I don't know," I said, realizing it was a stupid question. It wasn't as though she had gone to an academy to learn such things. So even if she did know magic, it wasn't likely the kind that polite people talked about.

I decided to change the subject. "What was it you said before? When I first came into the room?"

"Oh, yes. The opera. I was thinking of your mother, you know. She always had that quiet way about her, too. When she wasn't onstage, that is." Lady Pendrake reached out across the tea table, laying a cold hand on my cheek. "You remind me of her in many ways."

"In what ways?" I asked, leaning forward.

"I can see her in your face sometimes, in your expressions. When you think no one is paying attention to you, and your mind goes distant. She'd get that look about her, too. As though she were listening to some faraway music that no one else could hear. As though her own world was more interesting than the one the rest of us had to live in."

I sat back, and her hand fluttered to her lap.

"Oh, well," she said, "I suppose you can't help that."

"Will you tell me more about her? And the opera?"

"That was the first time I ever saw her. It wasn't a very good production, as I recall. The costumes were barely second-rate. I thought your mother could do better for herself, honestly."

"What was it about?"

"How should I know? Ask your father—he was glued to the playbook the entire time. I would visit him at university and practically have to *drag* him to the opera. I would virtually *throw* my pretty, unwed friends into his path, but to no avail; nary a match would be made." She shook her head in mock exasperation. "No, he told me he wanted to 'go have a look at the architecture of the set,' or some such nonsense, and that was that. The next thing I knew, she had ensnared him."

I imagined my mother standing in the prow of a skiff, wearing a long white dress. The water of a lagoon lay quiet all around her. With a graceful arc, she cast her net, and then the peace was broken as my father burst coughing and flailing from the water, as she dragged him into the boat.

"I don't think she would do that," I said, after weighing the probability of this scenario.

"You don't know what that woman was capable of," Lady Pendrake replied, picking up one of her magazines off the table. "Oh, I oughtn't say anything to you. She was your mother, after all."

"So that was how they met?" I persisted.

"I didn't even know until months later. Suddenly there is this opera singer sitting at our dinner table. And she has opinions! So many opinions. I thought poor Percy was going to choke at one point. It was his own fault, really. The man just kept going on, explaining to this curious creature of the stage the difference between various operatic styles. I had to whisper to him three times who she was. He's always been a bit deaf on his left side, you know."

"Did they dine with you often?" I asked.

She pursed her lips and flipped open her magazine —*Demimondaine*, I read, scrawled in an arch across the cover. Beneath the text, captured within an elaborate frame, a beautiful woman in a scandalously thin white gown seemed to float in a field of poppies. "Oh, all the time," she said. "I'm not saying I didn't *like* your mother. Once you got used to her presence, she could be quite a charming thing. But she was one of those women who needed everyone to love her. She always had to be special, if you know what I mean—like having a signature lipstick that she only wore for her performances. And sitting for portraits, of course. Such a contrivance. At least she gave that up when she married your father. A proper lady doesn't wear rouge on her lips, of course. But you could tell she resented it, as though her previous life was so much the superior. Well, in my mind, she would always be an actress, among other things."

"What other things?"

Lady Pendrake gave me a wistful smile as she reached for me again, smoothing my hair back from my forehead. "I only meant that she was a singer, as well. You do look very much like her. But you're a good girl, aren't you?"

I thought of my outburst against Alma Monti, and swallowed past the lump that had risen up in my throat. "I think so, La—Aunt Ellinora. I want to be."

"Of course you are. You're so quiet one hardly knows you're in the house. Perhaps I ought to put bells on your wrists, just so that I hear you coming."

"If you think you must," I said.

She laughed, her eyes curving into slits. "If only my own girls would be so agreeable. I hardly know what is to be done with them. I wonder though—" she paused, reaching out to give my hand a sudden, hard squeeze—"I wonder if you don't have a bit of the actress in you, as well."

I looked down at the hand gripping mine. I could feel her pulse racing in her fingertips. Something was wrong, but I didn't know exactly what. I reminded myself that she was a grieving mother, a devoted aunt, and I thought about all the questions I'd planned to ask her about the paintings upstairs. But my mouth had gone dry, and I found I couldn't speak.

"If it please you," I said, finally, my voice trembling, "I'd like to go back to my room."

She sat back, her face receding into the shadows. Her eyes met mine, and she smiled, and shook her head.

"Of course, child," she said. "I thought you would have

been asleep by now, anyway."

"I like to stay up sometimes," I said.

"We'll have to cure you of that. I was thinking of taking you girls into town tomorrow, if the weather is good. You'll be too exhausted after a day in town to lie awake and moon at the moon, or whatever it is you do. I thought you might pick out some new frocks. Would you like that, little one?"

I couldn't deny the little thrill of longing I had felt when I had passed the shops with their elegant window displays. Perhaps it would be enough just to touch the fabrics, to run my fingers over silky folds as soft as rose petals. But then I imagined myself wearing the gowns, looking as smart as Beatrice and Bianca as we all traipsed across the bridge in Rivene. No one would look at us and doubt that I belonged to an important family.

And yet, I felt again the familiar twist in the pit of my stomach, the sense of wrongness I couldn't explain.

"Thank you, Aunt Ellinora, but I like my old frocks. I don't want any new ones."

"Of course you do. I know your father doesn't care about fashion, and he's trained you to accept whatever you're given to wear. But I know that in your heart of hearts, you would be happier with a nice new frock."

She was so kind, I thought, feeling guilty for any misgivings I might have had. It was as though she could look right into the depths of my soul, and pluck out my secret desires. How could she know that I longed for pretty things, when I hardly even allowed myself to wish for them?

"Thank you," I said again, not wanting to seem ungrateful. "I'd like that very much."

She smiled, and I detected a trace of sadness in her manner that made my heart unfurl. "Of course, darling," she said. "You deserve only the very best."

❧❦

The next day at breakfast, Lady Pendrake and her companions discussed the possibility of going into town. It appeared that rain was on its way, Lady Fairlion observed, and she, for one, was not of a mind to ruin her coiffure. The others agreed that it would be best to wait until the following day.

"Are we going into town, too?" Beatrice asked.

"Of course, Honey Bee," Lady Pendrake said. "Your cousin is in need of a new frock, and I thought you might help her pick it out."

"Why does *she* get a new frock? I haven't had one in over a month."

"Because she's a very good girl," Lady Pendrake replied, looking at me over the rim of her teacup. "Aren't you, Miss Amardine?"

I looked down at my plate, feeling the heat of Beatrice's glower. I knew my aunt meant to be kind to me, but I wished she wouldn't say such things in front of my cousins.

"Does that mean we have to have lessons today?" Beatrice asked.

"Actually, I thought you girls could help me with something

else instead," Lady Pendrake said. "It's for the Ladies' Betterment Society."

"Bettering ourselves, bettering our future," Bianca chirped.

"That's right, Little B!" Lady Pendrake beamed at her.

Beatrice turned away from her sister, rolling her eyes. "Bianca doesn't care one whit about improving herself," she said, as a burst of rain hit the windows of the breakfast room, and a roll of thunder sounded in the distance.

After the dishes were cleared, Lady Pendrake led my cousins and me to the library at the end of the hall. Two entire walls were lined with bookshelves; the other two walls were covered with a dark green paper decorated with claustrophobic vines, not unlike the one my father had just torn down at home. A large table dominated the center of the room, cluttered with papers and ink pots and wooden stamps. Lady Pendrake led us over to the table, and I examined the items strewn over its surface. There were stacks of pamphlets which said things like, "*Please Be Advised*...Ladies Don't Slam Doors," and "*Always Remember*...Gentlemen Use Spittoons."

"What are these for, Aunt Ellinora?" I asked.

"We're going to take them to the chapel. And each week after the service, we'll hand them out to the less fortunate."

I looked down at the papers again, and must have appeared confused, because my aunt clarified, "It's to improve their moral character, darling."

She then went on to explain that we were to stamp every single one of the pamphlets with the official seal of the Ladies'

Betterment Society. One of the maids brought us fresh pinafores and gloves—not my own, I noted—and my cousins and I gathered round the table to work. It turned out to be a solitary labor. Beatrice abandoned the enterprise first, complaining that she felt faint from all the gummy smells. And Bianca, who had refused to wear a pinafore, made the bold move of spilling ink all over herself, just as I had once threatened to do. She excused herself to change her dress, and never returned.

I didn't mind the solitude. I listened to the voices of the men in the billiard room down the hall, and the muffled laughter of the ladies upstairs, and was glad I was under no obligation to respond. Perhaps this day wouldn't be so bad, after all. If I finished stamping the pamphlets before Lady Pendrake returned, there were plenty of books I could read to pass the time. I became so engrossed, I lost track of the time, and was startled when the door opened and Beatrice entered the library, wrinkling her nose.

"You're *still* working in here?" she said, walking up to the far side of the table.

"I'm not finished yet," I said, gesturing to the small pile of pamphlets I hadn't yet stamped.

"Well, aren't you Little Miss Perfect."

"I'm not," I said. "I just didn't have anything else to do."

Beatrice picked up one of the pamphlets and flipped through it. "*I just didn't have anything else to do,*" she repeated, her voice snide and mocking.

"It's the truth," I said.

"You want to join the Ladies' Betterment Society?" she demanded, fumbling to unpin her brooch with trembling hands. "Fine! I'm sure you'll be *much* better at it than me! Here! Have my pin if it means so much to you!"

She tore the brooch from the front of her dress and threw it hard across the table. It bounced once, spinning to a stop in front of me.

"Beatrice, it isn't like that. I don't want your pin," I said.

"Of course you'd say that. You act like you're so above everything, and everyone pretends you're so good and perfect! Well, I know what you really are!" She seized a handful of the papers and tore them in half, throwing the pieces down on the table. I could only look on in horror as she continued her rampage, destroying every single pamphlet I had so carefully stamped.

When she was done, she threw out her arms and swept the pieces onto the floor. Then she began jumping up and down, her feet snapping out to kick at them, but for all her effort, they only fluttered lazily out of reach.

"Look what you've done!" she shouted, pointing at me. "Let's see who gets a new frock now! Little Miss Perfect, indeed!"

"But you did this," I said.

"I did not. *You* did it. I saw you with my very own eyes."

"But Beatrice, that's just not true," I protested.

"Isn't it?" She crossed her arms over her chest and glared at me.

"You know it isn't," I said, as her eyes became a void of darkness. I could see that all reason had forsaken her.

"I know what you said to Alma Monti the other day. Are you going to say that didn't happen, too?"

"I could say it didn't happen," I said.

"But you wouldn't," Beatrice replied. "You'd probably faint if you told a lie like that." She went to the door, put her head out into the hall, and hollered, "Mother! Come quick! It's an emergency!"

I bit my lip and stared down at the mess she had made. Which "truth" would Lady Pendrake believe? A maid arrived first, but when Beatrice yelled at her to get out, she scurried dutifully away.

"Is she going to tell Lady Pendrake?" I asked, watching the woman duck into one of the reception rooms and softly close the door.

"She's probably hiding in a dark corner, pretending she didn't see a thing," Beatrice said. Then she poked her head out into the hallway again. "MOTHER!"

This time Lady Pendrake did appear. She took in the destruction, her face stricken, eyes wide and raving, like those of a mad, devouring god.

Beatrice pointed at me. "Look what she did!"

Lady Pendrake seemed to shake herself back to her senses. "Amardine! Did you do this?"

"No," I said.

"Liar!" Beatrice spat.

"Beatrice!" her mother exclaimed, her face further contorting with horror. "What's come over you? Why would you girls do this?"

"I didn't!" Beatrice wailed. She thrust her finger at me. "She did it. I don't know why. She's a wicked girl."

It was a convincing performance. If I hadn't known better, I might have believed it myself. When Lady Pendrake turned to me again, I thought I saw a flicker of doubt in her eyes.

"Is this true, Amardine?" she asked.

I shook my head.

"Just ask her what she said to Alma Monti!" Beatrice shouted.

"Don't you take that tone with me," Lady Pendrake replied, to my momentary relief. "Lower your voice, and don't try to change the subject."

"Why won't you listen to me? Why won't you be*lieeeve* me?"

"Because you're whining. You know very well how I feel about whining. And I know *you*. Just admit what you did, Beatrice Anne."

That was when the tears began to flow. For a moment I thought Lady Pendrake had cast a spell on Beatrice, that perhaps the invocation of her middle name had released them in a great blubbering torrent. Beatrice balled up her fists, sobbing, "I didn't do it. I didn't do it!"

Lady Pendrake grabbed her wrists, wrenching her hands away from her face. "Don't cry. You know your face gets ugly when you cry."

"Please, stop," I whispered. I could feel Beatrice's misery and frustration like waves of black energy, pulsing from her shuddering form. *Don't start feeling sorry for her*, I told myself. She had created the situation, tried to get me in trouble. And yet, it was almost too much to bear.

Beatrice hung her head, unable to help herself, her cries becoming softer, more piteous. Lady Pendrake let go of her wrists and took a step back, appraising her coolly. My stomach turned with a familiar sense of dread.

"You are seeing the truth of your cousin, Amardine," Lady Pendrake said, her eyes still fixed on Beatrice. "You see how wretched she is. How petty and vicious, how out of control. I ought to leave her home tomorrow while the rest of us go into town."

"Good!" Beatrice yelled back, raising her chin with a flash of her old defiance. She smeared her face with the heel of her hand. "I don't want to go with you anyway! I hate all of you!"

"Are you quite done yet?"

I cringed, as though the rebuke had been aimed at me.

Beatrice glared at her. "Yes, *Mother*."

"I've changed my mind. You *will* go, Beatrice," Lady Pendrake said, her eyes gleaming with triumph. "I want you to help Amardine pick out her new wardrobe."

CHAPTER THIRTEEN

I DREADED THE CARRIAGE RIDE. I sat wedged between Lady Chandray and Lady Fairlion, drenched in their perfume and the heat of their bodies. From the seat facing me, through her veil, Beatrice glowered at me. Her sister was wearing a bright, flouncy pink frock with a cascade of rosettes sewn onto the skirt, but Beatrice was clad in a plain brown smocked shift-dress which I could only assume was intended as a punishment.

We all wore veils to match our ensembles, covering our faces and arms, doused with lemon balm to ward away unwanted insects. The edge of mine was trapped beneath Lady Fairlion's leg, making it impossible to move.

Lady Fairlion glanced out the window as we made our way to the outskirts of town. "So many bright colors, even this late in the season," she remarked. "I wonder that the shops will have anything for my complexion."

"Perhaps you just need more sun," Lady Chandray suggested, but her cousin shook her head.

"It doesn't improve with more sun. You might look like a Kushrani princess by the end of summer, but I just get red and blotchy if I'm not careful."

"It's the same with me," Lady Pendrake sighed. "I have to have a parasol at all times."

The carriage came to a stop on a tree-lined lane near the river, and we all spilled out onto the street, untangling ourselves and rearranging our veils. The sun was already hot overhead, and the scent of flowers and perfume hung in the air, shifting on the slight breezes and wafting from the lazy beat of painted wooden fans. We descended a set of stone steps to a row of shops with plate glass windows. Standing before them, I could imagine I was in a great city, with a view to the ocean, and people walking the streets from all over the world, speaking in tongues I'd never heard of.

"Stop gawking," Beatrice said, poking me in the back.

Since the quarrel in the library the previous day, Beatrice had barely spoken to me. For my part, I had tried to remain invisible to everyone. As the others went ahead and turned off the sidewalk to enter a dressmaker's shop, I thought about disappearing entirely. We'd passed a public coach house on the way, and I'd made a mental note of its location near a cross street. I turned in that direction, my mind nearly made up to go through with it. But then I heard Lady Pendrake calling to me from the doorway of the shop. My stomach clenched as I followed her inside.

Between the rows of bright-colored silk and lace, I imagined I'd entered a labyrinth. I listened from behind a curtain as Lady Pendrake had her measurements taken for a new gown. She argued with the woman, insisting that her measuring tape had been "stamped out by a poppy fiend." She lamented the lax standards of labor in the workshops and manufactories, and the shopkeeper agreed that the only quality goods to be found were in establishments such as hers, run for generations by families serious about their craft.

When Lady Pendrake was at last satisfied with the design of her new gown, she took us children across the street to another shop while the other ladies went next door to look at the millinery. I had noticed the shop on the way to Pendrake Hall, for it displayed children's clothes in the windows, and sold dresses already cut. One of the display items in particular had caught my eye—a lavender silk dress with a pleated bodice and overlay of matching lace, embellished all over the skirt with silk violets and seed pearls. As we passed by the window on foot, the folds of the lace overlay caught the light, making it shimmer with an iridescent rainbow effect. I longed to touch the fabric and examine the details of its construction.

The inside of the shop was open and spacious compared to the previous one. There was even a little table set up in one corner, with child-sized dolls presiding over a porcelain tea set. Toward the back of the shop, a mannequin stood on a low pedestal, wearing a dress identical to the one in the window. I went to it immediately, trying to resist the urge to touch the fabric, to run my fingers over the lace and silk flowers. But when I realized it was the finest dress in the shop, I stepped back, ashamed by my own covetousness.

Then Beatrice was beside me, taking a handful of the lace overskirt in her hands and rubbing it together. It caught the light, gleaming like dragonfly wings.

"Do you like this one?" she asked me.

"It's the most beautiful thing I've ever seen," I said.

"I'm going to ask Mother to buy it for me," Beatrice said. "I need a new dress for the Ladies' Betterment Society Junior Ball. This one will do well enough, I suppose."

"I'm sure it will look lovely on you," I said. Of course Beatrice would have the gown. I berated myself for my brief pang of disappointment, pushing it out of my mind. Still mesmerized by the lace, I didn't even notice Lady Pendrake step over and put her hand on Beatrice's arm.

"Did you find something for your cousin?" she asked, sweetly.

"Not in this shop," Beatrice said. "But I saw a ragpicker a few streets back. Perhaps we can find something in his cart."

Lady Pendrake shook her head. "If you can't be nice to your cousin, I'm taking your whole wardrobe and giving it to that poor man. Perhaps you'll learn some humility once you see street urchins tearing round the town in your best clothes."

"You wouldn't dare," Beatrice said, screwing up her face. I thought she was about to cry, but at that moment, the shop girl approached, cutting off the exchange.

"The fabric is very fine, isn't it?"

Lady Pendrake startled, turning from Beatrice. "It is indeed."

"It was crafted by master silk weavers in Llimburie," the woman went on. "The lace is from Crimor and dyed with a special technique that makes it shimmer in the light. Truth be told, I thought of your younger daughter when I saw the color. I have it in several sizes, though, and I'm sure your eldest would look lovely in it as well."

"Is it mulberry or spider silk?" Lady Pendrake asked.

"The fibers come from a mulberry silk farm in the Frells. The Hellebore family produces it, have you heard of them?"

"Oh, yes," Lady Pendrake replied. "I have a family con-nection, actually. On my mother's side."

At that moment, the door of the shop opened, ringing the bell, and a trio of women in bright-colored attire entered, laughing among themselves. When they saw Lady Pendrake, they nodded and smiled at her, making little curtsies in her direction. Lady Pendrake greeted them in turn, calling them over to give their opinion of the lavender dress. They made the appropriate noises of wonder and appreciation, and then one of them turned to me.

"And who is this lovely child accompanying you today, Lady Pendrake?" one of them asked. "She has the look of a whisp about her."

"This is my niece, Amardine," my aunt said, then in-troduced the women, all members of the Ladies' Betterment Society.

"*I* know her," one of the women said. "Forgive me, but isn't she the daughter of the great Sephonie Mira? I saw her perform years ago—such a bright young thing." She turned to me. "I'm so sorry for what happened to your mother."

"Yes, it was a tragic loss for us all," Lady Pendrake said. "But sometimes, we make our own fates, if you know what I mean."

I tried not to react to the mention of my mother, so casually thrown out in front of me. But I felt like squirming away as the woman bent to examine me more closely.

"Yes, I can see the resemblance. Do you like to sing, child?"

"My papa doesn't like it when I sing," I told her.

"No? Well, perhaps it brings back painful memories for him."

"He did love his wife so very much," Lady Pendrake said. "In fact, I never saw anyone more infatuated with a woman. Very by-the-book, though, with all the flowers and exotic scents he lavished on her. I suppose she must have been appreciative, though, after the life she'd had."

"Yes, I did hear something about that," the woman said, frowning.

"But that's all in the past now," Lady Pendrake said. "No one can fault an innocent child for the mischief of her forebears."

"Oh, no, of course not!" the other ladies murmured, practically in unison.

"All children are born perfect," said another.

"It's all about the way they're brought up. That's what I always say. And with you looking out for her, I'm sure your niece will bloom into a most proper young lady."

"You're too kind," Lady Pendrake said, beaming. "I do what I can. Today we're looking at some new dresses for her. In fact—" she gestured to the shop girl, who had gone to fix a display nearby—"I think I'll take this one."

The woman hurried over to us. "For Bianca? Yes, I think that would do nicely."

"No, for my niece," Lady Pendrake said, turning to me. "You like it very much, don't you?"

I stood frozen, trying to work out the right answer, that which would make everyone happy.

"It's beautiful," I said, sincerely. "But I think—I think it would look better on Beatrice. The color suits her."

Lady Pendrake threw her head back and laughed. "Isn't she just the most charming creature? I swear, sometimes I forget her age. That's it—I'll take this one, and another as well, in the same size. Amardine shall have two new frocks."

The women continued their conversation, which turned to the subject of choosing their next charity fundraiser, as I was ushered behind the curtain to try on the dress. Off came my simple linen frock of green and white stripes, which Hespa had packed with such care. I stepped into the new dress, feeling its silky allure as it passed over my bare arms and settled over my shift and petticoat. I stared at my reflection as the dressmaker tied the bow at the waist, wanting to give myself over to wonderment. The garment truly was beautiful, perhaps too beautiful for someone like me.

As Lady Pendrake exclaimed about how lovely the dress looked with my coloring and blonde hair, I heard a sniffle from outside the curtain. When my aunt pulled the curtain back, I found Beatrice standing a few steps away, wiping her nose on the back of her hand. She looked utterly alone, defeated.

"What do you think, Honey Bee?" Lady Pendrake asked, handing her a handkerchief. Then she hissed, loud enough for me to hear, "Don't make a mess of yourself, dear."

Beatrice dabbed her nose with the handkerchief and turned away. As before, her humiliation was palpable, radiating from her hunched body, turning my stomach every time a wave of desolation rippled over me. Could no one else feel it? I wanted to go to her, to say I was sorry, but I knew instinctively that she wouldn't welcome any sympathy from me.

"I'm sure I can find something suitable for Beatrice," the shop girl said, looking uncomfortable.

"She just has a sun allergy, poor thing," Lady Pendrake said. "It makes her eyes water and her nose swell up. The doctors are certain she'll outgrow it."

"That's very good to hear," the woman replied. "The fit looks perfect for your niece as it is. Would you like me to wrap and box the dress for her?"

"That won't be necessary. She looks so lovely, it seems a shame to put her back into that old, frumpy dress."

We left then, emerging from the relative dimness of the

shop into the brilliant sunshine. The lace overlay on my new skirt sparkled and shimmered, making new rainbows with every step I took. *Perhaps you'll learn some humility once you see street urchins tearing round the town in your best clothes*, Lady Pendrake had said. Was that what I was to her?

I knew I ought to be thrilled with the dress. It was the sort of dress that was made to twirl in, to admire as the colors gave way from one hue to the next. But I felt no joy in the purchase, only an unsettling twinge of guilt, and that familiar clawing at my gut that was threatening to give way to panic.

༄༅

Lady Pendrake insisted that I wear my new dress for the remainder of the day. I would have preferred to put it away in a box, only to be removed once I was safely home at Guildenflore, but this was not the lady's will. I felt ridiculous and unnatural, sitting for afternoon lessons in such attire. Surely Beatrice was critiquing me out of the corner of her eye, finding the fault in my presentation, thinking her mother must be mad to put me in such a dress.

My only comfort was in learning that Alma Monti had other matters to attend to, and wouldn't be returning to Pendrake Hall until the following day.

But Beatrice did nothing to stoke my fears. She was perfectly well-behaved during our lessons, keeping her eyes on her work and listening attentively to Mistress Kettering. She smiled, when appropriate, and was quick to volunteer answers when prompted. They weren't always the right answers, but she accepted her teacher's corrections with unusual grace and poise.

I began to wonder if I'd misjudged Beatrice. I understood her anger at her mother's treatment. I understood her unhappiness, and that I was the cause of it. And yet now she seemed calm, even civil.

At dinner that night, she was quiet, as though in deep thought—a prospect which began to alarm me. She spoke softly to the servants who brought in the trays, then picked up her silverware. I waited for her to begin eating—my cue to do the same—but she set the knife and fork down again and folded her hands in her lap.

"Amardine, there's something I want to say to you," she said.

I set down my silverware as well, and waited for her to go on.

"I'm sorry about how I've been acting. It was wrong of me to try to blame you for the papers. I don't know what I was thinking."

"Oh, that's all right," I said, letting out my breath. "Nothing came of it, in any case. Except the poor people of Rivene won't know they oughtn't slam doors."

Beatrice laughed. "It's stupid, isn't it? As if poor people care about that sort of thing."

Bianca giggled.

Beatrice turned to her sister and said, "You should have seen Mother's face. She was *so* mad." She picked up her silverware again and this time began to eat.

"Are all mothers like her?" I asked, emboldened by this show of camaraderie.

"What do you mean?" Beatrice asked.

"I mean, she's not very fair to you. I don't even think she likes me very much. She just pretends to make you upset. Why do you suppose she does that?"

"She hates me, that's why."

"But that's awful," I said.

Beatrice shrugged. "It gives her something to do. Anyway, I just wanted to say that you look very pretty in your new dress. And I never should have been jealous that you had something new. I know how you never get anything like this at home."

"Thank you, Beatrice," I said.

"Though I do think you could wear it better," she went on.

"Oh?"

"After dinner, we should do something about your look. You could be a real fashion plate, if you actually tried."

"All right," I said. "If you truly think so."

The meal lasted a long time—the servants kept returning with more tiny dishes we were obliged to sample. At home I could have asked to be excused from the table, but here, we had to sit for a full two hours ("the better to prepare ourselves for our first formal luncheon," Beatrice explained, when I asked.)

Afterward she led Bianca and me upstairs. I thought she would take us to her room, but she turned at the top of the stairs and headed toward the other wing.

"Come on, we'll go to Mother's room. She'll be up late in the salon with the other ladies. And she has the best dressing table."

"Won't she mind if we go in her room?" I asked.

"Not if she doesn't know," Beatrice said. "So we need to be very quiet. No barking, baaing, or whinnying allowed."

"I wasn't planning on it," I said.

"That was mostly for Bianca. You want to be part of this, don't you, Bifa?"

"I'll be quiet as a mouse. Squeak, squeak, squeak, squeak, squeak."

Beatrice rolled her eyes. "Just don't squeak too loud."

I followed them down the hall, to Lady Pendrake's private room. Beatrice pushed open the door, then brushed her hand against the wall, flipping a lever. Light spilled from the aetherlamps as the brass rosettes enclosing them unfurled their petals, revealing a spacious chamber furnished with thick rugs and a canopy bed, a tri-fold screen, and a dressing table and mirror that occupied most of one wall. Its surface was arranged with dozens of glass vials and small jars. Beatrice approached it slowly, reverently, as though it were an altar. Bianca burst into the room headlong and flailing, jumping onto the bed.

"Bifa, *please*. You're going to get us in trouble."

"But it's a new bed," Bianca protested, flinging her arms up and down, rolling round on the coverlet. She began making *oinking* noises, snorting into the pillow.

"*Bifa!*"

"I'm pretending to be a pig in slop."

"I don't understand you. I'll never understand you." Beatrice turned to me, dismissing her sister's antics. "You see all of this furniture? It's all new. Mother has it replaced every couple of years."

"Why does she do that?" I asked.

Beatrice shrugged. "She gets ideas from magazines. There's always new styles and ideas. Why stick with the same old thing? Speaking of which, how long has your hair been like that?"

"Like what?" I reached for the back of my neck, grabbing the braid that hung down my back, and pulled it over my shoulder.

"Like that," Beatrice said. "Long and boring."

"You make her hair sound like it's a chapter book," Bianca said, giggling. She flopped over onto her stomach, resting her hands under her chin, the picture of innocence. All trace of her porcine mannerisms had fled.

"I don't know," I said, anxiously. But I didn't want to ruin things now that Beatrice was taking me under her wing.

"Sit down," she said, gesturing to the cushioned stool under the dressing table. I did as she instructed. In the light of the aetherlamps, my face looked pale and slightly yellow. Beatrice untied the ribbon from my hair and shook it loose. Still crimped by its time in the braid, it hung down in unnatural waves, cascading over my shoulders and brushing my arms as they rested in my lap.

She gathered it up in her hands, pulling it away from my face. Then she glanced to the side of my head, frowning.

"What's wrong with your ears?" she asked.

"What do you mean?" I replied, my throat going dry. But I knew what she meant. She wasn't accustomed to seeing them, as they were usually tucked under my hair or a bonnet.

"Why do they fold over like that? They look like dog ears."

"Let's see!" Bianca exclaimed, hopping up from the bed.

"See? See?" Beatrice twisted the tip of my ear between her finger and thumb. I flinched, trying to pull away, but she squeezed hard, causing a sharp pain to radiate from the pinch point.

"Stop it!" I said.

"You really are a freak," she said. "I should have told Mother what you said to Alma Monti. She might think twice about letting you stay here."

"Go ahead and tell her," I said. Maybe Beatrice was right. Maybe her mother would send me home.

"You're *unclean*," she went on. "You're not even human, are you?"

"You knew what I was," I said, through gritted teeth.

"Yes, but—"

"Freak! Freak!" Bianca said, bouncing up and down beside her sister.

Beatrice gave me a look of disgust and let go of my ear. Then she opened a drawer and withdrew a pair of scissors.

"What are you doing?" Bianca asked. "Are you going to cut her?" She was hanging back now, eyeing me warily, as though afraid I might unleash some strange power on her. If only that were the case. Beatrice turned the scissors over in her hand, and for a moment I feared she might do just that. I would fight her, if it came to it. I would scream, as loud as I could. I gathered my breath.

"No. It wouldn't do for her to bleed all over everything. Besides, Amardine ought to be proud of who she is. Don't you think, Amardine?" The scissors glinted in the light of the aetherlamps. "She oughtn't hide beneath so much hair."

Though I'd never thought much about my hair, I realized now that I very much wanted to keep it. I liked the way it flowed round me, like a cape. I liked the way Hespa would brush it out at night, ever so carefully, saving the strands that broke off in a porcelain jar. She was always so patient when she combed out the knots, as though it was something to be treasured. As though *I* was to be treasured.

"I don't want my hair cut," I said, the words catching in my throat. *Don't cry, don't cry, don't cry.*

"Why not? Beatrice asked. "Don't you think I know what I'm doing?"

I stared at her in disbelief.

"It's just, I thought we were finally getting on well," she said, pursing her lips.

"You called me a freak," I said, incredulously.

"I didn't mean it in a bad way," she said. "I just wasn't expecting it, that's all. Don't be a spoil-sport."

"I'm not. It's an awful thing to say, Beatrice."

Beatrice sighed. "I *said* I was sorry. What more do you want?"

"You didn't, though."

"Honestly, Amardine, I don't understand why you're being so difficult all of a sudden."

"She calls me a freak, too," Bianca said, sitting up on the bed.

Hespa's words came back to me then: *She's a child of keen feeling.* Perhaps I was making too much of this, getting upset over a misunderstanding.

"Can I do her hair?" Bianca asked.

"No," Beatrice said. "You can do her face, though."

"What's wrong with my face?" I asked, immediately regretting it.

"It's dull, for one thing," Beatrice said, grabbing a handful of my hair and pulling it back, so that she could examine the canvas she was making of my face. "It's all one color, do you see? You have no color in your cheeks, your lips, or your eyebrows."

Bianca pushed herself off the bed and skipped over to the dressing table. She picked up a jar and opened the lid, and was about the dig her finger into it when Beatrice stopped her.

"Use this," she said, handing her what looked like a small metal spatula. "We don't want Mother to know."

Bianca poked the spatula into the pot, then wiped white paint across my cheeks, first one side, then the other. She tried to rub it into my skin, but stopped before it was fully absorbed, leaving patches and streaks. I leaned forward in the mirror and tried to blend it with my fingertips, thinking all the while that it made me look like a ghost.

"I know what we need," Beatrice said. She pulled open a drawer and withdrew a small black tube of what looked like ebony. She removed the top. Inside was a dried out, waxy red stick. At the sight of it, my stomach began to clench, though I wasn't sure why. Perhaps it was something I had heard my aunt say once, about using paint on one's lips. I couldn't recall exactly. But then, perhaps I was confusing it with what Lady Chandray had said about perfume. There were rules, I knew, about what sort of ladies were allowed to wear certain cosmetics. And I had never seen my aunt, or any lady of rank, with ruby-colored lips.

"Lady Pendrake doesn't wear this," I said, as Beatrice scored the surface with a pin, removing some of the hardened skin that had formed over it.

"How do you know?" she asked.

"It's not...it's not proper," I said. Now I remembered. *A proper lady doesn't wear rouge on her lips, of course.* The tightness in my stomach was quickly turning to nausea. The little tube of pigment was out of place. It didn't belong in Lady Pendrake's dressing table.

"Are you saying my mother isn't a proper lady?" Beatrice asked, rubbing the stick on the inside of her elbow in a small circle, until it looked as though she had risen a welt.

"No, I just—"

She grabbed my arm and pulled me toward her, away from the mirror, then pressed the stick against my mouth. She wiped it one way, then the other, and as she did so, my vision darkened and her figure disappeared from view. I closed my eyes as the smell of castor oil filled my nostrils. The lights from the aetherlamps left little dots on the back of my eyelids, and my blood thrummed in my ears. Amid the ringing in my head, I heard a murmur of voices I didn't recognize.

An elegant hand passed before my lips—it was my hand, attached to my body, and yet it wasn't. It was wearing an emerald and gold ring I'd never seen before.

"Five minutes," someone said from behind me, and then another voice seemed to rise out of my throat, but it was a woman's voice, soft and silky.

"I'll be ready," she said.

The ring disappeared from sight as my vision darkened again, swallowing up the specks of light that danced behind my eyes. I felt a hand gripping my wrist. Beatrice was shaking me.

"What's wrong with you?" she demanded.

"Nothing," I said. My voice sounded breathless, though, and I knew I hadn't deceived her.

"You looked like you were about to swoon."

Bianca, illustrating her sister's point, threw up her hands and toppled to the floor with a thud and a dramatic flourish.

"Bifa! You're going to get us all caught," Beatrice hissed. Turning back to me, she asked, "Is it the color? Is it too much for you?"

I was a wretched sight. My mouth looked like a crimson gash across my face. The paint on my face made my new dress look even more ridiculous, a mockery of class and propriety. I was no daughter of a lady. I was the daughter of a stage performer, a woman who painted her lips like a scarlet flame. I was certain of that now, certain I had glimpsed my mother somehow, just for a moment, as the color flared across my own mouth.

I was the daughter of a stage performer, a woman who wore whatever she wished. Whose perfume and lipstick could ensnare memories of the senses. Whose presence transcended death itself. Despite my forsaken appearance, I felt a stubborn flush of pride.

"Where did this come from?" I asked, picking up the tube of lipstick.

"I don't know," Beatrice said. "Now, for your hair—"

"You're not cutting my hair," I said.

Beatrice frowned. "We agreed, Amardine."

"I didn't agree to anything. Sorry if I'm being *difficult*."

From the floor, Bianca chanted, "Cut her hair! Cut her hair! Cut her hair!"

"Shhh!" Beatrice hissed. "We *will* cut her hair, but we need to be quiet about it."

Again, I thought about screaming for help. I wondered for a moment if it would be better or worse if Lady Pendrake caught us in her private room. One glance in the mirror, however, settled the question. I was still wearing the lipstick, my mother's lipstick. I couldn't imagine any scenario in which Lady Pendrake would take kindly to that.

I turned from my cousins and tried to flee for the door,

but Beatrice seized me by the hair and wrenched me round to face her. I strained my neck, attempting to pull away, my hair pulled over my head. The scissors glinted on the dressing table, just behind Beatrice.

She dragged me forward, but before she could reach for the scissors, I snatched them up. I shoved them in her face as rage flooded through my veins. *A child of keen feeling, indeed.* I felt like poking her eye out. She would *not* cut my hair. I refused to give her the satisfaction, not after she called me a freak and then pretended I was the one with the problem.

"Give me the scissors!" she said, reaching for them. Bianca had latched onto my ankles, threatening to trip me. I kicked out, hitting her in the chest, and she fell back.

"*Oof!*" she cried out, scrambling to her feet. Then she tried to grab the scissors from me. In the struggle, I was turned round once again, my head wrenched back and forth, as Beatrice kept hold of a large chunk of my hair. She was pulling it at the roots, and I knew then what I had to do.

I reached up with the scissors, and before either of them could react, I cut my own hair, severing Beatrice's hold on me. She was left holding a long tail in her fist, her mouth open with shock.

I didn't waste a moment to mourn my hair. It would grow back, and the look on her face as I slipped beyond her control had been worth it. I fled the room, running down the corridor, past the top of the staircase. Where to go, though? Could I lock myself in my own bedchamber?

I made a break for it, my cousins in close pursuit. I got through the door and tried to shut it behind me, but Beatrice had caught up and wedged herself in the frame. She was stronger than me, and thwarted my attempt to close the door on her.

"I can't believe you did that!" she said. She was still holding my hair in her fist as she pushed her way into the room. "There's nothing I can do to fix it now, you know that, don't you? We're going to have to cut it all off."

"I told you!" Bianca said, as she bounced into the room behind her sister. "I told you to cut it all off."

I stepped backward, toward the window. The shutters were open, letting in a breeze, but there was a screen as well. I remembered a ledge outside my window, about a foot wide, with flower boxes, and a scaffolding tower nearby. If only I could get out, and away from them.

But where would I go? Hide somewhere on the grounds? I would have to face them eventually.

Beatrice followed my gaze to the window, and a slow smile came over her face. "If you don't want our help fixing your hair, I don't see any reason for you to be here. It's rude to refuse your host, you know."

"Let's push her out the window!" Bianca said.

Beatrice seemed to consider this for a moment. Then she said, "We'd get into a lot of trouble if we pushed her. But if she fell all on her own, that would be her fault, wouldn't it?" She marched over to the window and lifted a latch on each side of the frame, removing the bottom third of the screen. Moonlight shone through the gaping hole, its pale violet light spilling across the floorboards and soaking the coverlet.

"There, Amardine. It's your choice. Either get your hair cut, or go out the window."

I didn't hesitate, climbing over the sill and stepping out onto the ledge, into a bed of geraniums. Behind me, the shutters began to close. Beatrice stood in the window, her face obscured by the screen, turning a crank. Bianca crouched beside her, pressing the lower part of the screen back into place. As I watched, one of the shutters thumped me on the shoulder.

"You'd better get out of the way!" Beatrice shouted through the screen.

"She'll crush you like a bug!" Bianca warned.

I stepped round the closing shutter, steadying myself to keep from pitching over the edge. The wooden slats in the shutter flipped open, Beatrice's face pressed against them.

"Beatrice!" I said. "Let me in!"

"Have a nice night, Amardine," she said.

"What if I fall?"

"Then I hope you break both your legs."

The slats snapped closed. I looked down at the ground below. Because of the way it sloped, the distance was greater than the distance from the first floor. I judged the drop to be at least twenty feet.

But it had been my idea to escape through the window. Let

Beatrice and Bianca think they were tormenting me by leaving me out here. At least they were leaving me alone. I edged my way along the ledge, toward the scaffolding tower. The bars didn't quite line up with the ledge, and it was built for people with longer legs than I possessed. As I reached out for it, I realized I still held my mother's lipstick, clenched in my fist.

I slipped it into my pocket and grabbed hold of the scaffolding. I managed to slide my way down to the rung below me, and then the next, working my way slowly to the ground.

I landed in the grass and looked up at the window. The slats were still closed in the shutter. *Cowards*, I thought. My cousins might want me to fall, but they didn't have the nerve to actually watch.

I put my head down and slipped round the side of the house, staying close to the foundation. The ground sloped steeply down at the back of one wing, and I tripped in the darkness, stumbling and pitching onto the path at the bottom. I found myself standing in front of the kitchen door. I was in the herb garden. The air was pungent with the scent of mint and rosemary and verbena. The soil smelled freshly turned, and the rain from the previous day still clung in its pores and pooled in the leaves that lay scattered across the path. I snapped off a sprig of mint, rubbing the leaf between my fingers, and held it as a talisman—of what, I wasn't sure—and then I continued along the wall, to the back veranda that fanned out at the corner where the wing joined the rest of the house. There, the tall hedges of the labyrinth loomed before me like silent guardians, their shadows cutting across the lawn in the moonlight. I could rest there for a little while, hidden from sight. But then what?

A warm breeze lifted the long ends of my hair, flicking the back of my neck where more hair ought to have been. No, I thought, I had to start moving. I didn't belong at Pendrake Hall. Out here, amid the constant murmur of crickets and bullfrogs, I was safe.

It was time to make my escape.

CHAPTER FOURTEEN

THE LAWN SPREAD ALL ROUND THE house, with few trees or gardens to offer shelter as I made my way toward the treeline. I walked where it was darkest, in the blanket of shadow cast by the house. I'd hardly gone a quarter of the distance across the lawn when I stumbled on some object in the grass, arousing an angry squawk and a flurry of feathers.

A vakra staggered to its feet, head whipping from side to side as I leaped backward, its short wings beating furiously. Tail feathers unfurled like a fan, each one tipped with a depiction of the evil eye. The thing squawked again, snapping its beak toward me. I leaped backward, bumping into another dark lump in the grass. The second vakra didn't get up right away, but it screamed and lashed out at the darkness like a coiled snake. Others began to stir and make soft bleats of alarm, as the first ran back and forth in front of me, blocking my escape to the trees, its screeches seeming to echo over the whole countryside.

By now, most of the other birds had clambered to their feet and stood huddled together, their heads dipped low as if in conspiracy, their talon feet digging in the lawn, sending up clods of dirt. But the defender of the flock was still pacing and squawking and lashing out at me with its whip-like neck. I dodged this way and that, trying to get round the thing. Somewhere in the distance, dogs had begun to bark, and a light appeared in a window of Pendrake Hall.

I dashed toward the treeline, nearly colliding with the vakra. Ducking low, I felt its wings buffet me. Reflexively, I held up the sprig of mint I'd plucked from the herb garden, and it snorted through its beak, head snapping backward. For a moment it held my gaze, the red-slitted orbs regarding me with curiosity or contempt. Its beak gaped wide, then plunged down, straight at my face. I squeezed my eyes shut, thinking for certain my head was about to be popped off. The end of the beak bumped against my hand and severed the sprig of mint, leaving me holding just the stalk. I stifled a scream and dashed under its wing, finally making it past, trying not to trip on my skirts as the ground sloped down into the woods. Passing the treeline, I stumbled over a root and pitched forward, landing hard on my stomach, my hands disappearing into mist. The vakra hadn't entered the woods, but it was still pacing, huffing nervously and digging up the dirt. More troubling was the light of a lantern that had flared up some distance away, across the lawn. At the sight of it, the vakra turned and ran back toward the flock.

I got to my feet and began to run. The undergrowth was dense, catching on my skirt. I winced to hear the fine beautiful lace tear, but there was nothing I could do about it now.

Men's voices rang out upwind, toward the house. I hurried along a narrow path that animals had made as they traversed the woods. *What do they know of this place?* I wondered. *In which direction is Rivene?* Surely some of the forest creatures must know of the nearest center of civilization. But if there were any nearby who could be questioned, they hid well out of sight.

Everything appeared different now, in the darkness. I crossed a gap in the trees, an open field with a cottage at the far side. I'd come out into the field near a burn pit. The low, slumping silhouette of partially-collapsed logs looked vaguely like a crouching beast. There was an acrid scent in the air, strongest near the pit. Overhead, the waning moon seemed to stare down at me, unblinking in the cloudless sky.

I remembered suddenly that I wasn't wearing my veils. *Stupid*, I berated myself. If Hespa had been there, she would have scolded me all the way to the next week for going into the woods without them. I checked my arms, but there were no sign of cruorflies. Then I recalled that they were most active at dawn and dusk, and it was well past dusk.

I passed the cottage and climbed the remnants of an old stone wall. From the top of its crumbling ramparts I could see a road, snaking through the trees. Had the carriage passed this way when we had come to Pendrake Hall? It would have looked different from the road. I jumped down, tripping in my skirts. The dress was hopeless now, but it had ever been an extravagant dream.

The road didn't lead me through the town, as I thought it would. It wound through terraced fields, alongside wooden fences, past furtive cows. At the edge of a waterway it abruptly stopped, and I realized I had found the river. But I needed to be on the other side of it to get home.

I stumbled along through the thick weeds near the riverbank, cutting round stands of impenetrable shrubbery. With each step I questioned my sense of direction. What if I was going the wrong way, moving farther and farther from my destination?

At last, a bend in the river revealed the shadowy frame of a distant footbridge. I quickened my pace, and from its midpoint, stared down along the ribbon of water. A cluster of lights gleamed in the distance. I'd missed Rivene by a mile, or so I estimated. But I'd found a way to cross the river, and that was the important thing.

The woods lay thick on the other side of the bank. I had to find the road again, but it seemed as though I was plunging into the wilderness. I followed what paths I could find, searching for lights and houses, for a break in the trees. The low hills grew steeper, and I began to tire. My feet were beginning to sting in my slippers. How long had I been walking? The journey took over an hour by carriage, but that was on the road.

The moon rose as I walked, and it no longer shone through the trees. I'd lost my sense of direction, and still the road eluded me. My earlier relief at being alone in the woods was quickly turning to fear. What if I was wandering in circles, and never found my way out? I thought about curling up under a tree, and waiting until morning to continue my journey. But my stomach had begun to rumble, and I wasn't sure I would make it that long. Nor did I think I would get much sleep in the forest. Strange noises echoed through the wood, and snakes slithered at my feet, rustling through dead leaves.

I crested a hill and at long last, saw the glow of firelight in the distance. If there were people, I reasoned, then perhaps there was a road as well. I'd never felt so relieved to hear the sound of human activity. As I drew closer, the sound of drums and laughter made me forget about the pain in my feet, and I quickened my pace once again.

I reached the edge of the trees and drew near a cluster of cottages, some with peeling paint and sagging roofs. The vegetable beds looked like they hadn't been weeded recently, and various tools—rakes and shovels—leaned against a woodshed, exposed to the elements. I knew my father wouldn't have approved of such carelessness. But I was more interested in the sound of the drums coming from the field beyond, where the fire leaped high in an open pit.

I crept round the side of one of the cottages for a better look. About two dozen people—men, women, and children alike—were gathered not far away. None of them were wearing veils, either, so I judged that it must be safe. Most of them were sitting or milling round the fire, but a few were dancing and shaking metal discs. An old man with long, graying hair and papery-white skin lifted a strange instrument to his lips. A matronly woman wearing a yellow headscarf sat beside him, tapping a wooden stick upon a lap instrument with a graceful flourish.

I felt the insistent pull of the music, of the sense of belonging that these villagers seemed to have with one another. No one told the children to go play elsewhere. They were part of the group. I felt an urge to join my voice to this unexpected ensemble. I wanted to try my hand at the wooden stick, to feel the rhythm moving through my hands. I felt the music building in me, swelling round my heart. But as I stepped forward, I came face-to-face with a snarling creature as it emerged from the shadows of one of the cottages.

The creature's face was so distorted by menace that for a moment I failed to recognize that it was a dog. It was nothing like the excitable collie dogs that would try to fold me into the herd when I wandered out into the fields where the goats and sheep grazed. This animal, brute-faced and muscle-bound, looked like the sort my father's kennelmaster kept, for patrolling the grounds. Its ears were flattened against its head as it growled low.

I stood frozen against the side of the cottage. Then I took a slow step backward, hugging the wall. The dog held its ground, its growls turning to sharp barks. When I reached the other end of the wall, I ducked round the corner and began to run away, back toward the woods. The barking followed me, and when I stopped and turned round, it halted its advance. The music had stopped, and I could hear people calling out to it.

For a moment, I thought about calling back. But then I looked down and saw my tattered dress, and remembered my unevenly shorn hair and the bright red pigment Beatrice had swiped across my lips. What trouble would I get into if they saw me like that?

Instead, I turned and ran. I ran for the trees, the dog panting at my back. I was sure I felt the snap of its sharp white teeth at the back of my leg. I grasped the first low-hanging branch I found, scrambling up the silvery-white trunk of a squat old tree. I climbed higher, through the dense branches, trying not to get tangled in my skirt. The dog stopped at the base of the tree and began barking madly.

Men's voices sounded over the din. A branch snapped, and a lantern light bobbed at the edge of the woods.

"What is it, Trapper?" one asked, and the dog, hearing the familiar voice, turned round and began to whine.

"There's a thief about, must be," said the other. "That dog doesn't go mad over nothing."

The light flashed in the trees as the men came closer, their footsteps crunching softly on sticks and dry leaves. The dog circled beneath me, letting out plaintive barks.

I pressed myself against the trunk of the tree, feeling my heart pound in my chest. What would they do if they found me? Would they take me home? Or would they take one look at me and think I was a street urchin who had broken into one of the fancy shops in town?

Go away, I thought, as they picked their way through the undergrowth toward the tree. *Just go away, please.* I shifted my weight on the branch, trying to become smaller. It seemed as I pressed my ear against the trunk that I could feel a faint vibration running through it, a steady hum that somehow comforted me. I let my mind sink into the connection, as I had with the little potted trees in my father's house. *Darkness*, I thought. *Draw me into your shadows, oh mighty tree.*

A light flickered below as the men trampled the ground beneath the tree. The dog had quieted now, pacing back and forth, sniffing the ground, then looking up with a confused expression on its wrinkled face.

"There's something up there, that's for sure," one man said.

"Could just be a 'cherbil," said the other.

"Could be. I don't see anything, though."

"Could be a whisp. They can disappear into trees. Just climb up and *poof*, vanish right into them."

"Wouldn't that be something? I've never seen one, though."

"They don't be seen unless they want to be," the second man said. They both went silent then, listening to the sounds of the forest. Somewhere in the treetops an owl hooted, and another answered.

"Let's go," said the first man. "Come on, Trapper."

The dog stole one more glance up into the canopy, then huffed and reluctantly followed the man back out of the woods. I waited until I could no longer hear the murmur of their voices, then slipped down, branch by branch, until I was low enough to drop to the ground.

It seemed a miracle they hadn't seen me. I placed my palm on the trunk of the tree, giving it thanks. I didn't know if the tree had done anything besides providing shelter, but I figured it couldn't hurt.

Now, though, I still had the problem of finding a road. I wasn't worried about hiding from the men and women at the fire, but the dog presented a problem. The one I had seen was of a type bred for scenting intruders and guarding livestock, and they were a common enough sight. It would be best to avoid going near farms, even if it meant being closer to the road. Perhaps I could skirt near the edge of the woods, just keeping the cottages in sight.

Off I set, though I couldn't be sure I was going in the right direction. I began to imagine scenarios in which I never found my way home, and had to go door to door throughout the countryside begging for scraps like a stray dog. I thought of my great aunt Rosamund, the madwoman; as I cut through the middle of a dry creek bed, I wondered if I bore her features, her habits. Beyond this narrow track, the hills seemed to close in around me. My slippers, ragged and filthy, slid in the mud.

Have I gone mad? I began to think I'd made a mistake in fleeing Pendrake Hall, a gruesome, embarrassing mistake. I was lost, and worse, in an unpresentable state. There was no one I could go to for help, looking as I did. I stopped in my tracks, my eyes blurring with tears, swatting away the little flies that whined against my ear. There was no point in going on if an unlucky guess just took me farther away from home. The alternative, though, was staying in the creek bed, and that was unthinkable. I blinked away my tears—my hands were far too dirty to wipe them away—and grimly surveyed the terrain.

It appeared as though someone had worn a path up the side of the ridge, and I thought perhaps it would lead me to a better vantage point. I grabbed hold of the saplings, my feet slipping beneath me, as I made my ascent. At the top, the path turned and twisted along a narrow precipice. Below me, in the distance, the firelight had become a small orange dot, like a second moon. The wind shifted direction, carrying with it the last strains of music from the gathering. If I did have to live as a beggar in the woods, I thought, at least I could skulk round campsites at night and listen to music.

The ridge sloped down, and once again I found myself having to traverse the mud. Up and down, up and down, I climbed one hill after another, until it all began to look the same, and still the road was nowhere in sight.

I crested another ridge, pulling myself up by the branches of a wild rhododendron, which had strangled the trees round it and mounted quite a defense of the hill. I had to crawl through it to get to the top. As I emerged from the tangle of under-growth, my foot caught a root and I stumbled, pitching over the other side. My arms went out to catch myself, but I was tumbling now, my momentum carrying me all the way down to the bottom, through slick weeds, to a low swampy patch of ground. My slippers sank deep into the spongy black mud, and water pooled round me. The hum of insects was louder here, filling my ears with their incessant drone. Silvery wings flick-ered in the moonlight, rising from the water. They took wing in a scurrilous black cloud, the shifting swarm making patterns in the air: the head of a vicious, snarling dog gave way to a fam-iliar spiral, then transformed into a woman with blazing eyes and a sneering mouth, disgorging the stench of death.

This isn't real, I thought. This was my fevered imagination, playing tricks on me in the dark. But whatever I might make of the pattern of flight, the flies were unquestionably real. I tried to bat them away from my face as they swarmed over me, land-ing in my hair, crawling on my neck, feeding on the soft flesh of my arms. I felt the malicious sting of their bite, and I knew what they were. Cruorflies.

All the stories came back to me in a rush. I thought of the milkmaids and the children in the village, and the old man who had died beneath the tree. How I had feared for my father, who labored outside and took few precautions. And then I had wandered into a swamp, unthinkingly. How could I have been so foolish? How could I explain myself to Hespa, to my father?

I had to keep moving. I had to find the road. I swatted one fly that was feasting on my arm—its body was round and fat with my blood, swollen to the size of a pea. I pulled my foot out of the mud, losing one slipper in the process, but I hardly cared. I took off the other one and threw it into the water. I felt disoriented, as though the landscape had subtly shifted.

I scrambled for the nearest hill, my toes digging into the dirt. As I reached the top, an inhuman scream echoed through the woods, freezing me in place. Out in the blackness beyond my vision, the scream sounded again, and once again my blood ran cold. It was closer now. I huddled against a tree as the undergrowth rustled not far away. I could see nothing; whatever was coming for me, it was moving low, creeping through the brush.

I'm done for, I thought. This was it; there was no escape.

The horrible scream rang out one more time. It was definitely closing in on me. I listened, breathless, heart hammering in my chest, but the wood was eerily quiet now; even the bullfrogs had gone silent.

Then I saw it, slinking along the top of the ridge, a lean, graceful body, low to the ground, tail streaming out behind it like a dark plume of smoke. It turned to look at me, eyes glinting in the moonlight. It was a fox. I'd been frightened half to death by a fox.

I almost began to laugh, but I stopped myself, fearing the sound might frighten it away. There was something about those eyes that gave me pause. As relief flooded through me, I found myself inching toward it, moving ever so slowly, barely lifting my feet. The fox watched me with a steady gaze, seemingly unperturbed by my presence. It remained perfectly still as I approached, until I'd closed about half the distance between us. Then it turned, its tail flicking behind it, disappearing from view. I continued on, over the crest of the hill, and found it waiting for me on the other side.

"Who are you, little fox?" I called out softly. In reply, it opened its mouth wide, yawning, its sharp needle teeth gleaming white. As I approached, it turned and trotted away, then stopped and looked over its shoulder. "What are you trying to show me?"

The fox offered no reply. I continued after it, until we came to a narrow footpath that wound between the hills. I was too weary and footsore to think about where I was going. I had to believe that this fox had appeared for a purpose; I had no other source of hope.

Sharp sticks poked at my feet, and my arms and ankles were beginning to throb where the cruorflies had feasted. My mind began to drift, as though I were losing consciousness, though I remained on my feet, in a surreal fugue-like state. I wondered, for a moment, if the fox was leading me to the realm of the dead. Was that why it had appeared to me? It continued to trot through the woods, never too far ahead, stopping whenever my pace slowed, to turn round and look at me with those dark, glittery eyes. I remembered something

Hespa had said to me once: *If you gaze too long into the eyes of a fox, you will glimpse the underworld.*

But I didn't look away. The fox was the first to break the gaze, turning once more, its tail swishing behind it. I followed it down the next hill. Light glinted through the trees below me, and at first I thought it was water. Then I realized it was a road. I jumped the last few feet, landing on gravel. There was something familiar about the grove of conifers in which I stood. As I turned to look for the fox, it darted across the road, disappearing into the shadows too quickly for my eyes to follow. But it no longer mattered. Down the lane, not far in the distance, a light was shining at Guildenflore.

CHAPTER FIFTEEN

I POUNDED ON THE FRONT DOOR. From the floor above, the silk screens puffed up, then deflated, moving in and out as though the house was taking a breath. I heard my father's paleophone, the sound of violins rising and swelling on the night air. I sagged against the door, relieved to find the house still awake, even at this late hour.

A moment later, the latch flipped, and the door opened just a crack, Hespa's eye shining through the aperture. The eye widened in shock and recognition, and she swung the door wide.

"Kit! What are you doing here? What a state you're in! Quick, come inside."

I let her usher me into the front entrance hall. Her eyes roved over me, taking in my muddy bare feet, my expensive dress, now destroyed, my ragged hair and stained lips.

"Oh, child. What happened to you?"

I opened my mouth to speak, but suddenly it was too much, and I burst into tears, clutching her tight. She smoothed my hair, her fingers finding the ends that I'd chopped in my hasty retreat. Then she took my arm, prying it away from her waist, examining it in the glare of the aetherlamps.

"You've been bit," she said, her voice curiously flat.

"I got lost coming home," I tried to explain.

"Did you walk all the way from Pendrake Hall?"

I nodded, wiping my nose with the back of my hand. "Please don't make me go back there, Hespa. Don't let Papa send me back."

She let out a long sigh. "Let's get you into the bath, and you can tell me what happened."

She sent me to the washroom while she went to find Marguerite, to start heating the water for the bath. The two of them worked together, carrying the water up, stealing glances down the hall as they did so, communicating in soft words and gestures. Hespa helped me out of my soiled clothes, and both women gasped to see the red welts on my skin. I climbed over the side of the tub and sank into the warm water.

"Don't say anything," Hespa said to Marguerite, as she turned to go. "It's my place to explain." The cook nodded, and quickly exited the room.

"Do you think Papa will be angry with me? That I left the

Pendrakes?" I asked, as Hespa began to ladle the water over the back of my head. She handed me a cloth to wipe my face.

"No, kit. But whatever caused you to run away?"

"There's something wrong there," I said, watching the dirt float up onto the surface of the water. "Something wrong at the house."

"What do you mean?"

"Beatrice and Bianca—they tried to cut my hair, and then they locked me out on a ledge."

"Surely you could have gone to Lady Pendrake, though," Hespa said. "I can't see her standing for such behavior from her girls."

I shook my head. "There was something wrong with *her*, too."

"What do you mean?"

"I don't know—it wasn't safe there."

"If they ever do such a thing in this house, you *will* tell me, kit. I'll have a word with those girls."

The heat of the water was starting to become too much, and I put my arms up on the side of the tub. Hespa sponged the dirt from them and examined my cruorfly bites. They were swelling, rising up from my skin like angry red ant hills.

"When are you going to tell Papa?" I asked.

"As soon as you're out of the tub. He'll want to send for a doctor."

She finished the bath and dressed me in a clean chemise, then combed my hair, making sounds of dismay as she got to the chopped part. "We'll have to cut the rest of your hair to even it out," she said, eyeing the ends critically. "But never mind that right now. At least you're clean."

She marched me into the parlor and instructed me to wait there for my father. She was right—it was no small thing to be clean. Even the fearful implications of the cruorfly bites seemed less dire, now that I'd left behind the stink of the swamp and had a clean cotton shift. I was home now, and safe. My father would take care of everything else.

Under the harsh glare of the aetherlamps, the smoke from the incense burners curled and took on strange shapes. It was late and despite the terror of the last few hours, I began to doze to the sound of the ticking clock. I awoke as the doors creaked open, and lifted my head from the arm of the divan. My father took a few steps into the room and stopped, staring at me. Hespa remained holding the door, her eyes downcast. Silence stretched between us.

"Not all cruorfly bites precede illness," my father said.

"No," she agreed. "But I think a doctor ought to be sent for, as a precaution. There were...many bites, sir."

I waited for him to come over to me, to stroke my hair, to fold me into his arms. But he turned briskly on his heel and left the room, gesturing for Hespa to shut the door behind him. Though they spoke quietly, I heard every word from the other side of the lattice. Hespa's voice was urgent, hushed.

"Will you do nothing for the child?" she asked.

"There's nothing to be done. There is no cure for arrhemia.

Right now there are no symptoms to be managed. I would not have the doctor make a trip for nothing when he may have other patients in need."

"But you could speak to him, sir! If it is—if it is the worst, he would be able to prepare you—"

"If it is the worst, I am sure there is nothing Dr. Vidmont could say to prepare me."

My father's footsteps retreated down the hallway. The door swung open again and Hespa returned to my side. Her face looked ashen, all color gone from her normally ruddy cheeks. Her gaze was flat, but I recognized the determination in it. It was the same look she gave when her feet were hurting but she had wood to chop and buckets to carry, beds to strip, tea to serve, and on top of it all, a wayward child to tend.

"I'm sorry, Hespa," I said, as she gently roused me from the divan.

"For what, kit?"

"For causing such an uproar."

Her mouth twisted, almost becoming a smile. "You don't know the first thing about uproars. Come, let's get you to bed."

She was right, I realized, as she lay the coverlet over me and blew out the lamp. I'd expected my father to be angry, but his restraint was almost harder to bear. I lay in the darkness for a long time before falling asleep, feeling the bites on my arms and legs begin to itch. I knew it was bad to scratch them, and held out for as long as I could, keeping perfectly still, letting the tears leak from the corners of my eyes and track down to my ears. It was a hot night, but occasional breezes made the silk screens sag in and out, lifting the fine hairs around my face. I thought I would never get to sleep, but sometime before dawn, I drifted off into unquiet dreams.

☽☾

According to what Hespa managed to glean from the other servants, it was sometimes a week before a person began to feel the symptoms of arrhemia. Usually, though, it began after two or three days. The uncertainty of those next days were torturous. I went about my studies with the schoolmistress, since my father thought there was no need to disrupt the household routine. But all the while, the butterflies sliced at my insides with their familiar fluttery dance. *It's only nerves*, I would tell myself, as a twinge in my side made my heart bottom out. A touch of afternoon fatigue would claim me, and I would lay awake during respite thinking, *It's only the heat, of course it's the heat, that's why everyone takes respite!*

I imagined jagged black jaws ready to spring fast and pierce my lungs, waiting for me to jostle them just the wrong way as I reached for a pen or leaned forward to cradle my cup of tea. A malign bird roosted in the hollows of my chest, bristling in the darkness. Whenever my father wasn't present, Hespa would ask, anxiously, "Are you well, kit? You look a bit peaked."

And whatever ailment I might be imagining, I would answer that all was well.

That declaration felt like a challenge to Hespa's gods, though, and I fretted over that as well. I didn't want their attention. And yet, I kept dreaming of my flight through the night woods, and one morning I awoke with the feeling of a fox's eyes boring into me. Something had happened to me out there that wasn't entirely natural, and my dreaming mind wouldn't let me forget about it.

Hespa decided that morning to try to fix my hair. As she was combing it out at my dressing table, I said, "I got lost in the woods coming home from Pendrake Hall."

She picked out a snarl with her comb. "Why didn't you take the road, child?"

"A dog chased me, and then I couldn't find the road. I had to go round the swamp."

"But you did find your way back. That was no easy feat," she said, taking the scissors in hand. I flinched at the sound of their blades snapping together, as the recollection of the awful night at the Pendrakes flashed through my mind.

"I didn't, though. A fox found me."

"What do you mean?"

"I mean it led me back to the road."

"That doesn't sound likely," she said, making her first snip just below my shoulders. I watched the lock of yellow hair fall to the floor.

"It did, though. I don't think it was an ordinary fox."

"Did you look it in the eyes?" Hespa asked.

"Yes." Another lock fell to the floor. "It had beautiful eyes."

"Beautiful or not, that's not a wise thing to do. You know what they say about looking into the eyes of a fox."

"I know what *you* say about it," I retorted, a bit crossly. "I've never heard anyone else talk about it. How do you know it's a bad thing?"

"I don't like hearing about wild animals acting strange," she said. "It's never a good sign." By now she had chopped most of my hair off. The ends just barely brushed the top of my shoulders. I ran my fingers through it experimentally, trying to get used to the new look. "Be still," she said. "I want to fix the front."

She combed my hair forward over my eyes, then began cutting a fringe.

"But what does it mean?" I asked, from under my curtain of hair. "What does it mean when animals act strange?"

"I don't know," she said. "But I've heard it said that some demons can possess animals."

"Possess?"

"They bind their spirit to the animal, and can use its eyes and other senses to walk the earth."

"I don't think it was a demon," I said. "It led me home, after all."

"They're clever beings," Hespa said. "They might do you a favor just to put you in their debt. But there's nothing to be done about it now, I suppose."

"What would a demon want with me?" I asked.

"That, I cannot say," Hespa said. She pursed her lips, examining her handiwork. "It'll do until it grows back," she added, giving my hair one last run through the comb. "At least it won't tangle as much."

☙❧

On the third day after returning home from the Pendrakes, I had to be excused from my lessons. A wave of fatigue crashed over me as I was poring over the map in one of my history books, making my eyes blur until I could no longer distinguish the land from the sea. When the schoolmistress called upon me to name the Kushran princedoms of the southern coast, a roar filled my ears, drowning out the sound of her words.

"Miss Amardine, are you well?" she asked, removing her spectacles. We were in the parlor, and she sat across the tea table from me, her bright yellow cotton day dress swimming in my vision.

"I'm—not sure, Mistress Olbara," I replied, as my head suddenly dropped onto the open pages of my book.

Distantly, I heard the bell ringing, and Hespa appeared not long afterward to help me to my bed. I fell into a deep sleep, and woke that evening feeling better. It was past dinnertime, and I was ravenous. I ate two eggs and a bowl of soup, then dragged myself out of bed to my father's study.

The door was open a crack, which meant he could be interrupted. I knocked and then pushed it open. He looked up from his desk, raising his eyebrows.

"You're awake," he observed, sounding surprised.

"Yes, Papa."

"Did you need something?"

"I'd like to see Father Parquar," I said.

"Good God, Amardine, you're not dying," he replied, glancing down at his ledger.

"I never said I was dying," I said. "I just said I'd like to see Father Parquar. I must get an urgent message to Aneidis."

"Ha! What do you think he is, a postal courier?'"

"Please, Papa."

He looked up from his work, his brow furrowed, as though the sight of me was painful to him. "It's late," he said. "I'll send for him tomorrow morning."

But by morning, I knew it was all for naught. I emptied the contents of my stomach into the washbasin, then passed back into a feverish sleep and dreamed I was a sailboat, burning to the waterline.

CHAPTER SIXTEEN

I COULD NOT WAKE. I COULD not claw my way out of sleep. Something bad was happening to my body, but my mind remained trapped inside deep, sickening dreams.

Someone laid a cool, wet cloth over my forehead. Nausea plunged my stomach; I heard my own voice, begging for the basin. Later, a vision of Hespa, her broad face upturned, caught in the lamplight, looking as beatific as any of Lady Pendrake's cherubellum. Then the darkness covered me once again.

The next I knew, the room was flooded with daylight. My head throbbed. My father was outlined in the open doorway to the courtyard with a man I didn't recognize, and they jabbered and jabbered until their words fused together like a puzzle box.

Gradually the soft drone of their conversation resolved itself into speech.

"That's the problem with blood," said the other man, in an almost jovial tone. "It carries toxins all over the body. Why it's needed for continued life, we may never know. Ha, ha!"

"I've heard the Yfandi are making great strides in medicine," my father said, sounding desperate. "Are you familiar with their latest publications?"

"Bah. An excitable gaggle of themorogists, fouling up a perfectly good medical tradition with their mechanical devices and instrument thingy-majogs. Don't worry, Master Desmarius, I've seen this before. As soon as she's strong enough, I'll begin the treatment."

I pretended to be asleep, trying not to tense as the footsteps approached. I could sense the man's presence as he stood over me.

"That's all, then," my father said, from farther away. "I'll call for you if anything changes."

They left, closing the door behind them, and I drifted back into unconsciousness. It was hardly an escape, though—I only lapsed into more unsettling dreams. In one, I was passing through a vast courtyard, cut in half by a walkway raised upon crumbling stone arches, toward the halo of black mist that encircled it. As I approached, the mist ahead of me parted, revealing a figure standing before the edge of a wood. Her white gown rippled like a pennant in the wind as she held up her hand.

"Don't go that way," she said. "Go back, go back, go back from whence you came."

My body froze, and I could go no farther. She stepped forward, her feet blurring into narrow ribbons of light. When she drew closer I could see the blood stain in the center of her chest, the rope looped round one ankle, trailing over the pitted flagstones. The features were clear and familiar, the eyes luminous.

"Mama?" I whispered.

"I'm no longer her," she said, glancing round, as though her former self was lurking in the shadows nearby, just waiting to spring out and spook her.

"Mama, it *is* you," I insisted, trying once more to pick up my feet. It was no use; I was rooted to the ground.

"I see through her eyes," she said. "I see the things that she would see. But I am not her."

"It sounds like you're just confused," I said, still hoping to reason with her.

"There was something I left behind," she replied. "You never should have taken it. Go back, go back, go back to the maiden tree."

"What tree, Mama? I can't even move my legs."

"Poor child. I couldn't help that. I could do nothing but look on."

"What do you mean?" I asked, my voice rising as the figure before me seemed to break apart into hundreds of facets, gleaming like shards of glass. "What did you leave behind?

What couldn't you help?"

The image shattered, its shards flying, transforming in mid-air into a kaleidoscope of butterflies. Then my stomach heaved, and I tasted a metallic tang in my mouth. I began to retch as my mind made a jarring transition to wakefulness, but it must have only been in my mind, for my father remained undisturbed. He slouched in the chair in the corner, wearing his work boots and clutching his hat in his lap. A half-eaten pastry sat neglected on a plate beside him.

Then I saw the doctor standing at the foot of the bed, his head bowed over a slate. He was an aging man, bespectacled and nearly bald, with a mustache that looked like a tuft of milk-weed. There were dark rings of sweat beneath his armpits, staining his crisp white shirt. He glanced up and met my gaze. I looked away, feeling as though I'd been caught looking up the answers in the back of a primer.

"Child," he barked. "You gave your father a grave fright. What have you to say to that?"

Before I could answer such a bold question, my father dragged himself to his feet. "It's good that you're awake," he said, his voice frayed. "How are you feeling?"

"I'm well enough, I think."

The doctor, however, disagreed. "You were attacked by cruorflies during your misadventure, when you left the house of your esteemed relatives. Do you know how frantic your aunt has been, how many letters she's written in the past few days? I'd be surprised if you don't have a monstrous headache for the trouble you've caused. In fact, I'd say the first step in your recovery ought to be a sincere apology. Yes, an apology, child. It will lighten your soul and allow for a cleaner healing process."

"Dr. Vidmont, if you could endeavor to remain within the confines of your expertise, I'd be much obliged," my father said.

"I maintain that this *is* within the confines of my expertise, good sir. A patient's demeanor can greatly affect the prognosis. Humility, patience, contrition—these are the necessary qualities of the convalescent. Illness represents a great shift in one's Allotment. One cannot expect to recover from a physical ailment without an equivalent improvement of character."

"You don't truly believe that, do you?" my father asked. "All that nonsense about Allotment being the cause of illness and suffering?"

"My good man, I am merely speaking orthodoxy," said the doctor. "Surely your local priest would say the same."

"I doubt it," my father replied.

The doctor coughed, clearing his throat. "Yes, well. I understand the faith can be a bit more rustic in these parts. Never mind that, though."

I finally found my voice, and rasped out, "Where is Hespa?"

"I sent her to rest. She hasn't had much sleep," my father said.

"Am I going to die?"

The doctor clucked his tongue, as though I'd asked a vulgar question. "Nothing can be certain at this point, young lady, but

I'm going to give you something to help you rest. You'll need to stay very quiet for the next few days, though. Your maid is not to find you reading or doing lessons." To my father, he said, "In fact, sir, I recommend that you remove all the books from the room. Even the thought of books can bring a fit of distraction in the youthful mind, especially for females, as they are more naturally susceptible to umbral fantasies."

"Is there anything else, Dr. Vidmont?" my father asked, sharply.

The doctor rummaged in his medical bag and withdrew a bottle whose label read DR. VIDMONT'S MIRACLE OIL. "This will do the trick. It's very safe—even the child's maid ought to be able to administer it, given proper instruction." He poured a foul-smelling liquid into a thimble glass and waved it under my nose. "Drink the healthful tonic, child. It will aid your recovery."

I wrinkled my nose. "What's in it?"

"*Tsk, tsk.* Children are to listen to their doctors and not ask questions."

"What *is* in it, if I may ask?" my father asked.

The doctor mopped his brow. "It's a patented formula, sir. A family remedy, that sort of thing. You understand, I'm sure. What goes into pardesu extract, after all?"

"Pardesu oil," my father said.

"Ha! Quite right! Well, if you must know, this miraculous substance is a mixture of vetiver oil, gangro root, poppy serum, black anise, cinnabar, and several other rare herbs imported from across the Kethrean Sea. I'll have you know, Lord Pendrake is quite fond of this particular mixture. He finds that it helps him sleep when his gout is troubling him."

My father shrugged. "Drink the tonic, Amardine."

I let it drain slowly down my throat, leaving behind a trail of burnt licorice. Almost immediately, my vision blurred and my muscles went slack. I sank back into my pillows as the bed became a whirling parasol top and the bad dreams began to slink out from dark corners, scrabbling for purchase.

"No," I croaked. "I can't go back to sleep. I can't."

"You must sleep. It's essential for recovery," the doctor said.

"Please, Papa! Don't make me dream again."

"You will sleep," the doctor insisted, sounding irritated now. "Just be quiet and let the tonic do its work."

The darkness closed over my head.

‘’)(‘’

Voices sounded outside in the hallway.

My skin was burning, but the nausea had subsided. I hadn't dreamed at all.

"There is a concern here," the doctor said, "given the child's, erm, family extraction."

"I assume you are speaking of the mother." My father's tone was chilly.

"Hmmm, yes, the mother...it would be helpful if you could provide a genealogy, perhaps? I know many families in the county keep diligent accounts of such things..."

"She was feym'ari. Adopted by a good family in Miraval. I didn't ask to see her pedigree."

"Yes, well. Of course not." The doctor blew his nose. "Are you in touch with the family at all?"

"No. Sephonie left home at the age of fifteen. She rarely spoke of them."

"Not very grateful, if you don't mind me saying so," the doctor said.

"I don't think they exactly approved of her choices. What does this have to do with my daughter, anyway?"

"It may be relevant to the theory on the polarization of blood—I can have a copy of the treatise sent to you, to peruse —but to quickly summarize, it suggests that the blood, is, erm, energized, after a fashion, to attract either illness or good health. I'm afraid the infection your daughter has contracted may be drawn to her feym blood, you see, as it is a weaker strain, more—" he cleared his throat—"more prone to degeneracy."

"Is that your professional opinion, Dr. Vidmont? That the feym'ari are 'more prone to degeneracy'?"

The doctor coughed and blew his nose again. "I beg your pardon, good sir. It was poor turn of phrase. I meant no offense to your daughter, nor to your late wife, whatever ill-fated choices she may have made. I promise you, I will make this case my most urgent concern. I know of an excellent sanitarium in Cereval that specializes in the treatment of wasting diseases. I'll write a recommendation for admittance this very day, if you wish to pursue this avenue. Rest assured, you may call upon me at any time, day or night, and I shall be at your disposal. I don't wish to underplay the difficulty of the road ahead, no, but you shall have all the best resources, Master Desmarius. There is that to consider."

"There is that," my father said.

I lay in bed, listening to their voices and footsteps recede down the hallway. The glass doors of the nursery had been hung with heavy curtains, so I couldn't tell what time of day it was. I stumbled out of bed still half asleep, without any particular thought of what to do. I made it to the vestibule outside my room, where the hallway turned, before my legs quit, buckling under me. Pain shot up my spine. I crashed against the mirror hanging on the wall, knocking it to the floor, rolling away before it fell on top of me. I tried to draw my knees to my chest, but my lower limbs were in open rebellion now, trembling with agitation, refusing all marching orders.

Hespa found me, lying amid the shards of the shattered mirror. She lifted me off the floor. It hurt so much to be moved, I could hardly stand it. Then, from down the hallway, the ominous voice of the doctor boomed, "There's no time to waste! We must begin the treatment!"

Time *was* wasting, wobbling uncontrollably. A moment later, I was back in my bed. My father was there, too, hanging back in the doorway of the nursery as the doctor stood over me, regarding me through the lens of a monocle.

"We need to begin immediately," he reiterated. "The blood is already compromised."

I knew then that I had underestimated the doctor. I had found him slightly ridiculous, someone who could be easily managed by the likes of my father. But he was moving swiftly now, efficiently, withdrawing a roll of bandages from his bag along with a thin metal rod and a bottle of clear liquid. He paused, looking over me as though deciding on a cut of meat.

It was my father's turn to sweat and mop his brow.

The doctor pointed at Hespa and said, "Open the curtains, gussey, I need more light." Then he turned out my ankles, exposing my legs with shocking familiarity, causing a ripple of pain to cascade down to my calves. I hissed through clenched teeth. Hespa's bovine eyes didn't even blink as she grasped my ankles and stretched out my legs. The doctor held up the rod, a forked metal instrument, the prongs shining silver in the sunlight as though they were made to do right-eous work. He rapped my ankle with it and went up the leg, asking, "Do you feel this? How about this? Do you feel it here?"

Yes, yes, and yes I answered, through gritted teeth.

"I'll need you to hold the patient's legs while I incise the vein," he said to Hespa.

"Incise the vein?" my father echoed, in a threadbare voice.

"It might be best if you left the room, sir," Dr. Vidmont said, "as it may be a delicate sight."

"I'd prefer to remain here."

The doctor nodded and produced more implements from his bag: a cloth band and a bowl of fine white clay, curiously fixed with a spout, like one of Marguerite's batter bowls.

"Are you going to bake a custard, Dr. Vidmont?" I asked, my head beginning to swim.

He seemed to startle at the sound of my voice. "Sir, your child may be a bit mad. Oh, it's natural for the age. It is a poor strategy, though, to indulge whimsy in children."

There was a flash of metal in his hand.

"Papa, this man has a knife," I said, alarmed.

The doctor nodded at Hespa. "Hold her legs, gussey."

My father started toward me, but he kept his face turned away, as though he were ashamed.

"It's only a bleeding," Hespa said, and though she probably meant to be reassuring, the word sounded dire. I felt a scream rise in me, but the look on her face issued a warning and I closed my mouth, resigned to silence. How could I argue when all of the grownups thought this was a good idea?

As Dr. Vidmont tightened a band round my leg, I thought about the time the previous summer when my father had fainted. Two men had dragged him into the house, his body sagging between them. I'd thought he was dead, or dying. They brought him into the parlor and wouldn't let me see him. But I heard the laundry maids talking about it as they collected the bed linens, and learned that he'd only passed out. It was a hot day, after all.

"That's a true gentleman for you!" one exclaimed.

"Can't stand the sight of blood," said the other.

Earlier that day, he'd ordered a lamb for supper, and happened upon the shepherd while he prepared to slaughter it. Unable to find a graceful way to extricate himself from the scene, my father had just watched it all happen. It was then that he'd fainted. The servants had a good chuckle over it, but they stopped when they saw I was listening. No one ever spoke of it in my presence again.

But I could never eat lamb after that. Whenever Marguerite served lamb, I thought of scarlet ribbons of blood, spooling out endlessly from a gash in its throat.

That's what I was thinking of when the dull *thump* jarred me out of my rumination. It was my father, slumped in the door frame. He'd fainted again. Heedless of his fall, the doctor scowled in concentration, and the scalpel bit in deep.

My father had eaten the lamb, after all that, and he'd relished it, too.

CHAPTER SEVENTEEN

I WAS PUNISHED AFTER THAT, MY feet tied to a board.

Dr. Vidmont continued to administer his miracle oil, keeping my mind foggy, my sleep murky and dreamless. Hours crawled by and the shadows lengthened, the yellow twilight melting into dirty butterscotch. Voices slithered from one room to the next, like caterpillars slipping between dense plumes of leaves.

I heard bits and pieces of conversation as I drifted in and out of consciousness. "It's best to give the blood time to make its course throughout the body. But only a day or two ought to be necessary, for such a small child," the doctor said.

"Is that the only concern, then, with blood-letting?" My father's voice.

"Have you not had it done, sir?" asked the doctor. "It is a surprisingly neat practice, with an illustrious history."

"I've been very fortunate with my health," my father said.

"You are a rarity, then! A curious gem. But you needn't worry, Master Desmarius. It's a very common treatment, the best thing for the young and the old alike, never mind those fandy journals."

"I do try to stay current on the latest journals of discovery," my father replied. The divan in the vestibule creaked and I heard his boots thud against the tile floor. "But there's never time enough to read everything, is there?"

"No, indeed there is not! That's why Aneidis created clerks, or rather, I should say clerics," Dr. Vidmont replied, with an unfathomable chortle.

They went over a schedule of blood-letting and tonics and other treatments involving painful stretches and hot wool. Over the next few days, the doctor made sure my father kept to them faithfully, and instructed Hespa in some therapeutic exercises. It all transpired under the heavy haze of Dr. Vidmont's tonic, night shifting to day and back again with little sense of the passage of time.

But one morning, during a rare lucid moment, I recalled the dream I'd had of my mother. Was it only a fever dream, or had she been trying to tell me something? *There was something I left behind*, she had said. *You never should have taken it. Go back, go back, go back to the maiden tree.*

I wasn't sure I wanted to dream of her again. It hadn't been a happy reunion, after all. There was no sweetness in her affect, no gentle mother-love. Her eyes had been wild, her words nonsensical. I thought of the blood at her breast, of the trailing rope, and Bianca's vision of the woman hanging from the elm—was that what she meant by the "maiden tree"? Wherever her spirit dwelt, it seemed restless, confused.

You never should have taken it. I stared across the room at the wardrobe, where I kept the hatbox, full of secrets: her perfume, her papers and books. The silver stake.

If only I'd done more, when I had the chance. Perhaps I could have gleaned something useful from the perfume. I tried to turn onto my side, as though by adjusting my view I could somehow will it out of its hiding place, into my hand. But my feet were still strapped to the onerous board.

I sat up, feeling the muscles in my stomach straining from lack of use. It was painful to stretch my arms out, but I managed to reach the cord that bound my feet, and with deft fingers, worked it loose. The board flopped over onto the coverlet, and I tried to draw my legs up, over the side of the bed. They were still unresponsive. I could feel a tingling in my feet, but for some reason I couldn't wiggle my toes.

I was more frustrated than alarmed, wondering how long it would take before my legs returned to normal. In the meantime, I would just have to make do. I twisted at the waist and dropped my hands down to the rug, wincing as a sharp pain lanced through my disobedient lower limbs. After a moment it subsided, and I managed to pull my body out of bed, flopping gracelessly to the floor. I sat there for a moment, catching my breath, waiting for more pain to manifest. My body was weak, fatigued, but I had to hope the worst of my illness had passed.

When I was ready, I dragged myself over to the wardrobe and reached up, grasping the knob. But as I was pulling it open, I heard footsteps outside in the hallway. Dr. Vidmont's now familiar voice rang out, followed by Hespa's softer reply. The door opened and the doctor entered the room, followed by Hespa.

She gasped to see me on the floor, and immediately started toward me, but Dr. Vidmont held out his hand, stopping her.

"And what have we here? *Tsk, tsk*, child. Don't you run away on me, will you? Ha, ha!"

"Are you ill, kit?" Hespa asked. "Let me go to her, please, sir."

"You're being a very difficult patient," the doctor said, ignoring her. "Did I say you ought to remove the board from your feet, child? Did I say you ought to get out of bed?"

I looked up at him and shook my head. The hatbox was only inches away, but of course I couldn't do anything with it now.

"No," the doctor said, answering his own questions. "I did *not* say you ought to remove the board. I did *not* say you ought to get out of bed." He crossed the room to stand over me. "You are a very sick little girl. Do you want to get better, or not?"

I nodded, staring at his knees.

"Look at me, child," he said, bending down to grasp my chin, forcing me to meet his stern gaze. "If you want to get better, you need to do as you're told. Do you understand?"

"Yes," I said. I understood very well that this was the only acceptable response.

"I think what you need is another dose of medicine." He turned to Hespa. "Get the child to her bed."

Hespa knelt beside me and lifted me up from the floor. The doctor watched her with a satisfied look. "Where are you from, gussey?"

"I was born in Ungria, sir," Hespa said, as she eased me down onto the bed.

"Ah! I knew it had to be somewhere thereabouts. A lot of Vanzari blood in those mountains, isn't that right? When I first saw you, I thought to myself, 'there is a Vanzari giantess, if ever I saw one!'" He went on about the charted difference in heights across the continents. We natives of southern Atherlos tended toward the ideal range of height, that which produced the maximum health and industry, according to the doctor. Hespa listened to the diatribe, nodding her head in agreement, as he rummaged in his bag for the bottle of medicine. He poured a generous dose into the thimble glass next to the bed and held it out before me.

"Go ahead, child. Drink the tonic."

I flinched, moving my head away. "I feel better now. I don't need any more medicine."

"Are you a doctor now, child?" he asked, his voice dripping

with sarcasm. "Did you study at the most elite medical academy in Cereval? No? I didn't think so. I am the doctor, and you are naught but a very foolish little girl. Now drink the tonic, or I will be forced to tell your father how you misbehaved."

I looked to Hespa for support, but she was busy affixing my feet to the board. It wasn't a punishment after all; she later explained that it was only to keep my legs from twisting as the muscles contracted. Even so, the act seemed disloyal.

Then the doctor shifted, blocking my view, and all of sudden he was grasping my nose, pinching it hard. I opened my mouth with a gasp, and he pushed the rim of the glass between my parted lips. I coughed as he tipped back the glass, the fiery liquid burning its way down my throat.

"There, now. That wasn't so difficult, was it?" he said, stepping back with a satisfied air. His form separated before me, into two identical faces sharing the same body, and when I tried to turn my head to shake the illusion, it flopped back onto my pillow, too heavy to keep aloft.

"That's better," I heard the doctor say, before drifting into blackness. "That should quiet her mind."

ℴ™ɔʕ

I woke again in agony, with a spasm in my leg so painful it buckled me at the waist and left me breathless. I called out, trying to twist onto my side, but the slightest movement only made it worse. Hespa pressed a cool cloth to my forehead as I shrieked through gritted teeth.

"Try to breathe, kit," she said. "I know it hurts."

Tears stung my eyes as the spasm subsided. I felt the muscles go slack again. Hespa untied my feet from the board and began to rub my calves, loosening the knot.

"I ought to call for the doctor," she said, though she didn't sound enthusiastic about the idea.

"Is he here?" I asked.

"He's been living in the cottage."

"Grandame's house?" I asked.

"Yes, kit. He's agreed to stay as long as necessary, to help you with your recovery."

"Don't call for him yet," I pleaded. "I feel better now, honestly." I pulled myself up on my pillows. "How long will I have to stay in bed?"

"I don't know, kit."

"Can I have a book to read?"

"You know the doctor said you weren't supposed to have books right now," she said, as she grasped one ankle and stretched my leg, as Dr. Vidmont had shown her.

"But I'm bored."

"Perhaps it wouldn't hurt if you were to read a little," she conceded. "But you mustn't strain yourself. I'll bring you something after lunch."

She moved to go. I didn't want her to leave just yet. As she reached the door, I came to a decision.

"Hespa?"

She half-turned, her hand resting on the doorknob. "Yes, kit?"

"Have you ever heard of a maiden tree?"

Her eyes were steady as she looked at me, betraying nothing. "Where did you hear of such a thing?"

"In a dream," I said. "You told me the dead sometimes talk to us in dreams. I think my mama talked to me."

She took in a long breath, then nodded. "It would seem so, kit. I've not heard those words spoken together in Pheresian, though."

"What do you mean?" I asked.

Her gaze shifted away, losing its focus. I could almost see her mind working, trying to recall something from her past.

"*Avre'n as zavir,*" she said softly, almost in a whisper. "Tree of the maidens. I think that was what they called it."

"Who?" I asked. "Who, Hespa?"

"The Feym-ri," she said, finally looking back at me. "I heard of such a thing when I was a girl, in Ungria. It's a place where young women must make their offerings before they are allowed to learn magic. And in doing so, the tree's magic grows in strength as well."

I pulled the coverlet up over my shoulders. "What sort of offerings?"

"That, I do not know. The Feym-ri don't share such things with outsiders. I only know what I heard."

"Who told you about it?" I pressed.

"There was a Feym-ri girl who lived outside of my village. We would play together sometimes. Her sister was becoming *vardom*—one who is guided by spirits."

I sank back against my pillows, aware that I was gaping at her. A thousand more questions flooded my mind. But before I could sputter out any further inquiries, Hespa said, "That's all I know, kit. I promise. I haven't thought about that time in years. I didn't even know I still remembered those words."

"Are you going to tell my papa?" I asked. "That Mama talked to me in a dream?"

"No," Hespa said. "I wouldn't say a word about it."

She left soon afterward and returned with a tray of fruit and yoghurt, and a thick slice of buttered bread. Until I started eating, I didn't realize how ravenous I was. I finished everything on the tray, then asked if there was anything else to eat.

Hespa seemed surprised by my appetite, but she took it as a good sign, like my boredom. "There might be some chicken from last night. I'll go see."

She came back once more with a plate of cold chicken marinated in vinegar and lemon juice, a dish of roasted almonds, and two boiled eggs. As I was diving into the meal, the door opened, and Dr. Vidmont stepped in.

His eyes practically bulged out of his head as he saw me, hunkered down over my plate of chicken. Then he put down his bag, strode forward and yanked the tray away from me, setting it down on the dressing table with a rude clatter.

"What is the meaning of this?" he bellowed. "Why is this child eating solid food?"

"She was hungry," Hespa said.

"Of course she's hungry. Hunger is a symptom of her disease. We are trying to starve the sickness in her blood," the doctor explained, taking the tone of a schoolmaster instructing a particularly thick-witted student. He sighed and reached for his bag. "I thought we understood this, gussey."

"I apologize, sir," Hespa said. "I just thought it would help her recover her strength."

"Ah, yes, a common misperception. But what happens when the patient 'recovers her strength,' as you say? The illness flexes its strength as well. That is what most people don't understand. And so the recovery process becomes one of attrition. Which is stronger, the patient, or her sickness? That is what it comes down to, in the end." He sat down in the chair by my bed and withdrew a bottle with a label I didn't recognize. At least it didn't have a picture of his mustachioed face on it. "She'll require another bleeding soon, but first, we'll need to undo the effects of her irregular treatment."

"Ipecac syrup?" Hespa said, as the doctor poured out the dose. "Is that truly necessary?"

The doctor turned to her, setting the glass on the nightstand. I thought he was going to snap at her again for interfering, but his expression was calm, almost sly.

"Ah, I'd nearly forgotten." He reached into his bag again, and this time, he withdrew a dressmaker's tape. I frowned, trying to anticipate what he intended to do with it.

"You recall our conversation from some days ago?" he asked her.

"I'm...not certain, sir."

"Oh, dagnabit. When you told me all about your home-land."

"I only said that I was born in Ungria, sir."

"Yes, yes," the doctor said, impatiently. "I was thinking about our conversation, and I thought to myself, 'why don't we see just how tall a Vanzari giantess is?'"

"But she's from Ungria, not Vanzaroth," I said, confused.

"Never mind that, it's close enough. Stand against that wall, gussey, and we shall find out the truth!"

It was obvious to me that Hespa had no desire to participate in this exercise, but what could she say? He was the doctor. As she moved to obey him, I gave a loud groan. It was the least I could do for her, to create a diversion.

"What was that?" the doctor said, turning to me. He snapped his dressmaker's tape, looking annoyed.

I pulled myself up as straight as I could and began making unearthly noises, as though I were a witch in a storybook. I pulled a twisted, gleeful face and said, in the voice of an old crone, "You're going to diiieee, Dr. Vidmont."

It was a simple truth—I didn't see how anyone could fault me for stating it. But the doctor stared at me as though I'd gone mad. Sweat began to bead on his forehead, and he withdrew a handkerchief from his shirt pocket and began to wipe his brow. "What is the meaning of this?" he demanded. "What fevered madness do you speak, child?"

"You're going to diiieee. The spirits told me so."

Hespa abandoned her post by the wall to return to my bedside. "I'm sure it's just the illness," she said. She stole a furtive glance at me, biting her lip.

"Madness," the doctor said again. "And not the ordinary madness of children, no. This is a deeper, more dangerous sort of mania. Has she done this sort of thing before, gussey?"

"I don't think so, sir."

"Give her the ipecac. When she's done purging her stomach, you can administer another dose of my miracle oil. That will silence any spirits that have been riding in her blood."

I knew then, with a certainty, that if I continued taking Dr. Vidmont's concoctions, I would never get out of bed again. The doctor left then, and Hespa handed me the cup. While her back was turned, I spit the foul substance back into my water glass.

I did this twice again over the course of the next day, gradually recovering more of my senses. The second time, Hespa turned round as I was spitting into my glass, and looked me right in the eye. I held the cup in one trembling hand, my guilty gaze tracking every movement as she strode over to the side of the bed.

She lifted the carafe from the nightstand and rinsed the glass. Then she refilled it with clean water, speaking not a word.

ഇ)രു

Days and nights vanished in a torpid haze, the heat lingering in the thick walls of the house, sticking to my bed sheets. Over a fortnight had passed since I had first fallen ill, and I was still immobile, my feet tied to a board much of the time. This was to prevent deformity, the doctor said, but I would rather have been deformed. Nothing could be worse than spending the end of summer trapped inside a stifling sickroom, the curtains drawn up, unable even to lie on my side without assistance. My body felt like an unruly vine that had to be trained to a trellis, in order to keep its desired shape.

Boredom was my worst enemy during those days. Hespa brought me books to read, though we had to hide them whenever the doctor was present. She let me resume some of my lessons, but it was difficult to focus with the persistent discomfort in my body. I longed to get up and take a walk in the garden, but there was still something wrong with my legs. They didn't spasm as often as before, but they remained uncooperative, disobedient to my commands.

Father Parquar visited me often, bringing fresh flowers for the room, and honey from his beehives. He told me funny stories about the goings-on in the village, like how his cousin's goat had got loose and eaten the neighbor's petticoats as they dried in the sun.

I remembered something the doctor had said, and one day I asked Father Parquar, "Is Aneidis punishing me for my blood?"

"Who told you that?" the priest asked.

"Dr. Vidmont. He said that I have bad blood, and it made me sick."

"There's nothing wrong with your blood, child. Even the most virtuous among us are not immune to sickness," he said.

"But what about Allotment?" I asked. "I thought Aneidis made people sick because of their Allotment."

"Perhaps, but Allotment isn't a punishment for being bad. Think of it as a lesson, or a challenge. Even when life is abundant, and our Allotment is to be at ease, we still ought to consider what we can learn from our experiences. The irony is that when life is difficult, it's often easier to see what lessons we need to learn."

"I don't see what lesson I ought to be learning," I said. "How can I learn anything if I'm stuck in bed?"

He raised his hand, tapping his temple with one finger. "By using this," he said. "It all starts here, in the mind. No one can take your mind away from you. You can't always choose how your body feels, or what it's capable of, but you can choose what you think about it."

With that, he promised to bring me some books from his library, ones that he thought might spark my curiosity. He brought me atlases, and books about the flora and fauna of distant lands, about astronomy and cosmology. What I didn't understand, he would patiently explain. We sang songs together, practicing in rounds—my regular lessons had been suspended, for the time being, but Father Parquar thought that singing would help strengthen my core.

Dr. Vidmont returned to his practice in Rivene, but on the condition that he be called upon when I was stronger, and ready for my rehabilitation. I didn't know what he meant by this —I supposed he was waiting for my legs to begin working again. In his absence, my dreams returned, but they were confusing, frightening. I dreamed that I stood balanced atop the ferrule of a parasol, which spun endlessly in a black void. Filthy, cat-like creatures, their ears torn and their mottled fur a nest of mange, prowled about the edges, trying to claw their way into the center. Their lambent, golden eyes accused me from the darkness—how could I have neglected their care for so long? Yet their claws reeked of disease; I couldn't let them touch me. I felt dizzy, sick. The parasol wouldn't stop spinning. *Wake up!* my mind screamed, but now I was bound to the ferrule, tied up with dressmaker's tape. One of the cats had drawn so close, I could feel its whiskers scratching at the bare skin of my ankles. I struggled against my bonds. *Wake up!*

And when I did wake, my body was often bathed in sweat. At night, before I fell asleep, I would think of my mother, and try to call her up in my dreams. But she didn't return after that first fevered sleep.

I received many letters from Lady Pendrake, who had learned of my illness, and was thoroughly distraught over what had happened to me. She insisted upon visiting, but my father held her at bay, at least until I was stronger.

One evening before supper, my father appeared in the doorway of the nursery, bearing a small potted pardesu tree. It was still flowering, the blooms full and velvet-white. He went round the side of the bed and set it on the window sill, though the window was shuttered and no light shone through.

"This is a harvest bloom," he said. "It doesn't happen often, but sometimes, after the pardesu trees drop their seedpods, they flower again, though only briefly." He adjusted the pot on the sill for my viewing angle. "I just thought you might like to see them, before they drop."

His visitations had been rare, and brief. I sensed he was about to get up and leave. "Papa," I cried, ignoring the gift, "when will I be able to walk again? When can I throw this horrid plank into a fire?"

"Amardine." There was a note of impatience in his voice, and I knew I must have missed something important; I must have been slow to catch on. "Amardine," he started again, "you've reached a certain stage in your recovery—what I mean is, you're well enough now that certain things can be aired out, put out into the open. You're lucky to have survived, Dr. Vidmont says."

I waited for him to go on.

He cleared his throat. "The point is, I'm afraid...things aren't going to just go back to the way they were."

"What *things?* What do you mean, Papa?"

It was then that he explained about my legs. Imagine my muscles were like the strings of a viol. Imagine they've come unstrung—*twang!*—no longer taut, no longer capable of producing a sound. And I could imagine it, all too well. I understood his true meaning, almost instantly; I heard the hidden words knocking round between the careful layers of speech.

I was broken.

CHAPTER EIGHTEEN

"Just one more try, kit," Hespa pleaded, as I sprawled backward onto my bed. She reached out for me, but I jerked away and clamped my hands over my ears. Even that couldn't drown out Dr. Vidmont's chiding voice.

"You mustn't let the child get away with laziness," he scolded. "Children will do anything to avoid pain and suffering. It's their way. But someone must be willing to discipline them. Bring her over to me. We shall see how quickly she allows herself to fall when she has nothing soft to land on!"

Dr. Vidmont was doing his best to rehabilitate me. There was no reason, in his opinion, that I couldn't recover at least some of the function in my legs. Others had done so, he promised. He brought to the house a stack of thin, bound booklets which described case studies of arrhemia survivors, and another stack of pamphlets advertising the best in modern wheeled "spa" chairs.

But he warned my father not to present me with such a contraption too soon. "Once she's careening round the house in that doojigger, there will be no incentive to learn to walk again," he said.

I didn't think that was likely—after all, even the most expensive models shown in the pamphlets, those mechanical marvels with their dials and pumps and air tanks, had limits to their efficacy. The advertisements explained that they were designed to help their occupant up inclines and over uneven surfaces, but I couldn't see how I would ever ascend a flight of stairs, or go rambling in the woods. Besides, my father would surely opt for one of the less expensive ones, a basic model with a hard back and serviceable wheels, and congratulate himself on his economy.

But now, wilting beneath Dr. Vidmont's sharp gaze, as I was dragged from the bed by Hespa, I wished my father would just hurry up and place his order, no matter what model he decided upon. I'd been confined so long to the nursery that even the freedom of being able to leave the room by myself seemed a distant luxury.

Hespa propped me up, holding me under my arms in front of her.

"Don't let me go," I begged. "I'll fall."

"She can't stand, sir," Hespa said.

"She *thinks* she can't stand," said the doctor. "Go on, then."

Hespa released me, and I began to pitch forward. She caught me in her arms.

"No, no, no," Dr. Vidmont tutted. "I won't take my leave until I've seen you do it right."

The next time, she stepped back as soon as she took her hands off of me. I felt the retreat of her presence, the sudden emptiness at my back. And then I was windmilling helplessly, the floor rushing up to slam me hard.

"Again," Dr. Vidmont said, with a nod.

Hespa knelt down and hauled me to my feet. I struggled weakly as pain shot through my legs. This time when she let go of me, I could anticipate precisely how much it would hurt. I fell once again, trying not to cry.

"She cannot stand," Hespa said.

"You just keep working with her. One of these days, she may surprise you! One more time, now."

"No, please," I said, as the tears began to flow. Hespa lifted me up again, this time more gently.

"I'm putting the child to bed," she said.

"Then it will be your fault she remains a cripple," Dr. Vidmont said. His tone had shifted from its usual affable chiding. He wagged his finger at Hespa, scolding her as though she were a little girl. "You'll let a child manipulate you with her tears, and you will doom her to the life of an invalid. She will grow up helpless and crippled, a burden on her family. And when you are an old woman, when her father has passed, what will become of her? No, gussey, you don't want that life for her.

Let the girl fall."

"I'm sorry, kit," she whispered as she let go of me. Once again I felt my legs buckle, and the floor battered me up and down the length of my body. But it was no use. I couldn't figure out how to stop from falling.

"That's enough for today," the doctor said. "But you'll need to continue practicing three times a day for the next fortnight, for a half hour at a time. She'll tire of falling eventually. Where there's a will, there's a way, isn't that right, gussey?"

"I've heard it said," Hespa replied.

"But you have to believe it," Dr. Vidmont said. "That's why some people succeed, and others fail. It all comes down to the will."

The next day, Hespa tried to rouse me from my bed to do the standing exercise. I refused, gripping the bedpost in both hands so she couldn't dislodge me. My whole body ached with bruises, but the worst part wasn't hitting the floor. The worst part was the terrible dread that overcame me right at the moment of release, when I felt my muscles trying to engage, and there was nothing I could do to encourage them.

I read the booklets the doctor had left about those arrhemia survivors who had learned to walk again. Some had recovered fully, and others required the aid of a walking stick. Some could only walk for short periods of time before returning to a spa chair. But how had they done it? What command had they given their body to propel it back to a semblance of mobility? There was nothing in the case studies about the patients' battle of the will.

I tried again the following day, and the day after that. Hespa would let me fall once or twice, then help me back to my bed, and make another attempt a few hours later. But it was no use. My mind was soft, weak. I thought about Dr. Vidmont's prediction for my future, and one day, after yet another failed attempt at the exercise, I let myself give in fully to the terror of it.

What *would* happen to me when my father passed away? I wished he would visit, and tell me that the doctor was wrong. But I was alone in the nursery, with nothing but my books, and I couldn't even concentrate on them well enough to distract myself. My stomach began to lurch, as though a tiger had just leaped out from beneath the bed, except the feeling wouldn't recede. My heart raced and my chest tightened, and I couldn't think about anything except my own yawning chasm of a future. I wished, for the first time, that I had a thimble glass of Dr. Vidmont's miracle oil. At least it would have calmed my racing nerves.

For what seemed like forever, I lay locked inside my own body, which wanted nothing more than to flee the scene. I watched the shadows creep across the room as the sun passed overhead, wondering when I would feel the grass beneath my feet, or even sit on the veranda and watch the light fade over the treeline. Father Parquar had said my illness wasn't a punishment from Aneidis, which was a relief, but only until my mind circled back to my own culpability. If only I hadn't left Pendrake Hall that night and made my foolish trek through the woods. Of course it wasn't God's fault—it was my own.

I didn't move when Hespa brought my tea that afternoon. She set the tray beside the bed and I flinched as she touched my shoulder.

"Are you awake, kit?" she asked.

I didn't reply.

"I know you're awake. I know you're not very happy with me, either," she said. Still, I didn't answer. "I'm not going to make you try to stand. I don't think it will do a whit of good, even if you fall on the floor a hundred times."

I turned to look at her, my eyes blurry with tears. "I don't care, Hespa. Just let me die."

"Don't say things like that," she said. "You'll be out of that bed soon enough. Did your father tell you that he ordered a special chair for you?"

"No," I said, my voice quavering. "He hardly ever looks in on me at all. And why should he? I'm so stupid, Hespa. And now I'm a cripple, besides. You know he doesn't like broken things. He wants to get rid of me."

"No, no, no," she said, pulling out her handkerchief and wiping away my tears. "Don't ever say that. You're his only daughter, and he loves you more than anyone in the world. Why, just today he had a man come out and see about knocking down a wall and making your washroom easier to get into with your chair. Would he knock down a wall in his own house if he wanted to be rid of you?"

"But why won't he see me?" I asked. He hadn't visited the

nursery since he'd brought me the pardesu flower, and its blossoms had dropped days ago. "Why does he act the way he does?"

"I know there's been a lot on his mind," Hespa said, defending him, as she always did. "But I'll try to talk to him. In the meantime, you need to eat something."

"I'm not hungry," I lied.

"You need to keep up your strength."

"What's the point if I can't *do* anything?" I said, with a snarl. I hadn't meant to address Hespa that way, but a surge of anger rose from the pit of my stomach before I could shove it back down. She stared at me as though I had uttered the words in some demonic language, then averted her gaze.

"I know it's been hard for you, kit, but there's no reason to take a tone with me."

I scowled in reply. But even so, I knew I would have to shape up and learn to bite my tongue. I needed Hespa on my side, after all—I was helpless without her. When she offered me my tisane, I accepted it without further rebuke, and held it beneath my nose to inhale the fragrant steam.

As I picked at the biscuits on my tray, I heard the crunch of gravel on the drive, and the sound of heavy hooves making their approach.

"Is someone here?" I asked. My excitement over the prospect of visitors turned sour when I recalled all of the letters my aunt had written; I ought to have known she wouldn't stay away forever.

"I'll go see," Hespa said, leaving me with the tray.

It wasn't long before my worry was confirmed. Lady Pendrake's high, shrill voice rang from the front of the house as Hespa received her. There was quite a clatter as she dropped her boots to the floor of the vestibule and rattled the cupboard doors. She didn't wait for my father to be called in before coming down the hall and barging into my room.

"Oh, my poor darling," she said when she saw me, rushing to the chair by my bedside. "Did your father give you my letters? I wrote ever so many. It was the least I could do, to keep your spirits up in this dark time."

"Yes," I said. "But Dr. Vidmont thought it would tire me too much to write back."

"Of course, sweet one. Don't even think of it. I only want you to be well." She reached out and put a cool hand on my forehead. "Beatrice told me what happened. You can't imagine how distraught I felt about it. I wish with all my heart that you'd come to me, instead of running off into the night. What were you thinking?"

"Beatrice told you?" I asked.

"She said you girls were dressing your hair, and she tried to give you a more fashionable cut. But you weren't happy with it and got upset with her. Goodness knows, she had no business cutting your hair. But I'm sure we could have fixed it. There was no reason at all that you should have left."

"Did she tell you that she locked me out on the window ledge?" *Or that she pulled my ears and called me a freak?*

Her mouth drooped and her hands fluttered to her lap. "I didn't hear about that," she managed, finally. "But honestly. You could have just knocked on the front door."

Before I could find a reply, my father strode into the room.

"Ellinora," he said, by way of greeting. I waited for him to come over, to adjust my pillow, to tuck the coverlet up around me—something, anything, to reverse the deficit of his attentions. But he took a seat across the room, barely even glancing at me.

My aunt sniffled, and withdrew her handkerchief. "I'm sorry," she said, dabbing her nose. "This is so hard for me, you know."

"Of course," my father said. "It's a difficult situation. I wasn't sure when Amardine would be feeling well enough to have visitors. But there's been a lot of improvement."

Lady Pendrake shook her head. "I can't imagine. I can't imagine. It's awful, so awful."

"We're managing as best we can," my father replied. "I have a spa chair on order from Cereval, and I'm working on some renovations to the house to make it more accessible."

"Then—you don't think she'll ever walk again?"

My father finally looked at me. I met his gaze, giving him my most piteous expression, willing him to come over to my side. Surely he couldn't say what he was about to say without holding my hand, without smoothing my hair.

"I believe that window has closed," he said, without rising from his seat.

Lady Pendrake let out a great, shuddering sob, her thin shoulders trembling as she covered her face with her handkerchief. "I'm sorry," she said again, lifting her eyes from their concealment. They shone with fresh tears. "It's just—so hard to take it all in. And to think what *could* have happened—we ought to thank Aneidis that the poor child survived at all. Oh, brother, you can't imagine what it's like to lose a child. I didn't even get a chance to meet my little Theore. Be grateful you were spared that, at least."

"Yes, it could have been far worse," my father said, with a shrug.

"How can you speak so coolly?" Lady Pendrake asked, her voice rising. "I could hardly believe the letter you sent. It was so brusque, so matter-of-fact. As though you thought nothing of the effect your words would have on me. I've been beside myself for weeks, waiting for your summons, waiting to see my poor little niece. And all this time thinking of my own son, who never had a chance to draw breath."

"I am sorry that it affected you so," my father replied. He had drawn back in his chair, as though buffeted by dark wings. That was how I imagined Lady Pendrake's outbursts—as a demon flying forth to pummel anyone who drew her ire.

"I didn't eat for two days after I read your letter," she confessed, her voice dropping to a whisper. "You must have known I would blame myself."

"I don't blame you," he said. And then my father—the man who would not be moved by tricks or tears—rose from his chair, not to comfort me, but to lay a hand on Lady Pen-drake's shoulder, thus inflicting the worst betrayal of my young life.

She gave a violent twitch, then stood up and turned to him, pressing herself into his arms. He held her awkwardly as she practically collapsed into him, burying her face in his shoulder.

"Please," he said, "there's no need to be upset."

"No need! No need! You *don't* understand!" she wailed.

"This is too much for you. Let's go to the parlor, where you can sit more comfortably. I'll bring up a bottle of wine."

"Papa?" I called to him, as he escorted Lady Pendrake from the room. He turned in the doorway to look at me.

"Not now, Amardine," he said.

"Will you come back?"

He paused. "What do you need?"

"I just...wanted to talk to you," I said.

He gave a brief nod, then exited the room.

After the two of them had left, I turned over on my side and tried to curl up into myself as much as my body would allow. I tucked my arm round my knees and drew them up, wrapping my arms round one of my pillows. It smelled faintly of lavender and alfalfa, and the sun on warm grass. I buried my face in it and began to cry, unabashedly, now that I was alone. I tried to imagine that I was cradled in my father's arms, though I had no memory of such a thing to draw upon, and my body ached from the emptiness that enclosed it.

I cried until I was all out of tears, and when I had finally wrung myself out, I wiped my face and let my gaze settle on the little pardesu tree sitting on the nightstand. I reached out and touched the tight clusters of leaves, trying to connect to the tree's spirit, but I sensed nothing. "*Light*," I whispered, but nothing happened; the word wasn't powerful enough to overcome the darkness within me.

I didn't expect my father to return that day, but he did. My tears had dried by then, and if my face was still blotchy, he didn't remark on it.

He sat down in the chair Lady Pendrake had taken earlier, beside my bed.

"How are you feeling?" he asked.

I stared at him, giving him a tiny shrug.

"What did you want to talk about?"

Again, I didn't reply. Any movement, any attempt at speech, might trigger the return of tears, and I didn't want to frighten him away. No doubt he was at his limit, after consoling my aunt.

His gaze drifted out the window.

"You left earlier," I said, trying not to sound accusatory. I had to be careful with my tone as well, lest he feel wounded and withdraw.

"Your aunt needed me," he said, looking back at me. "She gets very emotional at times like these. It's hard for her, to see you like this. You know that she lost a child, several years ago."

"But it wasn't even born yet," I protested.

He shook his head. "That's an unfeeling thing to say, Amardine."

I winced at the unexpected rebuke. "I didn't mean to make her feel bad, Papa."

"I'm sure you didn't. I just wanted you to understand why it bothers her so much. It's the same to her, and that's what matters."

His voice had taken on a flat tone, making me think, for a moment, that he had fallen under a spell. But no, that was just how he spoke sometimes. I didn't know what caused his lack of affect, but I understood the disappointment in his eyes, that he could have produced this dozy, thoughtless daughter.

He was right, of course—I *had* been selfish to demand his attention when Lady Pendrake was in such a state. I had been unfeeling, not truly considering the extent of her loss. I was ashamed.

The chair creaked as he stood up, finished with the conversation.

"Don't be alarmed if you hear workmen outside your room tomorrow," he said. "They'll be expanding the washroom, and fitting a new door."

ℰℭ

By the time the chair finally arrived, the worst of the summer heat had lifted, and the nights had grown cool. One early afternoon, my singing lesson was interrupted by the sound of horses plodding up the drive. I fell silent and listened as the iron gate that connected the vestibule to the courtyard creaked open, and voices carried down the hall. My instructor, an alma who came from Rivene twice a week, tried to continue the lesson, but it was no use, especially when Hespa entered the parlor and told me she had a surprise for me outside.

She picked me up and sat me on a bench in the courtyard to watch the unpacking of the chair. Maslin broke open the crate with a hammer, spilling sawdust everywhere, revealing a strange assortment of pieces.

By now, a small audience had gathered to see it. Marguerite and Esmay slipped away from their duties in the kitchen, and Father Parquar walked up from his bungalow, no doubt alerted by the carriage. Maslin waited for my father to arrive, and then the three men went about sorting through the wheels and hoses and wooden bits on the flagstones.

The chair was comprised of two large wheels with double rims, and two small caster wheels. The back was made of carved mahogany, and was shorter than I'd expected, only rising up enough to support the lower part of my torso. But it had a cushion upholstered in wine-red velvet, shaped to fit round a small person's body. The seat came with two cushions, one covered in velvet, for cool weather, and another wrapped in silk, for summer. The arms, which were made of smooth curved wood, were removable as well, and there was a wicker basket I could attach to the side to carry sundries. But the most remarkable thing was the mechanism that gave the chair an extra boost of power. It had a hand pump that could be pressed whenever I was idle, and connected to a hose that looped round the back and attached to an air tank under the seat. The tank, inscribed with runes glittering with diamond dust, was virtually indestructible, my father said. There was also a lever I could pull that functioned as a brake, forcing air back into the tank.

My father pored over the instructions as the other two men set about organizing the pieces and trying to put them together. It took them until close to suppertime, because my father insisted on inspecting each piece and sanding down any rough edges, even though I couldn't see any, and the pressure through the hose had to be tested, and the wheels well-oiled. I could hardly stand the wait. When at last Hespa settled me in the chair and I pushed myself down the flagstone path, everyone cheered, and that night, Marguerite made my favorite custard with pardesu and rosewater.

I soon learned how to use the air pump, and when not to use it—once, I nearly spilled out of my chair trying to cross the threshold from the nursery to the courtyard when taking the step too quickly. After that, my father filled the step in with a ramp, and even removed the stairs in the courtyard leading up to the walkway that encircled it. He had them replaced with a zigzagging ramp, designed with regular flat intervals, making precise use of the power the air pump could provide. The workmen had to take out one of the oak trees, and remove a large flowerbed to do so, but I never heard my father complain about it.

By these means, I could access the second floor of the house through the balcony door, which led to the gallery at the top of the main staircase. Hespa shook her head and warned me to be careful when I raced from one end of the gallery to the other, but I was heedless, exhilarated with the heady rush of liberation.

My arms grew strong, even as my legs wasted away. I learned to lever myself from my chair onto my bed or onto the divan where I often sat to study my lessons. But for all this freedom my father gave back to me, he remained elusive. In his mind, I supposed, he had fixed the problem, to the full extent possible, and there was no reason for him to remain where he could not be useful.

Once, while sitting in the shade of the courtyard garden, I told Father Parquar about the visit with my aunt. As it happened, the priest was delivering some herbs for my father —ones he hoped would lift his melancholy.

"Why should *he* be melancholy?" I demanded, slamming my hand down on the pump. The air hissed through the hose. "How can he pity her, and not me?"

"Do you know what it means to appease someone?" Father Parquar asked.

I shook my head.

"It's when you give someone what they want, because you know they will make your life a misery until they get it," he explained. Then, lowering his voice, he went on, "I think you'll agree that Lady Pendrake can be quite miserable when she wants something."

"She's like a child," I said, then put my hand to my mouth as I waited for him to rebuke me. But he only laughed.

"Your papa doesn't care for you less than he cares about his sister," he said. "It's just that you haven't learned to get under his skin, as she has."

"But that isn't right," I said indignantly. "You oughtn't treat a person worse just because they're less troublesome."

"I agree."

"Then why does he do it?"

Father Parquar sighed. "You mean, why do people treat poorly those who least deserve it? I wish I had an answer for you, child."

"I suppose I'll just have to learn to make him more miserable," I said.

He laughed as a breeze stirred the wind chimes in the nearby mulberry tree, making a lonesome clatter, like coins falling from cold fingers.

"Oh, I'm sure you'll figure that out in time," he replied.

CHAPTER NINETEEN

"I SAY, YOU OUGHT TO SEND her somewhere, Desmarius," Lord Pendrake declared. It was a bright day in early autumn, though a recent rainstorm had left the air as clingy as a wet blanket. The parlor doors were open to the courtyard, and a carafe of wine sat on a low table. My father sat on one side of the table, smoking a cheroot, while my aunt and uncle, spaced out like bookends, occupied the divan. Beatrice and Bianca were scuttling a hoop outside as I sat by the latticed window, like a plant that cannot tolerate full sun, trying to work on my lessons. It was the first time since my illness that the Pendrakes had descended on Guildenflore in full force, though my aunt had made a few solo excursions to the house, just to make certain my treatment wasn't being neglected.

"Not to one of those brutish institutions in the city, though!"

she said, pouring her second glass of wine.

My father raised an eyebrow. "Brutish? Has your opinion of the sanitarium changed since you sent our aunt away?"

Lady Pendrake gave a little shudder as she raised her glass. "That was a family decision," she said. "And I don't mean to imply they're *all* bad. I just meant that it's too far for a child of her tender age to be away from home. Why, it would take a week just to get there, and who knows what could happen on the road? *I* say you ought hire a proper nurse and a proper governess. That's the first thing I'd do. Hespa is a dear, of course, but she simply doesn't have the training. And a good education will make all the difference for a child with such limitations. I'd be more than happy to help you find a suitable candidate."

"I'm sure you would," my father mused, tapping the ash out of his cheroot.

"Yes, of course, but until the walking issue is resolved, a more rigorous academic schedule would only be a distraction," Lord Pendrake interjected. "If she were my child, I would focus entirely on physical rehabilitation. I'm in agreement with Dr. Vidmont in this matter. God knows, my legs pain me as well, but I still get out for my daily constitutional. It's all about the will, I say."

"He read that in a book, you know," said Lady Pendrake, favoring her husband with a smile that perfectly caricaturized fondness.

My uncle took no notice of her. "When I was a boy, my grandfather, the first Lord Percy, used to go round in a spa chair.

They didn't have such sleek contraptions in those days, mind you. Now, *he* had some bad luck—shattered one leg in a riding accident when he was a young man, then lost the other foot to infection decades later. They had to saw it right off." He gave me a pointed look, as though nothing less than a series of trauma and mutilation could excuse my condition.

My father said, "Amardine, why don't you go out-of-doors and play with your cousins?"

My hands twisted the fabric of my dress. I hadn't told him everything about what had happened at Pendrake Hall. I'd left out the part where they had made fun of my ears—somehow I just couldn't bear the shame of recounting it. He seemed to accept Lady Pendrake's version of the story: that Beatrice had mangled my hair in a misguided attempt to improve my looks, and I had overreacted in a most dramatic fashion, fleeing without even giving my aunt a chance to rectify the situation. She was fond of bringing it up whenever she came to visit, as though to remind my father that my current condition was entirely the result of my own foolishness, no matter how she might wring her hands and insist on taking the blame.

And the more often I heard this story, the more the details of that night began to take on a dreamlike quality, until I almost doubted my own memories. I *had* been foolish and impulsive, and I would have to live with that now, for the rest of my life.

I was about to say that I was feeling ill, but was interrupted by the heavy *clomp* of hard-soled boots outside, as Beatrice flounced into the parlor.

"I'm hungry," she said. "Where is that cake you brought, Mother?"

Lady Pendrake clapped her hands. "Of course! The cake! Why don't you take tea with Miss Amardine?" she said. "She ought to have some fresh air, I think. You can sit at the table under the mulberry trees, how does that sound?"

Beatrice fixed me with a sullen stare. "I'll only sit with her if I can have cake," she said.

So it was arranged. We sat under the mulberry trees and Hespa brought out a tray bearing my miniature porcelain tea set. She hung back, keeping a watchful eye on us, for which I was grateful—she was the only one who knew the full extent of my cousins' abuses. But then a few of the neighbors arrived at the house, having spied the Pendrake's Cartouche on the road, and in the ensuing flurry of activity, she was called away.

I felt my stomach sink as Hespa retreated into the house, leaving me alone with my cousins. The sight of me in my wheeled chair had shocked them into silence at first, as though they didn't quite know what to say to me, but now they would be forced to confront the issue.

Not far away, Bianca was rooting round behind the herb pots, talking to herself and occasionally cracking a stick. Beatrice played with her spoon, tapping on the tiny cups to see if they rang—"that's how you know it's quality," she explained, and stared at me from under that heavy black fringe, as though waiting for me to acknowledge her superior taste. I tried to think of something clever to say, but all my thoughts pin-wheeled off like firecrackers under that baleful glower. Thankfully, the silence was interrupted when Lady Pendrake emerged from the shadows beneath the balcony, bearing a pyramid of petit fours and a glass of wine.

She served us by her very own hand, a single black ringlet escaping from beneath her bonnet, releasing the scent of jasmine. Beatrice popped one of the cakes into her mouth. "I'm bored," she complained, scowling at me as though it were all my fault.

Lady Pendrake patted her daughter's head fondly. "You just be a dear and keep Miss Amardine company, won't you? At least you don't have to entertain that dreadful Miss Hathervale."

For a moment, the sight of the cakes whisked away my unease, which had been growing ever since the Cartouche had rumbled up the drive. They were arranged with cappa sprigs on a plate inlaid with the amber glow of alchemical coldstones. Each wonderfully geometric morsel was decorated in exquisite detail, with tiny but identifiable flowers interspersed between satin buttercream and edible gold-leaf lace. "Who made these, Aunt Ellinora?" I exclaimed. "They ought to be in a museum."

Lady Pendrake smiled. "Oh! I'm pleased you like them. But I don't think they display cake in museums, dear."

Beatrice reached for one, examining it critically. "Doesn't your pastry chef ever make you petit fours?"

"We don't have a pastry chef," I said.

"Why not?"

"I don't suppose we eat enough pastries."

Beatrice frowned. "Well, you must eat them sometimes. You don't buy them in a shop, do you? I heard they put sawdust in the flour in a lot of those places."

"They do?" I turned to Lady Pendrake for confirmation.

"Now, Honey Bee, you mustn't frighten your cousin with such stories. I'm sure there's nothing wrong with going to a bakery, as long as you're smart about it."

"It's *true*," Beatrice said, reaching for another cake. "You said it yourself, I remember."

Lady Pendrake stood regarding her for a long moment, then gulped down her wine and snatched one of the petit fours for herself. She gave me a watery little smile and went back inside.

I took a long time choosing mine, and let it sit on my plate so that I could admire it while Beatrice toppled the pyramid and ate three or four more of the little cakes in quick succession.

"It's interesting what your maid did with your hair," she said. "But I suppose she had no choice but to cut it that short."

I didn't reply.

"You're a very dull girl," she said, watching me. "What do you do all day, now that you can't walk?"

"I read, mostly. I like to draw and sing, too." When I said it aloud, it didn't sound so terrible. But all the same, I missed the freedom of wandering the gardens and the woods. I wanted to show her the best path for skipping rope, or explore the old stone mill listing at the edge of the woods. I wanted to invent cities with her in the earthen warrens beneath the greenhouse flower beds. Well, I didn't want to do these things with *her* perhaps, but with a sort of ideal friend, who was good at making up names and other details.

"That doesn't sound like a very nice life," Beatrice said. "When are you going to be able to walk again?"

I felt my cheeks flush. "I don't know."

"Mother says you ought to go to an almary. I heard her talking about it with the Countess."

"Which one?" I asked, innocently.

"Lady Chandray," she said, frowning. "I'll have you know, they're working on a plan for you. Lady Chandray's father is a prelate, you know. They have connections in the Church."

I picked at a chunk of seashell-shaped frosting with my fork. I wouldn't ask. I *wouldn't*. What did Beatrice know, truly? She would lie about anything. Once she told me how my own mother had died, only it turned out she'd stolen the story from a news article about a whole different opera singer.

"Don't you want to know what Mother is planning? Or are you too dull to care?" Her mouth twisted in a smug little smile. "She's been writing to an almary to take you in. *She thinks she can get you healed.*"

My heart flailed. I turned the fork over and nibbled on my cake, but in truth I found it better to look at than to eat. The icing flowers were so sugary they made my teeth hurt, the buttercream so spiced with rosewater it tasted like a mouthful of shaving foam. Every time I took a bite, all I could think about was vomiting rose petals. I imagined a scarlet-black river of them, cascading out of my mouth and filling the courtyard.

"Do you want to hear something disgusting?" Beatrice asked, as though she had just read my mind.

I slid my plate away. "What's that?"

"Once—" she wiped her fingers on her handkerchief —"once, Bifa piddled in her petticoat, and instead of telling her maid, she just took it off herself *and left it on my bed.*"

I wrinkled my nose and made the appropriate noises of disgust.

"That's just what she's like," Beatrice said with a flippant little wave, and took more tea. Her hand looked huge, wrapped round the handle of the teapot, a grownup's hand almost, strangling the delicate stem.

"What was the countess wearing?" I asked.

"What?"

"When she came and talked to Aunt Ellinora," I said, cautiously circling back to the previous topic of conversation, hoping it would start her up again on the subject, so that I could glean more information without seeming desperate for it. "What were her clothes like?"

"You want to know what her clothes looked like?"

"Yes. Was her dress very fine?"

"Well," she said, warming to the topic, "if you must know, the countess looked very elegant. She wore a pale tangerine color, with cream-colored stripes. You know how all the ladies are wearing stripes this season? I'm having a few new things made up from the plates in the latest *Pattern Living*. Of course, my dresses will have to be made of lighter fabric, since we'll be spending the season in Carabilos." She chattered on about the upcoming trip, scarcely allowing me to reply. If there was one subject that could draw Beatrice out of her sour reticence, it was that of her own glamorous life. I realized I would get no further with her. Frustrated, I stabbed the icing seashell with my tiny fork, but the little dessert plate wasn't imbued with coldstones, and the icing had grown soft in the sun. All I did was smear it on the plate.

That was when Bianca marched over to us and spied the half-empty plate of petit fours. I'd nearly forgotten about her. She raised her stick in outrage.

"You've been eating cakes!" she screeched, waving the stick from the middle in a wild arc as I tried to duck away from the back end.

"We saved some for you," I said.

"You didn't tell me you were eating cakes!" She slammed the stick down onto the table, startling the teacups. Beatrice leaped back. Then, with a single swipe, Bianca knocked the contents of the table to the ground. My fine porcelain tea set cascaded over the edge and smashed to pieces on the painted tiles.

"You stupid brat!" Beatrice shouted. "You've ruined the cakes!"

"Ha!" cried Bianca, as she plucked one from the ground,

soggy and smeared. "Bet you won't eat them now!" She stuffed it into her mouth, her angelic features distorting into something horrid, like a blood-sucking bird. "Go on then, have your little tea party with the cripple. Oh, what a lovely tea party!"

"You know Mother makes me play with her. You get to do whatever you like because you're the baby. A great big, piddling baby!"

"Take it back!" Bianca shouted. "Take it back!"

"I won't! It's true and everyone knows it! Even *she* knows it," Beatrice said, with a sly nod in my direction.

Bianca flew at her sister, hitting her about the face with her smeary hands. Then Beatrice grabbed Bianca round the throat and began to throttle her.

"Stop it!" I cried, and began to call for someone, anyone, to put an end to this madness.

Bianca pried off her sister's hands and gave her a good kick in the shins. "You be quiet," she said, pointing a finger at me, "or I'll turn you out of that chair!"

"You wouldn't dare," said Beatrice, rubbing her injured leg.

"I would," Bianca insisted, and then began to chant in a singsong voice, "*Amardine, Amardine, skinny as a string bean. She lost her legs, now she's all pegs, and she will never be a queen!*"

Beatrice shrieked with laughter. "Let's see her peg legs!"

It was a shock to me, how quickly it all changed. One moment I was safe in my chair; the next, they were wrestling with it, tipping it back so all I could see were their twisted, laughing faces, dark against the brilliant sunlight. I clutched at the armrests so tightly that the oils in my hands left permanent imprints in the wood—long darkened fingerprints, inhuman-looking marks. I held on as they toppled the chair onto its side, jolting me and throwing me onto the ground, despite my best efforts to hang on. Then I was writhing in a pile of ceramic shards, my petticoats bunched up round my waist as I hugged the silk cushion to my chest. I couldn't curl up to save my life. I could only cringe as the two of them pointed at my braced legs and cackled together like magpies.

"Poor cousin," Beatrice said, when she had recovered herself. "I'm so glad I'm not like you. I make sure to thank Aneidis for that every morning when I write my petitions." She extended her foot and began stroking my ribs with the toe of her shoe. Bianca watched her with a hungry look, then stood over me with tentative glee, lowering her foot down onto my side, testing the weight of her own malice. Then she hopped back and dropped into a crouch. Hovering over me, she yanked my hair back with one hand, pinching my nose shut with the other.

"Help me hold her down," Bianca said. The elder sister's shadow fell over me as she crouched down, smoothing her skirts. I could do nothing as she wrenched my shoulder back, forcing me to lie face up and look at her. I could hardly even breathe. I felt as though I were melting into the tiles beneath me, leaving my body behind, as though I no longer belonged to this panting creature restrained on the ground.

Then Bianca was scooping up the cake from the ground and stuffing it into my mouth. I shook my head violently and tried to fend her off with my hand, but Beatrice grabbed my wrists and locked them within her iron grip.

I coughed and spat out gobs of sugary frosting, my mind working furiously. "My chair," I gasped, pointing one finger of my entrapped hand. That stilled them for a moment. "I need my chair."

"You want your chair?" Beatrice said.

"Please."

She released my wrists, then got to her feet. Still glowering at me, she bent and righted the chair, then pushed it awkwardly back onto the path. It turned my stomach to see her handling it, rolling it back and forth before her with casual cruelty. But at least she was no longer holding me down.

"Don't take it away," I pleaded. "I need it."

Bianca looked at the chair, then back at me, then back at the chair again. She leaped to her feet and scrambled into it. "Bigby, push me!" she shouted.

Her sister laughed and whirled her round, tipping the chair back as Bianca squealed in delight.

"Bye-bye, cripple!" Bianca said, waving over her shoulder at me as Beatrice began pushing her down the garden path, picking up speed. I heard my chair rolling away, the two of them laughing as they made for the courtyard gate, and disappeared from sight.

"*Amardine, Amardine, skinny as a string bean...*"

The tears flowed freely then. I trembled all over, my heart shuddering, my body wrung out like a limp dishrag. It was only then that I realized my petticoat was wet with more than just perspiration, and my face grew hot with shame. I tasted sugary frosting on my lips, and I thought I might be sick. I'd let them take my chair! I hated the mere thought of them sitting in it, yanking it this way and that, infusing the mahogany with the oils of their grasping hands. But at least they'd left me alone for the moment. That was all I really needed, just a moment alone, to pull myself together.

I twisted onto my side and pulled myself up on my elbows. I found an abandoned tea napkin lying on the ground nearby, and used it to wipe my face. Then I dragged myself over to the chair Beatrice had abandoned. I sat in front of it, straining to get my elbows up onto the seat. I could manage that step of the process, but the seat of the chair was too high; I couldn't get the leverage I needed to pull myself up. I sank back onto the tiles, my skirts spread out around me, and began picking the shattered bits of my tea set out of my arms, where they had poked in and stuck. I allowed myself a moment to mourn the ruined tea set. It had been a birthday gift from Grandame the previous spring, and I had loved how pretty it looked, when it was all set up and perfectly arranged on a white linen table-cloth. My dress was also ruined, encrusted with cake, stained with milk and tea.

Hespa, where are you? I expected her to come out any moment and collect the tea things. But no one came. I could hear distant laughter from the south lawn, and knew then that I was forsaken.

I lay back on the tile, cooling in the long afternoon shadows. The sun flicked through the mulberry trees, blinding me in sudden flashes. The branches above me trembled as crows took wing, cawing as they aligned themselves against the sky. They flew in a strange formation that reminded me of the cruorflies, rising up out of the thick sludge of the swamp, visible for just that brief instant as they blotted the reflected moonlight on the water. The memory of that night, when I'd taken flight from Pendrake Hall, came flooding back to me then. Was there something I could have done differently to avert my fate? What if I had been more agreeable, done everything they wanted, let Beatrice chop off my hair? What if I *had* gone back through the front door, and called upon Lady Pendrake for help?

The air around me felt stale, blanketing me in a strange yet familiar musk. In the mulberry tree, the wind chimes began to murmur. They were hanging from a bough only a few feet away, the painted wooden pipes clattering softly together, even though there was no wind. That was strange, wasn't it? Then the chimes began to mutter frantically, like a woman made hysterical by her own secrets. I squeezed my eyes shut, trying to shut out the scent of the perfume and the squawking of birds, to focus on that voice, to pick out syllables and will them to make sense. And then the noise seemed to sharpen, its random atonality converging upon language, and the voice said, *I'm listening, little one.*

I pushed myself up onto my elbows, lifting my head to listen. Had I imagined that, as well? Was there truly a voice in the chimes, or was someone lurking in the trees? If there was an intruder in the garden, I could do nothing to fend them off.

"Is that you, Mama?" I whispered.

The leaves on the trees didn't stir as the chimes rattled again, this time with a throaty laugh that did not sound at all maternal. *You don't have time. You don't have time. You don't have time.*

Time for what? I mouthed.

To be like thisss...

The voice was dissolving into chaos, but those last words went straight up my spine and my legs jerked as though controlled by invisible strings. I stood, for the first time in months, but I could not move; my limbs were under the command of another. Then my legs went limp, and I fell heavily into the chair, gasping. It all happened in an instant. I could only sit there with the perfect composure that sometimes accompanies a terrible shock.

"Who are you?" I called out. I craned my neck round. No one was there.

I tried to kick my foot out, to recreate what had just happened, but my legs seized up, refusing to cooperate. I was still as crippled as ever before. But I was still me, as well. I flexed my fingers in small, deliberate motions, just to be sure. I looked round again, still seeing nothing out of sort. The chimes had gone still, and above the sound of my racing heart, I heard the gate squeal open as my cousins returned from their revel. They raced up the path toward me and parked my chair several feet away. I was relieved to see that it was still in one piece, and apparently no worse for wear.

"Was Mother out here?" Beatrice asked, giving me a suspicious look. She did not expect to find me moved, and there was fear in her eyes; what if I had spilled all?

"No," I said, evenly.

"What about that maid of yours? That great beast of a woman?"

I stared at her, a faint smile cooling on my lips. "She hasn't been outside."

Beatrice stood dumb and still, as though the cogs in her head might stop turning the moment she moved from her place. Bianca was hanging back, thumb in her mouth. Her hair had caught the sunlight, and she looked like a wisp of flame, agitated, white hot in the face.

"Come along, Bifa," Beatrice said, waving her toward the door behind us. "Let's go inside and get something to drink."

Bianca followed her sister into the house, giving me a furtive look as she passed, as though she knew something strange had happened but could not put a name to it.

I couldn't explain it, either. I listened for the chimes again, half in anticipation, half in dread. I tried to slip back into that ordered vision, in which everything that had happened was part of a pattern and made sense. It was in that moment the chimes had spoken to me.

There was a slight rustle in the leaves above. I tensed, wondering what new terror was in store for me. The sound intensified as something fell through the branches behind me. *Just some berries*, I told myself, trying to quell my racing heart. A few of the berries had already begun to drop, staining the flagstones a dark purple. I craned my head round to see how close I had come to being splattered with ripe fruit.

A songbird lay on the ground, motionless, its feet curled up in deathly repose. As I recoiled from the sight of it, the rustling started up again, and another bird dropped from the branches. There was no chatter in the boughs, I realized, as the whole tree seemed to shake. And then they were falling all round me, pelting the flagstones, landing on my shoulder, on my lap. I covered my head with my hands as at least a score of brightly-colored finches dropped dead from the tree, as though their very life force had been drained away by the unseen presence lurking in the shadows.

CHAPTER TWENTY

I WAS STILL SITTING IN THE wrought-iron chair, the mess of broken pottery and dead birds at my feet, when Hespa finally emerged from the house, carrying a dustpan. She was about to toss the contents into the bushes when she caught sight of me, then looked at the birds littering the ground. Her eyes went wide.

"What happened, kit?" she asked, as she hurried over and set the dustpan on a nearby chair. Bits of broken crystal glittered purple in the sunlight.

"I don't know," I said helplessly, gesturing to the feathery lumps that lay all round me, to the shattered porcelain. I couldn't explain the dead birds. And the rest of it...it was best not to dwell on the humiliation. I was safe now, and that was all that mattered. "Bianca got a bit wild over the cakes."

"Too much sugar in those cakes," she said, pushing my chair over to where I sat. I told her I'd let my cousins play with it while I rested in the shade, but I wasn't sure she believed me. I turned the armrest and lifted myself up on my hands, sliding back into the comfort of the wheeled contraption. Hespa moved to help me, but I shook my head vigorously, fending her off with a glare.

"I can do it myself," I snapped.

"I know you can, kit. But there's no excuse for poor manners."

"I'm sorry," I said. "The cakes made my stomach hurt."

"No wonder. If something is too pretty to eat, it's probably poison."

"I—I need to change my clothes," I said. Hespa took one look at my face and didn't ask for an explanation.

"Let's get you inside," she said. "I set out a fresh frock for you, just in case."

I was allowed to take to my bed for the rest of the visit, on account of the stomachache, and was in far too much pain to say my goodbyes to my cousins. It was only a small lie. Then again, I'd been lying almost continuously to Hespa ever since she had found me under the mulberry trees. The falsehoods had come easily to me, but they prickled all the same.

She smoothed the coverlet over me. "You would tell me, kit, if those girls hurt you?"

I nodded, fluffing the blanket over me to conceal the fact that I was still trembling.

"You wouldn't be too proud to say something?"

"*No*," I huffed. She turned, about to take her leave.

"Hespa?"

"What is it?"

"How do you know the difference between a demon and a good spirit?"

She regarded me silently for a long moment. I knew she must be thinking about the dead birds in the courtyard. Would she take care of them herself? Would she tell my father? No doubt he would think they were infected, but he hadn't seen them all fall at once. Hespa knew the real score.

"I just want to know," I said, "how you can tell the difference. How you can tell if one wants to be helpful."

"You mustn't meddle with them," she whispered. "Not ever. Do you understand?"

"But you talk about spights and other phantasms," I protested. "You taught me about fennel and marsh-hock and sea salt."

"Because I was trying to protect you," she said.

"But what if it's too late and you need to know?"

She shook her head. "Oh, nothing is getting into this house, kit. I'll see to it."

She had that determined look in her eye that foretold certain, quiet victory. And I knew then I had erred in asking her too many questions. Now she was sure to button the whole house up with her circles of warding, drawn in chalk, consecrated with the burnt ashes of herbs. Not even an umbral demon-prince could get a message through her lines, I thought, with a twinge of regret.

I remembered something then—the dustpan she had been about to toss when she saw me in the courtyard, gleaming with broken crystals.

"What was it you were cleaning up?" I asked, suspiciously. "When you came outside, I mean."

"The aetherscope," she said, flatly. "The whole umbral ring —it exploded."

"What does that mean?"

"It means it wasn't made to handle such a spike in the flux," she said, turning to leave.

That night I drifted off into a dreamless sleep, and when I awoke, her circles were inscribed all over the walls.

✧

In the days that followed, I thought almost constantly of the voice in the chimes. Whenever I wasn't occupied with my lessons, or forced to make conversation with others in the household, the memory of that voice would come back to me with a little jolt, a frisson of anticipation. Then I would smile to myself, savoring my secret. I often sat under the mulberry trees, listening for the voice, especially when the wind lifted the leaves of the trees and rained down their silver devotions. I would sit and let them fall in my hair until long shadows swallowed the courtyard and the last ghost-pale leaf winked out in the deepening gloom. The chimes made a mournful babble, but uttered nothing intelligible. I felt no pull upon my limbs after that fateful day, and I didn't know whether to be grateful for this, or disappointed.

It was all Hespa's doing, I suspected. She had her methods, about which my father knew nothing. Sometimes I would find runes chalked behind the curtains that no one else had noticed. Or a swag of heather would appear on the banister, or a scattering of silver coins on the windowsills. Once, I asked her if she was a real witch, and she laughed. "No, kit, I've not that sort of power."

"But then how do you know so much magic?" I pressed.

Her face flushed. "It's just household magic," she said. "Where I come from, all girls learn how to protect their homes from spirits."

Whatever it was, it was proving effective.

I thought, too, of Beatrice's sly warning, that her mother was planning something for me. I danced round the topic with Hespa and my father, but neither of them responded to my furtive questioning. At night I lay awake, gnawed by the fear of being sent away, of the spirit returning to an empty courtyard, too late to be of any use. But what if I could be healed! For some reason I could not bring myself to believe it. It seemed too precarious an outcome, as though if I spoke of it aloud, the possibility might waft away on an errant breeze.

Sometimes all of these secret emotions wound so tightly round my stomach that I couldn't eat. I would lapse into long silences, just imagining all of the terrible and wonderful possibilities before me. I would shut myself in the library for hours, going over and over my mother's libretti, letting my head fill up with the music as I scanned the notes on the page. Then I would try singing it back to the wind chimes, thinking music must be their native language, but I never got it quite right; I couldn't get my voice to make the sounds I heard in my head. I began writing poems, because I knew that poems didn't have to make any sense, and so I was free to express anything I wished in them. My behavior worried Hespa, I think. I know my father thought I was going strange. That was only the beginning, though.

As the nights grew cooler, Lady Ellinora packed up her family and went to Carabilos. At the time of their departure, still nothing had been said to me about the almary. And despite my best efforts to summon it, the voice in the chimes remained silent all throughout the fall, and into the frostmoon. That tingle of anticipation I'd hung onto all the previous autumn began to recede, leaving me feeling like some hapless sea creature beached on a dreary spit of sand.

But there was something I could do. I thought about it often, during those months, but every time the urge came upon me, my courage failed. A few times, I got so far as to retrieve the hat box from the wardrobe, and withdraw the bottle of perfume from its hidden place. A tiny squeeze of the encapsulated bulb, not enough to intoxicate me, not enough to send me spinning through the past, into my mother's memories.

I was afraid of the tumult, the mental crash of sensations,

of what I might learn about her. And yet, I couldn't help but believe that she had answers for me, answers no one else would provide.

And so, one cold night as the rest of the household slept, as the moon shone bright upon the frosted tips of lavender bristling in the courtyard, I found my courage and opened the naked casement window, perfume bottle in hand. It was nearly empty; I would not get much more use out of it. As before, I was careful not to spray it into the room, where it might linger until morning. Instead, I aimed it out into the courtyard, letting it mist over the sleeping perennials, a breath of summer released into the chill air. I squeezed the bulb until only air hissed out. That was it, I realized with a pang, that was the last of it. I would never again smell my mother's perfume. I raised myself up on the arms of my chair and leaned out to breathe it in.

At first, I thought I'd let the perfume disperse too much. But I'd learned to be wary of the scent's potency. After a few seconds, a familiar tingling began to crawl up the back of my scalp, just behind my ears. I tasted a metallic tang in the back of my throat. The shapes of the flower beds, of the fountain, of the potted ornamental grasses, all began to lose depth, turning the courtyard into a scene of flat profiles limned in moonlight and shadow. Then the lines began to fade, the contrast between light and dark blurring, until I was looking out upon a velvet gray expanse, an empty stage.

My surroundings then began to take shape. They were familiar to me; I was in my own house, in the dining room.

When I looked down, I was startled to see that my legs were encased in trousers. Beneath my loose white shirt, I could feel a high corset pressing uncomfortably against my chest. I checked my reflection as I passed by a wall mirror on the way to the dining table—the face of my mother stared back at me. She was wearing the clothes I had found in the bottom of her wardrobe.

The moment I glimpsed her reflection, my perspective shifted; now I viewed her from a distance of a few feet away.

She sat at the table with an empty plate and a glass of wine, her booted feet slung over the chair beside her. My perception remained connected to her, though I witnessed her actions as an outside observer; I could feel the tension that belied her insouciant slouch, in the clench of her jaw, in the fingers that drummed against the wooden table.

Then the door banged open, the sound reverberating throughout the room, and my father walked in, grimacing, distracted, getting all the way to the end of the table before he finally registered her appearance.

"What are you doing?" he asked, stopping short. A half dozen empty chairs lay between them.

"What's wrong?" she asked.

"That...*ensemble*. Don't tell me you've joined the local theater."

My mother folded her arms over her chest. "If I had, I wouldn't breathe a word of it to you, for fear of you dampening my enthusiasm for such an endeavor."

He grunted in reply, pouring a glass of wine from the sideboard.

"It's just a new idea I had," she went on, her voice taking on a strange, sing-song quality. "I thought it would be more practical, for country life. After all, who is there here to dress for?"

"Your husband, I suppose," he said, taking a seat.

"Precisely."

He stared at her, then down into the wine glass in his hand.

"Don't be ridiculous," he said.

"I'm not ridiculing anything. I can keep an open mind—"

He leaped violently to his feet and hurried to the door, closing it with a resounding *thud*. "Do you always have to make a scene? Go put on some proper clothes, before the servants start whispering that you've gone mad."

"I'm not making a scene. You're making a scene."

"I don't need this," he said, turning to go. "I'll find somewhere else to dine."

"And walk away once again," she said, her voice rising with frustration.

He didn't reply.

"That's all you care about, isn't it?" she snapped. "Keeping up appearances. When I married you I thought I was done playing a role. You lied to me. You never loved me as a husband ought to love a wife. You've *humiliated* me, and you won't even own it."

It was the wrong thing to say. We both knew it, instinctively, as soon as the words tumbled out. He seized on the accusation, whirling round to hurl it back at her. "I'm sorry you feel that I tarnished your stainless reputation," he said. "I'm sorry I tried to give you a respectable life. That it wasn't enough for you after all."

"Is that how you see it?" She reached for her wine glass, grabbed it by the bowl. I felt her anger surge, long-held anger, exploding from some previously inaccessible place in her heart. I thought she would crush the glass in her hand, or fling it in his face. Instead she drank furiously, draining the glass in one swallow. "You think you rescued *me?*"

"I'm just being realistic. Admit it, your life was a mess when I found you. Drinking absinthe every night and smoking opium with anarchists and pimps. I suppose you've conveniently forgotten about all of that, though."

For a moment, her heart stopped, and her face drained of color. "I haven't forgotten," she said, quietly. "I remember what you said to me then, too. That you were different." She raised her chin to meet his gaze. "That you would never hurt me."

He looked away.

"Do you think I'm blind to your deflections?" she asked. "Do you think you can escape the truth by insulting me? Go ahead and drag my name through the mud. You wouldn't be the first. But it won't change anything, will it?"

"You're ill, Sephonie."

"You think if you say that enough times it will make it true."

"I'm not the one who refuses to see the truth," he said, getting up to refill her glass. "Your career was in ruins the moment your precious 'patron' died. No one was hiring you."

"You told me you would never hurt me," she repeated. "And yet, you have been as cruel to me as anyone. Not since I was a child have I felt so alone. The gods know, none are so accursed as those who lie in matters of love."

"I'm a monster," he agreed, handing her the glass. "It's true. Are you happy now? Is that what you want to hear?"

"*No!*" Her voice echoed throughout the chamber. Leaves rustled above as a single white blossom dropped loose from the balcony and fluttered down, landing on her empty plate. An amardine flower.

I saw the dining room through her eyes, then—a strange and beautiful prison, with doors she could walk out of at any time. She took in the great, twisted, mysterious trunks of those first pardesu trees, the clusters of flowers that hung down in graceful arcades. She scanned the rows of empty chairs at the long heirloom table. If she were to turn over her chair, she could read on a brass plaque the name of every Desmarius who had ever claimed it as their own. She didn't have a name on hers yet, but surely that was just an oversight.

She had been powerful, once, and the memory of her stage triumphs tugged at her. She needed something of her own. She picked up the blossom and clenched it in her fist.

"I don't even care any more if you love me," she said, wiping her tears away with her thumb.

"Then what do you want? What have I failed to provide for you?"

She shrieked in frustration, hurling her glass to the floor.

My father recoiled as it shattered on the tiles, drenching them in the dark red fluid. "I want honesty. I want to know who you truly are. I want to walk off the stage, *finally*, and wake up from this goddamned delusion."

He stared at her, unblinking. Then, without another word, he quit the room, leaving her alone at the great table, watching another blossom sail down like a plummeting star.

✌

My vision grew dark, and the tableau began to fade. Blood pounded in my ears, and the dim shapes of my own furniture slowly came into focus. The acrid taste lingered in my mouth, a bitter tang of desolation.

It would be years before I fully understood the relationship between my parents, the sacrifice they each made to complete the illusion of the other. But I felt the distance between them keenly, and the unraveling of my own illusions about their love. I recognized the cold, uncompromising look on my father's face, an expression I had always believed was a widower's mask of grief. But my mother had known it well.

Tears ran down my face as I gulped in the cold night air. The scent of perfume still lingered in the folds of the curtain, and I backed away from the window with sudden dread. I didn't want to know what lay in the past. I didn't want any more visions.

And yet, I couldn't bear for this to be my last memory of my mother. I could still feel her loneliness, her bitterness, her frustration, swirling in the air like the notes of her perfume. There might never be another chance. I had to go deeper into the vision, as deep as I could, one last time. I had to hold on to hope.

I closed my eyes, inhaling the scent. This time the vision appeared quickly, almost the moment I allowed it into my mind. Another scene began to take form in front of me. The wooden texture of a wall. Bookshelves, protruding out of the darkness. I was in a shop, transported right into the middle of the vision. My hands were sheathed in black silk gloves. An older man stood before me, behind a small counter cluttered with books, stacked in high, precarious piles topped with tea-cups and small, empty plates. The man looked familiar, but I couldn't place him. He wore a brown jacket with a fuzzy tex-ture and large, wooden buttons. He smiled at me, and his mouth moved, but his words sounded as though they were tra-veling to me from a great distance, through water, through time itself. The man turned and placed his hand on the wall, and the bookshelf slid on a hidden hinge, opening up a secret door behind the counter. He bowed, like the servant of some great house, and gestured me onward. I stepped through the opening in the wall.

The room beyond was small and windowless. The door slid closed behind me. Light shone down from a curtain stretched across the ceiling, fashioned to look like stars glowing in a night sky. It was enough illumination to make out the titles of the books on the shelf: *Pathways of the Umbra, The Rites of Binding, The Book of One Hundred Names, Circles of Abjuration.* The books appeared old, worn. Some no longer had titles visible; they had been rubbed away. One slender volume had only a symbol visible on its spine, an intricately stylized arched doorway, and I slid it out from its place. Flipping it open, I saw diagrams and strange runes, symbols whose purpose I could not fathom. *Yes,* I thought, *this is the one.* But the thought came to me in another voice, a grown woman's voice. I closed the book and tapped on the back of the secret door. It swung open, and the man appeared again, smiling, bobbing his head. Where had I seen him before?

I tried to examine the book again, but as I looked at it, it faded into a gray vapor, as though I were waking from a dream. I blinked. The courtyard was once again before me, still and silent, except for a lone owl that *who-whooed* in the distance. I shivered, the cold air piercing through my light woolen shift, and closed the casement window.

I realized then why the man had looked familiar. I hadn't seen him close-up, but I remembered the jacket, the oversized buttons, before the fire had consumed them. He was the man who had died beneath our elm tree.

CHAPTER TWENTY-ONE

IN THE WEEKS THAT FOLLOWED, I busied myself with my lessons, practicing my singing whenever I could. I took a renewed interest in the houseplants, which had become a bit listless, even for plants, in the months since I had been preoccupied with my illness. My father watered them the proper amount, pruned them and tended the soil, but he didn't talk to them like I did, and I could see the difference. Although I couldn't reach all of them in my chair, I did the best I could, and watched them perk up, rustling in my presence, restored to their old vitality.

Of course, my father would think I was mad if I told him my thoughts on that subject. Let him believe I was merely being helpful, a good daughter, making herself useful in her own small way. There were times when I longed to say something to him, to confide my secrets, and I had to remind myself that it wasn't safe. He would scold me and deny everything, tell me I was imagining it. Perhaps he would let Lady Pendrake send me away to an almary, or a sanitarium, like my great-aunt Rosamund.

And so, as the frostmoon waned, I kept my own counsel. The silverbell trees bloomed, their blossoms dripping in the moonlight like candle wax against their dark leaves. The house was turned inside out to let the sun scour everything that had molded throughout the cold season. Every scrap of fabric was removed from the cabinets—buttery soft tablecloths, furniture draperies, embroidered towels, bed linens, old handkerchiefs trimmed in yellow lace, all sorted and folded into labeled baskets for the laundress—weeks of work laid out in the breezeway. The carpets were dragged from the house and beaten with wooden paddles, all the dust and dirt of the previous season rising in the air and swirling away in the fragrant air.

The evenings grew long and languorous, the sky turning a deep plum color over the treeline as Hespa and I braided branches on the veranda. She had brought by the armload yellow catkins and trimmings from the silverbell trees, and we made wild bouquets to hang over the doorways to repel evil spirits. The new maid, Daphne, tried to take them down, but Hespa scolded her for it, and that was that. My father paid no mind at all; he only knew that we were engaged in some feminine nesting ritual, and was determined not to speak of it.

One evening, as Hespa and I were thus engaged, I looked up from my work to see my father walking across the lawn, his form a dark silhouette against the gathering gloom. He walked not from the greenhouses but from the road that led to the lower court, and as he drew nearer I could see he was carrying an animal pelt, draped over his arms. He ascended the steps to the veranda and stopped before me, saying nothing, as though he were waiting on me to acknowledge him.

"Yes, Papa?" I asked, trying to see better what was in his hands. But the light was fading and we hadn't thought to bring out lamps.

"Amardine," he said. "I just ran into one of my tenants on the road. He had something made for you." He unfolded the pelt, spreading it out so that I could see it more clearly. It had been made into a small square, a lap blanket, and was comprised of soft, light-colored fur.

I recoiled as recognition set in. "It's a fox," I said, my voice shaking, going high and shrill.

My father frowned and stepped back from me, rescinding the gift. "Yes, I've been told by several of the neighbors that it's been skulking round. Well, one of the tenants trapped it, and it will trouble us no more."

"He shouldn't have done that!" I said, to my father's astonishment. I felt Hespa nudge me with her elbow.

"You ought to say 'thank you,'" she whispered.

"It was kindly meant," my father said, stiffly. "If you don't want it, I'm sure someone else can find a use for it."

I began to cry. Hespa regarded me with alarm. "What's wrong?" she asked, laying a hand on my arm.

"He shouldn't have done that," I said again, my voice becoming a hopeless wail.

"I don't understand this," my father said, turning to Hespa.

"It's late," Hespa replied, patting me on the back. "I'm sure the child just needs her rest."

ഇന്ദ്ര

Knock, knock, knock. I rapped three times on the door of the workshop. The music of the paleophone swelled as the door opened, and my father stood in the aperture, regarding me cautiously. He'd barely spoken to me in days, not since the evening he'd brought me the fox pelt. It wasn't anger that fueled his reticence, though, at least not that I could sense. No, something else was troubling him. At dinner I would catch him staring off into space, as though in deep thought. At other times, he would look at me with a sad fondness, as though he were silently bidding me farewell. He'd never looked so fond of me, that I could recall.

That was what had given me the courage finally to go to him.

"What is it, Amardine?" he asked.

"I just wanted to see what you were doing," I said.

He turned in the doorway, ushering me inside. I hadn't been in the workshop in months, not since before I'd fallen ill. It looked the same as I remembered it—the crude wooden tables, stained with wax and dirt, littered with twigs and leaves, bowing beneath the weight of the potted pardesu trees; the cart parked next to the wall by the balcony doors; the incongruous gleam of the parquet floor beneath the high corniced ceiling.

"I ought to have had a ramp made in the courtyard years ago," he remarked, as I followed him to his work table. "It makes it much easier to bring the pardesu trees up here."

"Why do you work up here, Papa?" I asked.

He shrugged. "The view is pleasant, and the light is good. Besides, a room such as this oughtn't stand empty, don't you think?"

"You could have dances in here," I said. "Why don't you, Papa?"

"Because then I would have to move my tables and tools," he replied, picking up a pair of fine shears from the workbench. Critically, he eyed the small tree he was working on, then started snipping at one of the branches. I knew he was content to work in silence, and would not prolong the conversation without my prompting. *Courage,* I reminded myself.

"Papa, something's been happening," I blurted out.

"Yes?" *Snip, snip, snip,* went the shears.

I felt at a loss. I didn't know how to continue. Finally, I said, "Please don't let the tenants kill any more foxes."

He sighed. "This again? I can't very well tell them not to protect their hen houses. Foxes are vermin, in any case."

"No, they're not," I said, with more heat than I'd intended. "They've as much right to be here as anyone."

"They can stay out in the forest where they belong, and hunt mice and wild hares. A farm is no place for sentiment, Amardine."

"It led me home," I said, feeling my eyes fill with tears. "When I got lost in the swamp coming home from the Pendrakes, it found me and led me home."

He looked up from his work, eyeing me warily. "You saw one of the neighbor's dogs, perhaps."

"No. It was a fox. Papa, I'm sure of it."

He shook his head. "You were bitten by cruorflies. Sometimes the bite can cause disorientation. But wild animals don't behave that way."

"It's not just that," I went on, heedless now, too deep in the mode of confession to turn back. "There was that symbol under the wallpaper—"

"What does this have to do with a fox?"

"It's strange, Papa, isn't it?"

"Strange, yes. But you're getting upset," he said. "You're speaking nonsense."

Beneath the table, I balled my hands into fists. He was right, of course, I wasn't making any sense. But that was because I hadn't presented him with all the facts. How could I make him see the connection?

"There was a voice in the wind chimes. In the courtyard. And it went through me, and made me stand up. I—"

"Amardine, that's enough." He set down the pruning shears and stared at me over the top of the pardesu tree he was trimming. There was a sadness in his eyes, or perhaps disappointment, but in the way he braced himself against the table, I also read fear.

"You'll be nine years old soon," he said. "You need to start behaving like a young lady, and speak only what is truthful. I don't want to hear any more of your wild imaginings about foxes or wind chimes. Do you understand?"

I had one last gambit left to play. "That book you had in your study—you didn't get it from a tenant, did you? That old man had it. He sold books to my mother, too. She was using magic, and she did something you don't want to talk abou—"

"Quiet!" The harshness in his tone sent a jolt down my spine. His eyes were wide and startled, and his face had gone ashen, as though he'd aged two decades in an instant. "Who's been telling you these things, Amardine?"

"No one," I said. A tear slipped down my cheeks, and I wiped it away before he could scold me for that, too.

"You're lying to me."

"I'm not, Papa. She's been showing me things."

He sucked in a breath. "Your mother is gone. She left us, and nothing can change that."

My chest tightened as shards of hope formed like tiny icicles to pierce my heart. A mother who had gone away was a mother who could someday return. But as I watched my father attempt to regain control of his features, I realized I had misunderstood him. No, I thought, she wasn't coming back.

"What do you mean, Papa?" I asked.

"I mean that she took her own life," he said. "She left us of her own accord."

"I don't—I don't understand."

"*She killed herself.* I suppose you're old enough to hear the truth. She didn't want to be part of this world."

"No," I whispered. "I don't believe it. You said she was sick. You said, Papa!"

"She was sick," he said, quietly. "After you were born, something changed. I should have known she was never meant for motherhood."

I pressed my hands to my face. Emblazoned in the darkness behind my eyes, her image stared back at me, the only one I'd ever known, from her portrait in the library. I'd always thought she looked too perfect to be real.

"I'm sorry, Amardine. I'm sorry."

I peered out at him from between my fingers, but he wouldn't return my gaze. In that instant, I understood that it wasn't grief that had ensnared him after all—it was shame.

That night I cried myself to sleep, listening for the chimes between fits of tears, hoping beyond hope that my mother's spirit might speak through them and dispute my father's claim. I still couldn't believe what he'd told me. And yet—I'd felt her misery firsthand. I'd already been wrong about one parent. Why should I think she wouldn't abandon me? Perhaps it was childish to believe in the sanctity of a mother's love, just another foolish fancy I'd entertained long past its due. I would be nine years old soon, old enough to face hard truths.

No answers came from without. I heard only the rustling of the leaves, the scrape of branches as they lashed the courtyard wall. My father had taken the chimes down.

What was it the voice had said? *You don't have time to be like this...*

But the voice in the chimes was wrong, I decided, as the days passed, and nothing much changed. I had an entire lifetime to be like this.

CHAPTER TWENTY-TWO

EVERYTHING WAS BECOMING CLEAN AND NEW again—the house aired out, the linens washed and folded, the cornices repainted, the bric-a-brac removed from cabinets and scattered over sideboards and tea tables. The cabinets themselves had been pulled from the walls and stood huddled mutely together, awaiting polish. The portraits of dead relatives were propped against the balustrades, their faces beseeching as they stared out from their own little black voids. Every dark corner had been scrubbed and every window opened to let in fresh air and light. It was a yearly tradition, heralding the renewal of spring, but it felt somehow like a mockery. There would be no renewal for me, only a continuation of the malaise that had begun with my illness and deepened with every new revelation.

I still thought often of the voice in the chimes, though I pretended to have forgotten about it. I stopped asking Hespa questions, worried that she would further mount her defenses against the spirit realm. I knew I ought to be more afraid of trafficking with such entities. But whenever I thought of that day in the courtyard, all I felt was a wild surge of hope. It was like a secret power, dangerous perhaps, but without it I had no reason to believe anything in my life would ever change.

And so I kept my own counsel, even as the house gave up one final mystery. One morning, as I lay in bed, Hespa was going through my wardrobe. She found the tattered dress I'd worn during my flight from Pendrake Hall, wrapped in a towel and hastily put away. It had never been washed, but the fabric was so fine, she had saved it in the hope that it could be salvaged for another purpose. As she lifted it from the shelf where it had been stored, something fell out of the pocket and clattered to the floor. I leaned over the edge of the bed to see the tube of lipstick roll across the floor and disappear beneath the dust ruffle.

Hespa bent down to retrieve it, then stood before me, staring at the item in her hand. She removed the wooden cap to reveal its contents, looking more confused than ever.

"Where did you get this, kit?" she asked.

My mind raced, searching for an answer that would save me from a scolding. More than that, though, I didn't think I could bear for her to have a bad opinion of me. I could still feel my father's disappointment keenly, but he had always been difficult to please. Hespa, on the other hand, had ever been my champion.

But as I lifted my gaze and looked into her unsettled brown eyes, something in me broke. I couldn't hold back the flood of secrets any longer.

"I took it," I admitted. "From a drawer in Lady Pendrake's dressing table."

There was a sharp intake of breath. Hespa looked as pained as though I had slapped her in the face. It was all I could do not to wince myself.

"Kit, this is a grave admission," she said. "Whyever would you do such a thing? Why were you going through her drawers in the first place?"

"I didn't," I said. Now that I was committed to telling the truth of the matter, I would not spare my cousins. "Beatrice showed it to me. She made me put it on. But it doesn't belong to Lady Pendrake. She took it in the first place."

"From whom?" Hespa asked, her brow knitting in confusion.

"From my mother."

She let out her breath, turning over the wooden tube in her hands, as though examining it for some clue to confirm this wild accusation. Finally she said, "How do you know that?"

"Have you ever seen Lady Pendrake wear color on her lips?" I asked. "She doesn't—she wouldn't. Everyone knows it's not proper. But my mother wasn't a proper lady, was she? She's wearing it in her portrait. The same red. That's how I know."

Hespa regarded me for a long moment, her broad face devoid of any readable expression. I'd heard my aunt describe her once as "steady, but a bit slow." But I'd never doubted the sharpness of her mind—if she was slow of thought, it was only because she was determined to come to the right conclusion.

"Why would she take it, then, if not to wear it?" she asked.

"I don't know," I said. It was a reasonable question. "Maybe she only wears it in her dressing room."

"You mustn't speak such accusations to anyone else," Hespa said. "You don't know anything for certain. It's a very serious business, to accuse someone of stealing without proof."

"But you believe me?" I asked.

Again, she turned her attention to the wooden tube, turning it on its end to look at the bottom, where the date and the name of the maker had been stamped. "It's nearly a decade old," she mused.

"See? It could have belonged to my mother."

"Yes," she agreed. "It could have." She popped the cap back on, and then, to my shock, she handed it to me.

"You *are* a proper young lady, Amardine Sophia. You know that, don't you?"

I didn't know what to say.

"You're not to wear it under any circumstances. But I'll allow you to have it, as a keepsake only. Do you understand?"

"Yes," I squeaked, still too surprised to think of anything but agreeing to her terms. "Of course, Hespa. Thank you."

୧)୦ଓ

It gives me no pleasure to relate how quickly I broke my word to my trusting maid, but as I have said, I didn't truly think it through. I had been taught to be agreeable, and so I was. But that very afternoon, I took the opportunity during respite, when I was supposed to be napping, to examine the lipstick more closely.

I found iodine and strips of gauze in the medicine cabinet, left over from my convalescence, and managed to get them down without knocking anything over. This, I hoped, would remove the waxy substance once I was finished with my experiment.

For that was how I regarded it. It wasn't vanity that prompted my actions, but the hope of discovery. For some reason I couldn't fathom, both the perfume and the lipstick seemed to be tied to my mother's memories. Perhaps they had been made by arcanists, like the aetherlamps or the coldstones we kept in our ice box. Or perhaps my mother had imbued them somehow with her own magical powers. Whatever the case, I felt a connection to her through these objects, and despite some trepidation, I could not bring myself to leave them be.

It had rained steadily all that morning and afternoon, and the light in the room was a muted gray. I sat before my dressing table, lipstick in hand, staring at the colorless little face in the mirror, framed by short blonde hair. Hespa had left her pincushion on the table, and I used one of the pins to scratch the dried surface of the colored stick, the way I'd seen Beatrice do.

After scoring it several times, the dull red of the dried wax bloomed a bright scarlet, and I swiped it across my lips, rubbing it in, until it looked like a bloody slash against the paleness of my features.

It made me look older, or perhaps just more knowing, and less innocent. I felt a pulse of anxiety at the thought of Hespa walking in and catching me, thinking I was playing at being a grown woman. The blood began to pound in my temples, making me light-headed. I gripped the edge of the dressing table. Then my vision began to blacken, as it had before when Beatrice had made me wear the lipstick. It was happening. *What will you show me, Mama?* I wondered.

Then I was pacing back and forth in an elegant-looking room. The room seemed familiar to me, though I couldn't place it. It wasn't my mother's room at Guildenflore, of that I was certain. I wished I could turn and look for a mirror, but I had no control over the scene; I could only see it as though from my mother's eyes. She put a hand on the swell of her belly, and I could feel the arch of her back as she pushed her stomach out, walking, this way and that, almost experimentally. I sensed a flicker of triumph deep in her heart. Her hands were steady. She dropped to her knees before a covered basket on the floor, next to the bed, and lifted the lid. Something was swaddled inside, wrapped in layers of soft cloth. She cradled it in her hands and withdrew it from the basket. The cloth—tea towels, I could see now, embroidered with initials—fell away. In her hands, she held a large —what was it? It looked, impossibly, like a sausage casing.

She sat down on the bed, propping herself against a mound of pillows. She drew her knees up, then hiked up her skirts. She took a small knife from her nightstand. Then she put the sausage casing under her skirt, wedging it beneath her, so that she was sitting on it. I could feel the pressure as it shifted under her weight, as though it might burst at any moment. Then her knife hand went beneath her skirt. I sensed her probing with it, not for her own skin, but the casing. There was a swift jab, a feeling of release. A rush of warm blood, and the scent of vinegar. She wiped the blade on the empty casing and tossed them both into the basket, covered them with towels, and shoved the basket under the bed. Then she let out a scream.

There was confusion after that, a whirl of images. Dr. Vidmont appeared, accompanied by with a woman servant I didn't recognize. There were tears and admonitions. *She's lost the child*, a voice said. It was the doctor, speaking to someone behind the bedroom door. *I am sorry, sir.*

I saw before me a hand clutching a thimble glass of amber liquid, and smelled something caustic, medicinal. The hand tossed the liquid back, and I felt it smolder its way down my—her—throat. Darkness came over me. I blinked, seeing spots in my vision, and it took me a moment to realize the sight before me was my own face, staring back at me in the mirror.

I shook my head, trying to clear away the disturbing vision. What had I just seen? What had Dr. Vidmont meant, that she'd "lost the child?" Did I have some phantom sibling, like Beatrice and Bianca? But the bleeding had been fake. It made no sense.

I knew how animals were born, and I had a vague inkling of what it meant to have a baby, mostly derived from the sensation novels I borrowed from Hespa. Even so, it took great effort to work out the meaning behind the vision. When I finally did come to an understanding, it left me feeling more confused than ever.

There was no baby. There never had been.

Then I remembered the initials on the tea towels. Not my mother's initials at all. The letters embroidered on the towels were *EDP.*

CHAPTER TWENTY-THREE

I DIDN'T HAVE LONG TO WAIT before Lady Pendrake materialized once again in my life, heralded by the crunch of carriage wheels on the drive. It was afternoon when she arrived, and I was watering the plants in the entrance hall.

I retreated to the little parlor next to the vestibule, which had a latticed window set in the wall, so that one could see visitors when they arrived. All I could think of was my aunt's deception, gleaned from the vision in the lipstick, and the bizarre lengths she had gone to perpetuate it. If I'd had any doubt there was something wrong with her, the vision had chased it away and confirmed my worst fears.

But what could I do? I couldn't very well tell anyone what I'd seen, as I had no way to explain the source of my knowledge. I watched anxiously from the front window as Lady Pendrake stepped down from the Cartouche in a flourish of lime-green silk. She was wearing the most ridiculous boots—waders, I thought the term was—enormous black boots like those a man would wear, revealed for just a moment as she lifted her skirts. The cousins tumbled out of the carriage next, arguing loudly, the carriage doors slamming closed behind them.

My insides roiled. The feeling came on suddenly, in a moment of helpless dread. The razor-winged butterflies burst from the pit of my stomach, fluttering up through my chest. My heart began to race furiously. In a panic, I dropped my pitcher onto the rug where it made a heavy thump and splashed water across the floor. "Hespa!" I tried to call out, but the words wouldn't come; it was as though they were being held down and smothered with pillows. This was it—I was dying. I clutched the arms of my chair as black spots danced in my vision.

My head pounded. I gasped for breath. I crumpled in on myself as a crackling in my ears rose to a crescendo and then abruptly stopped.

You don't have time to be like this.

I put my hands over my ears and slumped in the chair. Or rather, I tried to, but something was stopping me, pushing me upright. The room spun. It was all coming back in a whirl of bright light.

Hespa was shaking me back to my senses.

"Amardine. Amardine!"

I blinked at her as a wave of nausea rolled over me.

"Are you all right, kit?" she asked, keeping one hand on my forehead as she bent to pick up the pitcher. There was still a little water left that hadn't spilled when I dropped it on the floor. She dabbed a handkerchief and pressed it against my face.

"Yes," I said, my teeth chattering.

"Seven mercies," she said. "I think you got rattled."

"Rattled?"

She draped a blanket over my shoulders, and I hugged it tight, still shaking. "It's when you're so afraid you feel like you're going to die," she said, then added, "or when a ghost passes through you."

"Where are my cousins?" I asked. I was so much in dread of their arrival, I barely registered the second half of her answer.

"The Pendrakes went straight to the greenhouse," Hespa said. "But I expect them to run back any minute now. They won't stand the heat much longer than that. Kit, you're too ill to have company. I'll let them know you're not well."

For a moment, I felt pure relief, spreading through me like the fog brought on by an elixir. I was safe. I didn't have to see them. But I hesitated in answering, and Hespa gave me a fretful look.

"Are you going to be sick?" she asked.

"No," I said, and realized it was true. "No, I'm all right, Hespa. I'll see my cousins."

"Surely not, kit," she insisted.

"I don't have time to be like this," I said.

She gave me a strange look. "Like what? Are you sure you're well?"

"I'm fine. Only, might we have some tea?"

"Of course. I'll be right back."

She left, intercepting the Pendrakes at the door. Just as she had predicted, Lady Pendrake and her daughters looked half-wilted in the heat. At least I wouldn't be the only one who was out-of-sorts.

Lady Pendrake stomped out of her waders and accepted the pair of slippers Hespa provided for her. "What a beautiful day!" she called out. Beatrice said nothing, but Bianca chattered on like a magpie.

Lifting myself up on the arms of my chair, I could just barely see through the bottom of the lattice window. The iron door from the courtyard opened, and my father stepped in from the other side of the entrance hall.

"We were just out at the old Colvern place. You remember, those charming gardens they used to have? They're all over-grown now, of course, but there's still a path down to the pond. We were hoping to see a checkered vireo. And we did! Didn't we, girls?"

I turned to one of the more fragrant potted plants and began clipping blossoms for a sachet, listening as the iron door swung shut.

"How very nostalgic, sister, coming back here in your waders. I haven't seen those in, oh, let's see, it must be close to twenty years. What do you want from me?"

"I want to *talk* to you, Martel. I have important news, but you must hear me out."

"It's about Amardine, isn't it?" my father said, quietly, and I nearly dropped my shears. He sounded resigned then, tired and a little old. "You've had an answer, then?"

She didn't reply at first. Then she said, "We'll have some wine under the pergola, Hespa, dear."

"One glass of wine," my father said. "Three-quarters of an hour. I'm setting the sand time, Ellinora."

"All right, all *right*. Seven mercies, you're serious, aren't you? Well, don't turn it over just yet. Girls, let's go find your poor darling cousin, shall we?"

Forty-five minutes, I thought, as I looked round the room for some prop to make me appear busy and composed. Then I remembered I'd left my embroidery in the emptied drawer of the credenza the day before, and there it still was, undisturbed.

I gritted my teeth. My father would keep his word. I could survive Beatrice and Bianca for forty-five minutes.

℘℘

I asked Hespa to serve us in the courtyard, under the mulberry trees. From there, I could just barely hear sounds of conversation from my father and aunt, though they were shielded from view by the walls of the house. Hespa arranged the cups slowly on the table; I knew she didn't want to leave me alone with my cousins. I understood her concern, but I smiled and thanked her, and told her we would be all right for the duration of their visit.

I hoped it was true. Beatrice stared at Hespa as she set the table, a hostile look in her eyes, clutching her reticule beneath one plump arm. Bianca, meanwhile, sat on the low stone wall nearby, plucking flowers from the bed behind her. From my pocket, I withdrew the sachet I had filled earlier and dropped it into the teapot. Then I picked up my embroidery, making a few stitches in the bright red poppy I was working on, but I couldn't concentrate on my efforts, and they came out tight and ugly.

"I found something in our library," Beatrice said triumphantly, after Hespa had left. "Something you might find interesting, Amardine."

This was all right, I thought, as relief began to loosen my stitches. I loved looking at old books. But I had to draw this out as long as possible. I couldn't appear too eager.

"Why should I find it interesting?" I asked. "I have lots of books here."

"Stupid children's books," Beatrice said. "I'll bet that's what you read. How old are you now, anyway?"

"I'm almost nine."

"I don't know if you ought to see it," she said. "I don't know if you're ma-*ture* enough yet."

"Has Bianca seen it?" I asked.

"Oh, yes. But she doesn't *understand* it. She's not...you know."

I confessed I didn't know.

"Do you *want* to see it?" Beatrice pressed, pouring herself a cup of tea.

I had to admit, she had piqued my curiosity. I was almost eager enough to throw off caution and let Beatrice draw me fully into her scheme. But I estimated there was still plenty of time left for her to torment me in other ways, if I gave in too soon.

"I'm not sure," I said, hesitantly. I brought my own teacup to my nose, inhaling the steam. "Do you really think I ought to?"

"Well. If you ask me, you ought to be prepared."

"Prepared for what?" I asked.

Beatrice ran her fingers absently over the corner of her reticule. "For the Change."

"What do you mean?" Now I was growing truly alarmed, for I had no idea of what she spoke.

"Amardine," Beatrice said, sipping her tea, "has anything strange ever happened to you on a full moon? They call it an umbral moon."

"That's not an umbral moon. An umbral moon has to do with the composition of the firmament," I said. Beatrice frowned, and I knew I'd made a mistake in correcting her. But surely her tutors had taught her this much. "I don't know what you mean about strange things," I went on, hurriedly.

From her perch on the wall, Bianca called out, "I want to see the book! Show her the book!"

"You have to promise not to talk about it," Beatrice said to me.

"I promise."

"Because I'll get in trouble if anyone finds out. And I'll know who told."

Beatrice opened her reticule and withdrew a thick, leather-bound book. The pages were rough-cut and yellowed with age, and they skittered across her lap as she turned them over, one by one.

"This book is about you, you know." She bit her thumbnail and wiped the fluid-laden digit all over the page, as though it were a cleaning rag. "It's about your real relatives."

"You're my real relatives," I said.

"Not our side. Your mother's."

My blood rushed to my feet, leaving my head in a pallid fog. Afraid I was about to get rattled again, I gripped the arms of my chair and forced myself to take a deep breath.

Beatrice opened the middle of the book to reveal a folded color illustration. "Alma Monti says the Feym-ri come from the Umbra, the same as demons. They lead people out of their houses with their evil music, and make them forget all about normal life. It happens every year on the first of Spring, when their power is greatest."

She gave me a smug smile as she said this, and handed the book to me. Gently I uncreased the page and stared at the picture, trying to decipher it. It showed a mob of strange creatures descending upon a village at the edge of a dark wood. The creatures were misshapen things, lurching along on goat legs and serpent tails, possessing human hands and the heads of other creatures: pigs and owls and bears, and horses with wild, rolling eyes. Some of them had wings and flew against a full moon, their toothy maws twisted with macabre glee. The village lay in the far right panel, where the sun was emerging over the horizon, and as the creatures approached the light they transformed, becoming like humans, but deceptively perfect and beautiful. They walked among wide-eyed peasants in their fields, dressed in fine clothing and casting arrogant looks all round. I flipped the page, needing to know what happened to the villagers. On the other side was a picture of a worried-looking man holding up a lantern in a dark forest, all alone as the shadows closed in around him. I closed the book to read the title that wheeled across its worn cover: *The Enchantment of the Feym-ri.*

"Is this real?" I asked, as Bianca got up and plopped down in the chair next to me. "What does it mean?"

"It's about what happened to the village of Two Trees," Beatrice said.

"What happened to it?"

"No one *really* knows," she replied. "But it's not the only town it's happened to. Everybody left. They just marched out into the forest and disappeared. Nobody knows why or what happened to them, but later, people found a doorway in the woods, made of twisted trees. And it looked just like the symbols the Feym-ri use."

Bianca grabbed the book off my lap. She flipped back to the panels and pointed to the monstrous horde gathered in the far left page. "I'll bet that's what you turn into at night," she said, giggling.

"So you haven't grown a tail yet, or anything like that?"

Beatrice pressed. "No wing stubs pressing out of your back?"

"Of course not." My skin was prickling all over, and I could feel the heat returning to my face, making it bloom.

"Because we could check," she said, slyly. "There's nothing you could do about it, is there?"

Reflexively, I wheeled myself backwards. "Lady Pendrake will hear me if I scream," I reminded her. "My papa, too."

"We'll make sure you don't," Beatrice said, ominously. "You could be hiding anything under those skirts and petticoats. Mother says you had arrhemia, but I don't believe it. I think you'd be dead if you had arrhemia."

"Not everyone dies from it," I protested, but Beatrice wasn't listening.

"So what *really* happened to you? Why can't you walk any more? That's what I'd like to know."

"Let's take off her dress and find out!" Bianca shrieked, as she bounced up and down, making her curls spring up round her head.

The air seemed unbearably hot to me then, leaving tiny barbed hooks in the skin of my back. Images flashed before my eyes of being dragged from my chair, pressed down upon the ground, unable to move as they stripped off my clothes. I thought about the embroidery needle in my lap, and for a brief second I imagined fending them off with it. But no, even if I hurt one of them, they could take it away from me, and then I'd be helpless in the face of their anger.

"I don't think you want to do that," I said, drawing upon

every ounce of will to keep my voice low and steady. I stared at Beatrice, forcing away the fear she invoked in me. I gave her a long, incisive look, dissecting her with my eyes as though she were some botanical specimen in my father's workshop.

She frowned as her stomach let out an audible gurgle. "And why is that?" she demanded, but the smugness in her voice sounded forced.

"Because it's almost the first of Spring, when the power of the Feym-ri is the greatest," I said. "And do you know what else that day is, Beatrice Pendrake?"

"No," she said. "What is it?"

"It's my birthday."

Beatrice stared at me, her reptilian black eyes becoming un-focused. She had blotted her face after coming in from the greenhouse, but sweat was beginning to bead up again on her forehead. She had not considered this, but she must have known it was true, for she had celebrated my birthday with me on multiple occasions.

She clutched her stomach. "I feel sick," she moaned, hastily returning the book to her reticule.

"You ought to have more tea," I said. "Perhaps that will settle your stomach."

"I think I need to use the privy closet."

Bianca watched her quit the room, then looked back at me.

"She won't be back any time soon," I said. "She won't have a pleasant ride home, either."

"How do you know?" Bianca asked, wide-eyed.

"Because I poisoned the tea," I said, removing the sachet with a spoon. "I told you that you ought to be careful about eating the wrong flowers."

Her mouth opened and closed silently.

"Do you still want to find out what I'm hiding?" I asked. "I can show you."

To my utter astonishment, Bianca burst into tears. "I don't want to see. I don't want to see!" She ran to the door, wailing, "I want to go *ho-ome!*"

I picked up my embroidery and went back to work, the scarlet thread flashing against the white circle of cloth, pulling smooth and even. Perhaps I would even have time to finish it before my father's sand timer ran out.

CHAPTER TWENTY-FOUR

BEATRICE DIDN'T DIE THAT DAY. SHE emerged from the house taking tiny, lurching steps, clutching her stomach in pain. She paused like a tragic heroine before the lily pond, staring moodily into the water for several seconds until Lady Pendrake prodded her onward. My cousin's illness would likely pass within a few hours—the aravilla flower I'd put in her tea wasn't toxic enough to do further damage—but I knew she would eventually discover what I'd done. Perhaps Bianca would tell her, or perhaps she would work it out for herself, as she lay in the darkness of her room, far from sleep.

I watched from the doorway, anticipating the familiar clench of uncertainty: *What would she do? Whom would she tell?* But instead I felt only relief. I wanted her to know. Perhaps in the future she would think twice about assuming I was helpless, just because I couldn't walk.

Beatrice tumbled into the carriage and settled herself by the window. After a moment she turned and peered round the curtain, giving me a glassy-eyed stare. My aunt must have given her some potion from her reticule. That was good, I thought, with a twinge of pity for her condition. It was better to sleep through such things.

"She always does this," Lady Pendrake said, pausing on the drive to have the last word with my father. "She's perfectly well. She's just using this as an excuse to go home."

"I don't see why. We'd already agreed on when you would go home."

"Oh, yes, I know. You said it loud enough, even my driver could hear. I thought when you heard the news, though—I thought you'd at least like to share a glass of wine. In celebration." She tilted her head and smiled, as I imagined she would have done as a young girl, standing in this very drive.

"We did have a glass of wine. One glass, as I told you," my father said. He cleared his throat. "What you've done is —remarkable, Ellinora. I'm still in a bit of shock, that's all."

"You oughtn't be shocked," she said, her eyes shining. "I told you we would do it. Those doctors couldn't do a thing for her, the poor girl. You just remember, when it's all said and done, that it was the Ladies' Betterment Society that came through."

I rolled my chair out to the edge of the steps and lifted my hand to get her attention. "Bettering ourselves, bettering our future!" I called out.

Lady Pendrake froze. "That's right," she said. "You're going to be healed, dear Amardine. *Healed.*"

„)CR

At dinner that evening, my father picked carefully at his salad, maintaining equal proportions of fiddleheads, peas, and pepper with each bite. He didn't speak until after he had finished and the main course was brought out. "That will be everything, Esmay," he said, and I knew what it meant, this dismissal. He wished to speak of private family matters. I'd been waiting for this all afternoon, ever since the Pendrakes had left. When I had asked him what my aunt had meant by her proclamation, he had twisted his hat in his hand and said he would tell me later. That had been hours ago. Perhaps he didn't mean to be cruel, though. Perhaps he had only wanted to take his time, to explain it all properly.

I tasted a spoonful of the spiced chicken stew, but it was still too hot to eat. The steam curled up my nostrils. I almost spoke up; I didn't think I could bear the silence any longer. But then my father said, "I told you we would speak about your aunt's visit. She had some important news for me today regarding your condition."

It's happening, I thought, my stomach flipping. My worst fear was coming true. "You're sending me away, aren't you?"

He coughed so hard, he had to put his spoon down and dab his mouth with his handkerchief. "How did you know about that?"

"Beatrice told me ages ago. I didn't think it would really happen, though. I don't want to go away, Papa. I'm happy here."

"The decision has been made. You'll be going to an almary near the coast."

"You don't even go to chapel," I said, my voice rising. "Why would you send me to an almary?"

"Take care with your tone, Amardine," he said. "As I said, the decision has been made. Your aunt went to a great deal of trouble to arrange this. You ought to write her a letter and thank her for her efforts."

"You don't know what she is," I said, without thinking. What sort of place was she sending me to?

"I know very well how trying she can be. Nevertheless, she is your aunt and she cares for you very much. You would do well to remember that, Amardine. I won't have you speaking ill of your elders."

I stared down at my bowl, feeling the tears well up, willing them not to fall into my stew. I knew what she was, but it wasn't enough. I would have to prove it, somehow.

"It won't be forever," he said, a bit more gently. "There's no need to be upset about it. This is your best hope of re-covering."

"But how?" I asked. "Dr. Vidmont couldn't heal me. Why should the almas be any different?"

"Your aunt has rallied her charity club on your behalf.

They've been petitioning the matron of this institution for the use of some...charm, or token, they possess. It isn't widely known about, but Lady Chandray has some connection to the family that gave it to the almary. The Souliere Benefaction, they call it. They've had it in their possession for over a hundred years, and it can only be used once."

"Used for what?" I asked.

"To gain an audience with Aneidis, or a close proxy."

"To speak with *God?* Is that what you mean, Papa?" I felt utterly unmoored, as though this were all happening in a dream.

"Many people claim to speak with God," my father went on, calmly. "Priests and almas meditate every day with the intent of establishing such a connection. The difference is that this token represents a promise, a sort of contract, made with the Church for a service the almary rendered them many years ago. Such tokens can only be created by the most powerful men in the Church, and carry the weight of their faith and service. They are not given out lightly. Lady Pendrake has convinced them to use it to heal you."

"Why would they use it on me, though?" I asked.

"The almary is...not what it once was. It's in need of renovations, so an arrangement was made. Your aunt was in correspondence for months with the matron of this place. It seems the use of a benefaction requires a consensus among the almas, and a long deliberation process."

"How does it work? I just go there and they use this token,

and then I'll be able to walk again?"

"It's...not that simple," my father said. "They'll need to prepare you for it. And even then, it's no guarantee."

"But it *can* work. You believe that, Papa?"

"I believe in keeping an open mind. It's worth trying, don't you think?"

My stew had finally cooled enough to eat, but I didn't feel hungry. I didn't know what I felt. A melange of terror and excitement, in equal proportion. The sharp bite of uncertainty. The faint sweetness of hope.

"When are we leaving?" I asked.

"In a few days," my father said. "Hespa will pack your things."

I thought that would be the end of it, but he picked up his wine glass and cleared his throat, and what he said next made my blood run cold. "There was one more thing I wanted to discuss with you before we leave."

"Yes, Papa?"

He swirled the wine in the glass, staring into its mysterious depths. Then he said, "I'm sorry about your mother. And about the way I told you about her. I imagined you would be older when we had that conversation. It didn't go as I'd planned."

I bit back the urge to tell him it was all right, that he hadn't hurt me. I was beginning to understand his reactions now, thanks to the vision in the perfume. My mother had shown me his fragility, his inability to sit with his own guilt. And that had freed me, in a way, from needing to assuage it.

I didn't have the words to articulate it at the time, only a child's instinctual awareness. My silence was making him uncomfortable, but I let it stretch out, until he spoke again.

"I can't say for certain why she did what she did. She didn't leave a note, never told anyone what she planned. It was a shock to everyone."

"How do you know she did it to herself?" I asked. "Or that it wasn't an accident?"

"It wasn't an accident. I believe she knew what she was doing. And the constable ruled out foul play." He sounded certain of it.

"How did it happen?" I asked, in a small voice.

"I don't think you ought to hear the details right now," he said. "Someday, perhaps. I just wanted you to know that she loved you, and that she did her best. And that I'm sorry I failed her."

"Did you love her?" I asked.

"Yes," he said, without hesitation. "Just...not in the way she needed me to."

To my shock, I saw a tear glisten in his eye. For a moment my heart bloomed with compassion. My hands went to my wheel rims, about to go to his side, to comfort him. Finally, he needed me.

Something held me back. He composed himself and sat, bereft and alone, just as I was. I watched him in silence, offering nothing.

My mother's presence seemed to hover over me then, and

for a moment I thought I smelled her perfume. But no, it was only the hothouse gardenias, arranged in a vase on the sideboard. She may have loved me, perhaps, but she hadn't loved me enough.

ഹോൽ

I sat upon the wall of the courtyard one last time the evening before our departure. The sky was a burnt orange above the line of cypress, fading to the color of a bruise. To the north, torchlight flickered through the screen of trees that separated the pasture from the lower court. There were occasional shouts and laughter, a baby crying, a dog barking, a shutter slamming closed. I could still hardly believe I would be leaving on the morrow. *Your papa wouldn't send you away for the world*, Hespa had said. I remembered her words exactly, because I'd written them down, even though she'd scolded me for the habit. She'd been wrong about that. But things had been different then, I had to allow.

The cool night air helped soothe my nerves as I kept my solitary watch. A sudden breeze made the outline of the cypress trees shiver. Across the field, on the hill where the ashes were scattered, the lone elm tree melded into the deepening twilight; warped branches transformed into a thousand hands grasping at the purple sky; palms turned upward on the wind, vaunting silver offerings of the underworld. The air smelled of wood smoke and witch hazel and the fires of antiquity, and I could imagine the gods of old that Hespa spoke of, who had roved these lands and still lurked in the hollow hills and handmaiden trees. A slight movement at the base of the tree caught my eye, and as I watched, the low, long body of a slinking animal moved from behind the trunk, its thick tail pointing straight out behind it. A fox.

As it turned its head toward me, it nearly disappeared into the outline of its body. Except for the eyes, which glinted with a knowing, inner light. As it stared at me, ears pricked, I knew without a doubt that this was the one, the very same one that had led me home on that fateful night. What did it mean, though? I held perfectly still, watching, waiting for an answer.

The fox stood, nose lifted to the wind, tail aloft with mocking elegance. *Vermin*, my father had said—an ugly word if ever there was one. The fox circled the base of the tree, once, twice, a third time, then disappeared from view. I hoped to glimpse it, bounding across the field, but it was gone, simply gone, as though it had slipped through the tangle of roots into some hollow chamber beneath the tree. *And why shouldn't it?* I thought. The tree kept countless other secrets; why not this one?

"You're not what they say you are," I whispered, my words falling away into the night air. "I know you're not." Tears blurred my vision as I reached under the cushion of my chair and withdrew the silver stake. I turned it over, reading my mother's name aloud. Was this the first time I had done it, spoken her name? The syllables felt so unfamiliar on my tongue. I said it again.

I am here with you always, little one, a woman's voice murmured, carried on an errant breeze. But it wasn't my mother's voice. I knew that now. It was the voice that had taken control of my limbs that day in the courtyard, and lifted me up when no one else had come.

"Who are you?" I asked, leaning forward, as though I might catch a scent on the wind.

There was no answer.

Perhaps if I said my mother's name a third time, she would appear and do battle with this trickster. I would have liked to see that. But then she would just scold me for removing the stake, and insist I put it back where it came from. I recalled her words from my dream: *You never should have taken it.*

It was too late now.

"I have to go away for a little while," I said, glancing round to make sure no one else was about. "Will you still be here when I get back?"

No reply.

"Thank you," I called out a bit louder, starting to get annoyed.

This was it, I had truly gone mad. I was speaking to empty air. Too old for imaginary friends, it seemed, but not for imaginary demons.

I turned to go inside, hiding the stake beneath the edge of my cushion. From under the pergola, Hespa was calling my name. No doubt she would insist I go to bed early to be well-rested for tomorrow's journey. I waved to her and made my way along the balustrade, ignoring her worried look as I approached the ramp. Soft, mushroom-gray moths flung themselves at the aetherlamps, batting my head as I passed beneath them. I paused, inhaling the scent of comfrey—weedy, sour, redolent of all green and growing things—and wished I could stay out just a little bit longer, to linger in the deepening night.

Acknowledgments

I want to thank my family for always believing in me, even when I wavered and doubted myself. You have shown me so much support over the years, in all of my creative endeavors. I am particularly grateful to my brother Tim, whose technical expertise made this print edition possible. I couldn't have done it without you guys.

I also want to thank my early readers: Andrew Cutter, Jayne Brown, Samantha Buccini, Tim Drumheller, Alexander Verbeek, and Bill Tracy. Even if the story wasn't your cuppa, your feedback helped me see what the story was missing and ultimately, make it stronger. And to those who cheered me on, your observations and comments not only improved the book, they made the whole process worth it in the end.

Finally, I would be remiss if I didn't mention the Writing Excuses community. Since my first retreat in 2013, I have learned so much from all of you, and have been inspired by the many success stories to come out of the group. I'm glad we could stay in touch and I hope to see some of you soon.

About the Author

Julianna is a writer of fantasy fiction, an illustrator, and a former potter. She spent over a decade touring the Northeast with an E-Z Up tent and selling her work at art shows. She never forgot her childhood love of writing and illustrating stories, though, and in 2010 she began working on her first novel. It soon became clear, however, that the book needed a prequel. And then the prequel turned into a trilogy.

You can find illustrations for The Maiden Tree at her website, www.juliannadrumheller.com. You can also follow her on Twitter, Instagram, or on her Facebook author page to get updates about new material.

Julianna currently lives in Western New York.